BEFORE WE TURN TO DUST

"A fresh new voice in literary fiction steps onto the stage."
JODI THOMAS
New York Times **bestselling author**

"Beautifully written and Shakespearean in scope, BEFORE WE TURN TO DUST is a stunning debut novel by Clara Sneed. Part family drama, part crime story, this piece of historical fiction will seduce and shock readers with its vivid portrait of passion and vengeance."

RICK TREON, award-winning author of LET THE GUILTY PAY

BEFORE WE TURN TO DUST

CLARA SNEED

This novel is a work of fiction inspired by true events. While certain elements of the story are based on real-life occurrences, characters, and settings, significant portions have been fictionalized or embellished for dramatic effect. Readers should bear in mind that this book is a creative interpretation and not a factual account of historical events. Some names and characteristics have been changed and some dialogue has been recreated.

Copyright © 2024

All rights reserved, including the right to reproduce this book or any portions thereof in any form whatsoever.

For information, address:
Blue Handle Publishing
2067 Wolflin Ave. #963
Amarillo, TX 79109

For information about bulk, educational, and other special discounts, please contact Blue Handle Publishing, www.BlueHandlePublishing.com.

To book Clara Sneed for any event, contact Blue Handle Publishing.

Cover and interior design: Blue Handle Publishing
Editing: Book Puma Author Services, BookPumaLive.com

ISBN: 978-1-955058-20-9

*To my mother and father, my sister Carly,
my son Sam, and my husband Kirk.*

Clara Sneed

CONTENTS

NOTE TO THE READER
By the author — i

MAP OF PERTINENT CITIES — iii

BEFORE — 1

PART 1: *Lena* — 5

PART 2: *Beal* — 115

PART 3: *On Polk Street* — 259

AFTER — 349

POST-SCRIPT — 359

SOURCES — 359

ACKNOWLEDGEMENTS — 360

ABOUT THE AUTHOR — 363

NOTE TO THE READER

I can barely remember not knowing some version of this story. John Beal Sneed was my great-uncle. His youngest sibling was Harold Marvin Sneed, my paternal grandfather; Cara Weber Sneed, Marvin's wife, was my paternal grandmother. In a family full of great stories and storytellers, this one was irresistible. Even if my grandmother—a mean storyteller herself—strenuously disapproved of the whole thing and wouldn't talk about it, most everybody else did.

In writing my own version, I made extensive use of primary sources, including letters, transcripts, newspaper accounts and interviews. I've stuck to the chronology indicated by the sources and incorporated verbatim quotes whenever possible. If I had to guess about events, I did so based on the sources. I invented only a few characters and none has any direct effect on the action. And though the novel was developed with the primary source material firmly in mind, I'm sure its characters' real-life counterparts would recognize my creation for what it is: Fiction.

Like any novelist, I've had plenty of time to think about the differences between fiction as a means of revealing truth and fiction as a means of denying it. Those questions are particularly acute in a story like this one, which ultimately goes far beyond the train wreck of a failed marriage and an adulterous affair to reveal layer after layer of the society in which the train wreck occurred.

The story itself does not directly involve one of the most fundamental layers—what W.E. B. Du Bois, writing in 1903, famously called the "problem of the twentieth century…the color line." Yet from the beginning, I thought an honest novel had to include it. And in a narrative written by a white woman, told almost entirely from three individual white points-of-view, I struggled with how to portray prevailing white attitudes toward Black people without using language—now considered highly offensive—that white people living there and then would have considered absolutely normal and routine. In the end, I concluded that while I could very significantly soften that language, in a few instances I needed to use the worst of it.

To flatter or soothe a contemporary audience by creating a fictional universe in which characters speak in ways that are anachronously benign—and false—is another way of pretending about the past and about ourselves. And pretending, sentimental storytelling, lying, denial, illusion, projection, pernicious falsehoods purveyed and/or accepted as truths . . . if ever a history spilled over with these, it's this one.

For the novel's primary characters and their three families, those particular oh-so-human tendencies have cataclysmic effects. And as their personal drama spills into courtrooms, newspapers and public opinion, those same "skills" are on full display, exposing how powerful social groups, attitudes, and ideologies can portray as necessary or even heroic behavior that is neither, and thus keep those with less power firmly in place.

This is very much a novel about flaws of all kinds. But it's also a novel about love, including most basically my own for this world and its people. I've done the best I can to create "true" fiction and to reveal the many layers of a dramatic and complex history. But that doesn't mean that the ghosts I've lived with while writing it don't think I got some things wrong. I've asked their forbearance. I hope you, the reader, will grant me the same. Any errors, whether factual or imaginative, are mine and mine alone.

Before We Turn to Dust

KEY CITIES

Clara Sneed

KEY CHARACTERS

Lenora "Lena" Snyder Sneed: *Maiden name Lenora Snyder; wife of Beal Sneed; born 1878*
John Beal Sneed: *Lena's husband; born 1877*
Albert "Al" Gallatin Boyce Jr.: *Born 1875*

THE SNEED CHILDREN

Lenora Sneed: *First child; born 1901*
Georgia "Georgie" Sneed: *Second child; born 1905*

THE SNEED FAMILY

Joseph Tyree Sneed: *Father of John Beal Sneed; born 1848*
Georgia A. Beal: *Mother of John Beal Sneed; born 1856; died 1884*
Lillian "Aunt Lillian" Itaska Beal Sneed: *Stepmother of John Beal Sneed; born 1865*
Joseph Tyre Sneed Jr.: *Older brother of John Beal Sneed; engaged to Bessie Boyce prior to her death; good friends with Henry and Al Boyce; born 1876*
Georgia Sneed Thompson: *Younger sister of John Beal Sneed; born 1879*
Harold Marvin Sneed: *Younger brother of John Beal Sneed; author's grandfather; born 1883*
Cara Carleton Weber Sneed: *Wife of Harold Marvin Sneed; author's grandmother; born 1880*
Joseph Perkins Sneed: *Paternal grandfather of John Beal Sneed; author's great-great-grandfather; Methodist circuit rider and first of Sneed family in Texas; born 1804; died 1881*

THE SNYDER FAMILY

Thomas S. Snyder: *Father of Lena; born 1839*

Lenora A. Bryson Snyder: *Mother of Lena; born 1848*
Dudley Wallace Snyder: *Older brother of Lena; born 1869*
Pearl Snyder Perkins: *Older sister of Lena; born 1870*
Tom Snyder: *Older brother of Lena; born 1873*
Eula Snyder Bowman: *Older sister of Lena; married to Henry Bowman; born 1877*
Henry Bowman: *Husband to Lena's sister Eula; birth date unverifiable*
John Wesley Snyder: *Younger brother of Lena; born 1882*
Susie Snyder Pace: *Younger sister of Lena; married to John Pace; born 1885*
John Alonzo Pace: *Husband to Lena's younger sister Susie; Snyder parents lived with them in Clayton, N.M.; born 1880*
John Wesley "J.W." Snyder: *Paternal uncle of Lena; Thomas S. Snyder's older brother; born 1837*
Dudley Hiram "D.H." Snyder: *Also known as Uncle Dud; paternal uncle of Lena; Thomas S. Snyder's oldest brother; born 1833*
William H. "Billie" Steele: *In-law sibling to Lena; Lena's brother Tom married Billie's sister Susan; Billie lives with his sister Nellie Steele; born 1872*
Nellie Steele: *In-law sibling to Lena; Lena's brother Tom married Nellie's sister Susan; Nellie lives with her brother Billie Steele; born 1877*

THE BOYCE FAMILY

"Colonel" Albert Gallatin Boyce, Sr.: *Father of Al Boyce Jr.; worked for Snyder Brothers prior to becoming manager of the XIT Ranch in 1885; retired from that position in 1905; born 1842*
Annie Elizabeth Boyce: *Mother of Al Boyce Jr.; born 1850*
William Boyce: *Older brother of Al Boyce Jr.; born 1871*
(James) Henry Boyce: *Younger brother of Al Boyce Jr.; born 1877*
Lynn Boyce: *Younger brother of Al Boyce Jr.; born 1879*
Elizabeth "Bessie" Boyce: *Older sister of Al Boyce Jr.; engaged to Joe Sneed prior to her death; born 1873; died 1906*
Mary Hamilton: *Live-in companion to Mrs. Boyce; born 1847*
Ira Aten: *Texas Ranger and later division foreman on the XIT; moved to El Centro, California, in 1904; born 1862*

PROFESSIONAL FIGURES

PHYSICIANS AND ATTENDANTS

ARLINGTON HEIGHTS SANITARIUM
October 17, 1911-November 8, 1911; January 13, 1912-January 19, 1912

Dr. Wilmer L. Allison: *Superintendent and resident physician in 1912 and 1913; brother of Dr. Bruce Allison*
Dr. Bruce Allison: *Resident physician and brother of Dr. Wilmer Allison*
Dr. John S. Turner: *Consulting physician; formerly superintendent of Texas state asylum at Terrell, 1900-1907*
Mrs. Watson: *Matron/supervising nurse*
Lillie Flowers: *Attending nurse*

JOHNSON'S SANITARIUM
Fort Worth, Approximately May 1, 1912–June 20, 1912

Clay Johnson: *Owner and doctor in charge; Cone Johnson's brother*
Mildred Bridges: *Superintendent and Lena's nurse; Boyce family friend*

JUDGES, TRIALS AND LEGAL REPRESENTATION

CANADIAN REPRESENTATION
T. J. Murray: *Andrews, Andrews, Murray & Noble, 1904-1908; Murray & Locke, 1908-1911; Campbell, Pitblado & Company, 1911-1912; own firm established 1912;*
  Representing Al Gallatin Boyce Jr. and Lena Snyder Sneed

HABEAS CORPUS/INSANITY HEARING IN FORT WORTH
Judge Tom "W.T" Simmons: *Presiding 1907-1912; 67th District Court, Tarrant County, Texas*

State Senator Offa Shivers "O.S." Lattimore: *Representing District 30, Texas State Senate, 1911-1919;*
Representing Lena Snyder on behalf of the Boyce family, in favor of release

State Senator W. A. Hanger: *Private attorney; Texas Senate, 1899-1907; Texas Senate president pro tempore, 1903-1907*
Representing Lena Snyder on behalf of the Boyce family with Senator Lattimore, in favor of release

W.H. Atwell, United States district attorney: *Texas Northern District, 1898-1913*
Representing John Beal Sneed and family, against release of Lena Snyder

W.P. "Wild Bill" McLean Jr.: *Law firm of McLean, Scott and McLean, founded in 1904*
Representing John Beal Sneed and family, against release of Lena Snyder

FORT WORTH TRIALS:
STATE OF TEXAS VS. JOHN BEAL SNEED

Judge James R. "J.W." Swayne: *17th District judge, Tarrant County, 1909-1916; Fort Worth city attorney, 1883-1885*
Presided over the trial of John Beal Sneed

Jordan Cummings: *State prosecutor*
Prosecution against John Beal Sneed

State Senator W. A. Hanger: *Private attorney; Texas Senate, 1899-1907; Texas Senate president pro tempore, 1903-1907*
Prosecution against John Beal Sneed

W.P. "Wild Bill" McLean Jr.: *Law firm of McLean, Scott and McLean, founded in 1904. Defense representing John Beal Sneed*
Walter B. Scott: McLean, Scott, and McLean
Defense representing John Beal Sneed

Cone Johnson: *Former Texas state representative, senator, and candidate for governor*
Defense representing John Beal Sneed
J. W. Henderson: *Sneed family friend, summation for the defense*
Defense representing John Beal Sneed

MEDIA PERSONNEL AND WITNESSES

Kitty Barry: *"Color commentator" for Fort Worth Star Telegram*
W. H. Fuqua: *Witness, prominent banker, and cattle broker in Amarillo; present at the Fort Worth trial before Judge Swayne*
E.C. Throckmorton: *Witness; Boyce family friend; son of Texas Governor James Webb Throckmorton, who served 1866-1867*

Clara Sneed

By the sweat of your face you shall eat bread, till you return to the ground, for out of it you were taken; for you are dust, and to dust you shall return.

Genesis 3:19

Clara Sneed

BEFORE

Clara Sneed

September 14, 1912. Milam County, Texas

I was sitting at the oak roll top desk, writing another letter and scheming away in the farmhouse that wasn't ours, just a ways up from the Brazos River. Somehow or other, I'd found paper and a pencil. Somehow or other, I'd get the letter to the post office. Somehow or other, it wouldn't get intercepted, steamed open, or destroyed. Somehow or other, we would be together again.

I had believed that for what seemed like a long time. But by then, I really only believed it while I was writing, so it was better to write than do anything else. *Oh my angel, I dream of you. With each breath I take, I am yours, body and soul.*

Out back of the house, my daughters were playing in the little fenced-off cemetery where the old preacher was buried. They liked it out there. They could steer clear of all sorts of things—including me—brush off the flat stones, and sit down without getting ambushed by chiggers or ants. Sometimes I'd see them pretending to take tea, like grown-up ladies. Lenora would pour from a banged-up tin coffee pot they'd found in the farm trash pile, and Georgie would hold up an imaginary cup and smile and nod. They'd chat a few minutes, then trade.

I'd about come to the end of my letter when I saw dust rising from the dirt track that curved toward the house and heard a puttering engine against the roar of the cicadas. Out of habit, I put a blank sheet of paper over the words I'd written.

By then, I was always nervous when people arrived unexpectedly. But when I saw it was cousin Cootsie, sitting beside a driver I didn't know, my heart lifted. I hadn't seen her in so long. She was on our side. I was sure of it. Maybe she had some good news or a letter for me—it had been a while. I smiled at her.

"Lena," she said when she reached the doorway.

She took my hands.

That's when I knew.

Clara Sneed

PART I

LENA

Clara Sneed

1

When something like that starts, you feel like you've found forever. The two of you are fated to remember or discover it from the beginning of time to its end. Everything else is just temporary.

But I've had plenty of time to wonder what would have happened if Albert and his brother Lynn hadn't left their cattle operation in Montana to come back to Texas and try things out in the Pecos. What if those dry years hadn't hit just when they did? What if Albert hadn't decided to ship some cattle up to Amarillo on account of drought and headquarter at his parents' house?

That was August of 1910.

His father—also Albert G. Boyce, but Sr.—had retired in 1905 as manager of the XIT Ranch and moved to Amarillo, where he built a big house on the fanciest stretch of Polk Street. Everybody called him Colonel. He wasn't and hadn't ever been one, but like a lot of those old men who'd lived through the War, he'd gathered the title somewhere along the way and stuck with it.

Back then, the only trees in Amarillo were the saplings in front of the courthouse and outside rich people's houses. Sometimes the buildings reminded me of naked people, all lined up for a parade along a grid of streets platted in the middle of what looked like nowhere. They could startle you like Palo Duro Canyon; you didn't expect to find either one out there on the plains.

All these years later, the trees have grown up and the city has filled out. It doesn't seem so surprising anymore. And no one remembers much about our Big Story—sometimes it's almost like none of it ever happened. There are times even I've felt that way. And the Big Story wasn't the real story. The Big Story was mostly a mess of lies. And when it wasn't lies, it was still the words of others. Not mine. Not his.

It took me a long, long time to make any kind of peace with all that.

I thought I'd managed. I really did. But lately I sit in church on Sundays, looking old and respectable and listening to the preacher talk about resurrection, and I just want to go back and do everything the preacher calls wrong all over again. I'd do it better this time, I swear. That was my real life.

But it's not what people generally mean when they talk about real life. They mean all the other things, like trees growing up and people moving on and how did I come to be in Amarillo in the fall of 1910 when Albert returned and how in the world did things go so wrong among old friends?

To start with the simple things: Beal and I moved to Amarillo in 1904 after he stopped trying to practice law in Childress. Our first daughter, Lenora, had been born there in 1901 and our second, Georgia, was born in 1905, soon after the move. We built a house on Tyler Street in the nice part of town, just a few blocks from the Boyces. Beal got into cattle, farming in Paducah, and working for W.H. Fuqua. Like the Colonel, Fuqua was another big wheel with another big house on Polk, though he and the Colonel didn't get along.

Amarillo had churches, schools, libraries, and social clubs, so it was a good place for ranchers and traveling men to stash their families while they worked. Beal spent a lot of time away, either in Paducah or traveling for Mr. Fuqua to the cattle markets in Kansas City, Fort Worth, and Denver. My father and uncles had done things the same way, so I was more or less bred to it. Wives often complained at first, but after a while we got used to it, and then maybe we started to like it.

I'd seen Amarillo for the first time on a special excursion train back in the 80s, when I was just a girl. My daughters loved to hear about that trip, at least before all the trouble. There was hardly a building in sight, but all sorts of people were camping in tents around the creek because the Fort Worth and Denver line had a new junction and everybody wanted in on the boom.

"You girls, though," I'd usually add, after I'd described the little girl I'd waved to from the train and the man in checkered trousers playing cards who'd gone for his gun, "you're Panhandle royalty. Your grandfather and great-uncles were out here way before that. They saw the Indians and the buffalo and the time of no fences."

I didn't tell the girls the less edifying bits: My father and uncles had come to Texas from Missouri in 1854, after Uncle Dud shot his stepfather. His mother swore it was self-defense and Dud was acquitted, but the judge made it clear the family was no longer welcome in Missouri. They all headed to Round Rock to live with their mother's father, my great-grandfather Hale. Dud was barely twenty, my father much younger.

That story is like mine has become. No one talks much about it. The official story drowns it out. It used to be that Texas was so good for that kind of thing. You could launder your past and change your story to suit yourself because no one in Texas knew anything about your old one.

Beal had family from the state's early days, too, because his grandfather had been a Methodist circuit rider. There wasn't much need to launder *that*. But though it was good for something in Amarillo, it wasn't the same as having forebears who'd seen Comanche and still had dinner with Charlie Goodnight on a regular basis.

So if Beal was around, I'd leave out the Panhandle royalty bit when I was telling stories to the girls. In fact, I didn't usually tell stories if Beal was around. The girls liked to hear his stories: What it had been like to go to college up north, the strange things Yankees ate and said and thought.

I liked those stories, too. They reminded me of our courting time, when Beal first told them to me. I liked watching him with the girls. They'd snuggle up next to him, just the way they did with me, but with that look in their eyes that little girls get when they're gazing at the daddy they adore, the one they don't get to see near as often as they see their mama—the daddy who is strength and security and protection.

My own daddy had been good with me, just like Beal was good

with our girls: Patient, funny, kind. "Those Yankees think we talk funny," Beal would say. Then he'd do his imitation of a Boston accent, followed by his imitation of a New Yorker, and all of us would laugh and laugh and try to do them ourselves, then beg him to do them again. Though he wasn't practicing law anymore, he'd retained the trial lawyer's ability to capture an audience. He could turn the simplest sentence—"That was a hard winter," for example—into something that had us laughing for half an hour. "That was a hod wintuh," he'd begin, then do the same sentence as if he came from the Bronx, from North Carolina, from Mississippi, and, finally, from Texas.

In the beginning, I mourned when the romance went out of our marriage. We'd been a brilliant match. Everyone said so. Good families. Bright future for Beal Sneed (so smart he'd gone to Princeton) and Lena Snyder (one of her season's most popular belles). I was nineteen when he came back to Texas. I was tired of the same old people, places, and things. I'd decided I didn't want to be stuck out on some dusty ranch with a bunch of barbed wire and ignorant cowboys. I thought Beal would be different, a way to launch my own life. And I thought I loved him.

"Do you still love me?" I used to ask him in the beginning, after the novelty of being in a house together with no one else around had worn off. I missed the ceremonies of courtship and the wedding. "You don't act like you're so happy to see me anymore. Do you remember how it used to be?"

"Lena," he'd say, taking my hand. "It's marriage. It's not that I don't love you, of course I do. You're everything to me, you must know that."

"But I like to hear it," I'd say. "I wish you would tell me like you used to." So for a while he'd try, and then he'd forget about it again. I didn't like it, but when I talked to my sisters and friends, they all said the same thing. "It's just men, sugar. Just be thankful he doesn't drink or beat you and he's got enough money that you're not starving. Sure he loves you. Men are just funny how they show it."

Bed never was any good, as it turned out, but I didn't have anything to compare it with, and if the women I knew ever talked about making love with their husbands—which they didn't much, and never in detail—I didn't get the impression that pleasure had a lot to do with it.

So I began to settle myself to him. The habits of daily life a couple builds, it seems like those are the leaves and twigs and bits of twine that make the nest. You say good morning and you say goodnight; after supper each night, he sits in that chair with the lamp casting a circle of light on his newspaper and you sit on that side of the divan with another lamp casting another circle of light on your novel or your sewing; you tuck your daughters in together; you take your clothes off and he puts his pajamas on while you get in your nightgown; you pull down the covers of the bed and you get in together and maybe you talk a little more, or maybe you go straight to sleep or maybe there is some groping and he pushes himself inside you and you do that thing together that everyone thinks before marriage is one of the main reasons you marry but which, in my experience of marriage, was the very least of it. It was the twigs and twine and leaves of everything else that made my marriage. At the heart, there was a great gap. I just didn't know it.

We did fight back then, of course, but at first the fights were like big storms on the plains in the summer, rolling in and rolling out: after a little while it was as if they'd never happened. Sometimes it felt like I'd dreamed them.

I remember Beal coming home late one night when we were still in Childress; Lenora wasn't yet a year old. I was at my dressing table wiping cold cream off my face when I heard him come in and head to the kitchen, open the icebox, and thunk down a glass on the counter. When he came upstairs there was milk above his upper lip; he couldn't ever seem to remember to wipe his mouth. Back then I was still chastising myself for being petty: Why did a little thing like a milk moustache matter so much? He looked at me with his jaw set hard and his chin thrust out and he nodded. I thought he was daring me to say something about the milk moustache, so I didn't.

"How was it?" I asked, making my voice pleasant, meaning the meeting with the client he'd said he was seeing.

"It was all right," he said. He sat down on the end of the bed and began to untie his shoes.

"You seem . . ." I was about to say he seemed unhappy or angry or irritated, but I wasn't quite sure what word to use. I didn't have to decide, though, because he cut me off.

"I don't *seem* anything," he said, and now there was no mistaking the anger. "I'm just tired."

I was tired, too, after a day of dealing with an infant, but I was sure he wouldn't understand that so I didn't say anything, which increased my irritation beyond what I was already feeling because he was acting gripey and hadn't wiped milk off his face.

I tried to keep my voice sympathetic. "Well, you're in the right place." I thought he couldn't argue with *that*. The bedroom was the right place to be tired.

He looked at me sharply. "What the hell is your problem?"

"What do you mean my problem?" I retorted without any effort to hide my anger. "You march in here in a nasty mood with a milk moustache and *I'm* just trying to be pleasant."

"Oh, for God's sake, Lena." He slammed one of his shoes down on the bedspread where it left a big muddy print. "I'm tired. *Tired*. Can't a man be tired in his own bedroom without his wife pestering him to death?"

"Who is pestering who?" I said indignantly. The only thing that kept me from shouting was the fear of waking Lenora. He put his head in his hands and shook it slowly, like I was the most unreasonable and nagging wife in the world.

"Lena," he said after a few moments. His head was still buried in his hands, but he looked up before he continued. I had the impression there was something he didn't say but wanted to.

"Did you get hold of the man about the back door?" he said instead. The door didn't shut quite right in wet weather.

"I'll do it tomorrow," I answered automatically, which I'd been doing for a while.

"Lord," he said, shaking his head. "You'd think the one thing a man asks his wife to do, she just might be able to remember, or find time in her very busy schedule to do."

I sighed heavily and rolled my eyes, then sighed again, this time more naturally. Lenora would wake up early as usual; I was at the stage of child-rearing when you feel tired pretty much all the time.

It was hard, though, to go to bed and feel easy when there was so much tension between us. Things kept going unsaid, and got harder and harder to say the more we didn't say them, and at the same time became louder and louder in their unsaidness.

Beal sighed, too, then stood up and began to remove the rest of his clothes. Despite his sloppiness in other ways, he always took great care hanging them, making sure the trousers were lined up so the crease fell correctly, buttoning the top few buttons of his shirts after he placed them on the hanger, getting the shoulders of his jackets to rest properly so the fabric wouldn't get stretched out in the wrong places. That night he didn't put his pajamas on, but came to bed naked.

"Be still," he said, urgently, a few minutes later after we'd turned the lamp down. "Turn around. Be still." I obeyed and turned away. "Don't move," he said. "Be still." I only knew to do what he said. He came into me, his breath filling my ear, and as he finished he groaned once, briefly. Afterwards he rolled away from me and onto his other side. Later I heard what sounded like muffled crying.

You learn to live with the unsaid and the strange moments you don't understand because there are the twine and twigs and leaves of habit to make sure that you can. Still, for a long time I kept trying to bridge the gap between us.

In Amarillo, I got in the habit of reading aloud to him. He'd sit in his chair with the newspaper spread over his knees and try to look like he was paying attention. One night not long before everything blew up, it was *The Shepherd of the Hills*, one of the big books around that time; most everybody cried reading it. I cried, too, and I wanted to share that, somehow, with Beal.

"*I loved her—I loved—her. She was my natural mate, my other self. I—I can't tell you of that summer—when we were together—alone in the beautiful hills—away from the sham and the ugliness of the world that men have made!*"

Styles have changed so much, I don't suppose anyone would do much but laugh reading a passage like that now. But at the time it gave my churning feelings some clear path out of my body. Life was tinged with grandeur again.

"It was so inspiring," I said to Beal. "It made me want to do so much good in the world."

"Well, dear girl," he said, a little absently, "you're the best wife and mother a man could ever ask for."

"Thank you, my love. But I mean I want to do something *truly* good, something fine, out of the ordinary. It's easy being a good wife and mother to such a good husband and children."

"We *are* lucky," he said, looking up into my face as if he was paying attention for the first time. "We're very blessed."

"Yes," I said, "we surely are."

Meanwhile, my mood of exaltation had shifted to one of frustration and slight irritation. I felt like there were voices in me that never got a chance to speak because the subject always changed. Then I reminded myself that the heroines in the novels that made me feel so elevated rarely got angry, especially not at husbands who were praising them, and if they *did* get angry they usually had a noble reason for it. I smiled at Beal and told him how wise he was to make me realize that the little blessings in our life were as important as the more exciting events in the books I'd been reading. But a part of me stayed mad, no matter what I told it.

Some days later—this would have been September of 1910—I walked Georgie to school for her very first day, just the way I'd walked Lenora a few years earlier. Georgie was less naturally timid than Lenora, but she still clung hard to my hand and said almost nothing on the walk. Just as I had with Lenora, I held back my tears until the teacher shooed the last child into the school, waved at the mothers, and shut the door. Another mother and I shared a hug and a little weep. *How fast time goes; how quickly they grow up,* we said to one another. The things mothers have said for forever.

We dried our tears and turned away from each other, and I walked home in the autumn morning, the wind blowing across the big Panhandle sky with its bright sun and wide-open views.

At our front door, I found myself crying again. The tears gushed up, with something in them as deep and dark as oil. I wasn't sure what all I was crying about—it didn't seem to be just Georgie's first day of school—and in a little while I stopped. But I felt something lapping under the surface for the rest of the day.

That night, when I went to check on the girls as usual before I went to bed, I stayed for a while. I watched their slightly open mouths, the steady rise and fall of the bedclothes, their sudden, unpredictable movements, their veiled eyes moving as they dreamed. I wanted to protect them, but the desire seemed more complicated than usual. When I returned to bed, Beal was snoring. It took me a long time to get to sleep.

2

It wasn't too long afterwards that the Boyces threw a party. I'm sure his parents thought it was high time Albert married—he'd just turned thirty-four—and that a party was a good way to kick-start the business. It was a fine September evening. The wind had shifted so we could no longer smell the cattle waiting to be shipped to Chicago. We could easily have walked, but Beal insisted on taking the new Buick. He was so proud of it. His clean hands with their even nails and diamond rings on the third and little fingers grasped the steering wheel like they meant business. I was glad the trip was a short one. Automobiles weren't a complete novelty, at least not in our circle, but just like a lot of the men in town who'd bought one, Beal hadn't quite mastered the thing.

I was wearing a new violet silk dress cut in the new slim lines, with a fringe of glass beads running down the back and dangling from the cap sleeves. I felt like part of the evening sky itself, violet and mauve, with stars beginning to prick out. I was in such a good mood that I didn't say a word about it when Beal jerked the car to a sudden stop in front of the Boyce house three feet from their sidewalk.

"We make a good-looking couple, Mr. Sneed," I said instead, smiling.

"It'll be nine years next month," he answered, reaching over to squeeze my hand. "Do you regret it?"

The question surprised me. So did the look on his face, which was uncertain. "Of course not," I said, squeezing his hand back.

Every single window in the Boyce house was lit up; the gabled dormer above the entry looked like part of a jack-o-lantern. Mrs. Boyce stood in the doorway to greet her guests. "How nice to see you all," she said, her face lighting with pleasure. "Lena, you look so pretty.

What a lovely dress."

An elderly colored man motioned me upstairs, where the ladies were removing their gloves and coats and adjusting their hair and faces in a spare bedroom. Sheer curtains billowed gently from the open windows. A young colored girl, the kind we used to call *high yaller*, greeted me. "Good evenin', ma'am. Can I get you anything?" She seemed shy, scarcely raising her voice above a murmur. Her hair was tucked behind her kerchief, and her honey-colored eyes were visible only in snatches.

"She hasn't been doing *this* long," Ethel Wallace muttered in an irritated tone as she removed pearl-studded pins from her hair and placed them in her mouth, its thin lines widened by the effort of holding the pins and talking at the same time. Those good at the job sensed without being told which women required what for their brief toilettes— hand towels, clean cloths, a place to put unneeded hairpins. This poor girl would soon have a line out the doorway of women waiting to check their hair and faces.

"Come on, girl," said Ethel, "we'd like to get to the party sometime this evening." The girl looked panicked and ducked her head, murmuring, "Yes'm, Miz Wallace."

"Oh, honestly, Ethel," I said, "you're not entirely helpless." I pulled a few cloths from a box the girl was holding and handed them to her. Then I turned my back and sailed out the door and down the stairs. I knew there would be talk later, but I didn't care. Back then, I liked causing a bit of a ruckus every now and again. This was one of those evenings. I could feel it like a burr.

At the parlor piano, a young man I didn't know was playing Tin Pan Alley songs while several young people sang along, including Ethel's daughter Cassie, who was wavering on and off key and looking jaundiced in her peach-colored dress. An old colored woman offered me a drink, but I shook my head.

"Well, Miz Sneed," I heard a voice say, "you surely are a sight a man is glad to see tonight."

I turned to find Lynn Boyce, Al's younger brother, standing behind me, tall and lean, with clear blue eyes and large features. His wife,

Hilma, was chatting away in the corner with old Mrs. Moore.

"Likewise," I said to Lynn, smiling and extending my hand. The singing at the piano had dwindled away and Cassie Wallace was talking. "Oh, no," I said quietly, "it's that story about the horse again. And your father is talking about my uncles' rules again."

Cassie's voice wavered as much when she talked as when she sang. The Colonel, who had several voices at his disposal, had unleashed the booming one to tell some Yankee-looking woman I'd never seen before all about how he got the XIT job. "The Snyder boys had three rules for their cowboys and they made sure they got followed. When I tell you what they were, you won't believe that was possible."

The Yankee woman murmured something I couldn't hear, which made the Colonel laugh and boom even louder. Lynn and I looked at one another and silently mouthed the words along with him:

"Number one: You can't drink whiskey and work for us. Number Two: You can't play cards and gamble and work for us. Number Three: You can't curse and swear in our camps and in our presence and work for us."

Lynn laughed, a low-pitched kind of snorting sound, sort of horsey itself, and rolled his eyes. To the small group gathered around her, the outskirts of which were trying to decamp, Cassie was saying, "Mama and I like to have died. That horse took off when he caught sight of the automobile, with the two of us just screaming our heads off."

On the other side of the room, the Colonel continued to boom. "Those Farwells were from Chicago. They had no idea how to run a ranch any more than you would. Half the cowboys were drunk and the other half were greenhorns. I helped out with the cattle count. Now I'm sure in your parts you think that's a perfectly simple thing to do"—the Yankee lady shook her head vigorously—"but it takes skill and practice. They don't just line up two-by-two like they're heading into the Ark . . ."

"At least he's got a new audience," I whispered to Lynn.

"He run right up the steps of the Methodist Church," Cassie said emphatically. "The doors were wide open and there were some workmen inside, thank the Lord, because otherwise I believe Mother and

I would have died right there with Darky heading up the aisle to the altar. Can y'all imagine the obituary?"

"Sometimes," I whispered to Lynn, "I swear I'd like to have read it."

Lynn whispered back. "You ask me, I think that horse just didn't want no more to do with fetching and carrying Wallaces. He went to church to ask the good Lord to save him."

"It would be awful to be so boring," I said.

"Oh, Miz Sneed, have a little mercy," came a man's voice from behind me. "She never was as much fun, and definitely not near as wicked as you are."

When I turned, there stood Albert.

"You always did have a soft heart, Mr. Boyce." I held out my hand. "You haven't been around *listening* to that story. Welcome home."

"I didn't hear it this time, either," he said, grinning. "Maybe I ought to ask her to repeat it?" His eyes, a dark brown, were two deep pools centering the room. My body pressed against my clothes.

"Mr. Boyce," I said, "would you be good enough to get me something to drink?" In his eyes, something flickered briefly, but he was too much of a gentleman to do anything but agree. "Coming right up," he said and headed off.

I bent close to Lynn's ear. "You got your gun?" I whispered.

He pulled back, looked at me sort of astonished, and then grinned. "What do you have in mind?" he asked joyfully. He sounded exactly like he did in Georgetown years earlier, when a bunch of us decided to do something we knew we weren't supposed to, just to break the monotony and a few of the rules. "Where's Beal? I don't want trouble."

"Don't worry about him," I said. "He's talking cattle with Bivins or somebody. He's . . ."

Lynn cut me off. "Come on out back of the house."

In the kitchen, the windows were steamed up from the heat in the ovens. Mary, the Boyces's cook, was talking to herself in a language no one else knew as she bustled around. I caught the word *Jesus*. They said she was part Indian with special knowledge and remedies; most of the farmers and ranchers consulted her about when to plant, harvest, brand, and tip. When Lynn excused us to her, she ignored him completely.

By now it was dark. Out near the garage, a knot of men stood smoking and drinking from flasks under the three-quarter moon. It was a feature at just about every party, even if—like the Boyces—the hosts weren't serving liquor. "Walked in, she was flat on her back, legs straight up in the air," said a Virginia-accented voice I didn't recognize. "Busiest whorehouse I ever was in. Soggiest whore, too."

"We got a lady out here," Lynn said in a low voice. The men began to cough and clear their throats.

"I beg your pardon, ma'am," said Virginia. "I naturally supposed . . ."

Lynn cut him off. "Now boys," he said, "Miz Sneed here would like some shooting practice. Real lively little gal. Known her since we was children."

As he moved out of the shadows and into the moonlight, I recognized the Virginian, a top hand out at the Triple L Ranch near Borger, known as Tiny because he wasn't.

"I'm sorry to intrude," I said, smiling.

Lynn pulled a tin can from the garbage and set it on a fence post. Then he walked back to me and held out a small pearl-handled revolver—his town gun, a .22. The men backed away as a group. I'm sure I made them nervous.

I hadn't fired a gun since back in Georgetown, where we'd done things like this every now and again without the grown-ups being any the wiser. There were goose bumps on my bare arms, and my dress rustled and shimmered in the moonlight. The tin can gleamed dully. I raised the gun.

Then a hand clasped my waist, an arm extended along mine, another hand stretched over my hand, fingers over my fingers, the trigger clasped and pulled—by which of us I never knew—and the can exploded off the fence post. He twisted the gun from my grasp and was no longer touching me when his voice came cool and easy.

"I brought you that drink, Miz Sneed."

My arm, my fingers, my waist where his hand had rested—the nerves were all erupting, wanting what they wanted, pulling the rest of me along. Albert had a funny look in his eyes, like he was the one pulling me to pieces, but it felt like tenderness to me, like all I'd ever wanted or could want.

The group of men evaporated.

3

Then Lynn was dragging me past the kitchen steps toward the other side of the house. "Come on," he said urgently, "we don't want Pa to get wind of this." I found myself with a drink in my hand, making strained small talk with the gawking men and women on the gallery. Albert had vanished.

The excitement died down some when it became clear that no one had been hurt or killed. But people kept chattering, the way they do after a little scare. Mrs. Moore, who'd dressed in black ever since Mr. Moore died thirty-five years earlier, announced disapprovingly, "Used to be the men were always firing off guns in town. You'd think they'd realize we're a lot more civilized now."

"It's the drinking, Miz Moore," said Ethel Wallace. "That's the reason why our club favors prohibition. There'd be a lot less of this if liquor was illegal."

"Don't get started with me, Ethel," snapped Mrs. Moore. She shook a huge-knuckled finger uncomfortably close to Mrs. Wallace's face. "I got kin in Richmond. Did you know they kicked Carrie Nation out of two churches there?"

Ethel edged away. Mrs. Moore had lots of money and bad breath; no one wanted to offend or get too close to her, either one.

"And you talk about shooting, now *there's* a town for it," Mrs. Moore continued. "Big shootout in the street a while back over votes for niggers. Governor came down to set 'em all straight and sent the Rangers in to finish the job. It's not liquor, Ethel—it's Texans. We just like to shoot."

"Well, now," said Ethel, searching for a point of likely agreement, "coloreds voting and electing other coloreds would make me take up a gun, too." She gave me a pointed look. "We had enough of *that* sort of thing after the War. It's bad enough this business of women wanting to vote."

Mrs. Moore looked at Ethel blankly as if she'd stopped listening. A few feet away, C.T. Herring and Lee Bivins were talking baseball. "Cobb's the better player," Lee said, "but . . ." His voice dropped and I couldn't hear the rest.

At that moment, Beal hustled through the gallery door. I smiled at him. "The real Wild West," I said.

"I think we better go before anybody else starts firing guns." He was irritated. "I've got an early train tomorrow."

Within thirty minutes, I was back in our bedroom, unclasping my necklace, laying my diamonds aside, stepping out of my dress and corset. Things still seemed scattered. I noticed the heavy curtains at the window, the dark armoire, my dressing table, the circle the lamplight made. Everything looked separate, like it didn't connect with anything else.

4

A few days after the party, turning his hat slowly in his hands, there stood Albert in my doorway. "Miz Sneed," he said, smiling. "Should I call you that? Or is it still Lena?"

His face was clean and smooth in the morning light. I hadn't exactly forgotten the business with the gun, but I'd managed to forget how I'd felt. It was just one old friend horsing around with another. The way we did when we were kids. He was family, just like Lynn.

"Why, Mr. Boyce, come on in," I smiled back at him. "Lena, of course."

We walked toward the parlor and sat down on the sofa a respectable distance part.

"Ma sent me over to borrow some books," he said, flushing slightly and looking down at his hands. "She believes I need some refining—spent too much time on ranches. She says you read the new books, and she and Pa only have the old ones."

"It sounds like Mother Boyce wants you to make a good impression on all those young ladies I hear have plans to settle you down," I said. I was teasing him a bit, but the young ladies—not to mention their parents—were plenty interested. He was as eligible as eligible could be: Handsome, wealthy, well-connected, and from a real good family.

"If you were one of those young ladies, Miz Sneed," he answered, "I'd sure enough be 'round to see you." Of course, everybody talked like that. It was the kind of compliment Southern males are trained to give from the time they can toddle. And it might have started out that way, but somehow it turned into the truth. Both of us knew it.

Yet when he left a half-hour later with a few of my favorite novels, everything between us seemed perfectly correct. I'd already put his comment in the same part of my mind where I'd stashed the gun episode. I thought it would be nice to talk with him about books, since Beal wasn't interested. It would remain a simple, reliable pleasure: The sound of his boots coming up the steps, the brief silence as he removed his hat, his knock, just the right amount of loud, and then Nettie's voice: "Mr. Boyce, how you doin' this mornin'?" And Albert's voice: "I'm just fine, Nettie, how about you? Miz Sneed home?"

Anyway, late in the fall of 1910, he left town again to deal with some cattle business. By then, Beal and I were quarreling more often—about almost everything it seemed—and I didn't forget about our fights the way I used to. I'd remember talking with Albert like taking a brief vacation to another, far more pleasant country. But that was all.

Then, in the spring of 1911, he came back.

5

Amarillo was changing—"Cowman to Plowman," as the new Chamber of Commerce slogan put it—and I was changing, too. I found myself reading things I used to ignore or skim carelessly. One morning, it was Lillian Russell writing about her fourth marriage in a week-old copy of the *Fort Worth Star-Telegram* I found in the front hall along with a circular advertising "300,000 FERTILE ACRES Ripped Up Into Splendid Farmland."

"If the adage, 'if at first you don't succeed, try, try again' applies to every other condition" Miss Russell inquired, "why not to marriage?"

Part of me was terrified by the idea of divorce, but another part piped right up: *Yes, why not?* And that part liked Lillian Russell (who had a complicated theory about why her fourth marriage was really only her second) a whole lot better than it liked the woman—Eva Somebody-or-other—sounding off in the column opposite: "A really nice woman will not marry many times. Frequent marriages confuse children, so to speak, and scatter property."

On Sundays, I sat with the girls—and Beal, if he was in town—in the Polk Street Methodist Church. Albert was in the First Baptist across the street at the other end of the block with all his family, except for the Colonel, who'd been raised Methodist and had a pew near us.

Like most everyone else, I'd heard the stories, things friends talked about in private.

"Well, I shouldn't repeat gossip, but she said he comes up the back stairs when her husband leaves."

"The bellboys at the Amarillo Hotel love to see him rent that room because he tips so well for just a few hours."

"Of course he don't admit it, but they say she sees a cowboy, just seventeen or eighteen. Can you imagine? I hope at least she makes him take a bath beforehand . . ."

Come Sunday morning, you'd never have guessed a thing. Row upon row of beautifully dressed men and women filled the church, enemies seated together like best friends, husbands beside the wives they barely spoke to. It was easy to picture Eva somebody-or-other in one of the front pews.

"What aileth thee, O thou sea, that thou fleddest?" rang the voice of Dr. Robinson one bright spring morning.

I know, I thought suddenly, *I know.* I looked at Cassie Wallace and her mother and some of the other women with their eyes and their hands bent so dutifully to their worship, and I knew I'd stepped outside that circle.

Albert and I talked about all sorts of things—the conversations flowed everywhere—and he told me a story I've never forgotten. Once, when he was very young, he'd gone lobo wolf-hunting with a few XIT cowboys. There was a bounty on those wolves; their skins carpeted the ranch house at Channing. He and the boys managed to track a mother to her den in the breaks, and Albert felt like he had something to prove so he volunteered to go get her.

"I could hear her panting and the pups whining and whimpering, and the smell—you got no idea," he said, looking like he was still there. "I wriggled in about ten feet to where I saw her eyes—that's what they told me to aim at. I never heard a gun so loud in my life. My ears rang for hours. She yelped once and I wriggled back out. The other boys fished the pups out with a hook and drowned them in the creek." He was quiet for a minute. "I left it to the professionals after that. You know I like hunting. But that wasn't it."

It still seems like that story said something about a whole lot of things, maybe including the ailing sea, even if I've never been able to work out what or why.

Sometimes we read aloud to one another, especially when the scenes seemed to give voice to our feelings.

"*Often when I have camped here, it has made me want to become the ground, the water, the trees, mix with the whole thing. Not know myself from* it." He put up a hand and touched her softly. 'You understand about this place. And that's what makes it—makes you and me as we are now—better than my dreams."

Albert looked up at me. "He says it. But I can't find how to…" He looked frustrated. "I don't mean all the foolishness people sometimes say. I mean it like a world I never imagined."

"I know."

I did, too. This thing had come upon us or we had come upon it, but whatever it was, it was nothing I'd ever dreamed of. Not because I couldn't imagine adultery, couldn't imagine the way things unfolded—although it's true, I didn't. But all those things sprang up in a world I knew, and this was different.

There were now many nights I stood at the window, unable to sleep, listening to Beal breathing the way he did, deep and then turning to snoring, then back to breathing again. The moon was all over the plains. I could see Albert as if he were there, his dark hair, lean hips, the look in his brown eyes, the clean, male smell of him. And at the same time, it was as if all that was just a disguise: there was his heart underneath, not only his body's heart—not even just the heart he gave to me—but his whole heart, the one he'd stand in front of God with. I never saw that heart in Beal or any other man, but I saw it in Albert.

That's what I know about love, the real thing. You can see the heart, the one God sees and most everyone else doesn't.

6

"I'm going riding with Mr. Boyce," I said to Nettie one Saturday morning. We did so a lot that spring, often in his automobile, sometimes on horses. That morning, it was horses.

Nettie's arms were plunged deep in soapy water, the windows steamed up in front of the sink. "Yes'm, Miz Sneed," she responded, just a beat too slowly. She had her ways of letting me know what she thought. Earlier that morning I'd heard her muttering when she knew I was close enough to hear but not so close I'd have to respond: "You got your nice life. Let that poor man go on and find his own."

By then, tongues were surely wagging. All up and down Polk and Tyler, people—women especially, who were home most of the time—watched as Albert left his parents' house and headed down to ours. He'd call out "Mornin', Miz Wallace" and "Evenin', Miz Bivins," just like he always had, happy in that way he could be, as if nothing in the world could prevent him from having a wonderful time with his girl on a beautiful spring day—not her marriage, husband, children, not anything at all. Lord, I loved that about him.

He knocked on our door without a trace of furtiveness and the girls clattered downstairs to greet him in their high-pitched voices. When I walked into the entry hall, he was swinging Georgia back and forth in front of him. She was laughing, but when he put her down, she looked at him as she often did those days, as if she were trying to puzzle things out. Lenora, who mirrored my own feelings more exactly, was smiling at him, happy because she knew I was.

Out on Polk, the streetcar tracks stretched in two straight shiny lines, but the rest of the street was a mess. The city was replacing the hodgepodge of dirt and gravel and private sidewalks with brick paving. The workmen were sweating away in the warm spring sun and the hundreds of private windmills in town were turning in the breeze, creaking like a strange flock of birds. We headed north toward the brakes. Outside the Amarillo Hotel, we spotted Mr. Fuqua. "Say hello to Beal," he cried out pointedly. I just didn't care.

Once we reached the edge of the playa lake outside town, we set the horses running. When we finally slowed to an easy trot near a few cottonwoods beside a sluggish creek, all of us were breathing hard. The air smelled of a clump of Herefords not too far off, crushed buffalo gourd, sweating horses, muddy water, and the two of us. Flies buzzed and birds called. A hawk wheeled slowly around the sky. And, of course, we could see for miles in the bright spring sunshine.

We dismounted under a cottonwood where the cattle hadn't made too much of a mess. Albert spread out a heavy blanket and went to unsaddle the horses. It was an old habit from our youth. Why not let them enjoy some freedom, too? I already knew there was a curry comb in the saddle bags to clean them up before we put the saddles back on. They ambled down to the creek for a long drink and the mare found a good muddy spot and began to roll. "That didn't take long," I laughed.

Albert stretched. I could see the sweat stains under his arms and his Adam's apple, veiled by its thin layer of flesh. "Sometimes, after a long ride, I think I'd like to roll around in the mud, too," he said, grinning. Then he ambled down to the creek, caught both horses by the bridle, led them up to higher ground and staked them. His movements were practiced and thoughtless and left me breathless. The horses began to crop at whatever they could find, tails switching.

The rhythmic sound of their grazing, the rustle of the cottonwood, the drone of the flies and the occasional hawk or bird cry, the flickering light and shade—it was all so soothing. As Albert sat down, everything about him seemed gorgeous to me: His unfashionably big feet, the ears that protruded a bit too much, his dark, well-kept hair, the lines at his eyes and around his mouth that told you he wasn't as young as he looked.

"I had the Harvey girls pack us some things," he said, reaching into the saddlebag to fish out several packages wrapped in brown paper.

"How did you manage *that?*" The Harvey House at the Santa Fe Depot was the most elite restaurant in town, and they didn't generally do picnics.

"I told 'em I needed it for a special occasion," he said with a wink.

He poured us tin mugs of lemonade that we drank down without stopping. Then he cleared his throat and gazed toward the creek. "Lena, I have something to say," he began.

My heart sped up.

"You know, I always thought I'd find a woman to marry. That's what people do, so I thought I'd do it, too. But nobody I met quite suited me. None of the women . . . it just never seemed like they'd fit in. I'd think it and her over and decide it and her would just be too much trouble. Ma wouldn't like her, or she wouldn't get along with Lynn, or she and Pa would butt heads, or some other thing was wrong with her."

He turned toward me and smiled in a wavering way. "But I'm starting to think I had it all wrong. I wasn't looking for a woman to fit in. I was looking for a woman who would make me feel that she was worth whatever I had to go through to be with her." He paused.

"The funny thing is," he continued in a moment, "you *do* fit in, or you would if you weren't married. But it wouldn't matter to me if you didn't. I love you and nothing is ever going to stop me loving you. For the rest of my life. Forever."

"I've waited my whole life to hear that," I whispered. I didn't know it was true 'til I said it.

It seemed like a long time, though I don't suppose it really was, before I stretched my bare hand up to his face. His shaved cheek grazed my palm, my index finger traveled the soft bulge of his lips. When he took my finger into his mouth, the pleasure of his teeth grazing my skin and his warm saliva and the restless muscles of his tongue made me dizzy.

By the time we got back to the house, Nettie had the girls at their supper in the kitchen. I could tell she was disgusted with me, but all she said was, "We was beginning to worry you'd fallen off that horse."

Albert smiled at her. "I'm sorry we scared you, Nettie. My fault. Went further than I meant to."

She couldn't help smiling back at him, a little mollified. "You want anything to eat, Mr. Boyce?" she asked. "It's right late."

So he sat down with us in the kitchen and had a bowl of milk toast. The scene has stuck in my mind all this time: The kitchen windows steamed up against the cool night, Albert and the girls and I eating warm toast with milk and melted butter while Nettie busied herself with the dishes, the girls asking about the ride and telling us about their day, and my own vast, unrepentant pleasure. In those moments, it was easy to believe that we would all end up happy, however things unfolded, because surely no joy as great as this could cause unhappiness. Even in recollection, I've never quite seen how it was possible.

We both had such faith. And we were so innocent. We believed the world could not possibly be a place that didn't make room for the two of us together; that love made the world and that we were its bones, muscles, breath, and voice.

I held onto that joy and faith as long as I could, then I held on to the memory of it, and after that I held onto everything connected to it, the things and people that had surrounded it —like hanging on to the setting because that's where the diamond used to be.

7

So here is forever:
We are out on the plains one warm evening in May, the breeze pleasant, our blanket spread out. We slide to the ground, his hand grasping my ankle, where the leather of my riding boots creases, then moving up my calf, pushing the riding skirt out of the way. My arms are around his neck, his tongue is in my mouth and the smell of him covers me: Whiskey and tobacco and his own smell, the one that only he has. His hand finds the big buttons along the inside of the legs of the skirt and he twists some of them undone. We speak simple, urgent words. "Oh, God, I need you, I love you." His hands push the heavy material aside, bloomers, my hair, my legs flanking his hand, cold at first, then warming. We stare into one another's eyes.

I say, "I can't wait anymore."

He says, "I didn't want it to be like this. I wanted a special place. I want to marry you, you know I want to marry you."

"I don't care. It's you, just you. In the eyes of God, we must be married. I am your wife."

He raises himself a little. "Are you sure?"

I pull him back to me. He tugs at his belt buckle. "Let me," I say, pushing the heavy leather up through the buckle, that little tightening around his waist as I pull the tongue back, watch the clasp fall free, then slide the tongue out through the other side of the buckle and undo the button on his jeans beneath. My fingers rub against the rough denim, and on his shirt, the buttons of bone. Pale skin with its own secrets, the line at his neck where clothes stop the sunlight, the nest of dark hair, his penis so hard, head smooth as baby's skin, stretched tight, wet at the tip. I bend my head down, his hair springs up against my mouth, his hands on my head, my tongue licking around the head, under its lip, feeling the opening. I have never done any of this before.

He pulls my face up to his. "Are you safe?"

"I don't know, I think so, I don't care." My bleeding stopped just a few days ago, and anyway, only this is real. He is slipping inside me, so wet it's easy, my hips thrust up to meet his, filled up, then tightening and gasping, crying, his spasms and my own in wave after wave rolling out.

Afterwards, we lie tangled together.

And then the rest of the world slowly seeped back in, the sky, the hardness of the ground, the horses with their mild curiosity, various birds. I began to plan how I must get Beal to bed, just in case—and soon—then thought I didn't want to get pregnant by Beal. I loosened myself from Albert's grip and squatted, letting him drip slowly out of me. No sense of shame, an entirely altered view.

That was the first time.

There were others before we escaped.

8

Mrs. Boyce looked at me in her direct way. I'd begun to speak, but she waved her hand to shush me. Her hair was dark, still barely streaked with gray.

It was Election Day, July 22, 1911, and the Colonel was out rustling up votes for Cone Johnson for governor. By then, my tongue had gotten to know every inch of Albert. I left nothing untouched, unlicked, unkissed, unknown: The recess under his lower lip, the taste of the sweat on his chest and his navel, the top of his spine.

I'd come to see if I could explain things to his mother in a way she would understand. We were seated in her parlor.

"I'm afraid for you both," she said. "I saw this start, but I never thought it would go this far. You're blinded, both of you. You're standing in one another's light." She shook her head as if to clear the whole thing away.

"It's forbidden fruit, Lena," she went on. "You'd come to hate each other." Her face was set so hard it almost quivered and she was squeezing her handkerchief 'til her knuckles turned white. "It's a blessing and a miracle Beal doesn't know, the way you two have been carrying on. I'm ashamed. And you must be too, Lena, deep down. You come from a fine family. You have a husband who loves you and two beautiful daughters who need their mother. Even if you can't think of Beal, or your parents, or Mr. Boyce and me, and the friendship among all our families that would surely be destroyed by this, think of your girls." The room was stifling.

"They need you," she said insistently, bending her head a little so that she was almost looking up into my face. "A mother's love is more precious than anything. I've often thought that some of the things you may not like so well about Beal are because he lost his mother at such a young age. Does it not make you compassionate to think of it?"

The truth was it didn't, or at least I didn't want it to.

"Would you cause your girls to suffer in the same way, depriving them of a father and mother together to guide them through the rest of their childhoods? Lena, you don't know how precious this time is." Her eyes filled, and her grip on the handkerchief loosened. "Your children's childhood is gone in the twinkling of an eye. And you will reproach yourself forever if you don't do everything you can to make the most of it." She began to cry silently, tears running down her face. I felt dizzy.

"You know how we still suffer from losing Albert's sister Bessie. You were so kind to me then. For the sake of her memory and your own children, please tell Albert he must go. I am *begging* you, Lena. I know it will be hard, but what you and Albert are contemplating would in a very short time be harder still." She took a deep breath, straightened, and the tears slowed. She looked away toward the curtained window and then back at me.

"Pray to God, Lena." She laid the handkerchief down and reached across the short space between us to put her hand on my knee. "He will smooth the roughest spots and help you bear the pain. He helps me every day." I noticed the crumpled heap of white cotton against her dark skirt because I needed something to notice that wasn't her.

"I can't criticize you for loving my son," she said. "I love him too. But you *must* give him up. It is your part, as the woman, to guide him to the right decision. He's in the grip of his feelings. You must be the strong one."

The tears rolled down her cheeks again, and I began to cry, too. She was right: I couldn't abandon Lenora and Georgia. I would pray and be kind to Beal, I would somehow learn to live with the ways I couldn't love him, if only for my daughters' sake.

"It will be harder than anything I've ever done," I said to Mrs. Boyce, gripping her hand in both of mine. "I love him so much—you don't know how much—but I will do it."

"Thank God." She sighed heavily and her body drooped with relief.

"Pray as hard as you can and God will help, I promise He will. We'll get Albert out of town on the early train tomorrow. Thank you and bless you, Lena. And your children, your lovely girls, if they knew they would thank you, too."

  I lay awake all night and I prayed, but when I heard the sound of the whistle in the early morning, along with the roosters and the mourning doves, I felt like my heart was on the train and not just my heart, but a whole invisible body, slipping past the porter, the name, *A.G. Boyce Jr.*, where was it, where was he, yes, there, hand over his face, the bump on the wrist he got from carrying all that wood for his grandfather's fire when he was a boy, not shaved this morning, drinking, I can smell it, eyes bloodshot. *Oh, my love.*

9

And then it was September again. It had been another dry year; the blooms of the bear grass were dark and rough, already split open.

Just a few weeks earlier, Beal had written from Paducah and talked in a vague way about a separation, that maybe it would be for the best for a while. It gave me hope that he'd concluded just what I had: The marriage was over. Briefly, I'd felt the return of warmth toward him.

It's not like it used to be, I thought. *We don't have to stay married to the wrong person. All sorts of things are changing. We can change, too.* But he didn't mention the letter when he came back from Paducah and neither did I. I thought it would be best to wait until Albert and I had fully settled our plans.

I decided to give a party. I don't really know why. It was something to do, I guess, something to take my mind off things. We'd had electricity in town just long enough for candles to be a novelty again and I thought I'd light the whole house with them. I thought of it all—the party, the candles—as a kind of distraction from the clamor of the undecided. I could pretend at least for a while that things were the way they'd always been. And at the same time . . . well, the candles were a way of telling everyone: *The world has changed. Don't you see everything looks different?*

"So pretty, Lena, just like you." People said things like that as they came through the door, with the last of the daylight slipping away outside in the windy evening and the candles at the entrance, bunched together and covered with hurricane glass, a nest of tiny fires. "So unusual; oh, how lovely; I don't know how you think of these things; it's magical, like a fairy story."

Beal had complained about the whole thing while Nettie and I and some other hired help were setting things up, but now he was beaming: Proud of his wife, proud of the impression we were both making.

Mrs. Moore appeared startled. Then she smiled, and gazed around her, looking almost rapturous before she composed her face into its usual opinionated grumpiness and said, nodding curtly at me, "Whatever gave you that idea?"

Mrs. Boyce arrived before I could answer. Of course, Albert hadn't stayed in New Orleans or anywhere else they'd tried to send him that was far enough away from me, but I suppose she thought if I was giving a party, I must be intent on staying married and she wanted to indicate her approval.

"It's beautiful, Lena," she said to me warmly. "Your house looks so beckoning, something the wayfarer can come home to," she continued, then looked embarrassed, as if the possible meanings of what she'd said had suddenly struck her.

People's faces looked different in the candlelight. As he leaned over a little table to bite into a tea sandwich, Mr. Fuqua's handlebar moustache was lit from below, his eyebrows heightened by the light, his eyes deepened. Cassie Wallace was softened, her sallowness erased. The Colonel, studiously avoiding Fuqua, stood bathed in pink light in a corner where I'd tied a rose-colored scarf around the glass holding the candle.

And then, in the middle of an evening I was proud of and enjoying and which briefly carried me away from my troubles, I felt sudden cramping, though it wasn't time for my monthly. I excused myself and went upstairs. When I looked, I saw blood everywhere.

I'd lost a child in the years between Lenora and Georgia's birth. It was too early in the pregnancy even to see the baby; he or she just slipped away on a tide of blood. But I hadn't recovered quickly; the doctor in Childress fretted over my grieving and the bleeding and prescribed a full month of bed rest. Beal had been good to me then, spoiling and cosseting me until I was well.

This time was different. He knew he couldn't be the father, even though I tried to convince him otherwise. "Dr. McMeans is wrong about the date. Of course, it's yours. How could it be anyone else's?" I cried. I swore I'd been true. But he knew better.

The story he and his lawyers came up with was nonsense, something to work around the awkward, messy details, something to support their simple tale of good versus evil. One of the only true things in it was that I managed to convince him, at least briefly, that Albert and I were through. "Never again," I promised tearfully.

Of course, I was lying. I'd come to believe that the miscarriage was God's punishment. I'd lost Albert's baby because I'd continued to live as if our secret world wasn't the real one, just like all the other hypocrites in Amarillo.

"Why should I keep acting like I believe this love is wrong?" I said to Albert when he came to see me, as I lay in the daybed downstairs, still weak from having lost so much blood.

Albert sighed. "He'll never let you go now, much less take the children," he said, then took my hand and kissed it gently. "Let me take you to Brazil. It's like it used to be here, great cattle country. When he sees how much your girls miss you, maybe he'll be willing to talk to you about having them. But we have to go secretly." He paused. "Maybe he's gripey and y'all are fighting and maybe he even sometimes wishes he was free of you. But he's a man. And now he knows some other bull's been kicking in his pasture. If you try to get him to agree to a divorce, after all this . . ." He shook his head and squeezed my hand.

"I'm sure I can talk him into it," I said. "He just needs a little time to calm down. We haven't been happy for ever so long. He might truly be glad, especially if he thinks getting rid of me will cost less than keeping me. And he wrote that letter, remember?"

The way things got pictured later . . . as if Albert and I had no sense of morality. It was the opposite really: if we'd been like others in town, we would have just gone on as we were. I think we could have easily managed it, maybe for the rest of all of our lives. But neither of us believed we should have to lie to love one another. Even Albert's plans to run away always ended with everybody learning and accepting the truth.

"Albert, you know I never . . . imagined any of this," I went on after a few moments. "I never thought it would seem right to do what I'm doing with you."

"I know," he said, gazing down at me. "You want everyone to see the truth and . . ." He looked away to the middle distance, the way he did when he was searching for the right words.

"I don't want to be the *bad woman*," I blurted out. "You know the things people say when they think a woman has gone wrong."

"But if we run off," Albert said, "you won't *hear* them talking."

There hasn't been a day since that I haven't wished at least once that we'd done as he suggested.

10

Although Albert and I didn't know at the time, later it came out in court that his brother, Henry, and Beal's brother, Joe, had taken the train down from Dalhart together in early October to talk the whole situation over—which by that time they realized was pretty dire. Joe was good friends with Albert and Henry, and he and their younger sister Bessie had planned to marry before she died in 1906. Joe was easy-natured, good with women, and generous. Beal used to say: "I look like a short, squat version of him, don't I? Only I didn't turn out handsome." That was back when he could count on me to tell him I thought he looked just fine.

On the train, after a long talk, Joe and Henry had decided to leave the problem to *the three old men*. That meant our fathers, who had decades of friendship and trust behind them and could surely work something out to keep the peace. Joe was supposed to wire my father once he got back to Amarillo, but instead he decided to wire his own.

"I don't want to get Old Tom all riled up," he told Henry. "Lena's his daughter and he . . . well, I don't think he's likely to be real reasonable about this."

And Henry said to Joe, "You think wiring your father is a good idea? You know how him and Beal are."

Henry was right: Mr. Sneed didn't really approve of Beal or of me. My father was an old-style Southerner through and through—idolized women, but expected to be boss; cried over the death of a good dog, but had no trouble hanging a horse thief; certain that nothing in the world was more important than honor and virtue and family.

But for Mr. Sneed, a rigid justice prevailed, whether you were family or not. It was kind of a Yankee Puritan attitude when you got right down to it, and he was happy to get right down to most things, especially if it involved correcting other people. He was a Methodist who tolerated Baptists—and to some extent Presbyterians and Lutherans—but was suspicious of Episcopalians and flat out horrified by Catholics. He seemed to think he was God's personal assistant. His job was to sit in judgement of human foibles, particularly those afflicting his own family, so the Lord didn't have to bother. "Face facts squarely," he often said, usually before he told you something unpleasant.

He'd been relatively pleased about our marriage at first. It was a good match between families, even if I was just a little too "lively" for his tastes. But he'd soured over the years. Most of the time, I called him Mr. Sneed, even when he invited me to call him Father. He asked like he thought it was the correct thing and wanted, as usual, to be correct, but I didn't think there was a shred of paternal feeling in it.

Before all the trouble, we mostly went to Georgetown to visit, where he lived with Beal's stepmother, the one we called Aunt Lillian. If he did come to Amarillo, he was more comfortable spending the night with Joe's family or his daughter Georgia's, both of whom lived a few blocks away. But on the few occasions he stayed with us, I was always anxious. I remember one visit when my Georgia was about two. He was due to arrive right after her nap and I told Nettie to get her dressed in a clean frock when she woke up. It took her a while to emerge from the world of sleep, and we both hoped she'd be less cranky than usual.

Beal headed off in the brand-new automobile to pick his father up at the station. I didn't think Mr. Sneed's temper was likely to be improved by the ride. A few minutes after they pulled in, I heard his voice outside the door. "Do you think such a purchase was really necessary, son? Seems to me the buggy suited you just fine and saved you some money, too."

Beal's answer—if he made one—was drowned out by Georgie, who was crying wildly upstairs as Nettie tried to soothe her. "Now, now, Miss Georgia, no need to bawl like a little heifer. Your mama wants you to act nice today, you hear? Your grandpa's coming. Won't that be nice?"

The sound of Nettie's voice was punctuated by Georgie hollering "Mama! Mama!" I was torn but decided Mr. Sneed might think me a rude, overindulgent parent if I didn't greet him instead of hurrying to my daughter.

"Mister . . . Father," I corrected myself, "it's so nice to see you. How was your trip? How is Aunt Lillian?" I had the habit of babbling in front of him, not the way I sometimes did to amuse myself and others, but because I felt his disapproval squatting like a toad under his smiles and cold, correct embraces. Georgie continued to howl, and I felt a spurt of irritation. *Couldn't she shut up just this once?*

"I think you'd better go attend to your daughter, Lena," said Mr. Sneed, giving me that sour smile that always made me feel I'd failed somehow, though I wasn't sure if he thought I should have comforted Georgie instead of greeting him, or that if I'd done a better job raising her, she wouldn't expect me to come running when she called. I always told myself it was just the way he was and he didn't mean anything by it, but I was usually thoroughly upset by the end of his visits. He saved the brunt of his criticism for Beal, though. In his view, the man was ultimately responsible for the behavior of everyone in the household: Wife, children, household help.

I rolled my eyes at Nettie as I walked into the girls' bedroom and held my arms out for Georgie, who quieted quickly. "Look at your face, sugar," I said. "You're all smudgy." Her small, warm body, with her face creased red where her blanket had been and her runny nose, which she twisted away from me when I tried to wipe it, was a comfort. Solid—she was always so solid, from the time she was born. "What do we care what he thinks?" I whispered, and just then, holding her, I meant it.

Lenora had come in, too, and stood looking at me with her deep, soulful eyes. "Don't worry, Mama," Lenora said, "it'll be fine." She was so young then, only about seven, but she knew I was worried and what I was worried about, even if I couldn't admit it.

"Of course I won't worry," I said, smiling at her and Georgie. "What have I got to worry about when I have my two girls?"

Nettie headed off to the kitchen and I led the girls down to greet their grandfather, who was standing in the entry hall gazing around him and saying, "There's a lot of money in this house, son. I know you feel you need to . . ." He broke off when he saw us and smiled his first real smile at the sight of the girls. Lenora led Georgie by the hand and said shyly, "Hello, Grandpapa." Georgie repeated the phrase, imitating her sister.

I was so proud. No matter what he thinks about me, I said to myself, he can't say I haven't got two fine children. He just beamed, squatted down, and opened his arms. It always amazed me to see the way he changed around them. They were his flesh and blood, but a generation removed, so he didn't feel quite so personally responsible for instilling a firm sense of proper behavior in them.

"I believe I might have something for two little girls in my pockets," he said to them. "Now wherever did I put those things? I hope I didn't lose them." He'd been doing this with Lenora since she was a baby, so she knew perfectly well he hadn't lost anything, and that this was her signal to help him look for whatever it was.

"Come on, Georgie," she said, "Let's help Grandpapa look for our presents. Try this pocket here." She helped Georgia put her hand into the pocket of his overcoat.

He'd brought two little dolls, tiny things with porcelain heads and stuffed bodies. Their faces were as white as my best dishes, their lips were painted red, their eyes were blue, and they had tiny white hands, dimpled like children's. "Oh, those are cunning," I said to him. "How thoughtful of you." He was so pleased with the girls' reaction that he actually gave me a genuine smile.

"I knew they'd like them," he said. "When I saw them, I said to Mother, 'Those will be perfect for Beal's girls.'" He looked around him and his mouth tightened again. "Not that they want for much, I'm sure."

His theme of late. I could tell we were going to hear about it the entire visit. Beal would end up coming to bed in a foul mood after he and his father had talked privately a while.

That chat happened after dinner. I listened from behind the half-open French door, peering through the slivered view to the dining room. "You can't let a woman dictate your purchases, son," Mr. Sneed said. "You've spent far more than you should have on this place. You don't *need* all these things. That crystal we had on the table at dinner—why, it must have cost a small fortune."

I made a mental note not to use the best things next time he visited.

"Well, Lena likes nice things, Father, and looking like you can afford it makes a difference in this town." I couldn't see Beal, but I could tell from his voice he was leaning forward, eager to convince his father, certain that just this once he could do it if he just talked hard enough and fast enough, the way he always managed to convince most everybody else. "Mr. Fuqua and I have started into business together. He thinks I have a fine future. Good judge of cattle, he says, shrewd dealer, hard dealer. He feels safe sending me wherever he needs someone to look after his interests." He paused briefly. "I don't have any debt I can't handle."

Mr. Sneed sat straight and stiff in his chair, the fist of his rectitude bunched up inside him. He reminded me of those fire-and-brimstone preachers who came into town ranting about sin, except Mr. Sneed never ranted. It would have been too voluptuous a use of his voice.

"Son, it's never a good idea to let a woman get too much control in marriage," he said, firmly. "They get ideas in their heads. Your mother understood her place and your stepmother does, too, although she doesn't always like it." He made a sound somewhere between a sniff and snort and shook his head. "A firm hand at the helm, son," he went on, "a firm hand at the helm. It's up to us to make sure our women don't get carried away by their desires."

"But Father—"

"Nothing but ruin can come from letting a woman have too much control," Mr. Sneed said, his tone ever more decisive. "It's a lesson you'd do well to heed, son. You've got a headstrong wife. She pulls at the yoke. I can see it, and it's trouble. Those Snyder girls always were a little too lively for their own good or anyone else's. And old Tom Snyder was a fool about Lena, right proud of the way she can charm a rattlesnake if she wants to. She charmed you, son, but she hasn't charmed this old man so much that he can't see that spending all this money on her frivolous desires is a foolish, foolish thing to do."

It would have served the old buzzard right if I'd stepped into the room. But I was so stung by his words that I just stood there.

Clara Sneed

11

It was a beautiful fall afternoon in October of 1911 when things came to a head. Beal came home for dinner, I met him on the gallery, took a deep breath, looked him straight in the eyes, and said, "You know I'm in love with Albert. I want to go away with him and take the girls."

He looked at me like he was from another country where they didn't speak English. He rubbed his forehead and then his eyes, as if he couldn't see, and sat down heavily on the porch swing. "What is *wrong* with you?" Out on Tyler, a mule plodded by pulling the Griffin Grocery wagon.

"Let me go," I said as evenly as I could. "You can't possibly want me. Why would you? Let me go."

He grabbed my hand and yanked me down into the swing beside him. "Lena," he said, and I could tell he was trying to sound patient. "You aren't well. You know that. You need a rest or—"

"Look at what *happened*," I interrupted furiously, pulling my hand away. "That's the truth. Anyway, you wrote me. You agreed to—"

"No, I didn't," he said emphatically. "Lena, you can't possibly mean what you're saying. I know I haven't been home the way I should, but we've been happy together. We'll be happy again. Let me send you to California. Take your sister and get away from . . . from all of this for a while. Living in this place, in this climate, it's no place for a lively woman."

"It's *not* the climate," I retorted. "It's the *marriage*. You've never cared the first thing about what I was thinking and you don't now. If you'd paid the slightest attention to me, maybe none of this would have happened. But you haven't for years. The truth is you've never loved me. You like having me here, taking care of the girls, giving fancy parties and charming the neighbors. You let me spend your money so you don't have to worry about me. That's not love. I know what love is now, and it's not what you've been giving me."

He stood abruptly, making the swing rock. "We'll talk of this later," he said in a tone I'd never heard before, then staggered toward the house. The screen door creaked and banged. I sat staring toward the street without seeing it. Then I started to cry.

It got worse that night. All the things that had lain beneath the surface for years came spewing up. I don't really remember how we ended up in our bedroom, but there we stood, facing one another, fists clenched like boxers. "You bitch," he hissed. He slapped me so hard that I toppled over onto the bed. The word bitch kept coming out of his mouth in a steady undertone, as if saying the word was how he managed to keep breathing.

He'd never spoken like that to me before, nor struck me. "What didn't I give you? What have we lacked?" he shouted. I saw his balding head, his stout body, the broad broken face, and red eyes. I tried to quell the abrupt ferocious pity tangled up with the fury inside me.

"I don't understand how you can have changed your mind," I said angrily, trying to get things back to just arguing like we used to. "You didn't want this any more than I did a month ago—"

"No," he said, clutching my hand so tight I cried out. "You can't mean this. It's impossible." He dropped to his knees and peered up into my face. I was trying not to look, but no matter which way I turned his head followed mine. We were like two snakes reared up and weaving before one another.

"Think of our girls," he said, desperately. "You must not leave us, please . . . We could go somewhere together, just the two of us, please. I'll do anything you ask. I'll give you anything you want, just stay." His pride was twisting away inside him. I knew it hurt him to beg.

I could feel ghosts in the room. Maybe they were the two of us in earlier times, or his dead mother or others we didn't recognize, but they were there. I sat on the bed where I'd fallen, cradling my slapped cheek. Beal was on his knees. I'd forgotten to draw the curtains and I caught a glimpse of our reflections wavering in the glass.

"Don't you have anything to say?" Beal cried, seizing hold of my thighs. "Don't you feel anything at all?"

Right then, I didn't. I was so tired. I just wanted the talking and the crying and the arguing and the pleading to end. I wanted to escape out the window into the streets. Beal rose to his feet, grabbed my shoulders, and shook me until my teeth rattled and I tasted blood.

"You can't do this," he shouted. "By God, I'll teach you not to do this to me."

With one hand, he pinned my hand to the bed and with the other he yanked the Colt out of the drawer in the bedside table. Everything slowed down. I knew he meant to shoot me—and for a split second I didn't care. But when he brought the gun up to my head and cocked it, I screamed as loud as I could.

Lenora came rushing into the room. She must have been right outside listening. "Don't shoot. Don't kill her," she shrieked, and Beal lowered the gun. She rushed into my arms and burst into tears.

"I'm sorry, I'm sorry, I'm sorry," I kept repeating.

Beal looked dazed, the way steers do right after being cut. He put the gun back in the drawer and shut it very quietly.

Then he sat down on the other side of Lenora and patted her back with a gentle repeated motion. "I'm sorry," he said simply, bending over her head, which was buried in my shoulder. "I won't do it again." She reached her hand out to his.

We remained there for some time, Beal and I, trying to comfort Lenora, repeating the same thing over and over: "It's all right, don't cry, it's all right." Why do we say that to children when we know it isn't true?

Later that night, when the house was cold and Beal was dozing on our bed in his rumpled clothes, Lenora asleep beside him, I went to the girls' room. Georgie was still young enough to sleep so hard that even my screaming hadn't wakened her. Her face—which could be so fixed and determined—was smoothed into the kind of beauty young children have, so great that you catch your breath over the clarity of the cut of their mouths, the smoothness of their skin.

In the movies they sometimes split the screen in two, show you two different things at the same time. That's what it felt like: Love for my children and love for Albert were separate scenes, no way to join them. My girls wanted their father and mother together. They wanted the parents they'd thought they had, the ones who never failed them, at least not in any important way.

I'd thought I couldn't live with any more lies. But that day—though I didn't know it at the time—was the start of a lifetime of them. It wasn't only the lies that Beal and all the rest told, nor the ones I told Beal and others. Eventually, I lied to Albert, too. I loved him and I lied to him. Sometimes I took Beal's money and told Albert I hadn't. Things like that.

Lying gave me room, and I ended up needing all the room I could get.

12

Although I tried hard to stop him, Beal wired my father to come down from Clayton the next morning. I didn't want him there. I knew he'd bring with him the presence of my whole family, the way each one of us led to all the others, like a big constellation. And this wasn't their business. For once. But of course my father got on the night train and came as soon as he could. I met him at the yard gate early the following morning.

It was going to be another beautiful October day in Amarillo, the air chilled but sure to warm, the light clear and golden. My father was worried because of the telegram—*Come as soon as possible, I need you*—but he didn't yet know the real trouble. I saw confusion in his thin, stern face.

I'd always been his favorite, though he never said so, the baby 'til Susan was born when I was six. And though he never realized it, he himself had trained me to want more than I got from my marriage to Beal; he'd let me ride bareback and shoot, turned a blind eye to various shenanigans, boasted about my brains, got a kick out of all the beaus I collected.

Now he pushed the gate open with a ropey-veined hand, the sun slanting up behind him, spiking its way between houses, making the white hair curling above his stiff collar shine. He looked bewildered when I burst into tears, threw my arms around his neck, and cried out, "Father, I have done no wrong."

I knew he couldn't hear what I really meant; it was like a canyon had suddenly opened up between us. And so my words turned into a lie the moment I said them. They came to mean something specific and untrue: *I didn't lie down with my lover.*

Over the next few days, all three families visited up and down Polk

Before We Turn to Dust

and Tyler to talk the thing over. There were *the three old men*: My father, Beal's father, Albert's father. There were Beal's brother Joe, his sister Georgia and her husband Terry Thompson, and Albert's brothers Henry and William. There was my sister, Eula, who came in from Plano. And there was Beal.

At first, Beal wouldn't see his father because he knew exactly what he was going to say: *Give her up.* It was so ironic that for once in our lives Mr. Sneed and I were on the same side of an argument. My own father blamed Albert and threatened to shoot him. Mr. Sneed and the Colonel blamed us both. Everyone was sorry.

With all the chaos, I'd forgotten that October 17 was our tenth wedding anniversary until Beal muttered something about faithless wives and sacred vows right before he stormed out the door. I headed to the parlor. It was the company room, and the one place I felt some coolness and a tiny bit of distance from the fevered family conversations. The shades were drawn. I sat in the semi-darkness with a sense of relief. Beal had gone I didn't care where. Eula had taken the girls downtown, and Nettie wouldn't bother me—she wanted nothing to do with any of it.

As I sat quietly in one of the guest chairs trying to get my heart to slow down, my father appeared suddenly in the shadowed doorway, startling me. *When had he arrived back at the house?* He walked in, holding himself even more erect than usual, his pale collar gleaming dully in the half-light. "Lena," he began, positioning himself directly in front of me. "We are taking you to a place in Fort Worth tonight."

I stared at him, confused. "What do you mean, a place in Fort Worth?"

He stretched a little taller, drawing his feet together as if he were on a parade ground. "A place where they can help you get well."

"But Papa," I said, "I'm not sick. What are you talking about?"

He cleared his throat, then went on in a louder voice. "You aren't thinking right. Your mother told me last summer when she visited she thought something was wrong and I see now what she meant."

He glanced toward the piano, as if its large dark shape was a respite, and then turned his stern gaze back to me. "You need a rest," he said.

Clara Sneed

"You're . . ." he paused, then seized on the easiest word he could think of. "You're nervous."

Despite everything, I laughed. "What do you expect me to be?" I asked. "*All* of you are treating me like I don't know my own mind or anything else. I want a divorce. I know that shocks you and you're ashamed of me for wanting it, and you think I've done wrong, but that don't make me crazy." I stood up, folded my arms across my chest, and glared at him.

"You be ready to go this evening," he said, glaring right back. "We've made up our minds. It's a nice place. They'll treat you well and you'll get a rest." He turned away and stalked toward the door, where he stopped to look back at me.

"I never expected," he began, then shook his head and walked out.

My mouth was as stiff as his own. *At least I'll get away from all this*, I thought.

That afternoon, I filled three trunks, packing as if I would never return. "You won't be needing a tenth of that," Beal said angrily, yanking dresses out, wadding them furiously into big, sloppy balls and hurling them on the bed. "This ain't a trip to Mineral Wells." I didn't bother to argue.

That evening, my father, Eula, and the girls all got on the train with Beal and me, though my father got off after an hour or so to head back to Clayton. He tried to hug me goodbye, but I turned away.

Once everyone else had fallen asleep, Beal returned to his earlier theme. "How could you forget our anniversary?" he hissed at me.

Really, at that moment, I almost liked the idea of the sanitarium: I wouldn't have to listen to any of them anymore—especially Beal. His face seemed to alternate between one of a man who would get what he wanted at any cost and the crushed face of a little boy, not hard at all, the lines and the pugnacious set of his jaw erased.

I couldn't love him. It was something animal, beyond my reach. I couldn't change it.

13

By noon the next day, Eula and I were standing in the wide lobby of the Metropolitan Hotel, watching the girls play a restrained game of hide-and-seek around the big armchairs. It was the finest hotel in Fort Worth—*only five minutes from your train*—three stories of red brick with all the luxuries: Gas, electricity, steam heat, and artesian baths. The property had been part of Hell's Half Acre not many years before and you only had to walk a short distance to find the Acre's bars and cribs. But in the Metropolitan lobby, that world hardly felt real.

Beal and Eula's husband, Henry Bowman, had left us to go track down a noted alienist. "Let's take the girls shopping," I suggested. Maybe I could explain things without them around to tell her I was wrong.

She gave me a worried look. I could see she'd been warned.

"Eula, please," I said, taking her hands. "I just want to pretend things are normal for a few hours. Let's go get you a hat. God knows I won't need a *thing* in that place they're taking me, but you should get something out of this trip." I smiled. "Please?" She smiled a little in return, but she was still on her guard.

"Lena, you know I can't let you run away, or wire Al, or use the phone." She gripped my hands and looked at me intently. "I'm not going anywhere if you don't agree to that."

"Oh, Eula," I sighed, "of course I won't." Her face looked so strained I felt sorry for her. She had to struggle to keep her distance from me in her heart, something she'd never before had to do. She wasn't fiery like I was and she'd had to listen to Henry and Beal go on and on about my behavior.

When the girls returned to us, bored with their game, I told them that I wanted us all to go shopping but that their Aunt Eula wasn't quite sure. Lenora said in the quiet, downcast way she said so much during that time, "Please, Aunt Eula. We all need something to do." Eula gave her a quick hug and agreed. She looked relieved. She could tell Henry that she'd gone shopping for the sake of the girls.

Like Amarillo's other fashionable women, I'd always come to Fort Worth to shop in the spring and the fall, and it wasn't too hard to pretend that this was the same kind of trip. The air was warm and the streets were busy and once we arrived at Jacksons, we all relaxed a little. "I *would* like you to help me pick out a hat, Lena," said Eula. "What with the children and Henry, I forget to take care of how I look sometimes." She sounded almost happy.

I sized her up, picturing something with lots of feathers, something to soften the sharpness of her features and the lines that worked too hard around her mouth and eyes. For a moment I forgot all about my troubles. "We'd like to try this, this, and this," I said to a saleswoman who fluttered into view like a butterfly making small, decorative gestures, her eyes undoubtedly taking in the size of my diamonds and the generally expensive appearance of my clothes and of my own hat—a large, high-crowned thing with stiff ribbons matching the ribbons in my dress.

"Please sit down," she said, pulling two chairs from against the wall into the center of the room. Then she carefully placed the hats I'd selected on top of the nearest display case with its rows of gloves and hairpins and combs. Georgie sat on my lap and paddled her feet out of boredom, but Lenora was old enough to look admiringly at the beautiful things around her.

"You have lovely daughters, ma'am," said the saleswoman. *She must be new,* I thought. *I don't recognize her.* She was a woman about my own age in a neat shirtwaist and skirt, a thin wedding ring on her finger. I wondered briefly what it must be like to work around such beautiful things and not be able to afford them.

Eula tried each hat in turn, and the three of us conferred on its merits as the afternoon light came through the open windows, along with the sound of automobiles and wagons and horses and mules, of people talking, of the newsboys hawking the *Star-Telegram*, and of the trolley braking at the stop below us. Everything seemed so normal. Only the way my stomach felt, as if it were floating somewhere, and my lack of appetite—I hadn't eaten since the night before—reminded me that things weren't.

We chose a much fancier hat than Eula was used to and that we had to convince her was becoming. She kept peering into the mirror, making tiny adjustments to the way it sat on her head, until finally she broke into a shy smile and said, "It does look nice, doesn't it?" The saleswoman placed it carefully in its box and Eula looked at it with pleasure, until she suddenly remembered that I was going to a sanitarium because I was ready to leave my husband for a man she'd known and trusted since childhood. She took herself and her innocent pleasure in hand and said, "Now, dear, we must get back to the hotel. They'll be expecting us."

That trip to Jacksons was my very last vestige of ordinary domestic life for quite some time. We drove out to Arlington Heights that evening. The girls sat on either side of me in the back seat of the open car, with Beal rigid and silent in front. Henry Bowman pointed out the lake and various amenities of the new suburb as if we were shopping for real estate. "And here we are," he said cheerfully as we approached a large pale house with a wrap-around porch on both floors.

It looked like someone's fancy home—that was the idea. A middle-aged woman who looked normal was seated in a garden chair beside a little fountain. "Let's just see what you think of this one," said Henry. "If you don't like it, we'll find something else."

Why I believed that I have no idea. Maybe I just wanted to be done with the strained talk and Beal's glowering silence. He took my elbow to steer me up the sidewalk, the girls and Henry trailing behind. A tallish man with regular features appeared at the front door, smiled warmly, extended one hand to shake mine and clasped my elbow with the other, as if greeting an old friend. "I'm Dr. Allison," he said. Beside him stood a stout, grim-faced woman in a nurse's uniform, obviously the matron.

"Here she is," I heard Beal say. Dr. Allison's grip on my elbow tightened and the matron caught hold of my other arm. I'd been trapped. My girls were the only ones not in on it. "You can't do this," I shouted. I tried to pull free, but they squeezed my arms tightly—the matron had the stronger grip—while Dr. Allison frantically gestured to someone down the hall.

By now, the girls were crying. "Papa, make them stop. Stop hurting Mama."

"Get the children out of here now," Beal hollered at Henry, who grabbed the girls' hands and dragged them away. Beal looked at me with some dark mix of feelings I couldn't sort out. Then he rushed out the door, slamming it behind him. "For God's sake, save her," he shouted from the porch. The matron jerked at my right arm and the orderly who'd just arrived jammed a needle in.

Then the light telescoped down and my screaming seemed to float away into the gray edges of the shrinking light.

I woke up in a dark room on a bed in my kimona, naked underneath.

14

They kept me in my kimona for the first few weeks. I smelled rank. They wouldn't let me take a bath, though I begged for one. I could hear the other inmates—patients, as they called some of us; guests, as they always referred to me, at least to my face—even from the other wings. It was worst at night, like all terrors.

"Oh, no," Dr. Allison later testified, "she was permitted to go wherever she wanted in the house." But I heard it: The key turning in the lock, the click and thump as the bolt moved into place. I stopped my own muttering and crying then, scarcely breathed, terrified, though of what I couldn't say exactly. They would never have entered the room. They just wanted to make certain they met Beal's most basic demand: *Keep her here.*

Outside the sanitarium's barred windows were the outskirts of Fort Worth and the autumn moon and stars.

It was Albert's name I said some nights, over and over, until I knew the shape of it as well as I came to know his body, the way it began like a cry or a moan and ended almost swallowed down, saved at the end from vanishing down my throat by my tongue against the roof of my mouth.

And some nights I cried for my girls. Beal had given them to the Bowmans *until this thing is straightened out.* What did Eula and Henry say to them about me? How awful it must be for them, plunged into a different household and a strange school in the middle of the year for reasons they couldn't explain. Dead or sick: Those were acceptable reasons for your mother not being there.

Run off. Committed. Those were a lot more difficult.

But after a few nights of stinking and crying, I found myself trying out words I'd heard men say under their breath if they realized women were around, or out loud if they didn't. Words I'd never dared speak aloud. And that made me feel better. *Sonofabitch. Bastard.* I felt my eyes narrow as I spoke. I pretended I had the power of my father or the Colonel—of truly powerful men—and that Dr. Allison or his brother, the other Dr. Allison, was cowering in front of me.

And then one night I tried the word *fuck. Albert, I love to fuck you.* I could feel my breath shorten in the dark, my cheeks burning, and I pressed on, said it again and again until it meant nothing bad, until it sounded soothing. *I want to fuck you. I love to fuck you.*

That one I shared with him later. I didn't mean to. The words just slipped out one night in a whisper—his ear so close—and they were clean in my mouth. I'd purged them in those nights at the Arlington Heights Sanitarium, when the doctors imagined I was getting well.

After four or five days, Beal's outside alienist, Dr. Turner, came to see me. He was a big deal in the world of Texas lunatics; he'd headed up the state asylum at Terrell, according to my nurse Lillie, who wasn't supposed to tell me he was coming but did anyway.

I was lying on the bed when I heard the key turn in the lock—and not at the usual time. They opened the doors a few hours a day because they thought it was good for all of us—except the homicidal types upstairs—to get out and interact with one another. Unless you were physically ill, you weren't allowed to shut the door until social time was over.

It was like the dances, which they also believed were helpful. Most everyone—excluding the homicidals and maniacal Baptists—had to attend, although they kept a sharp eye out for inappropriate behavior. Lillie told me some stories. I didn't have to go to those, praise the Lord. Maybe Beal worried what I'd do cutting a rug with a crazy man. Or maybe it was the Drs. Allison who were scared.

On his first visit, Dr. Turner brought a Dr. Gregory—his successor at Terrell—with him. I reckon they'd been comparing notes about the various maniacs they were in charge of and Dr. Turner had invited Dr. Gregory along to see this *very interesting case* he had over in the Heights.

Dr. Gregory was younger than Dr. Turner and looked more like a big farmer than an alienist. According to Lillie, he was obsessed with alcoholics. He traveled the state speaking about their evil effects on society, especially the increase in what he called *defectives*, on account of alcoholics breeding, the solution to which was sterilization, and the sooner we all realized it the better. It was our Christian duty. God knows what he was doing to the lunatics at Terrell, most of whom he was convinced were crazy as a direct or indirect result of liquor.

In only a few days, I'd reached the point where I no longer jumped off the bed if I thought someone was coming into the room. I'd lie there and look at them and wait to see what they'd do. Dr. Allison usually just sat down and started to talk. But apparently Dr. Turner thought it useful to pretend he was making a social visit. Unlike Dr. Gregory—who stood towering to the side—Dr. Turner was average size, with a trim beard and deep-set dark eyes.

"Good morning, Mrs. Sneed," he said in a firm voice, just this side of too loud. "What a pleasure it is to meet you at last." He extended his hand, which was, strictly speaking, a breach of etiquette since I was the lady, but I guess he felt that under the circumstances the rules could be bent. I stared at his hand, which oddly and suddenly reminded me of Albert's, similarly sized and shaped, and the bottom dropped out of my heart for a minute. Then I stretched my right hand to meet his, which he clasped so forcefully that he managed to pull me to my feet.

"Now Mrs. Sneed, I know you are troubled," he said, still holding my hand, "but for your own sake, I want you to make an effort to remember what a refined lady you *really* are." He stopped and stared at me with the piercing eyes, like he'd been told many times how effective they were. "I know you have been taught that a lady should never allow an unknown gentleman to see her"—he paused—"relaxing on her bed."

There was another tiny pause before he added, "Or any other gentleman, whether she knows him or not."

I hated him right from the start.

Dr. Gregory was standing there trying to look unobtrusive, which was difficult given his size. He cleared his throat and our eyes met.

Whatever I saw made me wish he was the one I'd be dealing with. There was a window there—it could have been attraction, pity, a desire to escape, or something else, but I knew I could have gotten to him. There wasn't a chance I was going to get to Dr. Turner.

"Now, Mrs. Sneed," Dr. Turner continued, pulling me round to face him, "your husband very much wants what's best for you. You're fortunate to have a husband like that. If you'd seen the kind of tragedy I have, you'd know just how true that is." He gazed out the window, like he was remembering those sad histories. Then he looked back at me. "Tell me, Mrs. Sneed," he said, giving me the direct eye treatment again, "what do *you* think of your husband?"

I'd had enough experience by now to realize that telling the truth wasn't what was called for.

Instead I asked, "When can I see my children? My youngest, she's only five, she's too young to be away from me this long."

Dr. Turner gazed silently some more while I stood there, hugging my arms to my waist, feeling how thin I'd gotten. "And yet," he finally said, "you were contemplating leaving them forever. How is that?"

"Not forever," I said. "I didn't want it to be like this." That at least was the truth.

"Sit down, Mrs. Sneed," the doctor said, gesturing to the chair beside the bed. I sat. "I'd like to talk to you about all these things. This man you are infatuated with, for instance."

Dr. Gregory was shifting his weight a bit, looking as if he wished he could sit down, too. Unfortunately for him, Dr. Turner took the other chair, pulled it closer to mine, and stared at me again, like he thought his prolonged gaze might hypnotize me into telling him everything. And I did have a brief fantasy of confessing, just so I could take a bath, put on real clothes and get away from the noise at night.

"I love him," I said. My eyes challenged his for a moment, but I could see that wasn't going to get me anywhere. His turned into hard black pebbles. So I folded my hands in my lap and tried to look as demure as possible.

"Doctor, despite what my husband says, this isn't a good marriage. He hasn't been happy either." I kept my eyes down and my voice low.

"You're an experienced man. You know what marriages can be. This is not a happy one. I think my husband . . ." I was going to say I thought it was all a matter of pride with Beal, but I sensed that would inflame the doctor.

"Mrs. Sneed," he said decisively, "I believe—from my experience, as you say—that your husband loves you. He realizes he neglected you somewhat in his attempts to make his business successful. But surely you can see how that was a sign of his love for you and the girls. He wanted to provide for you. Even now, he wants to provide for you."

He paused to look out the window in a melancholy way again. "He told me of the fine home you have in Amarillo," he continued after a moment. "Now he tells me he is willing to go anywhere you might choose to get away from this trouble and restore your happiness. I don't need to tell you, Mrs. Sneed"—he turned to face me again—"you are by all accounts a very intelligent woman, I don't need to tell you how much better off your girls will be if you and your husband can live amicably together.

"Divorce is not common in our society," he went on in a quiet voice, "although unfortunately it becomes more so all the time. But let me assure you, Mrs. Sneed, from my work with families, particularly among the classes where divorce is, sadly, a more usual remedy, that its effects on children are devastating."

I had a moment of seeing him not as my enemy, although he was, but as a man truly concerned about the things he spoke of. But if I gave in once, if I allied myself even for an instant with him, I knew I would be lost.

He wasn't stupid. He reached across the short distance between us and squeezed my hand gently, letting his own silence fill the space. I was tempted to squeeze his back—that hand so like Albert's—but I didn't.

Then he said, "Seduction is difficult, Mrs. Sneed," and he lost me right there, because I knew it wasn't seduction.

"Seduction is difficult," he repeated with a sigh, "I have only compassion for women like yourself who are the victims of these unscrupulous men who prey on your natural sentimental desires, particular-

Clara Sneed

ly in cases where there may be some marital discord. I am sure that, since this trouble started, many people have blamed you because they could not understand what might tempt you to believe you were losing your virtue only to gain something worth much more. I will not blame you."

He clearly felt this was very charitable on his part. He looked at me with mournful intensity, reminding me of a dog that wants you to pet it.

"I would like to help you, Mrs. Sneed," he said again. "I would like to help your family. I know this . . ." He searched his memory. "This Al . . ."

Even to hear his name like that, spoken by a man who could barely remember it, struck me the way power strikes the line it runs through. He was living and breathing somewhere; he wasn't a dream I'd had.

"This Al," Dr. Turner went on, "has made you feel as if life with him would be so different. But you know, marriage is marriage. There are always difficulties. I have heard many things, Mrs. Sneed, in the course of my years in this profession, and believe me, your marital problems are minor. And believe me, too, when I say that life with Al would not be what you expect right now."

He stood up so suddenly I started. His voice rose. "Before I see you again, I'd like you to think about what we have discussed."

We haven't "discussed" anything, I thought.

"In cases like yours," he concluded, "it is best if the patient is separated from all those she loves. It allows reflection. Consider carefully what you want for yourself and your daughters. I shall see you again in a few days. Charles," he said, turning to Dr. Gregory. It was strange, but I felt betrayed by his abrupt dismissal, though only a few minutes earlier I'd wanted him to leave.

Once they were gone, I lay down again. The light coming through the window was moving quickly toward dusk. I could smell myself, that thick animal stench, and I could feel my robe falling open, my hand beginning to travel down my belly, my legs parting slightly, then more; I didn't care, the shame was part of it, part of the pleasure, and the smell, so strong, so much the way it smelled with Albert and me sometimes, only without his. I could hear noises in the hall and still I didn't care, my hands and fingers rubbing and thrusting inside; oh my God such loneliness, such longing spilling all over, and the moaning no one would notice, too many other things to pay attention to—*Oh, my sweet boy, where are you?*—eyes closing to sleep.

Clara Sneed

15

Once I learned the kinds of things I needed to say to Dr. Turner and the Allison brothers about realizing the error of my ways, and wanting to go home to a husband who only wanted the best for me, they let me bathe and get dressed and walk around the grounds. They even let me go on little outings downtown with my nurse.

They also let me write letters to family. But they watched me while I wrote, took the pen and paper away once I'd finished, and though I always sealed the envelopes carefully I was sure they read the letters. I wrote to the girls and I wrote to Beal: *Please don't let Dr. Turner come here anymore. He don't know anything about me as he don't stay over 15 min., and I believe I would have seen you and the children if it hadn't been for him.*

My nurse's full name was Lillie Flowers. "Except it's L-i-l-l-i-e," she'd said when we met. I wondered what in the world her parents had been thinking. She came often to sit with me. She enjoyed reading the *Star-Telegram*'s little romances aloud—she'd acted in high school and liked voicing the characters.

"Heaven meant that we should meet and love each other, and it will not refuse us anything," she read dramatically one late afternoon, the light almost gone outside the windows.

My eyes welled up as Lillie continued with urgency: *"Go, dear Guy. Tomorrow, two hours after sunset, I will be waiting for you near the trap door."*

"Mrs. Sneed," she cried, when she realized I'd begun to weep, "Perhaps we shouldn't read these stories. They upset you so."

I wiped my eyes. "Lillie dear," I said and paused, looking down at my hands and twisting them in my lap, "I feel if I don't speak my heart to someone, I shall truly go mad. And I need to speak to another woman, not the Dr. Allisons and definitely not that awful Dr. Turner. Can I trust you?"

Her broad face with its blue eyes was a mix of curiosity and sympathy and a mostly suppressed excitement. For one thing, no one who wasn't nuts had ever called Dr. Turner awful to her face before. For another, she was surrounded by the insane and drug- and alcohol-addicted all day. I was a relief: Educated, wealthy, and clearly not crazy, no matter what the matron and the doctors said. And my husband was paying twice the going rate to keep me there. Lillie was dying for me to tell her my story, which she knew good and well wasn't the one she'd been hearing.

I used her boredom and her curiosity and her taste for melodrama. But it was also true that I needed to talk to someone. I needed to pour my heart out. It was one of my problems through the whole business.

"Oh, Mrs. Sneed," cried Lillie, crossing her hands over her heart, "I won't say a word to *anyone*." She put her hands back on her lap. "I've longed to tell you how sorry I feel for you—you seem so sad, I hope you won't be offended with my saying that." She blushed violently, a great splotch of color that bloomed like a peony and made the few freckles on her nose stand out.

"Of course not," I said. "I'm touched. It's true, I'm *terribly* sad. But before we talk more, perhaps I could ask you to do me the favor of calling me Lena?" I reached out and took her hand.

"Lena, I'd be honored," she answered, squeezing my hand encouragingly.

"If I confide in you, I want to believe you are my friend," I went on, plucking my phrases from the newspaper stories just like Lillie had. "And friends address each other by their Christian names. But there is another reason. The name 'Mrs. Sneed' repels me now. It represents a bond that has turned to bondage. In my heart, I am another's true wife." I was manipulating her—using the language of the stories, proposing intimacy—but I was also telling her the truth.

When is a marriage not a marriage? In the evenings in my room or walking on the grounds in the mellow autumn weather, we kept coming back to the subject. "I wanted to be a good wife," I told her. "But Beal's iron will and selfish ways slowly killed my love. When I met Albert again, it had been dead for years."

I didn't have to work too hard to convince her. She loved the story: Albert and I were mated souls who needed her help to escape my villainous husband. When I asked her to smuggle pen and paper into my room and mail a letter for me, she didn't hesitate. *For God's sake, Albert,* I wrote, *Get me out of this place. Contact my nurse Lillie Flowers. She is on our side.* I watched from my window as she walked out the front gate with that letter in her pocket and my heart lifted.

Then I went on saying all the right things to the doctors. *I tried to tell the truth, and you wouldn't let me,* I thought. *So now I'll lie and get what I want.* I begged to see Beal. I begged to see the girls. After a week or so of having to listen to me, Dr. Turner advised the Allison brothers that Beal could visit. I said all the right things to him, too. "I am so glad to see you. I want to come home. How are the girls? I miss you all so much." And after he left, I followed right up with a letter.

My dearest Beal, you simply can't know how terribly I was disappointed at not seeing you again before you left town. You never said a word about what the cattle brought nor what cotton was worth. I know you have been so worried over both and I feel that I am to blame for it, and I will try & be good to you and make up for it when I leave here. I am almost crazy to see the children. I guess you will think to drain the radiators for if it should freeze, they would break & ruin the floors. If there is anything in my letter you miss it is because I want to tell you instead of writing.

Lovingly, Lena

I sure didn't write that letter *lovingly*. Would a woman who knew she'd done her husband wrong and wanted to make it up to him talk about draining the radiators? Of course they all thought that was a good sign: I had home on my mind. But it was also true that after years of practice, the habits and vocabulary of affection were still there, sturdy, the way things are in long-term marriages—even bad ones. And I'd told the truth about the girls: I was crazy to see them. They all said I couldn't without seeing Beal. I thought I would prove them wrong.

Just a few days after his visit, I made another big show of begging to see Beal again. Then Lillie told Dr. Allison that I needed a distraction and she planned to take me downtown to see a matinee.

16

It was November 8, 1911. I stared out the window of the streetcar and tried to look calm. And then the car came to a lurching halt at the downtown stop we'd agreed on, and there was Albert, sitting on a bench with his hat pulled low and a newspaper spread open to screen him a little.

Ed Farwell—the assistant cashier at the Boyces's bank in Dalhart—stood a few feet away, young and fashionably dressed, with that banker's air of discretion and formality you could spot even at a distance. I gripped my bag so hard my knuckles turned white. Lillie was trembling too, but I could tell she was delighted. She hadn't expected *two* handsome men.

When they boarded the car, Albert tipped his hat to us like a polite gentleman stranger and looked away. Lillie's eyes were shining. Here he was—tall, dark, and handsome, with excellent manners—the crack shot in the Panhandle, as I'd told her repeatedly, rescuing his lady love from the prison of her marriage.

It was just a few stops to the train station. Albert and I whispered a few words to one another and Ed Farwell sauntered off to buy tickets while Lillie and I stood apart and I tried not to look at Albert. Then Ed returned, he and Albert conferred briefly, and they began to stroll slowly down the platform. Lillie and I followed at a distance. I had to force myself not to hurry. Ed nodded casually at a Pullman car as he and Albert passed it, and I was relieved to step inside.

Once we all got settled in the berth—Lillie and me first, Ed and Albert five minutes later—I began to breathe a tiny bit easier. I drank the sight of Albert like he was water in the desert.

He turned to Lillie. "You've been a good friend to us, Miss Flowers," he said, discreetly pressing an envelope into her hand, "and I appreciate it."

That blush of hers, which made her face look like blood was rioting to escape, swept over her. "Thank you," she whispered.

Ed Farwell stood by the window, looking out to the platform where the white-coated, dark-faced porters were loading baggage and passengers, singing out the way they did—*the way white folks like,* as I suddenly remembered overhearing Nettie say to the woman who came every week with the laundry—*they just love to think colored folks are happy.* Ed looked vaguely wary but also sort of bored, probably like he looked when a bank transaction required his presence but not a lot of his attention.

"Mr. Farwell," I said to him impulsively. "Could I ask a favor?"

He turned to face me, clearly surprised. His shoulders stiffened. "What can I do for you?" He sounded wary. Ed was by no means a fool. He knew the law was going to enter into this sooner or later, and he didn't want problems when it did.

"My diamonds," I said, beginning to pull off my right glove so I could remove my rings. "I don't have any money of my own, but the diamonds are worth something, and I would like my children to have them. Can you see to that?"

I could see how startled he was. And after he got over being startled, I could see how bad an idea he thought it. He turned into the sort of smooth-talking dandy he must have been at Saturday night dances in Dalhart. "Well, Mrs. Sneed, I hate to refuse a lady anything, but you can surely see that might not be such a good idea. Why would Beal let me see your children? And if I gave them anything, he'd surely take it back."

He was obviously right. "Ed's done enough for us, Lena," Albert said soothingly, "We'll find a way to get them to the girls later." So I gave it up. But later I wished a thousand times he'd taken them.

They made nothing but trouble.

That night, as Albert and I lay naked together in our berth, I cried for a long time. I was crying for everything really: My children, my marriage, the way I felt in the sanitarium, my injured pride, all the lying. Albert's body was close and warm and bigger than mine. And in the end, our bodies together worked as they always did, making my decision seem obvious and clear, and I fell asleep briefly, just before dawn.

    They found one of the colored porters later—a man named MacDonald—and got him to testify to my crying and mourning all the night long. And then he disappeared. The white men looking for him didn't know the colored world well enough to find him again.

17

We headed up the plains. "He won't expect it," Albert said. "Who would head north this time of year?" Those railroad-stop plains towns all looked pretty much the same: Wooden storefronts, stone banks, brick churches, the big here-I-am houses of the wealthy, other ordinary houses, and poor people's rundown houses and shacks.

In Omaha, I held Albert's arm as we walked, peering into the shops, watching clerks and shop girls getting ready to head home. It was a relief to be so open, to walk together and touch one another as if we had a right to it. My hands were gloved, but I could see the little ridge my wedding ring made. I continued to wear it because we always registered as married.

"My wife," said Albert to the woman at the front desk in the Hotel Rome, where we were Mr. and Mrs. A.J. Brooks from Montana, "is a little tired from the trip. Would you please send some tea up to the room?"

It was a detail that would never have occurred to Beal. "I didn't know a man could be so sweet to a woman," I told Albert.

Henry Boyce sent one telegram after another warning us to keep moving, that Beal had hired detectives and was on the trail. Every day was colder and darker as we ventured deeper into the darker dark and colder cold of the northern winter. Light and warmth seemed to have shrunk down to almost nothing by the time we crossed into Canada on November 28, 1911.

Once we reached Winnipeg and decided to stay for a while, we also decided it was time to buy our own rings. Of course Albert paid for them, but I insisted on choosing his by myself. I picked a gold signet ring with a pattern on both sides that could have been flowers, or maybe butterfly wings. There was a tiny pavé diamond at the center. "Engrave *B* on the face," I told the jeweler, "and inside I want *Forever, Lena*." His bright jeweler's light shone, illuminating the diamond and his agile, narrow fingers.

As I walked back to the hotel, I thought about my wedding ring—like a tiny link in a chain that led back to Beal. At the corner of a nearly empty side street, I removed my left glove and then the ring, clutching it in the other still-gloved fist. The snow was piled in dirt-pocked drifts. I thought how easy it would be to drop the ring into the dirty snow, then stoop down when no one was looking and dig a little hole for it. There that ring would stay, buried until spring. By then we'd be gone. I stood, imagining it all for a moment or two, then slipped the ring into my coat pocket, put my glove back on, and kept walking.

Albert and I exchanged our own rings in front of the fire that night. There had been sun dogs that afternoon, which old-timers said meant more cold, but the curtains were drawn and the shadows the fire cast made the room seem like a comfortable, warm cave. We felt safe. I could see no end to our love. I felt like we were flying above time and could see the whole design, the way years later I first saw Amarillo and the Canadian River from an airplane, and they looked beautiful and harmless.

"With this ring . . ." Albert slipped it onto my finger.

"When you look at your initial," I said, gazing at his hand, "always remember that it stands for the name I want to share, not just in my heart but before the whole world." I stopped and looked into his eyes. "With you, I am who I am meant to be. And someday I will wear your name"—I paused to try and get it right—"like a sign to the whole world that I am yours forever."

Oh, the way we talked. *Like a brand,* I might just as well have said. But it all felt so real—it was real. And I've never wanted anything more than I've wanted to go back to a time when such words came as close as we could to speaking the truth.

Of course, Albert himself wasn't using his real name when we talked about my sharing it. He was A.J. Brook, A.J. Brewer, and in the beginning—and occasionally afterwards—Joe Bush. All the subterfuge got under his skin. One night at supper in the hotel when we were dawdling over coffee, the silence lengthened and I realized he was angry. "Is something wrong?" I asked, trying to keep the fear from my voice.

He stayed quiet for a few more moments. Then he looked straight at me like he was coming up for air. "Of *course* there's something wrong." His voice was fierce, though he kept it low. "Do you think I *like* living like this—running and hiding and pretending to be somebody else?"

I was so scared I couldn't say a word.

"Most all my life," he went on, his voice even fiercer, "I've worked to be a good man—someone my family and friends could be proud of, a man another man could trust and a woman could depend on. And now look at me: Stuck up here in Canada like I'm afraid to go back to Texas, like I'm afraid of Beal, like I have something to be ashamed of." He brought his hand down on the table in a gesture that would have turned into pounding—something I'd seen his father do—except that he restrained himself because of our need to remain as inconspicuous as possible.

"What are you saying?" I whispered.

"What does it *sound* like I'm saying?" he retorted with a quiet fury. "I hate it."

This was the way the cautionary tales we all knew ended. *Seduced and abandoned.* I dropped my head and the tears started to roll down my cheeks.

"Oh, God," he said, looking at me. "Oh, God, don't cry. I never want to make you cry." My hands were clasped tightly in my lap. He reached across the table and made a small, beckoning gesture with his fingers. With his other hand, he signaled the waitress.

"My wife is unwell," he said when she arrived. "May we have the check please?"

She was a small girl who looked like she'd just come off some Manitoba farm and taken the Canadian Pacific into town to look for a new life and a husband. Her white apron was starched stiff and her red hair curled in frizzy masses around her face, which was still pimpled from adolescence. She peered at me, looked as if she were about to say something, then thought better of it. "Yes, sir," she said to Albert, and gave him a small, trusting smile. They all did that.

We made our way back to our room in silence. I took off my hat, unbuttoned and removed my dark shoes in a methodical, over-careful way, and lay down on the bed. Albert stood in front of the fire, his back to me, his hands clasped behind him where I could see the small clenching movements they made. I thought of my children. I wanted to be tucking them into bed and kissing their soft, smooth cheeks goodnight.

And then he turned to me, the anger gone from his face. He came and knelt by the bed. "Forgive me, Lena, please," he said simply. I inhaled deeply, as if with his words I'd started to breathe again. I nodded mutely. He took my hand and stroked it gently. The gold bands we'd exchanged shone in the firelight.

"How can I be selfish enough to complain when you have given up so much more than I have?" he said, his voice full of grieving. "You've loved me as I asked you to, and I've had the nerve and the ingratitude to complain." He bowed his head until it touched our clasped hands.

I stroked his brown hair like I was stroking away the pain in my own heart, touched the whorls and curves of his ears, the back of his neck where the hair thinned and his spine began. "I'm sorry," I whispered.

I knew again he was mine, that he would always be mine, no matter what. It was like a singing in me.

We fell asleep in our clothes, clasped tightly together on the bed, the fire burning lower and lower.

When I woke, it was morning. He'd put a blanket over me. He was sitting in the wing-backed chair by the fire, with the daylight coming in at the side of the heavy curtains, a thin, sharp beam in the darkness.

I knew the minute I looked at him that he was drunk.

He was sprawled in the chair, shirt unbuttoned, feet bare, looking at me with half-open, speculative eyes. I had some power in me, some residue of certainty from the night before, and I looked back at him and smiled. "Oh my love," I said. I stretched and sighed, then turned onto my side and looked him steadily in the face.

And all I felt was love and a sudden and complete compassion, able now to see how it was for him, as I had been unable to the night before. I saw the hurt pride and the anger, and below that, the fear. He was afraid of a number of things, but I knew at the moment he was most afraid he wasn't the man I believed him to be. He was drunk because of it.

"I'm drunk," he said.

"I know," I answered.

I watched him as he lifted the bottle and took another pull from it, holding it loosely between his thumb and fingers, and letting it drop to his side, then taking his other hand and wiping it across his mouth. His gorgeous long body was stretched out in the chair. I looked at him and I started to laugh, and it was real laughter, too, not some hysterical version like those writers often put in their novels.

"You're drunk and I'm ruined," I said, laughing. "God, I love you." It was like stepping out of my corsets at the end of the day. All my life they'd hammered on virtue and purity and self-control. And here he was, drunk, and we were committing adultery—no matter how many times we said we were married in our hearts—and I'd abandoned my children, and we were hiding out in some foreign country, and it was all right.

Albert walked over to me, steady as ever on his feet. He stripped off his shirt and dropped it to the ground, then undid his trousers and stepped out of them, and then began to undo the row of buttons on his long johns. I just watched. "Now you," he said, and I obeyed him, with a pleasure in obedience that had nothing to do with what was proper to my *womanly place*, and everything to do with some fervent, pleasure-seeking impulse. I remembered a line from Isaiah, *the treasures of darkness*. I took my clothes off slowly and he watched, and only when we were both stripped bare did we touch one another. *I want to fuck you. I love to fuck you.* He was too drunk to climax then. That happened later, with the sound of another blizzard outside our room, the heavy velvet curtains drawn and the fire crackling in the grate.

"I won't drink like that anymore," Albert said to me the next morning. "I don't want to do that to you again." His beard was a dark shadow on a face he hadn't shaved for two days. "Look at me," he said, standing suddenly and peering into the big mirror in the center of the dark armoire with a look of disgust on his face.

I suddenly remembered talking to Mrs. Moore the previous summer. She'd come calling and worked the conversation round to men. "Men hate doormats as much as they hate the woman who never takes orders, probably more," she rasped. "They like to feel they're bossing you around, but deep down they want to know you're running the show. It makes 'em feel secure. You can do pretty much anything you want with 'em as long as you make it look like they're in charge."

Mr. Moore had been dead a long time now, and she had so much money that everyone was going to act like they liked her no matter what she said or did, so she said and did what she liked. I had a hard time imagining her giving even the appearance of obedience. I looked away and smiled. She caught me and waggled her finger.

"Oh, I know what you're thinking, Mrs. Sneed," she smiled in her sour way, "but I wasn't always this old, this ugly, or this rich. And you won't always be this young or"—she looked at me doubtfully—"this pretty, and you might not always be this rich." She set her hands in a determined looking pile in her lap and brayed her hard, two-note laugh, the one her nephew Volney said made her sound like a donkey. "Right now you've got *at least* one of everything," she said, "and two of some things, so I hear." There was that laugh again. I remembered why people didn't like her.

But listening to Albert in Winnipeg, I recalled her words. I realized that, no, I couldn't be stuck up in Canada with a drunk. What would happen if Beal found us? All Albert's grace and legendary marksmanship might desert him. *We* needed him sober.

And it was in that kind of subtle way that our love began to pass from the realm of the ideal into the real world. Should he stop completely, or could he manage one or two on occasion? Did I tell him exactly what I thought or only a part of it, and how should I phrase what I decided to say?

At the time, it saddened me a little to see how the ordinary demands of living worked on this great and joyous love. But I was also grateful for the security of it, love woven into the tiny familiarities that living with someone brings: The way he smelled first thing in the morning, the way he talked late at night, the way when I watched him come down the street in his blue suit after he'd been to the telegram office I recognized the tilt of his head and his walk, knew without doubt it was him when I could still barely make out his figure.

18

The storms were early and heavy all up and down the plains that winter, and in Winnipeg they seemed to roll in without stopping. Even in Amarillo, the snow had been on the ground for thirteen days by the end of December. Sometimes when it stormed in Winnipeg I felt so safe; the wires and telephones and trains stopped functioning, and the roads became impassable. I'd snuggle up close to Albert and think, *They'll never find us.* But sometimes it frightened me: The storm seemed aimed directly at the two of us, sinning in our room, trying, like Adam and Eve, to hide from the God who was determined to find us.

We got a taste of home one afternoon when we went to see *The Immortal Alamo* and watched Santa Anna surrender on bare ground as a gray-and-white South Texas winter flickered on the screen. That morning, we'd gotten bad news from Henry. Beal had somehow finagled the Fort Worth D.A. into getting the Fort Worth grand jury to look into state charges of rape, kidnap, and abduction against Albert. He also had Will Atwell—the U.S. district attorney and conveniently married to one of my cousins—hard at work on federal white slaving charges. The argument being that since I'd crossed state lines with a man who wasn't my husband for *immoral purposes* I'd become a white slave.

The way the law looked at it, my consent was irrelevant. Whereas locked up at Arlington Heights against my will, or kept at home against my will, I was a *free white woman*. Beal and his lawyers presented the whole thing as a struggle for the soul of a *wife and mother*. I'm sure they loved the idea, the way those kind of men always do love the idea that putting them in charge of someone else's life is somehow part of God's best plan. But my soul was elsewhere, in some wild

Texas they never dreamed of.

By the time Albert and I left the theater, with visions of Texas still in our minds, the northern night had come once more. The sky was clear, stars stabbing it above the city lights, the cold a wall we walked into. We were silent until we sat down for supper in the Regina Hotel.

"You know it's worth it to me, don't you?" Albert looked at me in his serious way.

"And to me," I said, "it's worth it to me. You are. This is."

"But I miss home. I miss Texas."

"Me, too. Do you think it will always be like this?"

"No," he said. "Beal will get over it, someday, or . . ." He trailed off. "And even if we have to go to South America," he went on, "we'll buy some of that new cattle country and start fresh like our parents did in Texas."

That it was possible to wipe the past out, start over, choose to bring with us only what we liked . . how in the world did we ever believe it?

Just a few days later, two men approached as we were stepping out of the hotel elevator and down our names came crashing, like one of those traps that falls from a tree. "Albert Boyce? Mrs. Sneed?"

"Pardon me?" Albert said, his chin jutting out the way it did when he was ready to do battle, although he kept his eyes and tone of voice neutral.

"Albert Boyce," the other man repeated, "you're under arrest. And the lady, too." The stuff of cheap melodrama, like so much of the rest.

They weren't unkind about it. They'd come in plain clothes. There was nothing about the scene to make our situation obvious. They had an ordinary horse-drawn taxi waiting outside. We were just three men and a woman on our way somewhere together in the middle of another week.

I clutched Albert's hand, huddled myself against him. One of the men caught my eye and smiled in a small way. He was older and had a kind face. I could feel tears starting.

Drink it in: The way my lover looks, his ears, the dark hair, the

Clara Sneed

crease of his blue suit, his boots and the heavy overcoat, his hand holding mine, the bones covered in flesh and blood and skin and hair, the horse's hooves thudding along in the chopped-up snow. They caught up with us, and now it begins to unravel, those threads. Step along, step along, poor horse, it's coming, you'll get there, step along. Time going, unstoppable.

For years now, I've continued to see him dressed in that blue suit, while around me the background keeps changing, and the suit no longer fits the scene. *But you are still beautiful; I can still see you.*

Albert, my lovely boy, again and again stepping out into the winter light of the Winnipeg street.

19

At first they put us together in the Immigration Hall, but that ended quickly; I suppose they got pressure from Beal or Atwell. Albert hired a Canadian lawyer named T.J. Murray, another tall, dark, good-looking man but with a Canadian accent and a milder Canadian manner that didn't seem to go with his reputation as a young gun. Murray got us released. Then they rearrested us on different charges and he got us released. So when they came up with a third set of charges and arrested us yet again, we said goodbye, feeling confident that Murray would soon get us out of them.

By then, the newspapers had gotten hold of the story and the reporters—along with a few photographers—were clumped up in front of the hotel shouting questions and taking notes. I smiled in what I hoped was a shy, sad way that didn't make me look like the dimwit I was reported to be.

In the Hall, Murray offered fifty dollars to the guard at the door of my room to let Albert and me see one another, even if just for a moment. Stout, middle-aged, with broken veins in his cheeks, the guard seemed to hold whatever life he had outside his job far away, like he was in danger of having it stolen. He shook his head at Murray in a way that made it clear his *no* was final. "Don't worry," said Murray on his way out the door, "I'll have you out soon." There was snowy light coming in from the windows. I sat down and tried to compose myself.

A few hours later, the guard opened the door and in walked Beal.

I was so startled I screamed, then clapped my hands over my mouth and sat down hard, my heart pounding. He was thinner and looked exhausted. "Lena," he said, his voice quivering. He pulled one of Georgia's baby shoes—scuffed white leather and little laces—out of his trouser pocket and held it out to me. I burst into tears and clutched it to my heart like a talisman; if I wished hard enough, maybe my girls would appear as magically as Beal.

I cried for a long time. When I raised my head at last, Beal stood just inches away, his face tormented. He lifted his hand as if to touch my cheek, but when I flinched he thrust both hands behind his back as if I'd slapped them. And then he began to beg, though his voice was empty of feeling. "I'll do anything, go anywhere you say, buy you anything you want." Then he stopped talking and started pacing in tight circles around the small room. I felt sick to my stomach.

When he finally spoke again, his eyes were stone hard and his voice had come back to life, tight and angry. "Don't you know he'll hang?" He wheeled toward me. "He's been indicted in Fort Worth. If he goes back to Texas, he'll hang for rape and abduction. And then where will you be? People already think you're worse than a whore. Do you know what Annie Boyce is saying about you? Do you know what she wrote Aunt Lillian? Did that sonofabitch tell you *that*? She said I ought to go on and give you a divorce, seeing as you're such a low-down, worthless woman."

"You're lying," I answered angrily. "He can't possibly have been indicted on anything so stupid. The grand jury wouldn't fall for your nonsense. And she never wrote Aunt Lillian."

His voice was cold. "Just you wait and see, Lena." Then he whirled around and pounded furiously on the door for the guard to release him.

After that, Murray couldn't get us out. Beal hired his own Canadian lawyer who prepared deportation papers saying we were in Canada illegally because we'd used false names to enter. No bail possible on that one. And he also charged Albert with grand larceny, saying he'd stolen my diamonds—the ones I'd wanted Ed Farwell to take. Beal knew Albert wasn't a thief. But he was busy crafting his tale.

And he hadn't been a lawyer himself for nothing.

20

The immigration people made sure I didn't have paper, so I used the back of a menu I had tucked in my bag to write Albert. *Beal was here again tonight and brought the Burns detective with him. They tried to persuade me to go back to Texas and are tearing my heart out about the children. The Burns man said he would go with me to any point I wanted and leave Beal here, that we could go see the children, and that he'd leave when I asked him to. But of course I didn't believe one word he said.*

The Burns man's blue eyes had stared fervently and innocently into my own, while Beal stood stiffly by the window. The Burns man said, "Your husband is right, Mrs. Sneed. As things stand, he's likely to hang. Now, if you'll return to Texas, perhaps you might testify in his defense, say you had a momentary lapse of judgement. I know the families were all friends. It's tragic to see that ruined. I've had the pleasure of meeting your daughters, Mrs. Sneed, and I'm sure your heart must ache over them, and I *know* theirs ache for you."

He cleared his throat. It was a nervous tic; he did it a lot. He bent his thin-haired head closer to me and went on in a confidential tone. "You know what your youngest said to me, Mrs. Sneed, when I met her? She said, 'Mr. Burns,'—you see, she thought my name was Burns, so charming—'Will you help find our Mama? Keep her safe, Mr. Burns. We miss her.'"

I knew the Burns man—whose name I hadn't noticed either—was lying and trying to make me cry. But I couldn't help it. I cried anyway.

"I'll leave you now, but you think about it," he said in an almost tender voice.

Beal motioned him out of the room, then walked from the window, leaned over and put his hands on either arm of my chair, staring hard into my face, his mouth inches from my own. "If you don't come back with me of your own free will, here's what's going to happen. For starters, I'll get you deported."

I started to say that Murray could stop it. But Beal reached up and covered my mouth with one hand while he balanced himself with the other.

"Then," he went on, "I'll send you right back to that asylum. No one will believe any testimony a crazy woman gives about her lover, so you can forget about protecting him. And this time, you won't escape." Both his arm and his voice were shaking. He was so close I could see his dirty collar, smell the stale sweat and pipe smoke and the coffee on his breath. "And finally," he continued, his balance a matter of will now, as if propping himself up would prove that what he set out to do he would do, no matter what, "as long as you are with that man or say you intend to be with that man or want to be with that man, you won't see your children. Ever."

I was mute, my mouth clenched behind his hand, my neck straight and unbending.

"DO YOU HEAR ME?"

I was frightened and nodded and hated myself for it.

He straightened then, took his hand from my mouth, shook out the arm he'd been leaning on and pounded on the door. "Think about it." He spat the words over his shoulder on the way out, like he couldn't be bothered to face me and say them, like I was a ranch dog or horse that had misbehaved and he knew he had me under control.

If I'd had a gun I would have shot him right then and there. That's the truth.

But of course I didn't. I didn't even have paper to write on. So instead I wrote at the end of the note on the back of the menu, *Albert, I want you to kill Beal if they bring you back. He is nothing but a demon—I don't see how I ever married him. If I could kill him myself tonight, I would.*

There in the Hall, I swung so wildly from one thing to the next that I began to wonder if I really was going crazy. One minute I was crying over Georgia's shoe, the next writing Albert that I thought I wouldn't ever care anything about the children again, if only I could be with him.

Overcome with guilt, I wrote him another note on another piece of the menu. *I blame no one but myself. I loved you too much. I lost sight of what was best for you, while I would have so willingly given my life for you. If we are deported they will put me in an asylum first thing, and darling, I don't want you to kill B or him you. It would be all my fault and I would answer to God for it.*

Murray came to see me in person when his last appeal failed, which was kind. "I can't stop them from deporting you," he said with what seemed genuine sadness. "I admire your courage and am truly sorry I couldn't help you more." I started to cry from his tiny bit of praise; so few people saw anything to admire about me at all.

"Look here," he said, a little flustered by my tears. "You've lost the battle, but not the war." He lowered his voice so the guard couldn't hear. "I've some papers for you to sign. I'm no expert on American laws outside of immigration, but I spoke with a colleague and I believe you have a very valid legal case if your husband tries to incarcerate you again. These papers give the Boyces power of attorney so they can hire a lawyer on your behalf to mount that case." He handed me a pen and pointed at the place I needed to sign. I looked at him with astonishment and so much gratitude I had stop myself from kissing his hand.

"And another thing," he said, continuing to speak quietly. "Albert has hired Pinkertons to follow you, so we will always know where you are."

"Thank you," I said fervently, "thank you, thank you, thank you."

"Of course," he said, "I've seen enough of both Albert and your husband to understand your position." There were many times later when I would have given a lot of the world just to talk with T.J. Murray again.

He tried one last time to bribe the guard to let me see Albert, but once again his request met another firm no. "You don't know how he treats me," I said to the guard after Murray left, briefly heartened by our conversation.

"He treats you all right," the guard answered. The way he looked at me I knew he meant to say he would treat me much worse if I were his wife.

I submitted without resistance when Beal and the Burns man arrived the next morning. My only defiance was to refuse to take Beal's arm when he offered it. Thankfully, the press was absent; the Canadian authorities had kept their mouths shut.

It was the new year, January 2, 1912.

21

Beal sat across from me on the train picking at his overcoat, which I didn't recognize; he must have bought it for the trip north. Every now and then, he'd wad a bunch of it up in his hands and knead it, squeezing so hard his knuckles turned white. It was true what people said later: He didn't look quite right in the head. He looked like one of those crazy people who somehow manage to get hold of an expensive hat, good shoes, a fine suit. At first glance, you take in just one more ordinary man dressed the way men dress to indicate their ordinariness. And then you notice something off: The eyes, or the hair fixed in an odd way, or a hole in the heel of the shoe. With Beal it was the sloppy, visibly dirty collar, the red eyes, and the repetitive gestures: Kneading and picking at the coat, striking his thigh with his hand.

He managed to pull himself together at the border. The guards were forewarned and impressed, I could tell. "Here you go, Mr. Sneed, everything's in order for you and your wife." The very slightest emphasis on *wife*. They looked at me when they thought I didn't see. I could almost read their thoughts: *She's not anything special to look at, is she? Poor bastard.*

Whenever Beal glanced at the ring Albert had given me, his color rose and the overcoat twitching and kneading became more violent. Beside me, the Burns man's growing discomfort was obvious. His efforts to make small talk died in the stony silence. He was visibly relieved when he left us in Minneapolis.

When we pulled into the Chicago station, I was astonished to see my father on the platform. I didn't know whether to be angry or relieved. Ramrod straight as always, he raised his hand in a sort of half-salute as I got off the train, then hugged me. There was the very briefest melting. I refused to say anything at all, and he and Beal said almost nothing—either to one another or to me. They seated themselves on either side of me on a polished wooden bench and we waited in the cold air for the train south. I saw, really without wanting to, how tired my father looked. When the train arrived, they each took an elbow and steered me to our car.

"You must take her straight back to the sanitarium," I heard Beal say outside the compartment door. "Dr. Allison is expecting her." Until that moment, I hadn't realized that he was leaving us to head back to Canada. I felt immediate relief—I'd be done looking at him—followed by terror.

What would he do to Albert?

My father and I sat in complete silence and the train began to chug slowly out of the station. By the time we reached the fields outside Chicago, I thought if I didn't get some privacy, I would begin to scream, and that once I started, I wouldn't be able to stop. "I need to use the ladies' room," I said.

"I'll take you there," answered my father uncomfortably, shifting a little in his seat but making sure to look me right in the eye. I didn't bother to argue. Where would I have gone, anyway? He said nothing when we reached the door but I knew he'd be waiting when I came out. Inside, I stared at myself in the mirror. I seemed to have shrunk.

After what must have been a long time, my father rapped on the door, his voice low but urgent. "Lena, are you all right?" *He's afraid,* I realized. *He isn't sure he's doing the right thing.* I couldn't remember a time when my father had ever been unsure about anything. We made our way back to the compartment and sat staring out the window with all of it in the air between us.

At last, he spoke. "He wants you back in the sanitarium," he began without preamble, then glared at me. "I never in my life expected to be on an errand like this."

I started to say something, but he shook his head. "Your mother is beside herself with worry," he went on. "We've had reporters calling us at home in Clayton at all hours. Your girls," he said, leaning in and looking stern, "I don't begin to understand how you could have left them. They cry their eyes out over you, Lenora especially."

"I didn't want to leave them, Papa," I said. "Beal put me in that place and Dr. Allison and that awful Dr. Turner wouldn't let me see them, no matter how hard I begged. You know that. You agreed with Beal I should go there."

"He assured us the place came highly recommended," my father replied, "and that you would receive the best treatment." He glanced out the window at the glittering snow and then looked back at me. "I thought it would help you see things more clearly. Why would you break up a perfectly good marriage to a decent man who provides well for you and your children? You're old enough to know better, Lenora." He had lapsed, as he did when he was very serious, into my given name. "Your mother and I have had our share of ups and downs, you know. But we have always followed that rule, *Don't let the sun go down on your anger.*" His gaze turned toward a farm house, visible in the middle distance, the paint mostly peeled off, the wood gray beneath it. "You think I'm suggesting something too simple for your problems, don't you?" he said with an edge of sarcasm. "Old-fashioned advice. Nothing you could use. I told Annie Boyce I felt like putting you across my knee myself, and Beal ought to have done it long ago."

He faced me again, eyes fierce. "Has he ever beaten you, Lenora? He hasn't, those bruises you had from when he tried to phone in the wire to me, they weren't nothing. If your mother had ever done something like you did . . . " He shook his head. Then he barked: "What the hell are you so unhappy about anyway?"

I was shocked; he never cursed in front of family. I started to cry.

"You and Mama," I said through tears, "you don't have any idea what he's really like. He puts on the good show, and I've done the best I can for years, but I just can't go on. How can I make you all understand, the way he orders me around, and doesn't talk to me, and other things, things I can't talk about . . ."

My weeks of lovemaking with Albert had made the memory of Beal in bed a dim one, or at least the feelings about it seemed faded and distant, but I had those pictures in my head. How could I explain all that to anyone, let alone my father?

The heart wounds—those weren't totally real to him. He couldn't comprehend their gravity. He would understand only if I said Beal had hurt me physically, intentionally, repeatedly.

"Papa, listen to me," I said. "He's a liar. That sanitarium was terrible, they shot me full of morphine and when I woke up I was naked. They had me in a hall with crazy people. Papa, I don't mean people you might think are crazy like maybe you think I'm crazy, but people who really are crazy. You should have heard the place at night. The shrieking and the moaning and someone down the hall who just cursed all night long. They didn't let me take a bath for two weeks and then right before Beal came, they got me all cleaned up."

I reached across the space between us and grasped his hands. "Papa, please just take me home with you. Please let me go see Mama. Please, Papa."

His own eyes filled and he wrapped his hands around mine. "All right, my girl, don't cry, it's all right," he murmured. "Let me think for a little bit."

I joined him then on his side of the compartment, rested my head on his shoulder, and sobbed. He stroked my hair. "It's all right," he repeated, his breathing regular, his shoulder rising and falling gently beneath my head. "Well," he sighed after a while, "sometimes life don't turn out like we expect, does it?"

I laughed in a sort of choking way at the blatant truth of that.

"I'm not going to take you back to that place," he said, a bit louder. "Beal should have never gone public with all this and I'm not going to do his bidding just because of the circus he's turned this into. I have a horror of those reporters."

I remembered then—the way I tended to at odd times, since we never spoke of it—about Uncle Dud killing their stepfather. My father had experienced bad publicity and the shame that goes along with it, the way you read or hear a story about yourself and it seems to have nothing to do with you, it's someone they made up, using the incidents and circumstances of your life. I knew he remembered what that was like, back when he was too young to defend himself, before he was sure about much of anything.

22

We changed trains in Amarillo, walking quickly along the platform. Another life floated out there in the snowy, mud-gashed streets; I was just passing through now, like a traveling salesman. In a few minutes, we were on another train, headed toward Dalhart and then to Clayton, ten miles over the New Mexico border, where my parents lived with my sister Susie and her husband, a lawyer named John Pace.

Mercifully, there were no reporters to greet us at the Clayton station. It took them a while to figure out where everybody was and right then they were obsessed with the melodrama in Canada: Beal's return, Albert's whereabouts, the possibility of a murder.

"We've been so worried about you," said my mother once we'd reached the house. It was only four-thirty but dark enough that the lamp with the fringed shade on the little round table was already lit. The skies outside were low and gray. Susie's husband John was sitting nearby, so quiet that it was easy to forget he was in the room.

"We didn't know where you were and those dreadful news stories!" Mother tugged fitfully at a shawl wrapped round her shoulders. "I've hardly slept, Lena. I just keep wondering what went wrong. I know we never raised you to behave like you have—"

"Why would I do what I've done if I wasn't miserable with Beal and didn't love Albert?"

My mother gave her head a rapid little shake, as if trying to clear flies away. Then she said, "How did Beal treat you *before* all this, honey? Sometimes, you know, a reasonable man can act awful bad when he feels threatened. I can't approve what Beal has done, but I think of your dear little girls and I know they'd be happier if you and Beal could work it out, don't you think so?"

Clara Sneed

I took a deep breath. She wasn't like Mrs. Boyce, full of convictions and fearless about stating them. My mother was softer, used to forming her opinions by listening to my father. I'd almost always been able to talk her into seeing things my way. She was halfway on my side already, I could tell.

"Mama, I have been so unhappy," I said. "For *years*. Beal's never home. Still, I think I could stand that if I thought he cared about me. But after a week in Paducah, he'll come back and won't say three words to me all night. Then when it's time for bed—I don't mean to shock you, Mama, but he expects me to do my duty by him without even an endearment beforehand. And he'll leave the next morning and barely say goodbye. I tried, Mama, I did. I kept telling myself it was just marriage, and he *has* always provided for us. But now you're starting to see how mean and sneaky he can be, how he's got to have everything his own way, no matter what. Do you think *any* of this would have happened if he'd just been willing to give me a divorce?"

My mother shook her head again. "No," she said, "your father and I have talked about that. He knows as well as I do that you can't *make* someone love you and he don't see what Beal thinks he's going to have left in the way of a marriage when this is all over, even if he was to succeed in keeping you. Like my mother always said, *Love is a bird you can't cage.*"

She nodded, comforted in her distress and confusion by the thought of her mother's platitude, a little path she could take out of the woods.

"Mama," I said, stretching to take her hand, "you've known Albert all his life. You know he's not the kind of man they're making him out to be. Why Mama, if you could just talk to him, you'd see how truly he loves me. Beal isn't fit to shine his shoes. I know you can't want me with a man who don't really love me. I wouldn't want that for my daughters."

John twisted in his chair and cleared his throat. My mother and I startled. We'd forgotten he was there. "Lena, are you convinced Albert would marry you if you could get a divorce?" he asked.

"As convinced as I am of heaven," I said.

"What do his mother and father think?"

"I believe they want what's best for us both," I said, lying a little because I wasn't so sure they cared about what was best for me. "And anyway, Henry wired us that the Colonel was furious when Beal charged Albert with larceny. You know how he is. He's got his own ideas about things and he don't approve—"

I was going to say he didn't approve of Beal's scheming, but John interrupted. "If Beal shot Albert, the Colonel would think that was only justice; his son ran off with Beal's wife. But he don't think it's just nor honorable for Beal to say his son is a thief." He shook his head over the old-fashioned morality of the War generation.

I shivered involuntarily. "John, I came down here hoping I'd have a chance to testify to the grand jury that I went with Albert willingly and that he isn't what they say and that I'm not crazy. I want to save him." I paused before continuing. "And there's something else you all should know. In Canada, I signed papers to give the Boyces power of attorney and Albert hired Pinkertons to follow me. If Beal tries to put me anywhere"—I was saying Beal, but I knew John was smart enough to realize I was talking about anybody—"they'll let the Boyces know where I've been taken and the Boyces will hire a lawyer. They'll get me out."

I'd finally spotted the detectives across the street where one of Clayton's few automobiles was parked, making no effort to disguise their presence, two unsmiling men in city-boy bowlers, smoking cigarettes. "Look out the window, you'll see them." I heard my mother's sharp intake of breath as John rose and moved to the window, fingering the still-open curtain. He nodded as if to himself, then drew the curtains shut.

With a suddenly professional air, he stuck the tips of his fingers into his waistcoat pockets and pondered the middle distance in the parlor for a moment or two. Then he looked at me again and said firmly, "There's already more talk about killing than you probably realize. Almost everybody thinks one of those two men is going to die and that it won't stop there. As folks down here know, a whole lot less than this can start a feud."

To hear it all said so plainly and to know how much I wanted one man dead and not the other froze me up inside. For a minute, I couldn't breathe.

"Dear God, no," gasped my mother. "Surely it won't come to that. Surely it can be worked out so nobody gets killed. Don't you think so, John?" she asked pleadingly.

"Well, Mother," he answered, "here's my opinion." He sat down with a little, almost unnoticeable, flurry of lawyerly self-importance and rested his elbows on the arms of the chair, placing his fingers together so that his hands formed a kind of tent, into which he stared fixedly. When he spoke again, his voice had an air of objectivity, as if he had assumed the mantle of his profession and wore it as a kind of magic shield. It could save him—maybe save us all.

"I think you have two choices, Lena" he said. "The first and best is this—return to your husband. Write Albert and tell him to leave you alone. I reckon if he's convinced it's what you want, he'll do it. If you tell Beal you've made a terrible mistake but that it's over, and it really *is* over, I believe he will go on about his business and ignore Albert. Down deep, Beal don't want trouble if he can avoid it. It's why he ignored what was right under his nose as long as he did. But now he's riled up. He knows some other bull's been stomping in his pasture."

He raised his gaze from the tent of carefully arranged fingers. We locked eyes briefly.

"I'm not going back," I said flatly. "What's your other idea?"

He rose and cleared his throat again. "I have more doubts about this one, but here it is," he said. "Tell Beal you're staying here, or better yet, get your father to tell him. Let Beal know that if he tries to put you in a sanitarium again, habeas charges will be brought. Tell him you want a divorce but you don't want any publicity. Give him some time to think it over. Make sure Albert stays in Canada. Don't communicate with him. Let the press get bored. Let Beal start thinking about what it's gonna be like to stay married to you when you won't see or talk to him—more like something between the two of you and less something between him and Albert. I think in the long run it might work. But it would take time."

I took a deep breath and then spoke in a rush, trying to keep the rage out of my voice. "I hope Albert does stay in Canada right now," I said, "and I will certainly stay here, but John, you don't know what you're asking. I can't stop writing him. It would be like cutting my heart out."

He heaved a long sigh. "I was afraid you'd say that." The room was silent for a minute, his words hanging in the air. The clock on the wall struck five quick little notes.

"I don't think Beal will get very far pushing things on the legal side in New Mexico," John finally continued. He sounded dispirited. "The governor is a friend of mine and the Boyces."

"I plan to get mail here," I said defiantly. "I told Albert to use Mama's girl's name. Edith Rogers."

"No, Lena," he said firmly. "You can receive mail under your own name, but I won't aid you in using an alias."

I stood up and looked him full in the face, my hands on my hips. "John, you're so worried about bloodshed. Don't you think if I start receiving mail here under my own name it's going to make things worse? Do you think I'd even *get* my mail? They were opening the Boyce mail from the minute we left town. Beal told me they found us by hiding in Henry and Ollie's house and listening to them. You can't be serious."

He shook his head, spread his palms out and wagged them the way a fish might wag his fins; they seemed to indicate he'd done the best he could.

"Have him send it in a separate envelope," he said in a weary voice, "addressed to you on the inside, with the outer envelope addressed to me."

23

My sister Pearl arrived from Lake Charles the next day after stopping to see my girls in Plano, where she'd had a big fight with Henry Bowman over the whole business. "The nerve of that man," Pearl fumed. "And Eula just cowering in the background and trying to act invisible." She shook her head in disgust, while my mother made ineffectual calming noises at one end of the dinner table and my father sat at the other with his lips pressed tight together.

"He told me he wouldn't let Lena see her own children unless she was with Beal. He wouldn't give them the little dolls and things Lena sent—torturing those poor babies who are crying their eyes out every night, trying to make them believe their mother has forgotten them." Pearl's eyes grew damp. "Papa, you ought to go direct to Plano and tell Henry Bowman to cut it out or you'll bring those poor little girls back here. I told him I'm disgusted with this whole family. Al's family is sticking to him. Beal's family is sticking to *him*. And what are *we* doing? It will be a disgrace and a shame if we don't stick to Lena."

My father shook his head. "Beal says old Al has been saying terrible things about Lena around Amarillo. Terrible things," he repeated. "How can we stick to her and allow that? Do we really want her with a family who would say such things?"

Pearl snorted and was about to say something but I jumped in indignantly. "How can you believe *one word* Beal says? He's such a liar. Anyway, I'm not marrying Albert's family, I'm marrying Albert."

"No," replied my father, "it's not that simple. It never was and it never will be. You marry the family when you marry the man, especially in a situation like this. Do you really think they'll take kindly to you? Old Al knows way better than to say such things. But I know the man. He's talking that way because he's ashamed and trying to pretend he ain't."

He broke off and looked around the table with his oldtime fury and will. "But it don't matter," he said forcefully. "The man can't say that kind of thing about my daughter. He knows better than that. He *knows* better."

"Beal's lying," I repeated. "I don't know what he told you, but he's lying. I'm telling you, he lies about *everything*."

There was a sudden loud knock at the door, the kind that usually meant a telegram, often with bad news. We all froze. When Edith Rogers handed the Western Union envelope to my father, he tore it open, still angry, read it, became angrier still, and slammed the yellow paper down on the table.

"That high-handed, insolent . . ." he almost shouted. He looked directly at me. "Sometimes I think we should have drowned you all at birth." He read the telegram in a whiny voice. "Bring her to Fort Worth at once. Bring Mrs. Snyder. My expense. We must do all we can."

The commanding tone was partly the result of the terse conventions of the telegraph, but partly it was Beal's personality showing through; the stripped-down orders revealed something a letter could disguise. And that tone really grated on my father.

"I will not be ordered around by any son-in-law," said my father decisively. I had the good sense to keep quiet.

The next day I was so engrossed in writing to Albert—my pencil moving with its soft, steady scratch across the page, the household sounds muted, at times fading almost to nothing as I burrowed into the world of my love, submerged below the waves like the couple in the story Lillie and I had read—that at first I didn't hear John Pace calling from the foot of the stairs. "Lena, I have a letter here from Henry and Colonel Boyce."

I dropped my pencil and rushed to look over the banister at his upturned face. "They want me to meet them in Dalhart," he said and paused. I looked at him anxiously.

"I'll go of course," he said. I gave a little yelp of joy and rushed down the stairs to throw my arms around his neck.

"All right, all right," he said, patting me awkwardly. "Look here, you'll be pleased by this."

I read what he was pointing at. "Tell Lena," Henry had written, "that my father and I and all my family will do all we can for her. Tell her she has our deepest sympathy."

Tears filled my eyes. Albert and I had been fighting an enormous battle and the tide had at last turned in our favor. A few minutes later, another telegram arrived for my father. He came out of the library looking grave and handed it to me without a word. The Colonel was asking him to meet in Dalhart. He'd addressed my father as "Tom," and signed off as "Al."

"You will go," I said to my father, half-imploring, half-commanding.

"Yes," he said, "I'll go. Al and I have been friends for too long not to try to work this thing out."

Beal can't stand up to our two families united against him, I thought. The Boyces and the Snyders together, as they had been for years before the Sneeds ever showed up in Georgetown, back before the XIT, back to the War. Even Beal couldn't stand up against that.

That night I went to bed more certain of happiness than I'd been for a long time. As I looked out the bedroom window to the two nearby peaks named after a chief who'd died there, I felt a sliver of peace wedged like moonlight into my heart. Above the clouds, the same stars shone down on Albert in Winnipeg, and he thought of me as I thought of him. I found his heart and knew he found mine, despite the miles and miles between us.

As it happened, I got a letter from the Canadian lawyer Murray the following day, enclosing a cheering editorial from a Winnipeg paper. I loved it so much I memorized it. All these years later, I can still recite my favorite sentence. "It is a fine thing—and, oh, what a manly thing!—for a mushy emotionalist to slop over in writing of the 'injured husband' and the 'erring wife'—but officials of the Canadian government and of the police department in Winnipeg are not paid their salaries for the purpose of serving the ends of wife-chasing husbands who attempt to exercise a tyrannical authority by locking their wives up in insane asylums in the United States because those wives fail to 'love, honor and obey' a male of the human species whose conduct, on his own admission, would make love impossible, honor a confession of depravity, and obedience an encouragement to brute force."

It was a view from another world. When I read it, I thought maybe people in Texas could learn to see it like that, too.

But the next morning's mail brought a copy of the *Fort Worth Star-Telegram* in an envelope addressed to my father, with no note attached to identify the sender. As he read, his face tightened. "That bastard," I heard him say under his breath. "And she's worse."

"Lena," he cried out, "take a look at what your very good friends the Boyces had to say in Fort Worth." He was practically snorting he was so angry. "Just listen to this." He began to read, his voice a sarcastic, high-pitched imitation of a woman. *"If we had not accidentally heard of the grand jury investigation we would not have been here today and the indictment would have been returned without anyone raising a voice on behalf of our son."* The words sounded just like Mrs. Boyce, the quivering furor at injustice, her protectiveness. *"Albert was hypnotized by that woman. She hypnotized her husband, too, or he wouldn't have offered a big reward for her. She has ruined her husband and my son and has broken my heart."* My father's voice whined, though Mrs. Boyce never did.

I was so hurt I couldn't move.

"She was as sane as anybody," my father went on in the same high-pitched whine. *"She planned the whole business herself. I am sorry for her in spite of all the ruin she has brought upon us."* He rattled the paper furiously as he turned the page. *"I only hope that Mrs. Sneed will go back to her husband and two little children. She has been used to having her own way—her husband always granted everything she asked, whether it was a new piano, a victrola, or more diamonds. She was headstrong and only more determined to have her way after her husband tried to separate her and my son."*

I had a sudden view of myself as she described me: Spoiled, conniving, self-indulgent, willing to destroy the happiness and peace of everyone around me for the sake of my foolish desires. She lived for her family, and she rebuked me. She was a righteous woman, as I was not. My shame turned quickly to anger, but it never entirely vanished. It's been there all along, like an alternate map to a place you believe you know well. For the rest of my life, in bad moments, I have heard her voice: *She has ruined her husband and my son and broken my heart.*

I lost track for a few seconds, but when I caught the thread again, my father was still speaking, his voice now masculine and outraged: "... no right to talk about you like that, as if that boy of theirs had nothing to do with it. *Hypnotized.* Hah. I will not meet with that old man. What father could send his child to a family thinking that way about her, just so's they can make their son happy and get him out of the trouble he got his own self into?"

I began to cry, and Pearl put her arms around me. "It's just like I said, Papa. The Sneeds are sticking to Beal. They're"—she nodded her head in the direction of the newspaper—"sticking to Albert. She shouldn't have said it, Papa, but she's his *mother*. If Beal hadn't accused Albert the way he did and charged him with rape and theft and I don't know what all else, Mrs. Boyce would never have said those things. She's upset, Papa, we all are. She's mad and she's scared or else she wouldn't talk like that."

But my father was having none of it.

"I'd be failing in my duty as a father if I agreed to talk with those people," he practically shouted. "Al and Annie have never been shy about saying what they think, either one of them. Al knows what an insult this is. He knows a man don't ever forget that kind of talk." He beat the newspaper against the wall like it stood proxy for his old friend.

"Now he wires me," he went on, "and wants to meet and talk this thing over. There'll be northers in hell before I meet that old man to talk about my daughter." He pounded the wall some more.

I tried to change his mind and Pearl did, too, but it was no use. Beal had told him all the awful things the Boyces had said about me. "He's lying," I'd said to my father. But it turned out he'd been telling the truth.

A few days later, my father set out with Pearl to meet Beal at D.A.

Atwell's office in Dallas. "Come at my expense and see the sanitarium for yourself," Beal had written. "Dr. Turner says they all say things that make it sound like they're being tortured. It's a common mark of insanity."

The way my father now saw it, Beal had told the truth about the Boyces and I'd said Beal lied. I told him the sanitarium was terrible and Beal said it was all right. Maybe it was. The way my father now saw it, as mad as he was at Beal, being on Beal's side ended up being the best way to be on mine. Beal was proclaiming he just wanted to do what was best for me and that I wasn't responsible for my actions because I was crazy. As a story to protect my reputation—what was left of it—it looked a whole lot better than what the Boyces had come up with.

For my father, love, passion, unhappiness—those things came and went. But reputation and virtue were like precious, magical birds. Once they flew away, they never returned and a whole flock of troubles flew in to replace them. Little troubles, like being snubbed on the streets or left off invitation lists. Big troubles, like eternal damnation.

The preachers loved to thunder about it—it was the kind of thing they stuck in with the temperance sermons. *"Woman, if you are virtuous, your heavenly Father will reward you, no matter how great your troubles in this life. But beware if you betray the bonds of holy matrimony, no matter how great the temptation, for you there will be no reward but the flames of hell itself. There will be no light save from that terrible fire."*

24

The minute he walked in the door after he came back from Fort Worth, I saw there was no use trying to change my father's mind; I recognized *the look* from earliest childhood.

"We've got to go along with Beal and the sanitarium," I heard him say to my mother later. I was listening quietly outside the door of their bedroom, as if I were still a child.

"But Tom," my mother said, "she *isn't* crazy. You know that."

"No," said my father, his voice sagging, "I don't think she's exactly crazy, either." There was a brief silence. "Dr. Turner says it's common in cases like this that they don't *seem* crazy." Another pause. "But it can't hurt to have her think about this for a while. If she gets a divorce—and I don't believe Beal will ever agree to one—and marries young Al, I don't see how I can ever be civil to old Al and Annie again."

I could imagine the way he rubbed his eyes to clear his head. I imagined him slumping, allowing his spine to loosen and curve with the weight of his fatigue and confusion. He had his softness, more than the Colonel and certainly more than old man Sneed.

Throughout their long marriage, my mother's own softness must have been like a pillow or thick feather mattress for him, a place where he could occasionally ease his aching head, rest for a few moments, allow the burdens of rectitude and certainty and manhood to slide from his shoulders. She, who seemed so much weaker to all of us most of the time, must have become the strong one in those moments, the one who understood the country he so rarely visited, knew the customs and the language and could say, *Don't worry, it's like this. Follow me.*

"Tom," she said in a voice so drenched in accustomed tenderness that it seemed the young woman and young man they had been long ago were revived and contained in it. "You should try to get some sleep. It will look better in the morning." There was a faint rustle behind the door as she drew back the bed covers. I imagined her patting the bed, trying to coax him in, as I remembered her doing when I was a child, worn out but too wound up to know it.

Inside their room, the years they had passed together settled like a flock of chickens or doves, something homely and simple, rustling their feathers, roosting, making their little night sounds. And outside their door, like wild animals, were my own pity and shame and rage and envy and passion.

I fled, almost running down the hallway, trying to find the place inside me where the truth lay, where I could touch Albert, feel him breathing, many miles north, longing as I was longing. Now even that northern cold and darkness seemed like a paradise, the world as it belonged to just the two of us, a place where I didn't have to stare at other people's pain over what we were doing.

I knew what John Pace said was true. I had only to write to Albert to stop all of it. He would leave me alone, because I asked it of him. And all the pains we'd caused would stop. Except our own.

I sat hunched over in the little chair at one end of the hallway, far from the light in the wall sconce at the other end, my eyes dry and wide-open and my teeth clenched so hard my jaw hurt. I started when I felt Susie's hand on my back and heard her whisper, "Lena, are you all right?"

"No," I said, and began to cry harshly, the sobs pounding like fists inside my ribs. "Can't you run away with me, Susie? There must be some place we can go." I squeezed her hand so hard she winced. "Please . . . Susie . . . please." The words spurted out between gusts of crying.

"Hush," whispered Susie, stroking my head. Deep down, in a place she struggled to deny, she was probably glad I was proving so troublesome, because she'd always felt our father preferred me. But she was also—her voice and touch so soft—truly sorry for me. "You can't run, Lena. He's got people all over. Anyway, the Boyces will get you out.

Don't you think so?"

"Albert will," I said, my chin thrust up, "no matter what. He loves me, Susie." I knew how tired they all were of hearing about Albert and his miraculous love for me, but I didn't care.

"Do you think Beal loves you?" Susie asked timidly. She reminded me of our mother, fidgeting when she spoke of uncomfortable things, smoothing her dressing gown over her knee.

"No," I said. "How could he treat me like this if he loved me? Would John treat you like this, Susie? You know he wouldn't."

In her silence I heard the answer she didn't make: *I don't know what he would do if I did what you have done.*

"Susie," I said, "Listen to me. No matter what Beal says, this ain't about love. This is pride, or . . . or hate, or I don't know what, but it isn't love."

"Lena, look at it this way," she said earnestly. "If the Boyces get you out this time, then Beal won't be able to confine you again. Maybe he'll get tired of all the trouble."

I wanted to believe her. "I need to lie down."

Susie walked me to the spare bedroom where they'd put me. There were a few books beside the bed and the bed itself, with its dark-stained wooden headboard and the chenille bedspread over wool blankets. Blank, like any other spare room, a place where family odds and ends go—the novel everyone has finished reading, the old dressing table—a room where the life of the family recedes quietly, like water evaporating from a playa lake.

I was surprised when Susie followed me in. She shut the door carefully so as to make no noise and watched me light the bedside lamp. "Lena," she said, "there is something I want to ask you." I could see her blush, even in the lamplight. I climbed up on the bed and sat cross-legged on it, the way we used to when we were girls, and she came and sat beside me. I'd been like her little mother, so proud of her accomplishments and of my own ability to correct and inform her. We stepped back into those years as if they'd been there all along, just waiting for our return.

"Lena," she said again, "what is it like? I don't mean to pry. You don't have to answer." Her voice dropped almost to a whisper, despite the closed door. "I don't know anyone else to ask. John is a kind husband, you can see that, but that part of marriage . . . I was so unprepared. I didn't have any idea what to expect."

She looked at me suddenly, straight in the face. "You know how Mama is. I couldn't ask her. I've wanted to ask Eula sometimes, but since she married Henry, you can't talk to her at all. And sometimes I think I could ask Pearl, but she still treats me like a baby. She likes you better. She doesn't know what to do with a big coward like me."

I leaned over and put my arms around her, just the way I used to when she was small. "You're not a coward," I said. "You're just shy." It was a relief to comfort someone else.

"And no one talks about it," I went on. I knew what she was asking. She had married young. Sometimes, with her husband's body on top of her, inside her, she felt so small and alone. He seemed to have turned into another creature, something she didn't recognize. Sometimes she didn't recognize herself either; she was as strange as he was.

"With you and Albert, what is it like?" She paused too briefly for me to answer and covered her face with her hands. "I'm sorry. It's not my business."

I wanted to answer her, but I found it harder than I expected. It would have been easier to talk about how it was with Beal.

She took my hesitation for rebuke. "Please don't be offended, Lena. I—"

"I'm not angry. I just don't know how to describe it. I feel like it's the way it should be. With Beal, it was just something I went through and—"

"Yes," said Susie eagerly, "I love John, but that part of our life, I feel like it's for him. I do it for him and sometimes it's nice to be close and I love him, but I don't really understand it." She started to cry very softly. "Sometimes I think there's something very wrong with me, because it seems to make him happy and I want to be a good wife to him and I . . . I don't understand it," she finished up, weeping and wiping her hand across her eyes.

"You must love Albert so much, to do what you've done," she went on after she stopped crying. "You were always so brave and free. I've always admired you, no matter what they're saying now. I never *could* stand all they're saying." She pulled a handkerchief from her dressing gown and blew her nose. "I'd be terrified. I've always thought not understanding all this was a sign I was a good woman, but now you understand it—I can see you do—and so many people are saying you're bad, but I know you're not, and I don't know *what* to think anymore."

Her honesty and humility touched me. I didn't know how to answer.

"I don't know," I said finally. "I . . . Albert . . . it's home. It's how it's supposed to be." I started to cry again. "How could Mrs. Boyce say those things about me, Susie, when all I've done is love her son?"

We cried together on the bed and then, after a while, we began to laugh a little because the world of our childhood was once more around us.

Sinking into bed later, after Susie had left me at last, I pulled the quilt up around me and whispered goodnight to Albert somewhere in Canada. Then I slept well, at least for a few hours.

25

When I woke, I could hear Beal and Henry Bowman downstairs. I made up my mind. *This time, they won't see me scream and they won't see me cry.*

Beal was seated in the living room beside my father and John Pace. Henry Bowman's stout figure filled up another chair; he gave a tight-mouthed nod when he spotted me in the doorway. I didn't respond.

My father greeted me sternly. "We're taking you back to Arlington Heights," he said without preamble. Whatever doubts he'd expressed to my mother the night before had left no visible trace. "I'm now satisfied that it's the best place for you."

I turned to Beal. "You've lied," I said coldly. He opened his mouth to say something, glanced at my father, and thought better of it.

"I've explained the legal situation on your end," John Pace said. I knew he meant the power of attorney part. I expected him to say more, but he looked away and was silent.

"Then you know," I said to Beal, "you can't keep me there this time."

Still he said nothing. He cast his eyes downward and did what he was learning to do so well: Suffer with dignity, as if he had never threatened, hit, or cursed me. He suffered as if it were all my fault.

My mother came through the door just then to offer coffee. The room was so silent that when Henry Bowman took a sip the sound exploded. I could smell bacon frying in the kitchen.

"Well, look at you all," I said contemptuously, "ready to tuck into a big breakfast so you've got the strength to march the little woman off to the nut house."

"It's for your own good, Lena," Beal said in a low, hurt-sounding voice. "Dr. Allison has seen many cases like this"—his voice grew a bit stronger—"and he don't see one reason why you should be unhappy with this marriage. He has spoken at length to your father and we all agree this is best."

The last part sounded like a hint to my father, who cleared his throat. He looked tired, but unlike Beal, his shirt was clean and pressed and his shoes were polished. His wife was there to make sure of it.

"Your husband is willing to forgive all that is past," said my father, "if you will give this man up." He continued in a louder tone, blustering where he felt his ground to be least solid. "I have visited the sanitarium myself, and I don't think they have treated you as you have led us to believe."

I gave him a hard look. His eyes wavered like I'd hit him and then they hardened too. "Get yourself ready to go," he ordered, "and don't try any tricks. I've wrangled balky cattle and stupid sheep. Don't think I can't corral one crazy daughter."

How had Beal managed it? He'd somehow gotten my father to do the threatening and ordering for him. He didn't have to worry that my father might feel sorry for me if Beal did it himself. He had a power I was only starting to recognize, something dug real deep in unlikely country, just pumping away while other wells ran dry.

A few minutes later, I cornered Susie and scribbled out the wire I wanted her to send to Henry Boyce: F*or God's sake, protect me. Beal and Henry Bowman are here to put me in an asylum by force.* She agreed, but she was frightened and her timidity wasn't touching anymore. She would still be with her husband in Clayton while I would be on the train to Fort Worth.

Beal and my father flanked me as we headed to the automobile. At the station, Beal grabbed my elbow to pull me out. "Let go," I muttered. "What do you think I'm going to do? Run off so you can shoot me?"

He loosened his hold just slightly. "Don't try anything stupid," he muttered right back. Henry Bowman pressed into me on the other side and my father walked right behind. It really was like herding. I saw the train ahead, steam swathing the engine like a cloud, the engineer stretching his legs on the platform, laughing suddenly at something one of the porters said.

Ordinary life—my sudden longing for it cut like a knife. My teeth began to chatter.

It smelled like snow again.

26

On the train, my father was in one compartment, and Henry Bowman and Beal and I were in another. It was an odd arrangement, but I guess Beal wanted the backup. After supper, the two of them climbed into the berths without undressing. I sat up and watched the snow start to fall in flurries, the flakes appearing like ghostly faces in the dark outside the window. From the upper berth, Henry began to snore. I heard nothing from Beal. After a while, I began to doze. It must have been about two or three in the morning when Beal sat up suddenly and said, "You'll never get away from me."

I was so startled I gave a little scream, even as I realized it was Beal speaking and not some monster out of a dream.

After I got my heart to slow down, I asked, "Why won't you let me go?" My own voice surprised me; it sounded calm, like I was just curious.

"I don't know," he answered across the darkness. His own voice had changed: it was flat and quiet. I knew he was telling the truth.

"You know I'm not crazy," I said. It wasn't even a question.

"No."

"Then why are you doing this?" I asked again. The train rocked on in the night. Our conversation seemed to take place outside of time, in some ancient room God reserves only for the truth. We spoke quietly above Henry's deep, slow snoring. The snow hit the windows in wet splotches. "What good is there in all this for you?"

"I don't know," Beal said again. He paused. "Our family," he said. "The children." I knew *the children* hid and exposed it all at the same time, whatever it was.

I saw their faces. I remembered what Eula said about the way Lenora cried.

"You know I don't love you," I said after another silence.

"Oh, love," answered Beal, "I don't need that kind of love. But I won't let you go."

For a second or two, I accepted what he said because I knew it was true. But truth like that is so unbearable you can only take it in short bursts—after that you have to struggle for a long, hard time before you can accept it once and for all.

"Why not?" I asked again, but my calm was evaporating. And in that subtle way in which people understand each other through so much more than words, he also shifted.

"You're my wife," he said. "I'll kill you both if I have to." His voice was cold and certain.

"He's more of a man than you are. And he's a much better shot."

Beal stood up. I couldn't make out his face, but his smell stood in for it, disheveled and dirty.

"Don't push me, Lena," he said harshly.

"You push yourself," I said in a fury. "All you had to do was let me go. You know you weren't any happier than I was." I stood up, too, ducking quickly to one side before he could catch hold of me. I half-noticed that Henry had stopped snoring.

"In my heart, I belong to Albert. And someday, we'll be married before the whole world." My voice was low but angry. I waved my left hand to make the point clearer.

"I've seen just about all I want to of that ring," he muttered low and fierce, grabbing my arm and pulling me up close to him. His breath was so strong I almost gagged. "Take it off," he demanded. "Take it off, goddammit."

"You have no right," I said, my voice as enraged as his own. "Don't you ever again tell me what to do. You go to hell." His grip on my arm slackened for just an instant—he didn't know about the words I'd learned to say—then tightened again. "You go to hell," I said again for good measure. "Why would I want to belong to a man like you? You're a liar and a bully and a whiner and I'm sick of you. *Leave me alone.*"

113

With a sound coming out of his throat like nothing I'd ever heard from a human being, he pushed me onto the lower berth and brought the heel of his hand down hard on my palm, pinning it to the crumpled sheets. Bit by bit, pulling so hard he was panting, he wrenched Albert's ring from my finger. I pushed at his chest with my right hand but I couldn't work myself free, then he had the ring, and full of that stinking hard breath he went to the window and pushed it open, high enough for his whole arm to reach outside. "God damn you to hell, you sonofabitch," he shouted as he hurled the ring into the snowy night. "God damn you to hell."

"Beal," came Henry Bowman's voice from the upper berth, "shut the window, man." I just lay where I was, crying from pain, my finger sprained and dangling. Beal's breath slowly quieted. He shut the window. In the midst of our silence, the whistle blew, that wild sound, lonesome and moaning, floating across the plains like their own voice.

Henry said, "It won't do you no good to hurt her, Beal. I can't let you hurt her." He was telling him for his own good. Nothing to do with me. We were all awake the rest of the night, but no one said another word.

PART II

BEAL

27

She had *no* idea what it was like.

The entire night I'm listening to her cry and play the victim on the train, and then there's the trip back out to the san with everybody squeezed together like chum in Allison's car and old Snyder acting standoffish like maybe he's *still* not sure. Watching her walk upstairs behind the matron, I swear I thought, *I am glad to be done with you.* Even though I'm telling everybody I'm not.

It was Henry Bowman who suggested the Metropolitan. He and Will *I'm-the-D.A.-and-you're-not* Atwell were ready to relax. Who wouldn't be? But when we walked into the lobby, there was old man Boyce, setting in one of those big chairs like he owned the world. He spotted us and waggled his finger at Atwell to come on over to talk. Like he hadn't done enough talking already.

I went right back out the revolving door, Bowman in tow behind me. It was cold as the devil's left nut outside. We stamped our feet to try to keep warm and waited on Atwell.

Next thing I know, they're dragging me down the street to Joseph's to try and convince me to eat some supper. Atwell sits cutting his steak into tiny pieces like he's some kind of goddamn old maid with a delicate constitution, while he drones on and on. Which he is good at. The Colonel said *this*: "I just got the state to drop Beal's bogus kidnapping charges." The Colonel said *that*: "I've got twenty minutes before I head out to the station. I'm going home tonight. That's all I need, Will. Just give me twenty minutes of your time. I'll prove to you what kind of woman she really is." Those parts I heard. The rest I didn't.

God, how it hurt me. It twisted in my gut like a broken bottle, so no matter which way I turned, it cut me up some more.

I don't remember leaving the restaurant. I was talking but not out loud.

Old man, you've caused trouble enough. Just stop talking. Go straight to hell and stop talking.

FORT WORTH STAR-TELEGRAM
FORT WORTH, TEXAS, SUNDAY, JANUARY 14, 1912

BOYCE-SNEED ELOPEMENT ENDS IN TRAGEDY

The sensational elopement of Mrs. Lena B. Sneed, wife of the wealthy Amarillo banker, and Mr. Albert G. Boyce, Jr., had its still more sensational climax Saturday night when John Beal Sneed, the husband, shot to death Colonel Albert G. Boyce, Sr., aged father of the man who eloped with his wife.

The shooting took place in the lobby of the Metropolitan Hotel, Ninth and Main streets, shortly after 8 o'clock. The lobby was crowded at the time and panic followed the shooting.

Colonel Boyce was seated just a few feet from the Main Street entrance where Sneed entered. Eyewitnesses to the tragedy say that Colonel Boyce was not aware of his presence until Sneed fired the first shot with a .32 automatic from about eight feet away. This shot missed Boyce, and he jumped from his chair, evidently with the intention of running, when another shot sent a bullet crashing through his abdomen. Three other shots, fired rapidly, struck him in the stomach, and he staggered forward, falling about twenty feet from the chair where he was seated.

Sneed never spoke and Colonel Boyce uttered

only half-audible groans. A man grabbed Sneed from behind. He made no resistance and was shoved toward the door to Main Street and walked briskly toward Eighth. Here Officer Cogdill placed him under arrest and took him to the central police station.

An ambulance was immediately summoned and Boyce taken to St. Joseph's Infirmary, where he soon died.

28

They put me in a cell by myself. I lay on the bunk and listened to the noises around me—men snoring, a little talking, one short argument—and felt quiet for the first time in a long while. My mind just ground to a halt, which was a blessing after all the furious scrabbling and digging and running around it had been doing for months, even when I slept.

There was part of a moon out that night—we were between storms—shining through the high window in my cell. I watched its slow movement with my heart going regular and easy, knowing I'd done something that couldn't ever be taken back or undone. I fell asleep feeling peaceful.

It wasn't 'til the next morning that it started to sink in: I'd done this thing that wasn't going to be all that easy to get out of. If I'd just killed that sonofabitch Al, it would have been easier, at least in Texas. But shooting his father, an unarmed and peaceable old man, five or six times in the lobby of a fine Fort Worth hotel—it wouldn't be easy at all. In fact, it might be impossible. Bill McLean Jr., the high-priced lawyer that Atwell had sent over to the jail to deal with me, made that clear.

McLean had no interest in small talk or soothing manners. He just got right to it. "Beal, you need to tell me exactly what happened. And you better be honest with me because I'm going to be honest with you. You've got yourself in a real jam here. I'm as good as they get, but there are a whole lot of other good lawyers in Texas and the Boyces will be hiring 'em fast as boll weevils hit cotton to help the D.A.—Jordan Cummings? you probably know him—no slouch himself."

He waved a cigarette in my direction, raising his eyebrows quizzically. I shook my head. A match flamed between his fingers so fast I barely saw him strike it. He lit up, drew deeply, exhaled a cloud of smoke through his nose, then shook the match out sort of contemplatively—the only time in the entire visit when you might have applied that word to anything he did. He even quit tapping his foot the way he'd been doing since he sat down in the cheap chair they'd provided in the room they set aside for lawyer conferences.

"Just so you know," he concluded.

Well, the truth was, I didn't exactly know what had happened. All these years later, I still don't. I didn't walk into that lobby expecting to find the old man there. Atwell said he'd headed home. I expected . . . maybe I thought if I saw that he'd gone, I'd feel some relief. But when I saw him sitting there, I didn't think about anything at all, I just pulled the gun out of my overcoat pocket and started firing.

It felt good. That's the truth, too. The moment I shot the Colonel, something inside me got bigger and surer and everybody I had contact with afterwards acted like they understood that. Even my father recognized the change. He marched into that cell with his Bible-toting pastor in tow and his old-fashioned beard and ramrod-straight bearing that looked like a rebuke to everybody about pretty much everything. I could see he was about to unwind a real corker and then he looked at me and sort of sagged. The steam went out of him like a baked potato.

"Son," he said, "what's all this about?"

The Reverend Nelms didn't say a word. He understood right away his presence was superfluous.

"I shot him," I said without elaborating.

29

Just as Bill McLean had predicted, by the time it was all said and done there were a lot of big-name lawyers working on my case. Cone Johnson, who'd run for governor the year before, was probably the biggest. People jammed the courtroom to listen to his closing speech about tracing the river back to its source.

These days, I seem to be tracing it back myself. I'm old now. I look common as dirt. No one pays me any mind in a crowd—I'm just another worn-out-looking old man. But I remember how free I felt in that Fort Worth jail. I go over and over what went on in court. I dream people are hanging on my every word again. I can't exactly say I want to go back, but there's something back there I miss. Notoriety? The story? A missed opportunity? I can't quite put my finger on it. But I know one thing. It's not just the poor you have with you always. You have the dead, too. They slither around like snakes. You might not see them for a long time, then all of a sudden you do.

Of course, any intelligent man realizes that the river traces all the way back to our unhappy first parents, Adam and Eve. But let's say my part of it branched off when I was seven years old and our mother died. Joe had just turned eight, Georgie was almost six, and Marvin was less than a year old. Our mother—Georgia, like my sister and my youngest daughter—wasn't yet thirty. She never got over whatever went on when she was pregnant with Marvin. I don't know what that was. No one ever talked about it.

In those days, mothers and fathers often died before their children were raised, and children often died before they were grown. But tragedy being common don't make it less tragic. You can tell yourself that it's just the way things are. You can tell yourself—or more likely the preacher will tell you—that it's the will of the Lord, which for some unfathomable reason the Lord prefers to keep to Himself. You can tell yourself that your mama is an angel in heaven and so sweet the Lord just called her home early because He missed her so, but none of it much helps.

She's there. You need her. She's the anchor in your world. And then she's sick and people are always telling you to be quiet, not to bother her, she needs to save her strength and get better.

Then, ten days before Christmas, she dies.

There's a thing it does inside you. I guess the best way to put it is that you never again feel sure about anything you really care about. No matter how long it's been. The more you care, the more certain you are that who or what you care for will be taken away—with very little, if any, warning. The Lord will make one of His mysterious decisions and decide to mess with your life.

We moved off the family farm in Milam County and into Georgetown not too long afterwards. That's where I first met Lena and the Snyders, and Al and the rest of the Boyces. It's where Joe met Bessie Boyce, the girl he wanted to marry and couldn't because she died, and where we all became friends. And it's where my father started riding me—about everything, it sometimes seemed.

When I cried because I didn't want to go to school the first day or he caught me moping or reading when I was supposed to be doing chores, I was in for it. It wasn't the switch. He used one like most everyone else, but he didn't get carried away. It was what he said and how he said it, like he almost couldn't bear to look at me.

"Are you crying *again*? Do you think you're the only one who misses her?"

"Do you think this is how your mother would want you to behave? Do you think this would make her proud?"

"I expect you to act like a man, son. You have to grow up now."

Sometimes it felt like I'd lost both parents. For about a year, I tried desperately to please him, hoping that would make him love me again, but I finally realized it wasn't going to work. Helen, the colored woman who took care of us, didn't say too much, but I think she felt sorry for me. Sometimes she'd let me lick the batter spoon when she was making cake, and she soothed me when I cried.

And Joe stood up for me. One afternoon as I passed by the study, I overheard him. "Father, you're too hard on Beal." I froze outside the door, holding my breath. Joe's fear was obvious—his voice wavered all over the place. "It isn't fair."

I thought our father would surely explode with anger. Instead, there was a long silence. And then he sighed so deeply that I could hear him through the closed door. "I expect you're right, son," he said. "I wish all this were easier."

I crept away because I was afraid if I heard more, he'd spoil it.

I never told Joe I'd heard him, and Joe never told me what he'd said. But things were a little easier after that; I could see my father was trying. And when I started winning prizes—debating prizes, writing prizes, reading prizes—he began to treat me like I had something valuable to contribute. He even started to boast about me, in that way that didn't look like boasting but you knew it was. By the time I got into Princeton—Woodrow Wilson's school—I was known as the brightest of all the Sneed children and one of the very brightest young men in town.

In '99, not long after I'd graduated and come back home, I ran into Lena at a party. I was paying a lot of attention to girls, not just for the obvious reasons young men do, but also because I thought my next step ought to be marriage and I wanted to check out the local options. I was plenty eligible and I knew it. Lena had turned into quite a belle—she wasn't the prettiest girl in town, but she had . . . something. Those eyes, for one thing. They gave a man the impression he could drown in them and be happy going down.

When I first spotted her at the party, she was talking with the town librarian and a philosophy professor from SMU. The librarian was a middle-aged woman with a mouth she appeared to keep under strict control, and the professor had long white hair in the Bill Hickok style. Lena was wearing a pale blue dress, which billowed around her like she was swimming in her own personal lake. She never took her eyes from their faces when they spoke, listening like they were angels come down from God. The first thing I ever wanted from her was to watch her listen to me like that.

When I next saw her, she was bent over with laughter with a school of boys, thirteen or fourteen years old, swimming around her, all laughing too. The second thing I wanted was to make her laugh like that.

The third time I saw her, she was sitting in the porch swing outside the house, fanning herself slowly and looking like she was a thousand miles away. That time, I wanted to sit down next to her, so I asked her if I could and she said yes.

"It's good to see you again, Beal," she said, after we'd gotten a nice little rhythm going on the swing. She touched my arm lightly, smiled and looked me straight in the eyes, which cheered me. It's not often you want something and get it just like that.

"Likewise," I said. "I see you've gotten prettier."

She responded, "And you've gotten handsomer." The usual compliments.

But then she hitched her legs up in the swing and turned to face me more directly, putting her hands together in her lap. "Tell me," she said, "what was it like up there? What did you think of it? What did they think of you?"

I told her. I talked for a long time and she never took her eyes off my face. She asked all kinds of interesting, intelligent questions. They were things I'd asked myself. I think she probably was genuinely curious, even if she was also husband-hunting. I could see she was smart enough to have gone to Princeton herself if she'd been a man.

I told her what it was like to open my mouth and have that accent come out when most everybody else sounded different. I told her that people didn't act like we did, and they all thought different about the war. I told her sometimes I got so hungry for fried chicken and greens and grits that I wanted to take the next train out to come on home. I told her that people thought we were all stupid and ignorant, even though they had to admit I wasn't either one.

"They don't know about coloreds," I told her. "They have all these ideas about 'em, but they mostly don't know any. And they want to tell you they do, especially some of them people from Boston.

They're sure if you come from down here you probably eat colored baby sausage for breakfast."

"What did you say when they started in on you?" Lena asked.

"Mostly I tried to stay out of it," I said. "I figured I was up there to get an education, not fight the War all over again."

"Lord," she said, "there's sure enough of that down here. I didn't know they did it up north, too. You'd think one of these years—maybe now that we're about to start a different *century*—people would realize we really did lose that thing."

That made the conversation a bit more private. You really couldn't say much about the Confederacy or Lee or Jackson or Bedford Forrest or anything else that wasn't pure praise and sorrow, and you couldn't get impatient with anybody else's praise and sorrow. Lena and I had grown up listening to our elders reminisce, complain, and weep about the war.

"Exactly," I said. "Up north, they don't talk about it all the time like we do. They won it and they don't have regrets, and anyway, they mostly ain't the type. But when they got around me, it would spark 'em. Sort of like poking at a bobcat or an armadillo. They wanted to see whether I'd bite or curl up." I made biting gestures and then curled my body into a ball so that the swing rocked a little harder.

Lena giggled and pretended to poke me. "So, Mr. Sneed," she said, and now she was definitely flirting, "which are you, a bobcat or an armadillo?" She cocked an eyebrow and looked straight into my eyes some more.

"Miss Snyder," I answered, taking hold of her hand, "I'll have to take you out for ice cream tomorrow afternoon so you can study on that. But I warn you, it's not an easy thing to deduce. You might need to be studying on me for years."

And so we went out for ice cream the next afternoon. With some of her family along, we went out to supper the night after that. We saw one another the next day and the day after. There weren't any doubts about the suitability of the match—two good families, friends for years; two young people with a brilliant future ahead of them. I had the education, the brains, and the family to end up a big wheel in the state. And Lena was the smartest, most charming girl in town.

When something goes so easily at the beginning, it's natural to believe that the future will roll along in the same pleasant way.

30

It was up north, feeling lonely and out of place, where I'd begun to see young colored gals every few weeks. It made me feel less homesick. You don't see coloreds all over up there; that was part of what made it seem foreign. And I'd already discovered in several outings to cat houses with Joe that I often liked the colored gals best. I could leave the world I'd learned to live in and go somewhere else.

I figured I'd give up the habit when I came back home. But I didn't. So when I began to court Lena, I was also seeing a gal in Georgetown every now and then. She couldn't have been much more than sixteen. I don't remember her name. But she was a sweet girl and she liked me, too. I was young and I got still younger when I was with her. When I was on the everyday planet—the one where Lena lived—I couldn't ever talk about the colored planet. But on the colored planet, I could talk about the Lena planet, and I did.

One early morning, this young gal and I were lying together watching the light brighten, the frayed velvet curtain pulled open a few inches to let in some air. Chickens were clucking just outside and the housedog was barking in the dirt lane. "Everybody says it's a wonderful match," I said to the girl, whose head was resting on my shoulder. I was admiring the contrast: Pale skin with dark skin against it. I liked the soft springiness of her hair.

"What's she like?" the girl asked sleepily.

"She's everything she could be," I answered. "She's smart and pretty and a great favorite with everyone. She comes from a good family—the Snyders, you know them?—and she's just twenty and lots of fun."

The girl sighed and wrapped her arm around my torso. She was a tiny thing with hardly a speck of meat on her. I could see the jut of her hipbone under the sheet. "Are you happy with her?" she asked.

It was just an idle question. She probably figured I'd be talking for a while and she could drift off with the comfortable vibration of my voice coming through to where her head rested on my shoulder.

But it brought me up short. On the Lena planet, the answer was yes. But the danger of the colored planet was that sometimes I'd feel so happy and comfortable, I wouldn't want to leave. After that, I'd have to stay away for a while 'til I got my bearings again.

Her eyes were closed and her breathing was slow and steady. "I'm as happy as I'm going to be," I said.

She was less asleep than I'd reckoned. She twisted her head up to get a good look at me. "That don't sound all that happy," she said. "What you want to marry her for if she don't make you happy?"

I patted her head back down on my shoulder. "It ain't that she don't make me happy."

"Well, it don't sound like it," the gal said, sounding sleepy again, but carrying on. "I don't understand white folks. I don't understand you. You got money, you got family, you educated, you young, you a man, you can do whatever you want, so why you want to tie yourself up with a lady who don't make you happy?"

I couldn't think how to answer the question. I vowed after that to stay away from the colored gals. *But when I was a man, I put away childish things,* as the Bible verse says. In honor of my bride, I'd leave the colored planet behind.

Lena and I got married on October 17, 1901. I looked into her dark eyes as we said our vows and I saw melting tenderness and standing tears and my heart soared. When I touched her that night in our dark hotel room, she was eager. She was a virgin, of course, but she caught fire while we were kissing. I tried not to remember other arms and other bodies. But there they were: If I imagined them in the dark beneath me, I caught fire, too. But when I remembered who I was making love to, the fires died down. I was never able to change that.

Still, it took two years and the birth of our first daughter before I went back to my old ways. Lenora had just been born and I was practicing law up there in Childress. Clients were scarce and those I had never seemed to pay off very well. One old lawyer I knew—drunk but brilliant—said I made things too complicated. "You keep trying to be fancy," he told me when I asked his advice. "It's a problem with being smart like you are. A lawyer is better off being kind of a dummy like me because most of the judges are dummies and just about all the clients are, and that goes double for juries. You got to keep it on a level they can understand." Of course, he was no dummy. But he had a point. You were better off keeping it simple.

One night, feeling discouraged about my practice and proud and scared about having another mouth to feed, I just quit fighting temptation, headed to the tiny Colored Town in Childress, and found me a young woman the way a man finds water after days in the desert. After that, I didn't quit the habit again until all the troubles. I figured I'd tried to change my tastes and it didn't work.

Anyway, if practicing law teaches a man anything, it's that most folks have secrets. They say things to get along with their neighbors about what they believe and how they live, about what their families and God and His son, Jesus Christ, mean to them, and all like that. And then they do things that kind of run beyond the borderlines of what they say. I wasn't any different.

Life went on—the way it does—and by the fall of 1910, I thought things were pretty good. Our house in Amarillo was finished. I'd given up lawyering and gotten deep into business with Mr. Fuqua and farming out at Paducah. We'd had plenty of rain. Speculators were selling ranch land to nesters as fast as they could get a trainload of them out to see it, so my property values were rocketing up.

Lena seemed happy enough. I hadn't been raised to think that well-bred white women were very interested in the physical side of marriage, so I figured I gave her all the things that really mattered to her. She had beautiful dresses and jewelry, and our girls were cared for like princesses. The house was fixed up how she wanted. I always kissed her goodnight and good morning. I said thank you after every meal, even though Nettie did the cooking. I always told Nettie thank you, too. And I tipped her big at Christmas. I figured she knew things I didn't want her telling.

But by then, to be honest, Lena bored me most of the time. I wanted her to look good and I wanted us to make a good impression in town and I wanted her to be a good mother to my children, but I really wasn't interested in *her*. She kind of wore me out with her parties and her ideas and wanting to talk over all those silly novels she read.

Every now and then she'd say, "I miss you. I wish you were in town more. The girls miss you. I want it to be the way it used to be between us."

And I'd try for a while to accommodate her. But my heart wasn't in it. I liked our routine. I didn't really remember all that much how it used to be.

So when I heard Al Boyce was coming 'round to see her in the spring of 1911—which I *did* hear from a few people—at first I was actually sort of relieved. As dim-witted as that sounds. I figured it would take the pressure off me. I suppose it was about as foolish a fantasy as hers was; that just because I wasn't hardly sleeping with her and was gone all the time, I wouldn't care if she humiliated me in public.

And when we first got to talking about separation and possible divorce, I didn't think it was necessarily a bad idea. Lena was never an inexpensive woman and there's no alimony in Texas. Once the divorce was final, I'd just be paying for my girls. Even though I knew some of that would end up going to Lena, I thought I could probably make myself look like the bewildered, grieving husband and then go on and do whatever I wanted.

And then Dr. McMeans said, "Your wife was pregnant."

We were standing near the front door. Lena was asleep in the daybed—he'd given her a sedative—so he spoke in a low voice. "She wasn't far along, maybe a month. But with all that bleeding, she lost the baby. I'm sorry, Beal. I don't know what's troubling her—it may be the climate—but if you all want to try again it would be better if she was less nervous."

"Are you sure?" I asked.

He misunderstood the question. "I'm sorry, Beal. There's no mistake. She lost the baby."

I hustled the man out as fast as I could. Then I just stood there in the hallway with my forehead pressed against the door and my mind exploding. I'd been drifting toward divorce with a foggy view of Lena in my mind. It was like she was a mountain covered with clouds and all of a sudden the view had cleared and I could see what I'd been blind to. She'd gotten pregnant by Al Boyce and been hoping she could get me to agree to a divorce before she started to show.

When she came to, I was sitting in a chair I'd pulled right up to the bed, so worn out by all of it I was half-asleep myself. There was just a moment, as she weakly called my name and I opened my eyes, when I thought, *Oh, what the hell. We were talking divorce anyway.*

But that didn't last any time at all.

"Bitch," I said, almost conversationally.

She startled like I'd struck her.

"I don't know what you've been thinking and I don't really care," I continued, "but thank God you lost that bastard's bastard. This here is the end of the whole thing. Do you hear? The end of ALL of it."

She started to cry, hanging her head and balling her fists over her eyes the way little kids do.

"You're gonna write a letter to that sonofabitch and here's what you're gonna say: '*I never want to see you again in my life. I have done my husband wrong. I am going to spend the rest of my life trying to make it up to him because he don't deserve what we did. Go away and leave me alone.*'

"And if you ever see him again, if you so much as try to telephone or wire him or anything else, I swear to God I will kill you both."

Lena sobbed, saying over and over in a weepy voice, "I'm sorry. I'm so sorry."

It softened my heart a little, I have to admit, even though I didn't want it to. Something inside me said, *You have some responsibility for this situation, you know.* I didn't really want to listen, but I couldn't ignore it completely, either.

"Look," I said in a quieter tone, "I'm a forgiving man." At the moment, I liked the idea of being magnanimous. "But how am I supposed to forgive *this*?"

She looked up at me and burst out crying harder and sobbed to me, "You were gone so much. I should have been stronger and oh, please, please forgive me. It will never happen again. I swear it. Give me the paper and I'll write whatever you want."

If I'd been a more sensible man, I would have realized that speech sounded way too much like something in those stupid novels. I would have been suspicious of how easily she was giving in. Because not a month later we were out on the gallery and she was telling me she'd never loved me and wanted to marry Al Boyce.

There was a moment that night when I thought maybe she knew about my habits. We were in the bedroom, still trying to keep our voices down for the sake of the girls. I hadn't yet picked up the gun. "How could you have done something like this?" I hissed at her. "You're a decent woman. You know better."

She glared at me. "*You* are asking *me* that question?" she said angrily. She snorted and shook her head. "The Sneeds. There's always one of y'all around to tell the rest of the world what it ought to be doing. Seems funny to me that God would put Sneeds in charge of that, when some of y'all have such peculiar ways." She drew the word *peculiar* out, making it sound dirty. Then she started crying again.

I let it drop. I've always wondered, though, why she didn't use it, if she really knew. Maybe she did, privately, with the Boyces and with her family. Maybe she brought it up to her lawyer and he advised against it: "That stuff rubs off. You'd have the niggers and he'd have his father, and your father, and all sorts of other upstanding white citizens, and you'd end up looking even worse." If he told her that, he told her right. They went after me just for having that colored porter testify. The story wasn't supposed to include elements he could add.

And maybe, despite everything, she preferred the story I started telling. She wanted to believe that if I was a demon, it was because I wanted her, since she knew deep down I didn't and never really had. That kind of knowing is animal, just the way everyone knew in the jail they couldn't mess with me anymore.

Anyway, I laid off once all this got started. I knew it would be stupid to get caught with any woman, let alone a colored one. The funny thing is, I didn't really miss it. I became the man who wanted his wife. On a terrible December day in New York after she'd disappeared, I stared out my hotel window to the gashed-up snow on the streets below and poured out my heart in a letter to Fuqua.

Why does God want me to suffer and suffer and yet live? If Lena was here and herself, she would help me as no one else could, instead of killing me by degrees. I am sure it will only be a matter of time until she will be the most miserable of human beings and probably become more insane. Or should she recover her mind by some act of providence, she would be just as miserable and probably destroy herself. And, of course, I want to take care of her, and I could not be true to myself without doing all on Earth I can to find her.

All that felt like the truth when I wrote it.

31

I spent most of December of 1911 looking for Lena and Al or dealing with legal angles in Fort Worth. But I had to come back to Amarillo every now and then to see about the house and the cattle business and to check in with Fuqua.

Mid-December, I visited him at the First National Bank. His office was warm from the fire and the radiator—one popping and hissing, the other popping and gurgling—but outside was bitterly cold and windy. Every now and then, a big gust rattled the windows in their sashes. It had snowed a little the night before and everything was iced up.

I'd pulled my wooden chair so close to his vast wooden desk with the big blotter that my knees hit the front of it. My eyes were rimmed red from lack of sleep, as I'd seen when I'd made the effort to shave that morning, which I hadn't for a few days. A lot of what was left of my hair had fallen out; a few strands stuck to my coat. My collar was dirty and I stank of tobacco and old sweat and nerves.

"I have some disturbing news, Beal," Fuqua said without much in the way of the usual greetings. He reached across the desk like he wanted to pat me, but the desk was too wide, even as close as I was pushed into it. "I want you to promise you'll stay calm."

"Oh, for God's sake," I said angrily. "Just get to the point. When is the news not bad these days?" I was so wrought up by then that people tended to forgive my rudeness. Fuqua just ignored it.

"You know I don't want to add to your burden and I never talk ill of others if I can avoid it," he went on, pressing his mouth into a long line that gave him a strange look, simultaneously priggish and elated. "I don't want to repeat precisely the terms Al's father has been using in public about your wife, but they are such that the lowest woman in town would be insulted by them."

"What?"

Fuqua cleared his throat some more. It's not my belief that he liked to hurt me. But he liked telling tales on the Colonel and feeling saintly while he did it. Those two had hated each other for decades. Fuqua always began by saying he disliked talking ill of others and assuring you that a larger purpose was involved: Your own good, the good of the city, or some such thing. The Colonel, on the other hand, didn't say much about Fuqua, but when he did it kind of exploded out of him in a shower of cussing, no preliminaries required.

"It shocked me, too, Beal," Fuqua said. "But I've heard it from Sam Slade and others I consider reliable." All the good bankers in town had men like Slade to keep them up to date on gossip—a necessary asset when it came to making loans and extending credit. "It's not my place to sow discord, as the Good Book puts it," Fuqua went on in his usual vein, "but I've always said old Al Boyce is a man who can't be trusted. He thinks he can talk in town like he'd talk to the cowboys in the bunkhouse. Well and good, you may say," he continued, though of course he knew I wouldn't, "but there are times when talk is as bad or worse than bullets, and I'd say this is one of them."

"How can he be talking like that about my wife when it's his own son that's run off with her?" I asked incredulously.

Fuqua took a deep breath through his nose and thinned out his lips again. Then he exhaled and looked at me with melancholy eyes. "Honestly, Beal," he said, "I don't know." I don't think he did, for all his bad opinions of the Colonel.

It was only a week or two later that the Burns detectives found the lovebirds. I was trotting up the Fort Worth courthouse steps to testify to the grand jury about the state abduction charges when Dr. Allison—who never did stop feeling guilty about losing Lena—hollered at me from below and sprinted up the stairs to tell me the news.

That very afternoon, I walked into Anderson's Guns and tried out a .32. For a few minutes, firing it in a long, well-padded room at the back of the store, I could see a future where I triumphed. Feeling good like that didn't last—it dried up like desert rain a few blocks from the store—but it began to change things.

"What name shall I put down on the receipt, sir?" the clerk asked. He was a sandy-haired, middle-aged man about my size and I could see the answer made no difference to him.

"John Smith," I said. He looked at me skeptically over the edges of his steel-rimmed spectacles, but said nothing and wrote down the name.

I bought my ticket to Winnipeg that evening.

32

Canada was tough. For one thing, there was the cold. Folks in the Panhandle like to say there's nothing between them and the North Pole but a barbwire fence. They have no idea. Canadian cold is epic like Texas heat, and that was a particularly brutal winter. Cattle were dying in fenced-in snowdrifts all up and down the plains. I was freezing inside my heart, and the Canadian weather went right along with that. *You are correct,* it seemed to say. *Life is cold and hard and the darkness goes on a real long time.*

Every now and then, I'd wonder what it would be like to be playing the whole thing out in Cuba, say, which is where we first thought they might have gone. At least it would have been warm. And I didn't think the Cubans would have been giving me lectures about not shooting Al. Canadians don't understand Texans, nor Southerners for that matter. They understand even less than Yankees do—that cold has worked deep into their blood.

"I want to be entirely clear with you," the immigration official said in his clipped Canadian voice when we met in his chilly little office. He stared at me with eyes the color of a blue-eyed sled dog's as I lay my gun on the desk between us. I was wearing gloves and an overcoat. The official was young and strapping and stripped down to his shirtsleeves.

"Here in Canada, we don't necessarily see things the way you do in Texas, Mr. Sneed," the pale-eyed official continued. "I have, of course, as we all do, great sympathy for your position in this matter. But you must understand one thing *very* clearly—if you shoot Albert Boyce here in Canada, you will hang. There should be no doubt in your mind about that. There aren't going to be any 'accidents,' any 'self-defense,' any 'heat-of-passion,' 'heat-of-the-moment' excuses. You shoot him, you hang. Full stop."

He reached across the desk and took hold of my gun. "You won't be needing this while you're visiting us," he said. "I'll tag it and keep it until you're ready to head home."

I knew there wasn't any point to protesting. It wasn't like I planned to shoot Al up there anyway. The thought had crossed my mind, but it hadn't laid down tracks.

I figured to keep hammering on the legal side; for the Canadians, abduction and white slavery weren't extraditable offenses, but larceny was. That sort of sums up their attitude toward things in general—and you have to wonder about their priorities—but it's what I had to work with, so I did. I found out Al had a couple of her diamond rings in his pocket when they were arrested so I swore out a warrant saying he'd stolen them, and that they were worth over ten thousand dollars or whatever the extraditable minimum was—at the moment I don't remember exactly. The argument being that since she was feeble-minded and all, he was taking advantage of her in every way he could, including stealing her jewelry.

Unfortunately, it was that theft charge that got Al's father so riled up. The Colonel didn't mind that I was trying to get his boy charged with rape and abduction. But he minded like hell that I was saying he was a thief.

That's not quite accurate. He didn't think the rape and abduction and white slavery charges were *right*, but he could understand the basis for them. He had his rules, same as he'd had 'em at the ranch. What his boy, Al, had done to his neighbor, Beal, would justify Beal and Beal alone in killing him. That was a rule. If anyone else got involved, the Colonel would make sure they paid full price for their stupidity because no one but Beal had a right to Al. That was also a rule. Beal had a right to exact a price for his own stained honor and his wife's tattered virtue, but it had to be a price that kept to the terms of the discussion. He couldn't be bringing in all sorts of insulting, extraneous, penny-ante things like diamond theft and larceny. That was another rule.

The Colonel was an old-fashioned man. So was my father. So was

Lena's father. So was Al, when you got right down to it.

I wasn't, though I did a real good job of pretending I was. It gave me an advantage it took everybody a long time to figure out I had.

33

And now, after all the arguing and crying and threatening and chasing her all over creation, where was I? I was in the Fort Worth jail with my father and the Reverend Nelms and Bill McLean Jr., realizing I'd done this thing that might get me hanged. And everybody was treating me with a whole lot more respect. I'd stopped being the pathetic husband, offering rewards and hiring detectives and trying to get grand juries to indict for one damn thing or another, and I'd turned into a dangerous killer. I hadn't killed the lover, either, who was the obvious target. I'd killed his *father*. It gave me that bad hombre, crazy factor your Billy the Kid types have.

I'd had enough of the why-does-God-want-me-to-suffer-and-suffer business. I'd broken the murder commandment, which appeared to be judged more serious than the adultery one. I waited to see what God would do about it. It turned out God was like my father and everybody else: He knew when He couldn't mess with you anymore and He laid off.

"Reverend," I said, turning to face Nelms. Clean-shaven and clutching a small, worn-looking Bible, he looked a decade or so younger than my father.

"Yes, son," Nelms responded. His voice was deep and powerful, though he spoke quietly. No wonder he'd become a preacher. That *son* grated on me.

"I have been badly wronged," I began. "No matter what I did, they would not stop wronging me." I felt a strange jubilation inside me; the old Sneed preacher blood was finally speaking up. "That old man spoke scurrilous things about my wife on the streets in Amarillo after his son had seduced my wife in the very castle I'd built for us, the nest I'd constructed, asking her at every turn what might best please her. I have tried everything within the measure of the law and of medicine to separate them, to restore her to her right self—the woman I know would be horrified by what she is now doing. I have paid for the best care, I have asked the authorities what to do to help her. I have been willing to move, to go wherever my wife might wish. My own father has advised me to give her up and I have not, despite all these wrongs she has done me, the wrongs she and her lover and her lover's family have done me. And why not? Because I believe that the vows I made her on our wedding day were made before God and are not to be broken."

I fixed my eyes on the reverend. I could hear McLean furiously scratching notes, his foot tapping even faster. I didn't look at my father.

"Reverend," I went on, "I traveled to Canada to bring her back home and found her with our youngest girl's shoe tied around her neck, crying because she missed her old life. I found her with a lover who had taken her jewelry—jewelry I'd given her—for 'safekeeping.' I sent her home with her father, an old man who traveled in the dead of this terrible winter north to Canada to try to help restore his daughter to a good, honest life and to her family and children. I thought she would return to the sanitarium where they could care for her again, but instead she lied to her father and mother and convinced them of all sorts of terrible things about the place I'd put her. 'Please,' I said to her father when I found out. 'Come visit the place. My expense. If you aren't reassured, we can put her anywhere you say.'

"Her own father sees that the sanitarium isn't the prison his daughter has described, and agrees to send her back. And then they tell me that she has given power of attorney to the Boyces so they can get her out. The very man who is saying such vile things about her and his son who stole her from our home are now in charge of her future. She flaunts a ring she is wearing instead of her wedding ring—a ring that fiend gave her—in my face.

"And when I finally get her back to the san, we see that smut-talking old man at the Metropolitan. He calls Atwell over and says he can prove 'what kind of woman' my wife is. I can't eat my dinner. My guts are in turmoil. I stop back at the hotel afterwards because I suddenly need the john. I don't expect to see the old man. Atwell said he was heading out to catch the train back to Amarillo. But there he is.

"And I shoot him."

There was an impressively quiet pause.

"Now, here's my question, Reverend. Did I do right or wrong? What do you think God reckons? He gave Moses Ten Commandments. Thou shalt not commit adultery was one. Thou shalt not covet thy neighbor's wife or goods was another. Thou shalt not kill was a third.

"How do you weigh it up, Reverend? How do you think God weighs it up?"

The reverend's eyes had filled with tears. McLean slapped his pencil on his legal pad so hard he broke it.

"Well, well, *well*, Beal," McLean said, delightedly. "I don't usually make this decision so early and usually I decide against it, but in this case—we're putting you on. Good God, man. You'll be the best witness on murder one I ever had."

He leapt from the chair to shake my hand and pound my back. He was beaming. He didn't look like he even remembered a man had been killed.

"Mr. McLean," my father said in a strained voice, "I'd ask you to remember that there are serious things at stake here." But Bill McLean Jr. was a force of nature even my father couldn't douse.

"Yes, sir, of course," he said to my father, still grinning. "And one of 'em is saving your son's neck. That's still a serious subject, but I'm feeling a lot more optimistic about it."

Then he began to pump my father's hand. "And you, yourself, sir," he continued joyfully. "Just look at you. Look at that posture, that . . . that firmness of character and morals every bit of you proclaims. No jury will believe that a man like you could raise a son to kill without reason. It's simply not possible." He began to pat my father's arms as if he'd just finished dressing him and wanted to admire the effect. My father couldn't help it. He started to laugh. It seemed I had a miracle-working lawyer.

"Mr. McLean," my father said, trying to stifle his laughter, "your reputation did precede you, but I have to admit, it didn't really prepare me."

"I hear that a lot," McLean said modestly. By then, I was laughing and so was Reverend Nelms. We all laughed for longer than anything was funny because the tension had gone out of the air. When I glanced at McLean, I saw he looked satisfied.

The man was a pro, no mistake.

34

She sat in the witness chair wearing a blue suit trimmed with red ribbon I didn't think I'd seen before and figured that bastard had paid for. I was wearing the same clothes I'd been wearing when I'd dropped her off. No one had thought to bring me a fresh set. We were both in court for habeas hearings, hers to get out of the san, mine to get out of jail. They'd delayed mine to deal with hers. The place was crawling with reporters. We were now front-page, above-the-fold news, the biggest sensation in Texas.

The reporters wrote that they only knew I was tense was because I was clutching an unlit cigar. They said Lena only looked agitated when Dr. Allison said she didn't love her children. But I could tell she was nervous. Her right hand strayed to tuck her hair under a new-looking fur hat way more than it needed to. And the little finger on her left waved around in her lap like a butterfly antenna, a habit she'd had since I'd known her. When she noticed it, she'd set it down and cover her left hand with her right, like she was trying to keep it from flying away. But after a little while, she'd get caught up in the testimony and that finger would start waggling again.

She never once looked at me. I knew her lawyer—another big wheel, Senator O.S. Lattimore—would have advised her to ignore me because it was safest: Nothing for the press to write about, no clues for the judge. But it still stung.

She turned out to be a better witness than I could ever have imagined. All the histrionics and drama were gone. She was calm and stuck to the instructions Lattimore must have given her: "You're not up there to talk about your husband, your marriage, or your lover. Stick to the san."

"I wish only to tell the court about my experiences at the sanitarium," she said, looking at Judge Simmons, hands clasped in her lap, little finger entirely still. With Lattimore leading the way, she told all about it: The knock-out injection forced on her when we dropped her off, the lack of baths, crazy people, no treatment, how hard she begged to see the children.

My side brought out the facts about the miscarriage. She had to answer a number of questions that must have been excruciating: How did she know the child was Al's, could it have been someone else's, were there other lovers? But she managed to appear entirely calm, only blushing becomingly on a couple of occasions, which did nothing but make her look normal. That part never made the papers; in those days, they kept things like that back, especially if they involved a white woman in her social position.

But then things really went to hell. It started when Lattimore pushed Dr. Allison about what medicine he'd given Lena and Allison's only answer was calomel. Several reporters snorted and someone in the back of the courtroom laughed out loud. Calomel was one of those purgatives that mothers or other concerned females administered every spring to clean you out and tone you up. It's out of style now since it's mostly mercury, but back then it was considered harmless and routine. It sure wasn't known as a cure for crazy.

Next Lattimore tucked into moral insanity—such a useful thing in its time, for the same reason it wasn't that day; it was pretty hard to prove she wasn't but it was also pretty hard to prove she was. "It is a difficult diagnosis to explain," Allison began.

"I think so, too," retorted Lattimore. "But you are the expert—what do you mean?"

"I mean a person that has lost their moral sense to a certain extent," Allison answered. "A woman who has been reared under every proper surrounding might show less inclination for her home. She may manifest a disposition to spend most of her time visiting with her neighbors and may neglect her children."

Things just went from bad to worse: "Did she speak incoherently? Are all liars insane?" Etcetera. The good doctor was either too arrogant or too slow to do anything but dig himself in deeper. By my side,

Atwell fumed silently. *The man is an idiot,* he wrote on his legal pad, turning it so I could see.

"Surely anything as serious as this . . ." Lattimore paused effectively. "This moral insanity would have physical signs. After all, it was serious enough to be treated with calomel."

"Objection!" Atwell jumped to his feet, relieved to have some way to express his frustration.

"Sustained," said Judge Simmons. "Counsel for plaintiff will stick to questions and refrain from commentary."

"Yes, Your Honor," said Lattimore, unperturbed. "Allow me to rephrase the question, Doctor. What were the physical signs of moral insanity that Mrs. Sneed exhibited?"

"They were subtle," Allison responded. "Her pupils were dilated and she had almost an expressionless countenance."

Lattimore let that one speak for itself and switched gears. "Isn't it a fact that you regarded her as insane because her husband told you to keep her from going away and agreed to pay you sixty-five dollars a week, twice your usual rate?"

"Certainly *not*," Dr. Allison answered. By this time, his physical signs weren't so good: Damp upper lip, white knuckles. Atwell scribbled furiously: *You should have shot him, too, while you were at it.*

Judge Simmons had Lena examined by three outside doctors for the best part of an hour—all of whom said she wasn't crazy—but you could tell he was convinced long before that. He announced his decision with a little flurry of restrained judicial disgust. "After hearing this testimony, I could not conclude there was a semblance of insanity developed here in this case and I will discharge the applicant."

Though Lena must have been thrilled, she maintained her composure, looking down modestly at her hands in her lap. With Lattimore at her side to shoo reporters, she made her way down the aisle and out of the courtroom.

She never once turned my way.

35

"I know things didn't go like we wanted this morning," said McLean, talking away in his rapid-fire way before the guard had even finished opening the door, "but I've got some good news. Old man Snyder will say something to the press this afternoon."

"Where's Lena?" I asked. It had all come swarming back: The way I'd believed the letter she'd written from the san, the bleeding in the daybed, the way she'd lied.

"She's over to your in-law Billie Steele's," answered McLean, patting my arm awkwardly. "Don't worry. He and his sister Nellie will keep her in line." He removed his gloves and rubbed his hands together vigorously. It was clear he didn't want to be distracted from the topic at hand. I sat down on the cot and tried to focus.

"This hasn't been easy for ol' Snyder, has it?" said McLean, looking up at the light coming in through the room's high windows. "Especially with that weak heart." He grabbed the chair and straddled it, turning to face me.

"There at the office, he got to pulling on his collar and looking so peaked, I thought he was gonna keel over," McLean continued. "I finally went out and told the girl to get a doctor to come set outside the door just in case. We sure don't need him dying on us right now."

He said this almost to himself, then looked as close as Bill McLean Jr. generally got to looking embarrassed and said, "I'm sorry. It's just how I am when I get going on a case."

"No offense taken," I said. There wasn't.

"I'm not sure what brought him around," McLean went on. "There's things he ain't telling. But he can't forgive old man Boyce for talking how he did, nor his missus for sounding off to the papers about Lena hypnotizing y'all, etcetera." He snorted. "Like one of those melodramas my wife and her sister are always going to see."

He paused. "Not that it ain't," he added. "A melodrama, I mean."

"It qualifies," I said dryly. I was starting to pull myself together—acting the way lawyers act when they're working together, the strategizing, the little jokes. The image of the daybed faded.

"He's not over-pleased with you, either," McLean said bluntly, "and he surely is upset you shot the man to death. He came right out and asked why you didn't shoot Al instead, said everybody could've understood that. Said no matter how mad he was at Annie Boyce, she didn't deserve this sorrow to come upon her in her old age. I just had to let him ventilate for a while."

"I got an earful a few weeks back," I said. "He blamed me for going to the newspapers, making his daughter unhappy, locking her up and abusing her, worrying his wife to death, and keeping my girls away from their mother. He asked why I wouldn't give Lena a divorce since she doesn't love me and from the way I'd been acting he didn't believe I loved her either. He said he'd come to the conclusion it was the most sensible solution, and he wanted to know why I wouldn't do it."

"What did you tell him?" McLean said. He hadn't ever bothered to ask the question directly; my giving Lena up wasn't good for his case. Still, he had to be curious. He stopped his incessant foot-tapping and looked at me expectantly.

"I told him I loved his daughter and believed she was insane and had been preyed upon by her lover and that I would walk on my heart for the rest of my life for her good if it was necessary, but that I was bound to protect her from her own illness and her lover's evil ways," I said.

"What did he say to that?" McLean asked, looking vaguely disappointed. His foot started tapping again.

"For a few minutes, he didn't say nothing. Then he started asking about the sanitarium again."

McLean took a puff of his cigarette and flicked a piece of lint off his lapel, puffed away some more, and then looked at me directly. "He don't like you much—excuse me for saying so, but it's true—and he believes you've abused his daughter. But at this point he thinks she's better served by our story—she's insane and her lover took advantage—than anything else."

"Did you know his oldest brother shot their stepfather to death back in Missouri?" I asked. "He got off because their mother swore it was self-defense, but the judge made the whole bunch leave the state. They don't ever talk about it—any of 'em—but Tom Snyder knows what it's like to stick to a story in court."

McLean looked startled. "I did not know that," he said, appreciatively. His foot tapped even harder. "Could be useful if he tries to buck, but I don't think he will. I think he's worked it out in his own mind just like I said."

He was quiet for a moment, then brightened. "And we may have more good news later," he said. "Billie Steele is bringing Lena over to the offices so Walter Scott and I can talk her into testifying for you. He and I are a good team when it comes to balky witnesses. It's one reason we're partners." He sounded so optimistic that he carried me along; I could see all the reasons testifying for me made sense. I could even picture her doing it, could imagine how I'd feel listening to her.

But when McLean walked into my cell again a few hours later, he shook his head. "No deal," he said curtly, looking tired and frustrated. "She's tougher than she looks."

"You tried the children?" I asked.

"First thing," said McLean. "I got the impression I rubbed her the wrong way, so I let Walter do all the talking. He was real polite. Pulled out her chair, poured her coffee, real respectful and sympathetic. Said he knew she must miss the children and wouldn't she like to see them. And of course the idea that their father might hang would naturally prey on their minds. And if she would just testify that the Colonel knew where she and Al were, then she could save your neck. And afterwards y'all could deal with your marriage as you both saw fit, but that there wasn't no point to robbing her children of their father. Tried to convey that she could still go on and get a divorce after she'd done the charitable thing and saved you from hanging."

"She's never gonna get a divorce," I said coldly.

"*I* know that, Beal," said McLean. "I'm just telling you the argument

Walter was making. He did good, too. Unfortunately, she knew as well as we did that the thing didn't make no sense."

My stomach knotted. "What did she say?"

McLean sighed. "She got all high and mighty. She said she didn't have nothing to tell and if she did she wouldn't tell it. She said you might be a liar, but she wasn't and she wasn't going to lie to save you and if she was to lie, it wouldn't be on a dead man. I got in on the act then," he continued with the tone of self-satisfaction he generally had when speaking of his lawyer doings.

"I told her if she testified for us we'd make sure to defend her reputation just as fiercely as we could. I told her that all those questions at the habeas that couldn't go in the papers—that was just for openers. I told her she had no real idea what was being said about her, and who we'd have to put on the stand, but that if she'd testify for us, we'd spend less time on those witnesses and more time protecting her from the worst of it. I told her Al was up in Canada and couldn't do her no good, and anyway, how could she possibly be sure he'd still want her after all this. I told her life is long and passion don't last, but reputations do. Just look at all the stories you read where women break up their marriages and then realize they left a good husband for a bad one and commit suicide and things of that nature. I told her that her father was doing everything he could to stand by *you* because he thought that was the best thing he could do for *her*, and how could she be so selfish and hardhearted as to watch that old man, her own dear father, cry the way he did, in public, because of all the shame and trouble she'd brought to the family."

"Well," I said, "that about covers it, don't it."

"Oh, no," said McLean cheerfully, "I'd just gotten started. I told her that her whole family was against her, and your whole family was against her, and obviously the Boyce family didn't think much of her either, and really, looking at the thing pretty objectively, she didn't have much choice. If she took the long view—which I strongly recommended her to do—being your wife was the very best alternative, and why not begin to undo all the damage she'd done by testifying on your behalf."

"So how did she react?" I asked. There was a part of me that was truly curious and another part of me that didn't want to know. It was an uncomfortable mix. It had been so much easier when I thought I knew her.

"She's tougher than I thought," McLean said again, almost admiringly. "And she's smart. She got pale and real still, but the first thing she said when I got done was, 'Mr. McLean, don't tell me stories about who and what you won't use in court if I come with you. We both know you're going to have to use that testimony so let's not fool around pretending you won't.' I told her I could use less of it or soften it, and she looked me right in the eye and said, 'You'll do exactly what you need to do to get him off, no matter what it is and what you tell me in here. That's your job and I hear you're good at it.'"

"She's right about that," I said with a weird and sudden pride. My wife was smart enough not to be taken in by two smooth-talking lawyers and tough enough to fight. The pride made no sense at all. A few seconds later, I was ashamed of it.

"Yeah," said McLean. "And we both knew it. So I told her I didn't want to argue and it didn't matter anyway because all the rest of what I'd said was right. She sat there staring into her lap for a minute and then she looked up and said, 'Mr. McLean, this is very simple. It's just gotten complicated because Beal doesn't want to accept the truth, which is I want a divorce. I want to marry Al Boyce. Al Boyce wants to marry me. I've stood being put in that asylum, taken from my children, escaping to Canada and being deported from Canada. I've stood lie after lie after lie, and if you all think talking to me in this office is going to change my mind, you're stupider than I think you are. Quit pestering me.' That was pretty much that. She got up right quick and walked out."

"That sounds like Lena all right." I felt low again.

But that evening, McLean brought me the *Star-Telegram*. Just as he'd promised, old man Snyder had staked his position that afternoon. With tears in his eyes and reporters hanging on his every word, he'd said: *I and my entire family will stand by Beal Sneed, who has stood by my daughter in a manly way. I have four sons-in-law and all are first-class men, but none is better than Beal Sneed. He has always provided everything that any father could wish for his daughter, and has been kind and loving to his wife and his children.*

It warmed me to read the words.

36

When two officers brought me up from the tunnel out of the jail into the courtroom for my own habeas hearing, I felt about the way a prairie dog must feel when he comes up out of his burrow to find a bunch of hawks waiting for him. My heart beat all out of time with itself and my knees felt ready to buckle. Al's three brothers—Will, Henry, and Lynn—were sitting in the front row behind the prosecutors' table. Lynn looked something like a blond, blue-eyed version of Al and stared at me fixedly as he sliced perfectly thin white strips off a sheet of paper with a pocket knife. They fluttered to the floor. On the other side of the aisle, my father and old man Snyder sat in the front row behind the defense table. My father gave me a small, tightlipped smile.

Somehow I made it to over to McLean. He stood respectfully, his hands clasped before him, looking like he was paid to look; why, he'd never had a finer client, nor met a finer man. Grasping my hand, he heartily said, "Ready, Beal?" Under his breath, he muttered, "Don't worry, it's normal the first time. It gets easier." I sat down at our table and tried to get my heart to stop jumping around. Then Judge Simmons came in and everybody stood up, things got started, and I relaxed a little.

Simmons was more sympathetic to my side that day. While he made sure we knew that he "could not condone shooting down Colonel Boyce, an unarmed old man"—"We don't concede he was unarmed," McLean piped up—Simmons granted bail at thirty-five thousand. "In Sneed's frame of mind, doing all he could to protect his wife, I cannot conceive that he was cool and deliberate. I have great sympathy for both sides in this case—they are all good people—but I can understand how Mr. Snyder feels. He can't conceive that his daughter lost her virtue before she lost her mind."

Behind me, Snyder was weeping quietly. He and my dry-eyed father stood clasping hands.

I went to see my girls at Henry Bowman's house in Plano that very afternoon. My heart warmed when they ran into my arms. I don't mean it the way people do, just a saying. My heart literally felt warmer, like the sun shone in there, at least for a few minutes.

After Georgie went to bed that evening, Lenora nestled beside me on a sofa in the parlor, her head on my shoulder and my arm around her. "I'm so scared, Papa," she said softly. "I go to bed but I can't sleep, and when I do I have such dreams. I want to go back to before."

"I do, too," I said. "You don't know how much. And I promise, sweetheart, someday we'll all be together again. Your mama will be herself again."

Lenora began to sniffle. "Papa, I never thought you could kill anyone, especially not Big Uncle Al." She pulled away to look at me intently. Her eyes could do the same thing her mother's did: Turn into bottomless dark pools in her face.

"I don't suppose I'm really myself either," I answered, feeling at sea. "But when your mother is herself again, I'll be myself, too. Sometimes, people get sick in their minds just like they do in their bodies."

"Yes, Papa," Lenora said impatiently. "Everybody has explained that and I understand. But when we saw our Mama again, she didn't seem crazy. She seemed sad. She cried and she wanted to take us with her, but Aunt Eula said no."

"Did you want to go?" I asked.

"Yes," said Lenora, sticking her chin out a little because she knew it wasn't what I wanted to hear. "I miss her. She was always with us before."

"Your Mama might seem like herself," I said, "but she isn't. I know you don't understand this."

"No, Papa," Lenora said, "I don't. I ask Aunt Eula why Georgie and I have to suffer because you and Mama can't get along and she never has a good answer, either. She says she knows my Mama doesn't want anything but the best for us. Then I ask why we can't see her, because that's what's best for Georgie and me. Then Aunt Eula says, 'Oh, your Mama isn't herself. That's why she ran away.' But Papa, she still seems like my Mama to me and I want to be with her."

"Your Mama didn't run away," I said. "She was stolen."

"Papa," said Lenora with a trace of grownup asperity, "I don't think that's how Mama looks at it."

"That's what I mean," I said emphatically. "If your Mama doesn't think so, it's because she isn't herself. If she was herself, she would." Lenora looked confused. "Listen, sweetheart," I went on, "you know your Mama was the center of our home."

"Yes," said Lenora, starting to cry again, but harder, "and I want it to be like that again."

"It will be," I said. "I promise you. If your Mama was in her right mind, why would she want anything else?"

Lenora was never as bullheaded and argumentative as her sister, but she didn't lack her own perspective, no matter how sensitive and pliable she appeared.

"I don't know," she said, an edge to her voice, "but she does."

"I'm sorry," I said. "I know it's hard on you and your sister."

"You *don't* know, Papa," she said, standing up from the sofa abruptly to face me with her hands on her hips. "You've been up in Canada and in jail and in court and in Amarillo and all over creation like Aunt Eula says. You're gone all the time, just like you were before, except more, and when you're around you mostly don't pay no attention to us."

"Any," I said automatically. "*Any* attention."

Lenora gave me a withering look and rolled her eyes. "All you do," she continued, "is stare out the window or talk to Uncle Henry in the study or talk on the telephone. For *hours*. So you *don't* know and don't say you do. I want to be with my Mama," she finished up loudly.

"Well, you can't be," I said, feeling aggravated. "It's not possible. Your Mama ain't right in the head."

"She's as right in the head as you are," Lenora shouted. "She don't look half as crazy as you do, Papa. That's the truth."

"Do you want them to hang me?" I shouted back. "Is *that* what you want? Because they could. If you want our family back together and your Mama and Papa back to themselves again, then you got no choice in this matter but to do as I say. Otherwise you're gonna end up with a dead Papa and a Mama who never sees you because she's still crazy and has new babies with her new husband and don't care nothing about her old ones."

"My Mama will always want me," wailed Lenora, running from the room. "I hate you, Papa. I hate you all. I want my Mama." There was a pause, and I heard her sobbing in the hallway. Then she shouted, "*Doesn't,* Papa, *anything. Doesn't* care *anything* about her old ones." She ran upstairs, bawling.

At that moment, I wanted someone to take me straight back to Fort Worth, clap me in a jail cell, and throw away the key.

37

Jury selection started at the end of January. None of the three available judges wanted anything to do with the case since it was sure to be a circus, but we'd ended up with the one McLean considered the very worst choice. "John Swayne spent *years* as D.A.," he fumed as we strategized in his office, "most of it prosecuting gambling cases in Hell's Half Acre with juries so rigged he couldn't get a conviction no matter how good his case was. It made him a real hard ass about law and order. *And* he's liable to take it personal that you shot the man in a fancy hotel where the Acre used to be because he believes he's part of the reason it ain't there anymore."

McLean took a puff off his cigarette, which had its usual calming effect. "Besides, he don't like me. He thinks I'm a loudmouth. Can you imagine?" He smirked. "We'll file a change of venue motion today. And one to continue—we'll say we need time to get Cone fully briefed." Cone Johnson nodded gravely, then winked. He'd joined the team a day or so earlier. He and McLean were going to work the courtroom together.

"And we can throw in a motion to dismiss," McLean went on.

"How do you figure *that*?" Cone asked.

"The grand jury process was *obviously* tainted," McLean answered, looking immensely self-satisfied. "The stenographer was in the room during deliberations." Cone threw back his head and laughed.

Of course none of it worked, but we thought it had been worth the time and trouble. "It lets the prosecution know we'll fight over everything," said Cone.

They were ready to fight right back. Jury selection was one long, dragged-out battle. The newspapers ran humorous stories about the whole process: Confused veniremen, lawyers who confused themselves when their questions got too complicated, the amount of time the whole thing was taking.

"Do you believe in the protection of the home against the world? Do you believe that a man should be allowed to use weapons in the course of protecting his home?" Those were the kinds of questions my side asked.

District Attorney Jordan Cummings, on the other hand, wanted to know: "Do you believe in enforcement of the law?"

But that was only the beginning. Those veniremen got asked all sorts of things: Whether they had preconceived ideas about the case, obviously, but also where they went to church; how long they'd been married; the ages of their children if they had them; whether they wanted children if they didn't; and a bunch of hypotheticals, like what would you think if . . . ?

We knew exactly who we wanted—married men, ideally fathers, preferably Texans but at least Southerners, with strong ideas about home and family—and we ended up with a jury we liked. The youngest was twenty-three, the oldest forty-five, eight of them were married, and seven of those had children. Four were native Texans, four came from the deep South, and we had one each from Tennessee, Kentucky, and Missouri. The twenty-three-year-old had been born in Michigan but moved to Texas at ten months, so he'd had no time to be contaminated. Half the men farmed and the rest—except for Michigan—were small businessmen: A car repairer, a wood dealer, a salesman, a grocer. Michigan was a railway mail clerk.

"I'll get those men walking in your moccasins, Beal, just you wait and see," McLean said cheerfully as we left the courtroom. And that evening we got more happy news. The son of old Governor Throckmorton had just died. A friend of the Boyces, he'd been chatting with the Colonel in the Metropolitan lobby and had testified to the grand jury that I'd stood over the body, pointing my pistol and sneering, "Now you're out of it."

Naturally, there were all sorts of rumors. Throckmorton's son claimed two mysterious men had slipped something into his father's whiskey. Eventually the grand jury requested an autopsy, but the family had already had him embalmed, so it was too late. Anyway, we had nothing to do with it. We just got lucky. His own doctor said he'd died of water on the brain from drinking.

38

Every morning, three deputies stationed at the door of the courtroom searched everybody for firearms, including the horde of reporters and photographers who swarmed my arrival so aggressively that my lawyers got in the habit of surrounding me in a flying wedge formation as we came up the courthouse stairs. People got used to reading and talking about us, and I think they forgot we were real. Sometimes they talked like we were characters in a movie and wouldn't pay them any mind, or couldn't even hear them.

"There he is."

"Where?"

"The short, bald one next to that heavy-set, dark-haired man."

"You'd never think he was a killer, would you, to look at him?"

"Well, you never can tell, can you? Maybe something around the eyes or the jaw?"

"*Oh*, I see what you mean. Who's the heavy one?"

"That's Henry Bowman. He and his wife are keeping those poor little girls. And that one—with the pocket knife? That's Lynn Boyce."

"Isn't *he* handsome? I wonder, does his brother look like him?"

"Darker hair and eyes."

"That Lynn looks dangerous."

"I wonder how much more killing there's going to be."

"My husband says bad feuds get started over much less."

"Oh, I hope not."

But you could tell they sort of hoped so.

Once Judge Swayne entered the courtroom, though, things always settled down. With his brilliantine-shined hair and his full mouth turned down at the corners, he looked like he was used to considering serious things and wasn't going to tolerate any nonsense while doing so.

He had a bad cold throughout the first part of trial, and right out the chute you could tell McLean aggravated him. But by the time we were a few days into it, anything with a license to practice law in the state of Texas was pissing him off. The courtroom battles were fierce and personal; after just a few days, opposing lawyers no longer even nodded to one another in the morning. Swayne was constantly adjudicating attorney disputes when all he really wanted was to move the trial along. He'd blow his nose and pronounce his ruling, not necessarily in that order, and look darkly at the lawyers like he could think of better things to pound with the gavel than the block.

The women aggravated him, too. As a courtesy, he reserved the front two rows for them but asked that they remove their hats so people behind them could see. Very few obliged, so he had to make it an order. If he told them that the next day's testimony would likely be unfit for their delicate ears, they'd show up anyway and he'd have to waste time shooing them out. They always left as slowly as possible, casting longing glances at the witness they were about to miss.

On account of all the rain and snow that winter, the courtroom was stuffy and always smelled faintly of Listerine and wet clothes. On days when Swayne ejected the ladies, it smelled of tobacco. The second the last big hat was out the door, there was a chorus of matches being struck, and within a few seconds at least half the men present were puffing like dragons. I myself had a little brown pipe I smoked or chewed on, depending. McLean had a habit of lighting matches when he couldn't smoke, letting them burn down, and then shaking them out, as if the act itself might magically summon a cigarette.

Almost all the reporters smoked cigarettes that dangled from the sides of their mouths as they tried frantically to keep up with fast-paced testimony or lawyer squabbles. When things got really heated, the ash sometimes burned so long that it fell of its own accord. By the end of the day most of the reporters' shoes were covered with it—adding to the general sloppiness of their pencil-stained cuffs and bad haircuts—and the polished floor around them was grimy.

The exception to journalistic slovenliness was Kitty Barry. She had a byline for the *Star-Telegram* and was neat as a pin. Her cuffs always looked spotless. I don't know how she did it because she was always scribbling too. She was paid to describe and opine and you could tell she enjoyed both, especially the latter. According to Kitty, the hordes of women attending my trial were not part of the *rapidly growing class of American women interested in things outside the feminine sphere, including the judiciary system. Only the personality of the trial strikes the fire of their attention. During the routine of the examinations, they are looking at the toes of their shoes or fumbling with their dress accessories or whispering very quietly to each other or calmly staring at people who sit in the enclosure in front of them.*

A lot of the men got bored, too, and I didn't think they were any more interested in the inner workings of the judiciary system than the women. But they didn't tend to fool with their clothes or whisper to one another.

Just as McLean had promised, I got over my initial jitters quickly. I soon found something soothing about the courtroom rituals. Partly, it was my feeling of professional competence. I liked thinking like a lawyer again; it kept me from thinking like a cuckold. And then there was the story we were building. I liked all the legal detail and strategy that went into building it. I liked dreaming I was the man at the heart of it.

"How do you plead?" asked Swayne.

"Not guilty." My voice surged out of my throat, and those words felt sure and true.

39

The state went first, of course, and one of their starting witnesses was Ed Cobb, a former neighbor of the Boyces. Like Throckmorton, he'd run into the Colonel at the Metropolitan and was chatting with him when I showed up before supper. By the time I came back, Cobb had left, but the state wanted his testimony about the Colonel's state of mind.

Because he was an early witness, I hadn't yet gotten used to something that happened occasionally. I'd be sitting there listening to a witness like a lawyer, and all of a sudden I'd lose the thread. I'd find myself recalling or imagining the scene the witness described. In Cobb's case, I didn't remember seeing him at all. I got so distracted trying to find him among my memories that McLean was on cross before I checked back in.

"Didn't Colonel Boyce say, 'There's Sneed now. I am going to have his wife and my son back together in thirty days?'" McLean asked.

"Not to me," said Cobb, sticking his chin out a little.

"To Throckmorton?"

"Not in my presence."

McLean badgered him a while longer and Cobb got more and more confused, and then Cone Johnson stood up and strolled to the witness chair. Sometimes I almost felt sorry for the witnesses. McLean was like a buzz saw—on cross he set their teeth on edge instantly. They'd see Johnson coming, looking so relaxed and calm, and you could almost see them thinking, *Thank the Lord, I'm done with that sonofabitch*, meaning McLean. Then Johnson would get started, and he'd be as bad or worse.

"Did you not hear Throckmorton say that Al Boyce and Mrs. Sneed would be back together inside of thirty days?" Johnson asked, without any of the usual good-morning-Mr.-Cobb preliminaries.

"It seems that I remember that, but I can't be positive. I was simply a listener," said Cobb.

Cone took full advantage of Cobb's confusion, doing his very best to lodge the words "back together in thirty days" firmly in the jury's mind. "You mean you're not sure who said it but one of them did? That language was used? Back together in thirty days?" Cobb got so frustrated he balled his hands into fists and his knuckles went white.

He thought he remembered things clearly, just like I did, but by the time McLean and Cone got done with him, everything he knew had been all twisted up and he didn't recognize any of it anymore. The very next morning, Swayne announced before the jury came in that Cobb wanted to correct his testimony. All the lawyers objected, Swayne swatted them down, and Cobb stared fixedly at Swayne, like he was afraid that even glancing at the lawyers might mess him up. "I didn't intend to say that Colonel Boyce ever said anything about Mr. or Mrs. Sneed in my presence."

The battling over Cobb took more time than anything else in that phase of the trial. The state was in a rush to conclude; they just wanted to prove I shot him, which was easy enough.

Both sides knew the real battle would come later.

Cobb was just a warm-up.

We'd decided to begin with old man Snyder, but he arrived so ill and exhausted that Swayne had to delay court to give him time to recuperate. Once in the chair, however, he sat perfectly straight, his snow-white hair and firm mouth all in order. His memory seemed clear and specific. He quoted exactly the telegram he'd received telling him I'd shot the Colonel, quoted whole conversations, etc. And he stuck to the story.

"The Boyces said that Al was a cigarette and alcohol fiend who wouldn't listen to them," he testified, his voice quivering with emotion. "I told them: 'This is a fearful thing to come on folks in their old age. Why didn't you all tell me about this? We have been friends for fifty years.'"

"And what was the answer?" asked McLean.

"Well, Colonel Boyce said, 'I thought I would. I told Ma we should, but . . . we were afraid that some of Lena's brothers would kill Al. And we know that the Sneeds love money and we were afraid that they would sue Al for all of his.'"

McLean shook his head, as if in regret at the missed opportunity to avert all the tragedy, and the Colonel's insistence on protecting his ne'er-do-well son.

"Later I met Henry Boyce on the train," Snyder went on. "I told him that we had sent Lena to a sanitarium and that Beal was going to leave Amarillo and start over somewhere else, but that he'd need to come back to transact his business and that if he ran into Al it would be like waving a red rag at a bull. Henry told me he and his father had decided they would swear out a writ of insanity against Al and have him put in a sanitarium even if they had to shackle him. Henry promised to let me know if they didn't. But they didn't and they didn't tell me." Snyder's voice was full of indignation. "Instead they bought Al's cattle so he'd have money to steal my daughter away."

McLean sat down looking satisfied. Beside him were a bunch of burned-down matches that he'd piled up on a handkerchief. W.A. Hanger—the high-priced prosecutor with a tranquil manner and a whip-sharp mind that the Boyces had hired to help the state—got up to try to make things look better for his side. McLean lit another match.

"Didn't Colonel Boyce say they had thought it was an infatuation that would wear out and that he would have rather followed Albert to his grave than to see him involved in such a thing?"

"His wife did," answered Snyder.

"And didn't Colonel Boyce say he hoped you would put Mrs. Sneed in the sanitarium, and didn't he go on to say, 'But Tom, you know she isn't crazy.' Didn't you reply, 'I know it, Al. She's the smartest child I ever raised'?"

Snyder looked stricken. His eyes filled. "No," he replied. "Colonel Boyce was the one who said she was the smartest. He said that if she had been a man she could have revolutionized the world. He said she could do anything with Al, that Al wouldn't go to church with his mother unless Lena told him to."

I felt it again, that weird pride. She's my wife.

"Now, Mr. Snyder," said Hanger, "I'm going to ask you a question but I don't want you to answer it until the court has had a chance to rule on it. Do you understand?"

"Yes, Senator," replied Snyder.

"Did not Mrs. Sneed at Minneapolis beg you not to take her back to the sanitarium, but instead to your home in Clayton?"

"Objection," cried McLean and Johnson in unison. "She can't be a witness in this case," added McLean, shaking his head. "There is not a man in the defense of this case but who honestly believes that the woman was insane and is insane now."

"We of the prosecution think Mrs. Sneed is entirely sane," Hanger retorted forcefully.

What followed was a long skirmish over the rules of testimony as it applied to my wife, which Swayne ended as he had to—by ruling in our favor. Lena couldn't testify *against me*, even second-hand. All we could do to explain why she wouldn't testify *for* me was say she was insane.

And just like that, I went from strange pride to full-on shame again, the salt of the fact that my wife wouldn't say a word in my defense stinging an open gash.

I clambered back into the story we were telling, like a shipwrecked man climbing onto a raft.

40

That night after supper, as I was taking off my shoes and tie, there was a knock at the hotel room door, composed of the coded beats we'd all worked out so we'd know we weren't about to get ambushed by reporters. When I opened the door, there stood my father, upright as always. "Son," he said, giving me his brief, formal embrace.

He looked round the room as he always looked at things—like he expected to find something wrong. Then he perched himself on one of the two chairs and got down to business.

"You know my opinion in this matter," he began. "I have told you from the start that you need to let your wife go." He didn't sound angry but his fists were clenched and his voice was just slightly higher than usual—both signs I recognized from way back.

I sat down on the edge of the bed.

"The wisdom of my advice has been made abundantly clear by subsequent events," he continued, his voice rising a tiny bit more. Diction that formal always meant something serious was coming.

"Tomorrow," he went on, "I will be placed in the unpleasant position of having to testify at my son's trial for murder." He shook his head and unclenched his fists in a deliberate way and placed an open hand on each knee. "You always were nervous and prone to doing unsteady things in the boat, Beal, but this is beyond anything I ever dreamed. You have, as usual, been so absorbed in your own situation that you have failed to consider how terrible this is for the rest of the family, not to mention how much money it's costing us. This *whole thing* could have been avoided had you agreed to give that woman up. It is through your stubborn pride and pigheadedness that all of us— myself, your brothers and sister, your stepmother and half-brother and sister—are suffering."

"But—"

"You're about to say that if Al Boyce hadn't run off with your wife all this would never have happened. True, but if your wife hadn't gone wrong or if you had done the sensible thing and got rid of her, Al and Annie Boyce would never have got involved as they did."

"But, Father—"

"But nothing. I will do as I agreed to—get up there tomorrow and say my old friend Al Boyce was plotting to get Lena for his son. But I don't believe a word of it. And neither do you."

I tried to call up the power I'd felt in the Fort Worth jail, but I couldn't.

"I'll stick with you through this trial because you're my flesh and blood," my father went on. "But I want to make three things very clear. First, you will give that woman up once we get through this or I will cut you out of the inheritance. Second, if you get yourself involved in any more shootings, you'll be on your own when it comes to paying lawyers. And third, I won't be so accommodating a witness next time."

"But—"

"No." He struck his thigh with his open hand. "No buts. I know perfectly well that unless they hang you, this business isn't finished." He repeated slowly, "When this trial is done, you are going to give her up and leave her and Al Boyce alone."

I bowed my head so I wouldn't have to see those terrible eyes.

"And if you don't," he continued, "I won't do another thing to help you. Is that clear?"

I just sat there on the bed with my head hanging down.

"Do you hear?" He stood. "Not another thing. Think it over before you shoot anybody else." He stalked out, slamming the door behind him.

True to his word, the next day he sat down in the witness chair and spoke in that firm voice that proclaimed everything he said to be the gospel truth. "I brought all the pressure I could to bear on my son. I told him my family could have nothing to do with his wife, that we wouldn't receive her or recognize her. He said he couldn't help it"—here his lips tightened—"that he would put her in a sanitarium. He said he only asked that we wouldn't cut his children off. I supposed he meant that I wouldn't cut them out of any property I might leave and I told him I wouldn't. He said he was convinced his wife was guilty of no criminal wrong. I told him I was certain she was. I tried everything I could to get him to leave her."

McLean nodded in a way that looked sympathetic. He needn't have bothered, except for the jury. My father didn't require sympathy.

"What kind of husband was your son, in your opinion and observation?" asked McLean.

"He was the best of fathers and husbands," my father announced, sounding almost proud, which surprised me and pleased me, too, with that reflexive pleasure I'd taken since childhood in his rarely granted praise.

"Was he measly or liberal in providing for his wife?" asked McLean.

"He provided not only liberally, but extravagantly."

My father's mouth tightened and my heart sank again.

41

"We need to get your girls to court," McLean said as we sat in his office after a long day with my father on the stand making me sound exemplary and the Colonel conniving. "Murder one, you bring on the babies, if you're lucky enough to have 'em. Get up in front of that jury, wave that baby around, and plead for mercy. 'If you hang him, gentlemen,'" McLean whined in a high-pitched voice, "'this poor innocent child...'"

Cone Johnson snorted through a cloud of smoke. "Most of the time, the kid would be better off if his Daddy swung."

He added hastily, "Not in this case, of course, Beal."

"Let's bring 'em in tomorrow," McLean said. "They won't understand a lot of the testimony, so we won't look like monsters for putting 'em through it."

Did I think about telling McLean no? I didn't. I'd never had a case where I'd had to wave babies, but it was standard practice. If you had 'em, you waved 'em. And in my case, it made all the sense in the world. But when I informed the girls, Lenora looked at me with those dark eyes and said, "Papa, I don't want to."

"You come, Nora," said Georgia, bouncing up and down. "You come, too." She was excited because it meant a day off school.

"Please don't make me, Papa," Lenora begged. "I don't want all those people looking at me."

"We don't have a choice," I answered. "It's what the lawyers say we must do."

"But Papa," she said, taking hold of my hand. "You can tell them no. Please."

I clasped her hand tightly. "Don't you want to help?" I asked.

She pulled her hand away from mine and started to cry. "I want it to be over," she sobbed.

The evidence that next day turned out to be anything but innocuous. We introduced photos of pages of hotel registers where Al and Lena had signed in as Mr. and Mrs. A.J. Brooks. Georgie remained oblivious, but Lenora was plenty old enough to understand and tensed up beside me. And after the registers came Ed Farwell.

Farwell's blue suit was well-cut and pressed and his cuffs and collar were so clean and white it almost hurt to look at them. He inspected the witness chair briefly before sitting down, then shot his cuffs, crossed his legs, and turned to face Cone, cocking his head slightly and gazing at him with an exaggerated respect that had the effect of conveying its opposite. He was our witness, but he didn't want to be. Cone had to pry information out of him like he was an oyster. Was he in Fort Worth with Al when he met Lena? Where were they headed? Had Farwell purchased the tickets? Establishing those few basic facts took way longer than it should have. At one point, Farwell took the Fifth, then reversed course and answered the question.

His attitude changed completely once he was in friendly hands on cross. "Why did you go to Fort Worth in the first place?" asked Hanger.

"Henry Boyce sent me," answered Farwell, "to see if I couldn't get Al to go on and leave Mrs. Sneed alone."

"Objection!" McLean shouted, but it was too late. The words had flown away to perch inside the jurors' heads.

"Sustained," said Swayne wearily.

"Did you see Colonel Boyce when you returned to Dalhart?" asked Hanger.

"I did," answered Farwell. "I had lunch with him at the Dalhart Hotel."

"During that lunch, did Colonel Boyce express himself on the subject of Al and Mrs. Sneed?" asked Hanger. McLean objected, naturally, but was overruled.

"Yes, he did. He said this matter had caused him more trouble than anything in his life and had broken Al's mother's heart and that he hoped he would be able to keep Al in Canada where he would never see Mrs. Sneed again," said Farwell, the words spilling out in a rush.

"Objection," shouted McLean and Johnson in unison, but they were overruled again.

"In your presence, or in your hearing, did Colonel Boyce ever express any wish other than to keep Al and Mrs. Sneed separated?" asked Hanger. The objections followed like thunder after lightning but to no avail.

"He did not," answered Farwell.

Throughout most of this, Lenora was trembling beside me and Georgia was wriggling around in my lap. I did feel bad, I have to admit.

But it all paid off.

The next day, the *Star-Telegram* printed a photo of me coming down the courthouse steps, a daughter on each side clinging to my hand. Kitty Barry devoted a whole column to them. *The two little girls, silent and a little fearful, followed directly behind their father when he entered the courtroom, and seated themselves, Lenora in the chair to the left of Mr. Sneed, and the little one plump on his right knee.* She went on to describe various charming moments: Lenora ducking her head shyly when a prosecutor smiled at her, Georgie exploring the area around our seats as best she could.

"Tell your daughters thank you," Cone said gravely after reading it. "That jury don't see Kitty's columns, but Kitty's columns likely express better than they could what they *did* see."

42

By the time Fuqua sat down in the witness chair the next day, Swayne had excluded all the women, even Kitty Barry. We'd run through a few preliminary witnesses, and the courtroom was thick with smoke. I didn't feel well that morning—my throat hurt and my head felt clogged. One reporter called it the "illness hoodoo." It hung, just like the relentless rain and snow and cold, over the whole trial: The judge, a lot of the lawyers and witnesses, and even some jurymen fell ill. There were always people coughing in the crowd.

I had to force myself to listen to Fuqua's testimony about the gossip in Amarillo. I didn't like to remember how I'd felt when we'd talked in his office in December.

"I told Beal Sneed I'd heard that Colonel Boyce had said some very obscene and uncouth things about Mrs. Sneed, very smutty things. I didn't go into detail." Fuqua looked pleased with his tact. "But what I'd heard was that when they were all standing on a street corner, someone said, 'As cold as it is in Amarillo, it must be awful in Winnipeg.'"

"And what was the response?" asked McLean.

"Colonel Boyce answered"—and here Fuqua did the lip-thinning thing but even he looked embarrassed—"'Not when you got some nice, hot pussy to keep you warm.'"

I could see that street corner in my mind, wind blowing, men stamping their feet to get up some warmth and everybody laughing. I was still drifting there a little when Fuqua stepped down and McLean called up Sam Slade. Slade had a peculiar way of swallowing hard, then clearing his throat quietly before he spoke. His thick brown moustache bounced a little every time. It was so odd that it got me focused again.

"Colonel Boyce and I shared a buggy home from Richardson's Drug Store," Slade said after his throat-clearing ritual. "He said that Albert was terribly stuck on Mrs. Sneed, just the way dogs get stuck on bitches and can't get unstuck. He said she must have one of them dick-gripping pussies that get hold of a man and don't let go." Slade blushed to the roots of his receding hairline. He couldn't look up he was so embarrassed.

I saw the buggy, the cold wind blowing, the Colonel talking because he wanted everybody to know he was still the same down-to-earth man with a rough manner of speech when the situation or people called for it. Even if it was his own son and Lena Snyder Sneed. I remembered then that I'd liked him. He was one of the men who'd helped me feel like a man when I was still just a boy. And one of the ways he did it was by talking just that way in front of me. And I'd killed him. All he'd been doing in Fort Worth was sticking up for his son on charges I knew as well as he did didn't make any sense.

By the time Lena's brother-in-law, John Pace, got up to testify that I was acting crazy in Clayton—just in case we needed to use crazy as a defense—I was starting to think maybe I really was crazy. And maybe crazy was better than just plain no good.

Fortunately, my lawyers had decided to call Dr. Turner—the alienist I'd hired to diagnose Lena in the sanitarium—immediately afterwards. They wanted to get the jury thinking about crazy on Lena's side and how that might have fed into any crazy on mine. Seeing him on the stand took away the sick feeling.

Unfortunately, though we all thought Dr. Turner would hold up better on cross than Dr. Allison, it turned out that Allison had been Hanger's warm-up act. As stately-mannered as he was, you could almost see him lick his chops as he started in on Turner. "Didn't you tell Sneed that she was morally insane, but you couldn't convince any jury of it?"

"It was a difficult case for the ordinary person, or even many physicians, to judge, Senator," Turner answered in a patronizing tone. Quite a bit of testimony along the Dr. Allison lines followed. And then Turner claimed that Lena's constant complaining proved his diagnosis.

Hanger pounced. "Is it not natural for a person put in a place of that sort to complain?"

"If the person were entirely responsible for being put there, the person would not be resentful," replied Turner, imperturbable. "I myself would not be, in such a case."

McLean snapped his pencil in two and began stabbing one of the pieces into his pile of burned-out matches.

"Tell us, Doctor," said Hanger, in a bland tone that always meant trouble, "how many inmates were at the Southwestern Insane Asylum when you took charge?"

"One thousand forty," said Turner, looking relieved at the apparent change of subject.

"And when you left?" asked Hanger.

"Two thousand."

"One thousand forty when you took over and two thousand when you left," said Hanger, stroking his chin. "And at Terrell, how many when you started?"

"Two hundred," answered Turner, looking a little less unflappable.

"And when you left?"

"Seven hundred," Turner said then paused. "Over several years time."

McLean had made a small pile of pencil pieces and was now lighting matches around it.

"Two hundred to start, seven hundred to finish?" asked Hanger. The tittering in the courtroom was low but audible.

Turner looked annoyed. "Tarrant County has the second greatest number of any county, Senator."

"Which county has the most maniacs?"

"That would be Dallas County," answered Turner, stuffily.

"And you live in Dallas County now?" asked Hanger with studied casualness.

The whole courtroom, including the jury, burst into guffaws. I bent down to fiddle with my shoe and met McLean under the table pretending to do the same thing. We couldn't look at each other. Swayne pounded the gavel, but even he looked like he was struggling not to laugh.

When we finally escaped for the evening, McLean fussed for a bit about whether Turner had hurt us, but finally he just threw up his hands and began to laugh. "My Lord," he said when he caught his breath, "these doctors! When Hanger and I are friends again, I'm going to buy him a drink and we can compare notes on making experts look like idiots."

43

"Look, there he is," I heard one boy whisper to another as we passed through the big courtroom doors. Back then, they ran court on Saturday if the case warranted it—mine definitely did—so the boys weren't in school that morning.

"He's sort of short," the other piped up, then remembered where he was and giggled while his friend jabbed him with an elbow.

I winked at them, which made them both giggle more. Lord, I wanted to be that age again, running around with Joe, doing what boys do, getting into mild trouble that feels monumental, instead of monumental trouble that I had to try to wrestle down to size.

Judge Swayne peered round the room, spotted the boys, and looked stern. "Young men, I'm going to ask you to leave," he said. "You surely have something better to do with your Saturday." You could tell the boys didn't agree, but they shuffled out.

We were waiting on Will Atwell, who was a big-deal witness. He'd been my lawyer. He'd put watches on the Boyce mail. He'd had contact with the Boyce boys. He'd talked to the Colonel before the shooting. He'd run off after it. Not to mention—as he almost always did—that he was a United States district attorney and a post office inspector. Who'd written a recognized textbook on the Mann Act that we were trying to charge Al with violating.

The courtroom was packed with people eager to see the show: a hard-nosed prosecutor on the stand himself. When he finally strode in, he had a big bundle of papers under his arm. "It is the contents of the entire S file in my office," he said when McLean asked about it. "I was employed by Beal Sneed from one to three days after the abduction of Mrs. Sneed—"

"After the *elopement*," Hanger interjected loudly to emphasize the state's view of the situation.

"You can use your terms, we'll use ours," snapped McLean. "Your honor—"

"I'm not saying he can't describe it that way," interrupted Hanger, "I'm just telling you we don't agree with the term."

"After the *abduction*," McLean continued, turning his back on Hanger, "you were employed by Sneed. Is that correct, Mr. Atwell?"

"Yes," said Atwell, his round face still pink from the cold. "I was hired to ascertain Mrs. Sneed's whereabouts and to apprehend and prosecute her abductor, as well as to represent Mr. Sneed in any other matters which might grow out of the abduction."

"Elopement."

"I appeared before the Tarrant County grand jury," continued Atwell, "with regard to the charges of rape, abduction, and kidnapping against Al Boyce Jr. I also began federal action in my own jurisdiction on a charge of violating the white slave traffic statutes, which are applicable in a number of ways. One is a statute against the taking and paying the transportation of a woman, not the man's wife, into another state or territory for immoral purposes."

McLean nodded his head thoughtfully, as if critiquing and approving Atwell's analysis. "In such a case, is the consent or sanity of the woman relevant?"

"It is not," answered Atwell firmly.

"What other steps did you take to assist Mr. Sneed to recover his abducted wife?"

"Eloped wife."

"In my official capacity," Atwell responded, casting a brief but withering look in Hanger's direction, "I called the post office inspector in charge of the Amarillo and Dalhart district. I asked him to put a watch on the mails in order to check postmarks and dates on any mail sent to the Boyces."

With McLean guiding him along, Atwell went on to claim he hadn't authorized that any mail be opened. "In fact," he said with an air of prim rectitude, "I ordered a special investigation when it was reported to me that mail to the Boyces had been opened."

After that, they got into all the strings he'd pulled to get Lena extradited and Al charged in both Texas and federal court. "As United States district attorney and as attorney for Sneed, I sent telegrams to the secretary of state of the United States, the United States commissioner of immigration, Texas congressmen, and others to get them amenable to state and federal processes."

The jurymen, who had started out interested because of Atwell's importance, were beginning to look bored. But they perked right up when the subject got round to the Metropolitan.

"Colonel Boyce asked me to come to his room to talk," Atwell recounted. "He said he had a lot of money and about five years to live, and he was willing to spend all of both on the matter. He wanted me to drop the federal slaving charges. He said he could prove what kind of a woman Mrs. Sneed was. I told him that my actions in the matter would be determined in my own official heart."

I heard a very tiny snort from D.A. Cummings. Hanger was stretched out in his chair with his eyes closed, which was always a dangerous sign. But the jurymen looked rapt.

"What happened after you left Joseph's?" McLean asked.

"I was standing on the corner near the Metropolitan," Atwell answered, "when I heard explosions—it sounded like a motorcycle or an auto—and then I saw people running. I ran, too, and went through the saloon because the front door was fastened. They were calling for an ambulance. I overheard a man at the clerk's desk say that Sneed had shot Boyce."

We'd worked especially hard with Atwell on what came next. "I'll be honest with you, Will," McLean had said. "It's going to smell a little fishy to the jury, you being right in the vicinity and Beal's lawyer and all and taking off the way you did."

Atwell had looked at McLean like he wanted to strangle him. "Yes," he sniffed, "I'm aware of that."

"You got to put the jury in your shoes," McLean went on. "Let 'em hear your thoughts about it, make 'em think about what it would be like to be in your position. Be humble, sound perplexed. What you don't want 'em thinking is *accessory*."

Atwell wasn't all that good at sounding humble under any circumstances, and he didn't have much in the way of a perplexed act, but he tried.

"Knowing that Sneed was my client, I wondered if I should try to find him," Atwell continued, looking briefly at the jury as McLean had instructed. "I decided that I had not been employed by Sneed to defend him if he should kill someone and so I went out and caught my streetcar."

"It sounds weak as hell," had been McLean's opinion when Atwell had tried this out the first time.

"What were you employed for?" asked McLean now, which is how they'd decided to deal with the problem.

"As I understood it from Sneed, I was employed to use all lawful means to punish the man who had abducted his wife."

Hanger's eyes popped open. "*Eloped* with."

Atwell looked sniffy and went on. "I had accepted the employment, not only because it was not inconsistent with my duty as United States district attorney, but was right in line with it." Humble and perplexed had disappeared completely by the end of that pronouncement.

In the crowd that day there must have been at least a few people who'd been on the wrong side of an Atwell prosecution. They must have enjoyed the show on cross immensely. Atwell outdid himself splitting hairs over what words like "discussion" or "realize" meant. We objected to almost every question. Hanger asked Atwell repeatedly about statements he'd made at the habeas hearing. Atwell repeatedly said he didn't recall what he'd said or couldn't recall what he meant when he said it. There was occasional muted laughter from the spectators, which Swayne had to gavel silent, though he didn't look all that annoyed. The reporters could scarcely keep up, but even so I'd catch them smirking. One of them was using hash marks to keep track of all the instances of "I don't remember."

It was late in the afternoon when Hanger got around to a line of questioning that worried me, but fortunately he didn't push it.

"Once again, with regard to your . . . recollections, you testified this morning that you had represented Sneed since early November. Yet did you not testify at the habeas corpus trial: 'I had been consulted six or seven months ago by Sneed about his family matters.'?"

"I can't say what I testified to at the habeas," Atwell replied, "but the fact is my employment with Beal Sneed began a day or two after the abduction by Al Boyce of Mrs. Sneed."

"Elopement," said Hanger firmly. He paused to look at the clock for effect. And then he moved on. "Now, Mr. Atwell, I'd like to return to your decision to leave Mr. Sneed on his own and catch the streetcar home after the murder of Colonel Boyce."

"Objection!" shouted McLean and Johnson in unison.

"Sustained."

"After the *shooting* of Colonel Boyce, Mr. Atwell, why did you choose to return home without ascertaining anything more than that your client had shot the victim?" Hanger looked satisfied; the objection had allowed him to make his point all over again.

"When I heard the pistol shots, I thought at first it was the explosions of a motorcycle engine. If I had thought that Beal Sneed was going across the street to the hotel to kill Colonel Boyce"—his voice rose dramatically—"I would never have let him go."

Another thing that had returned to me from my lawyer days was the ability to gauge how a witness was coming across, and this jury couldn't stand Atwell.

By the end of the afternoon, even some of the lawyers were struggling not to laugh.

44

Feeling just like one of those boys let out of school, I sat in the tub a long time that Saturday night and listened to the radiator gurgle. For a while, the day's battles over evidence ran round in my head. I was especially worried over Hanger's question about when I'd first consulted Atwell; the true answer was I'd talked to him in the spring of 1911 because I'd been considering divorce.

There wasn't an easy way to explain to a jury how one day you were thinking about divorce and then your wife has a miscarriage and tells you she's in love with someone else and you don't react the way most men would—which is to be even more convinced that divorce is a good idea or maybe you kill her. Instead, you decide she's going to stay married to you forever.

"Don't worry about it," McLean had said when I mentioned my fears. "That jury is so confused, what with all the arguing about what he thought and what he felt and what he realized and him not remembering shit, or not admitting he remembers shit—Jesus," he interrupted himself. "I don't like Atwell, but he could take us all to school on 'I don't recall.'"

He shook his head, smiling like he'd just thought of something funny he wasn't going to share. "Anyway," he continued, "those jurors are going to be thrilled to be done with him. Did you see Estes roll his eyes about the sixteenth time Atwell said he couldn't recollect?"

He lit his cigarette and took a few contemplative puffs. Then he brightened. "It could work in your favor, you know," he said. "They might feel sorry for you—stuck with a lawyer who took off when you needed him and who is obviously mostly interested in saving his own professional hide."

As I soaked in the tub, I got to thinking McLean was right. There had just been too much fighting and confusion for the jury to notice the discrepancy. And the state wouldn't push it because it was a minefield for them, too. It made it seem more likely that the Boyces were hiding what they'd known and when they'd known it.

Once I hit the bed, I fell asleep almost instantly. The sun was shining through the drapes by the time I woke up. I opened them, ordered up coffee, and looked down at the street—people in their Sunday best, horses and wagons, dogs, automobiles, newsboys hawking the paper, a shoeshine boy snapping his rag at the hotel entrance, a pretty blonde walking into the lobby on the arm of a young man—and felt refreshed.

When Joe arrived about noon, he looked surprised to see me dressed and smiling. "Let's get the hotel to make us up a sack lunch and take a walk along the river," I said.

"Sure thing," he said, "but pull your hat down. We don't want people recognizing us." He didn't need to remind me, but he was my big brother. He couldn't help it.

The staff let us out the kitchen so we could avoid a few reporters lurking around the front entrance. We walked a while, and then ate lunch on a bench overlooking the river and talked about the women walking by, just the way we did when we were in school. "Headlights coming on the left," I said, reverting to our old system. Joe swiveled his eyes to the left to take in the nice big bosom of an otherwise unremarkable, mousy-haired matron about our age. "Yup," said Joe, "headlights, but no caboose. We got to do better than that."

"Contest," I said. "First one to spot headlights, caboose, and a ship-launcher all in one package wins."

"No," said Joe, "it can't be just a ship-launcher. She's got to be a thousand-ship-launcher."

"In Fort Worth? We'll be here all night," I said. "Hell, we'll be here all winter. 'Judge, I'm so sorry I couldn't be present at my trial where y'all decide whether to hang me, but y'all got too many ugly women 'round here.'"

We both started laughing and couldn't stop for a while. "There are some right pretty ones in court," Joe said. "You ever notice that redhead who mostly sits second row back? She ain't bad."

"The one who favors blue?" I asked. "She's all right. But you know who I really like?"

"Lemme guess," said Joe, squinting speculatively at me. "That dark-haired Italian looking one up in the balcony?"

"No," I said. "Kitty Barry."

Joe burst out laughing again. "You know what? Me, too. I can't figure it. She ain't all that good-looking. She got small headlights, no caboose to speak of, and I don't see more than a couple of canoes or maybe some paddleboats getting launched for that face."

"Yeah," I agreed. "But there's just something about the way she walks in and starts taking notes and acting all business-like that makes me want to help her get to *really* know the defendant," I said, more to amuse Joe than because I really meant it.

"Or his brother," Joe added. He swiveled his head toward a blonde heading our way. "Hey, check out the caboose over there," he said in a stage whisper.

We strolled through the park for hours that afternoon. No one ever won the contest, even though both of us claimed to a few times. But one of the rules was it had to be unanimous. If either of us thought she didn't qualify, she didn't. After a while, we sort of drifted into other subjects.

"Do you ever think about Bessie Boyce?" I asked after we'd started walking again. I could tell the question startled him.

He paused before answering. "Lately I have been quite a bit." He didn't need to say why. "We were both so young. I've been wondering if it would have made any difference." He didn't need to say what he meant by that, either. There was another silence.

"It hurts me, Beal," Joe finally said in a rush of words. "She was my first real love. And Al and I have been out I don't know how often and Henry . . . They were like my other family. I hate sitting across from them in court and knowing I won't ever speak to them again."

I looked at him and saw his eyes fill up. "I just feel so bad, Beal," he went on. "Every day I want to cross that aisle and say to them, 'I'm so sorry for your loss. I'm so, so sorry all this has happened,' and I can't.

I loved those people." He paused again. "I still do, you know."

I saw him the way I always had: A handsomer version of me, a man women loved, in part, for that tender heart of his, that easy generosity.

Our feet sounded on the gravel pathway over the silence between us. "I'm sorry, Joe," I finally said, but I knew it hadn't come out sounding like I meant it.

"Why the old man?" said Joe, stopping and turning to look at me. "None of us understands that, no matter what McLean and them are saying. It just don't make sense. Al makes sense. Even the old man wouldn't have had nothing to say about that. Henry told me so."

"When did you talk to Henry about it?" I asked sharply.

"What difference does it make?" Joe said in exasperation. "After Lena took off with Al, I talked to him a few times about the problem, if you really want to know. He was my friend. He still would be if—"

"If I hadn't messed things up so badly," I interrupted, suddenly furious. "I bet y'all talked about how stupid I was and why wouldn't I go on and give her a divorce. Jesus, Joe, why the hell did you talk to Henry?" I was so angry I stood there glaring at him, my hands bunched into fists.

Joe started walking again, forcing me to walk, too, if I wanted to keep arguing with him. "I thought it might help," he said evenly. "Why did you shoot the old man?"

"I thought it might help," I said, mimicking him.

"No you didn't," Joe said, irritated and emphatic. "You just did it because . . . well, I don't know exactly, but here's what I bet. You saw him and you lost your temper like you're doing now and you had a gun in your pocket. I don't think there was one thing more to it than that. You had a temper tantrum and you had a gun when you had it."

I don't know what it was with me and Joe, but he could say things like that and it would have the opposite effect of what you'd think. I sort of collapsed like a balloon. "You're probably right," I said. For some reason right then, it struck me as funny. When I repeated, "I just had a temper tantrum with a gun," I had to stifle my laughter.

Joe looked sideways at me. "It *ain't* funny."

I turned my head to the river. After a few minutes, I got myself under control and said, "You heard the way he was talking about her."

"Yeah," said Joe, "but come on, Beal, he was always like that. And Father don't think no different about her."

"He don't use the words the old man did, and he don't go blabbering all over town," I said. "Anyway, *you* like her, don't you?"

"Yeah," said Joe, "I do. I always have. But I don't think she's worth all this trouble and you didn't think so either. I don't know what changed your mind." He stopped walking again, put his hand on my arm and looked at me intently. "Father says—"

"I'm very well aware of what Father says." I pushed his hand away.

"So why the hell are you hanging on to her?" Joe was more than irritated now—he was truly pissed off. "You know this thing between her and Al ain't goin' away. Henry says he's never seen Al like this over a woman. He says when Lena talked about divorce last summer, Mother Boyce tried everything she could to talk her out of it. You know those two old people didn't want this. You got all them lawyers saying something you know ain't true about people who've been friends most all our lives. Lena . . . hell, Beal, one of the reasons I *like* Lena is she's smart. And she's acting like a fool over this man. Now why would that be?"

He gave me no time to answer. "Because *she loves him*. Christ, if she'd just wanted fun and games every now and then, like some of them ranch-widdas, you wouldn't have known a thing about it. Why would a woman that smart decide to talk to the man's mother? Why would a woman that smart get herself pregnant? *Because she loves the man*. That ain't gonna change, Beal. Get through this trial, hope you don't hang or go to prison forever, and then give her a divorce and get on with your life. Find you another woman who will love *you* and not be in love with some other man for the rest of her life. Because that's what this is—it's one of them rest-of-your-life type things."

He put his hand on my arm again and positioned himself where I couldn't avoid his gaze. He said very slowly, "Why are you doing this, Beal?"

I thought of the answers we were using in trial, but I knew I couldn't use them with Joe. "I don't know," I said equally slowly. I stuck my chin out at him. "But I'm going to keep doing it." I paused. "So y'all best get used to it."

"You know it ain't worth it," Joe said flatly and started walking again.

After a long silence, I said, "It's a thing that's got to be done. It's got to be finished."

45

First thing Monday morning, Atwell started complaining. "Your honor, I object to the way my testimony was reported in the Saturday newspapers, particularly the *Star-Telegram*. I'd like to correct some things."

McLean raised his eyebrows as high as they would go. "Oh, good Lord," he whispered.

Hanger, stretched out in his chair in his usual brown suit, got to his feet lazily. "With all due respect, Mr. Atwell"—he paused and brushed something imaginary off his sleeve—"the jury here didn't *see* the newspapers." Another pause. "If you start correcting things, that's a way of making them aware of what was reported." He paused again. "Indirectly." Yet once more. "If you see what I mean."

Swayne tilted his head and gazed inquiringly at Atwell. The jurors looked delighted.

"Upon consideration," said Atwell, his pale face now pink, "the . . . uh, I withdraw the request."

Hanger shuffled some papers for a few long moments, cleared his throat, paused again, then said in his stately way, "I'd like to return this morning to what you remember of the scene at the Metropolitan."

Back they went to the same old ground. There wasn't a single substantive thing in the whole deal. The always-cool Hanger was finally so exasperated with Atwell's innumerable I-don't-recalls that he snapped. "About the only thing you have remembered in the whole trial is the streetcar you took back home after your client killed the old man."

"I answer 'no,'" Atwell snapped right back.

Hanger resumed his paper-shuffling for a second or two before continuing. "Perhaps we could review once more the . . . fine distinctions made between your duties as Sneed's lawyer and your official capacity as district attorney."

McLean was getting ready to object when Atwell said, from way up on his high horse, "You are making this personal, Senator," and began a long-winded explanation about the way work was taken in at his office, how cases were filed and handled, and the means of determining possible conflicts. By the time he was done, juror Cowley was snoring gently. Several others had their eyes closed.

"Be that as it may," Hanger said the second Atwell paused for breath, causing a ripple of laughter. "Be that as it may," Hanger repeated, "will you please refresh my failing memory"—more laughter—"as to which portions of your acts in this case were performed as Sneed's attorney and which portions were performed in your official capacity?"

"Surely, Senator," Atwell said with exaggerated courtesy. The veins in his neck looked ready to burst. "I was paid by Sneed to locate his wife and assist in prosecuting her abductor. That employment did not include my official duties, for which I was paid by the government."

"Let's see if I have this straight," said Hanger. "When you wrote the post office inspector in Amarillo to put a watch on the Boyce mail and enclosed the request in a government envelope, that was ...?"

"An official act," said Atwell sanctimoniously. "My two duties were entirely harmonious and moved along together."

"Yes, indeed," said Hanger dryly. "To proceed with the subject of correspondence and your division of duties . . . as it were . . . when you went to see the bank cashier in regard to correspondence that he had aided Henry and Al Boyce to carry on, did you tell him you were asking officially?"

"Yes, I did," answered Atwell, appearing relieved for some reason that was entirely unclear. "I told him that if he didn't tell me about it, I would have him summoned in front of the grand jury to force him." He stopped with a look of intense self-satisfaction.

"That's all," said Hanger, abruptly.

"Mercy killing," McLean muttered, nodding and giving the thumbs up sign to Atwell as he made his way past our table. Even Cone Johnson—in no mood to see the humor in things since he'd been in bed all day Sunday with a bilious attack and his mother was very ill—remarked under the cover of the coughing and chair scraping and general adjustments that went on between witnesses, "In all my professional life, I've never seen such a display of . . . of . . . "

"General overeducated idiocy?" suggested McLean in a low voice. "Sorry, Beal, I know you're related to him."

"Distantly," I said. "By marriage."

We had Henry Bowman up after that, which was a relief for everybody, except possibly Hanger. In his down-to-earth way, he told about Christmas at his house, how my girls were crying on my neck for their mother, how I'd worried over them, how I'd said, "I don't know where Lena is, but she must be very miserable tonight."

By the end, several jurors had tears in their eyes.

46

We spent the evening after Bowman's testimony at the McLean offices rehearsing mine. "Try to get a good night's sleep," Cone said as we stepped out into the dark.

He headed off to see his ailing mother, but McLean walked me back to the hotel. "You'll do fine," he said yet again when we reached the doors. "Just remember to keep your temper with Hanger. He's going to do his best to make you lose it." He gave me a sort of awkward, professional hug as we parted.

I climbed the stairs to the second floor and stood for a moment overlooking the lobby. There was a lingering smell of roses. I wondered what it would be like to be someone else: The woman who wore too much toilet water, or the bored-looking bellboy who was lounging in his cap and jacket against the front desk. That night, in addition to the usual front-page coverage of my trial, there was news of another Fort Worth killing. One young man had shot another over a pretty twenty-year-old. As I turned the heavy key of the bolt in the lock to my room, I sympathized with that young man, sitting in jail on a cold night just like I had.

The bed I'd left rumpled was perfectly made and turned down, and the table lamp was lit. Over the desk, a painting of nymphs by the side of a stream was only dimly visible. I took off my shoes and tie and stretched out on the bed. Around me, the nymphs fluttered and whispered. I strained to hear their words.

When I woke up, I was cold but I felt completely calm.

It was Valentine's Day 1912.

On the witness stand, I kept my voice even, made no obvious emotional appeals, spoke simply. McLean asked the bare minimum to move the story along. The jurymen were entranced from the moment I began.

Defendant John Beal Sneed:
My name is John Beal Sneed. I am thirty-four years old. I was born in Milam County, Texas. My father moved to Georgetown in 1885 when I was about seven years old. The Boyces lived just across the street and the Snyders also lived nearby. That is where I first met Lena Snyder. In 1901, I married her.

My married life was all that anyone could wish — happy up until a few months prior to this when my wife's health was so bad. I thought I was the most fortunate man in the world, and she seemed...she was the same way. I heard her say lots of times that she had so much to be thankful for, with her home and her children and everything, and in looking back over it I don't know that anything could be added to the ten years to have made it any happier than it was.

The first time I learned that there was anything wrong was on Friday, the thirteenth of October, 1911. I went downtown in the morning, made some arrangements to take some men out to the ranch at Paducah to show them some cattle that day. I phoned up to my wife to have an early dinner.

I went home about eleven-thirty, and my wife says, "Well, come on out here on the gallery," and she sat down in a swing and proceeded to tell me about this infatuation with Al Boyce. She told me she had decided to go to South America and live the rest of her life with him, and take the children.

Before We Turn to Dust

I, of course...looking back at it, I did not — could not — believe...could not realize what she was saying, and she probably repeated it to me two or three times. Finally I said to her, "What in the world are you talking about?" I kept asking: "What on earth is the matter? What do you mean?"

I appealed to her, told her of our home and of our children and of our struggles in life together and all that we had done and what we had been to each other, and I repeatedly asked her what had come over her. I finally realized she was serious about the matter.

It had only been once prior to this time, some two weeks prior, that there was any question of improper conduct between Al Boyce and my wife. My wife had been in bed a couple of weeks for an operation for a trouble that she had had. When I came home at noon, I noticed him standing by the bed as I came in at the door — well, it was not a door, it was an opening between the parlor and the hall and bedroom, they were all thrown together in one large room.

As I came in, he sat down in a chair by the bed. We sat there and talked for ten or fifteen minutes. When he got up to go, I let him out.

When I came back in, I asked my wife, "Wasn't he holding your hand standing there?" and she said, "Yes, I asked him to look at my nails, how purple they were." She had been sick a couple of weeks and the nails were right purple or blue.

I said to her, "What on earth do you mean?"

193

and she says, "Why, I do not mean anything." "Well," I says, "I do not understand it," and she commenced crying and asked me if I thought she meant anything, and I told her "No," but she kept crying and called me to her bed and embraced me. And while I knew it was imprudent on her part and it stung me, still I never dreamed anything being wrong at all.

The day she told me she wanted to go with him, I asked her how long this had existed. She said, "Some six or eight months." I asked her if he had taken any liberties with her, and she said he had put his arms around her and kissed her. I asked her repeatedly if they had gone any further, and she said no, even declared by her children. She convinced me that there had been no really criminal intimacy between them.

But that night — I do not now recall just exactly how it happened — but that night we had been talking along the lines indicated, and finally I was so desperate, or wrought up, or was not myself — I do not know what — I started to kill her. She grabbed hold of me, and in trying to get her loose from me so I could kill her and then kill myself, she screamed several times, and the older little girl ran into the room, and I caught hold of the pistol and I put it away.

Someone had given me Dr. Turner's name and the next day I phoned him in Fort Worth and he recommended the Arlington Heights Sanitarium. Henry Bowman and I went out there and talked to Dr. Allison for a couple of hours.

I told him I wanted my wife to have anything money could give her that might help. We had intended to leave the younger little girl with her mother, and the older girl with the Bowmans. But Dr. Allison said that it was absolutely essential to take all the loved ones away. He said they had tried leaving their children with the parties in such cases, but they always had to take them away later on.

Later, I met Dr. Turner at the Elks Club in Dallas. I told him I wanted him to examine her thoroughly and that if he knew of anybody anywhere that could help her, or help him, to just name the man and I would get him.

Dr. Turner went to see her three times. After the first visit, he said he couldn't give me a definite answer about her condition. After the second, he said he wasn't absolutely sure, but he thought she was insane. After the third visit, he said her condition had improved, that she was making a noble effort to pass this man out of her life, and he thought that it would only a few months until she would be entirely well.

The doctor told me that she begged so hard to see me and the children that he thought it would be best for me to go see her. I told him her good must come first, and he said it would probably help her to see me, and I went out there and saw her after she had been in the sanitarium about two weeks.

I talked with her all evening and brought her downtown and took her back after supper. Based on little things that I do not suppose any human being on earth could describe or reproduce, I judged from the entire conversation, her actions and demeanor toward me, that she was more affectionate — in other words she just simply looked like she was her old self again.

But a few days later, when I got a wire in Quanah from Henry Bowman saying to come to Plano at once, I knew right away something awful had happened. I got to Fort Worth about four-thirty in the afternoon of November ninth and Henry Bowman and Dr. Allison met me at the station. They said, "Your wife got away from the nurse last night and said she was going to Plano, and we have not been able to locate her." We went straight to the sanitarium to talk to the nurse. She said she and my wife had been downtown to a moving picture show, and afterwards, as they were walking along the street, the interurban car comes along, and my wife said, "I am going to go to Plano and see the children."

The nurse claimed she argued with her and tried to hold her, but she broke loose and got on the car, and that the nurse told the conductor not to let her on but the conductor reached down and helped her up. The nurse said she tried to phone back to the sanitarium but it took her an hour because she could not find the number and the first place she tried the phone was out of order.

From the way she talked, I decided she was not telling the truth. I said to her, "Bowman and Allison have seen the conductor and he says no such party got on that car. Now tell me the truth about it, no one will hurt you."

She got mad and said she was telling the truth. She was sitting in a corner of the room and I walked over to her. I think I took her by the arm, that is my recollection, and I took out a pistol and told her, "I am not going to hurt you if you tell me the truth, but if you do not, I am going to kill you."

I expected to scare the truth out of her, that was my object. She commenced screaming, and I guess Allison and Bowman thought I was going to hurt her — they interfered and she dropped out of the ground floor window onto the gallery and ran away.

The rest of them thought she was telling a straight story. We decided my wife was probably hiding somewhere in Dallas, with a view maybe of seeing or getting in communication with this fellow.

I went to the pawn shops. I thought perhaps she might have pawned her diamonds for money. I had officers at Dallas search every kind of boarding house. But late Friday, Mr. Bowman discovered by investigations at Jacksons Department Store that the nurse's story was untrue, that my wife had bought a suit, and bought the nurse a suit, and that she had a large roll of money with her.

So we all went down to the depot. The nurse pointed out the tracks and we tried to find out who sold the tickets. Finally the Frisco ticket agent described a man whom I took to be Farwell. One of the tickets was sold to St. Louis and the other one to some point this side of St. Louis.

I also talked with the Pullman porter. He

spoke of the man's incessant cigarette smoking. He described her crying off and on all that night. I learned from him that they went to St. Louis and I went there Sunday but did not learn anything. From there I went to New York, because the St. Louis ticket agent said he had sold a ticket to New York to someone who matched the description of Al Boyce.

  I remained in New York about ten days. I had private detectives and city detectives to try to locate them. I was neglecting my entire business, my own cattle and Mr. Fuqua's, and cotton, and all that needed my attention. When I returned to Amarillo, Mr. Fuqua told me that old man Boyce was making vile talk all over town about my wife — things Mr. Fuqua would not humiliate me by repeating.

  I spent Sunday and Monday, December twenty-fifth, in Plano. The girls always asked about their mother and wanted to go where she was. The little girl was left under the impression she was still over in Fort Worth in a sanitarium, but Lenora worried so much I thought it would be better for her peace of mind to tell her, and I said that her mother had lost her mind and gone away and I did not know where she was. On Christmas Day, she several times threw her arms in the air and cried out that everyone had a mother but her, and wanted to go where she was.

Everybody told me that evening how well I'd done, how hard it must have been, how taxing emotionally, but the truth is it was one of the highlights of my life.

  I got to *be* the man in the story I told—a noble, long-suffering husband who loved his wife so devotedly that despite her betrayal of him, despite his own father telling him he should give her up, despite her constant rejection, despite warnings that no one would respect him, he clung to his faith and his marriage, convinced that his poor wife was insane and would, one day—if he would only stay true to his purpose—return to her rightful home and family.

I got to see the beauty of that man reflected in the audience's eyes. His truth rang out of me like the trumpet an angel blows. "And my wife had one of Georgia's baby shoes tied around her neck in Canada. She crushed it to her chest and cried." Out of the corner of my eye, I could see tears running down several jurymen's faces.

McLean was masterful when it came time to go over what had happened in the Metropolitan. He asked his questions in a low, respectful voice, and gave me time to make a show of collecting myself before I answered. "I had walked twenty or twenty-five feet into the lobby when I heard someone say, 'There's the sonofabitch now' or 'There comes the sonofabitch.' I looked to the left and saw Boyce and Throckmorton rising from their chairs and I pulled my pistol and commenced firing as fast as I could."

"How many shots did you fire?" McLean asked.

"I don't know."

"What occurred to you, mentally or physically, when you heard that remark in the hotel lobby and turned and saw Boyce and Throckmorton rising from their chairs?"

"Why—I thought of all that had ever happened. I thought like a flash of how he had helped that man take my wife away, of what I had gone through to bring her back, and how now he wanted to take her away from me again and send her back to the life of shame from which I had rescued her. I went—I went all to pieces and commenced shooting."

"Take the witness," said McLean.

Hanger was in a terrible position when it came to cross. He had to try to impeach a witness who'd made a bunch of grown men cry. Those men wanted to believe I'd told them the truth. It shamed and confused them to think anything else.

"Didn't you write to her from Paducah and ask her what wanted to do about a separation?"

"I have no recollection of such a letter."

"Didn't you talk to your brother Joe Sneed about Al Boyce being at your house so much?"

"I do not remember such a conversation."

"Didn't you tell the Canadian lawyer Murray that if he were in Texas, you would blow the top of his head off?"

"I said nothing of the kind. I told him that he wouldn't be able to do what he was doing for them if he were in Texas. That they didn't have the same morals up there we have down here."

"Get out of killing people easier down here than up there?"

"I didn't say that. I said the laws were different."

It was hopeless. I think Hanger himself knew it. That kind of little, messy, realistic detail just gets run over by a story as strong and simple as the one we were telling. Twelve men locked away from their wives don't want to look all that deeply into the picture of a failing marriage, especially if you claim the husband had *no idea* anything was wrong.

47

We all went to supper afterwards. What with all the lawyers and relatives, it was a big group. My father and Marvin and Joe all had business to attend to, and Tom Snyder begged off due to feeling poorly. But Marvin's wife, Cara, was there, along with a couple aunts and Henry Bowman and some Bowman cousins. We had escaped the reporters on the way out of the courthouse and met up in the hotel lobby. The women crowded around me, reminding me of a flock of parakeets, with their high-pitched voices and colorful feathered hats. "How well you did." "It was so impressive." "How did you *ever* stand the strain?"

I strolled through the lobby surrounded by that flock and thought if I could just sail along through the rest of my life like that—with a bunch of women who were on my side fluttering and twittering around me—I'd do just fine.

The hotel staff put us in a separate dining room to keep reporters from eavesdropping. My spirits were the highest they'd been in a long while. I felt the lingering, warming effects of the jurymen's tears and compassion, and the nobility and faithfulness of the man I'd been on the stand. And then there were the women, with their compliments and their sometimes silly comparisons and the foolish things they say that nonetheless warm a man's heart and make him feel like he's king of the world.

"I never knew a man to be so devoted under such difficult circumstances," chirped one of the Bowman cousins. "I felt a thrill of . . . of gratitude to know that a man can protect and cherish a woman so. I'm sure Lena will one day recognize what a jewel she has in you." She squeezed my hand and said to those around us, "Don't you think she *must*?"

"She certainly *will*," replied my aunt, tartly. "If she has the slightest bit of sense left in her."

I looked down at the table modestly.

Cone Johnson tapped a spoon on the side of his water glass. "This brave man," he began when the chattering had quieted, "deserves our commendation and applause, not only for what he has stood today, but also for the way that he has stood *by* his wife, and stood *up* for his home and his family, and thereby stood up for all of us who fight for and believe in our families and homes here in the great state of Texas, and in morals and honor in a world where the light of both at times seems dim."

Cone really didn't know how to talk to a group without making a campaign speech, but his words still swelled me with pride.

"Clasp this good man to your bosoms," he continued, his voice quavering with emotion. "Succor him in his hour of need. For this good man is fighting the forces that threaten us all: Failure of honor, looseness in women, divorce, moral laxity, and the creeping liberalism of the North which is so alien to our hearts."

I bowed my head while everybody cheered.

"Speech," cried one of the dimmer cousins, but Marvin's wife, Cara, shushed her.

"He surely doesn't want to give any speeches," she said. "He's been talking all day."

By the time the last dinner plates had been cleared, Bill's father, Judge McLean, looked exhausted, and even Bill seemed to have deflated like a cold soufflé. Cone took the cue and announced, "We should call it a night. We have another busy day tomorrow."

The chairs scraped and the maître d' made sure everybody got their coats and we all said our goodnights. But at the foot of the lobby stairs, Cara took hold of my arm. "Beal," she said quietly, "I need to talk to you."

I tried to put her off. "Cara, it's late. Can't this wait?"

"No," she said, "it can't." Like Lena, she was an intelligent woman and a strong one. She ran Marvin's household like she was head of an Army post. "We both know this thing isn't over."

I strove for a light tone. "That jury may decide to hang me."

She was having none of it. "They won't," she said firmly. "Your lawyers don't think so and neither do I."

There was no mistaking her seriousness. There she stood and there she'd stand 'til she'd said whatever she had to say, a very pretty woman with a full mouth that looked so soft it took you a while to realize that she herself mostly wasn't.

"As you must know, everybody thinks you've started a feud," she said in a low voice. "People say those Boyce boys are just biding their time, hoping that jury will convict you, but that nobody will be able to hold them back if they don't. And they won't."

"I hope you're right," I said, still trying for the light touch.

"I'm right," she answered, but not as if it was her main point. She turned and faced me squarely. "I don't want my husband involved in any feud. Marvin looks up to you and he'll do whatever you ask—and I don't want you to ask him, you hear?"

"Yes, ma'am," I said. I don't know why I kept it up, since it wasn't working.

"I mean it, Beal," Cara said firmly. "Keep my husband out of it. You've put the whole family at risk and I will not lose my husband over this."

"Does he know you're asking this?" I countered.

"Of course not," she snapped, "and you're not to tell him."

"I can't promise you anything, Cara," I said without beating around the bush anymore. "I have no idea what will happen next."

She glared at me and snorted. "All that claptrap about what a hero you are," she said furiously. "You are nothing but a selfish little man who'll do anything to have his own way. You don't fool me one bit."

She dropped my arm abruptly and walked away, smiling cordially at my aunt sitting in a lobby chair a few yards away as if nothing in the world were wrong. Her hips swayed as she minced along in her hobble skirt.

She gave me a chill, that woman. It was like listening to one of the old fates talk at you.

You don't fool me one bit.

48

First thing the next morning, we rested our case and the state put Henry Boyce on to start rebuttal. He was large and round and tanned and talked like a Westerner. When Hanger asked his opinion about the power of attorney Lena had given the Boyces, Henry said, "I didn't want to see Lena shot full of dope and Al railroaded to the penitentiary."

"What was your father's attitude toward Albert's involvement with Mrs. Sneed?"

"He was sore—talked about disinheriting him," Henry answered in a businesslike tone.

"Once you became aware of the relation between your brother and Mrs. Sneed, did you talk to anyone in the Sneed family about this matter?" Hanger said, inching his chair a bit closer to Henry.

"Yes," answered Henry. "On October sixth, I met Beal's brother, Joe Sneed, in Dalhart to talk the business over. We decided to send for old Tom Snyder and get him to meet with my father to see if something couldn't be done to break it off. But Joe telephoned later that he'd decided to send for his father, too, and let the three old men settle the trouble. I told him I thought that was a mistake, as Beal and his father didn't get along very well. About a week later, Joe and I decided that Joe should take Al to Mineral Wells to separate him from Mrs. Sneed."

That was news to me. Joe hadn't ever mentioned it. It's never fun to find out what other people have been saying behind your back about your business. You've got your own story and it often includes a bunch of stuff about how confused or misguided other people are. Then you listen to someone like Henry Boyce and you realize that pretty much everybody thinks the way you do—that they know best—but they think they've got it right and you're the one who's confused. Mostly though, you don't have those moments when you're on trial for murder. That made things quite a bit worse.

"When they took Mrs. Sneed away," Henry continued, "I told Al that they had taken her to a sanitarium. He promised me that if Mrs. Sneed told him she was reconciled with Beal, he would pass out of their lives. But he said, 'If she writes me that she wants to go ahead with our arrangements, I'd be a damn dirty low-down man to lay down.' He was in Santa Rosa when he got a letter from her on November second saying, 'For God's sake, please come take me away from this place.' He caught the train to Fort Worth that night. Once they eloped, I helped him, but my father and mother never knew where they were."

Henry never once looked at me. Even when McLean was cross-examining him from our table and he had to look in my general direction, his gaze never once touched me. It must have taken enormous discipline but it looked natural. *He* looked natural. And even with McLean doing his absolute best to rattle him, he never got ruffled.

"What did you have in mind when you wired Al in Canada, 'Stay there and fight it out. Tell Lena we will see her through. Father is here: Beal's last step puts him in the game.'?"

"Pa got involved only after Beal made the diamond theft charge," Henry answered. "I knew they couldn't stick Al on the Fort Worth kidnapping charge, but I didn't want him to come back. I thought if he and Beal ever met, there would be one man killed and the other would go to the penitentiary for life. And I didn't want anyone else in on the act. Pa always said that if Beal killed Al he wouldn't take to the warpath, but that 'if anybody else butted in, there wouldn't be a greasy spot left'—that was his expression."

"Who did you fear would butt in?"

"My mother worried all the time that Beal would hire somebody to kill Al."

"So your father was happy for Al, the crack shot of the Panhandle, to fight it out with Beal, but warned that if anyone else took a hand there would be trouble?"

"You can't tell who'll be hit when both parties have guns," Henry countered. "I saw Jim Keeton shoot five times at a fellow in Amarillo and never touch him, and there's not a better shot around than Jim Keeton. That's because the smoke was coming from both ends."

He made me feel the way the Boyce boys always had. Like my brother Joe, they were the real men, the ones who knew how to talk the way real men talk and do things that real men do. I was only a feeble imitation.

But that's not true, I told myself. I've proved it.

49

And after Henry came Mrs. Boyce. All in black, she entered from Judge Swayne's office with Henry and Lynn on either side. Lynn helped her out of her coat, laying it carefully on the arm of the chair, and Henry gently lifted her black veil. I was shocked at the sight of her. In just a few months, she'd gone completely gray.

"Would you state your full name?" asked Hanger, rising to address her.

"Annie Elizabeth Boyce," she answered in a voice that rang through the courtroom.

Hanger made quick work of the rest of the usual preliminaries and got right to it. "When was the first time you learned of the affair between Beal Sneed's wife and your son, Albert?"

Mrs. Boyce laid her black fan in her lap and looked at him directly. "The first act I didn't approve of was when he took her to the Opera House matinee, about the end of October in 1910. He phoned for a cab and I asked where he was going. He said to the Opera House. I asked him who with and he said..."

"Objection. Hearsay," Cone interrupted.

Mrs. Boyce looked at Cone a little perplexed and said politely, "If you talk a little louder I can understand you better."

Judge Swayne said to her gently, "It's only a protest to the court about what it is permissible for you to say. You needn't respond."

"We'll get at it another way," said Hanger. "Mrs. Boyce, did you say anything to Albert to express your disapproval of his going to the Opera House with Mrs. Sneed?"

"I did," Mrs. Boyce said, taking hold of the fan again. "I told him, 'This is not New York City and the Four Hundred Society. Beal Sneed wouldn't like this. It's imprudent.'"

"Were there other incidents to cause you concern at that time?" asked Hanger.

"Albert went away that night to attend to a cattle deal and wasn't home much for a while after that. But in the summer he commenced going up to her house in the forenoon and the afternoon," Mrs. Boyce said. "And then I heard something on the twenty-second of July." She looked over at Cone. "Mr. Boyce was downtown electioneering for Mr. Johnson." Cone bowed his head slightly as if to thank the Colonel retroactively.

"How did the information which made you uneasy come to you?" asked Hanger.

"Mrs. Lena Sneed came and talked to me," answered Mrs. Boyce, lightly tapping her fan on her lap.

"Objection," said Cone. "Her acts as well as her statements can't be used against her husband."

McLean was listening intently with one leg over his knee, repeatedly stroking a match against the heel of his shoe. As Cone objected, the match suddenly caught fire.

"Your honor cannot permit this witness," McLean had begun vociferously when the flame reached his fingers and startled him. He dropped the match and stamped it out.

Swayne looked severe. "Mr. McLean, you know the rule against smoking."

"Yes, your honor, I struck the match by mistake. I apologize. I won't play with matches anymore," said McLean in a rare moment of contrition. The crowd tittered. Mrs. Boyce sat still, looking like nothing in the world would ever make her laugh again.

"Order," Swayne said sternly. "Objection overruled."

"As Mrs. Sneed is not a witness in this case, witness can't say what Mrs. Sneed said," McLean said, "as your honor knows."

"It's admissible," Hanger snapped. "You know it is."

They tussled a few moments longer, then Swayne ruled that Mrs. Boyce could tell what she herself had said but not what Lena had.

Hanger went to work extracting information bit by bit. It reminded me of gutting a fish, though nobody in the room except Mrs. Boyce and the prosecutors knew what that fish really looked like. Mrs. Boyce appeared more and more frustrated. Of course I knew we didn't want the jurors to see the fish, but part of me wanted to scream: *What did my wife say about our marriage? What did she say about me?*

"I said to Mrs. Sneed, 'Oh, Lena, I knew you were imprudent, but I never thought of such a thing as this. What would Beal think?'"

I knew Mrs. Boyce was telling the truth because I knew her. Or I had known her. No matter what happened now, I would never know her again.

"After Mrs. Sneed left, did you tell anyone about the conversation?"

"Yes," answered Mrs. Boyce, "though I worried about telling Mr. Boyce because of his nervous spells. But when he came in I said—"

"Objection," McLean and Johnson cried in unison. "Inadmissible."

"Objection overruled," said Swayne, with by now well-practiced exasperation.

Mrs. Boyce looked at Hanger with a mix of confusion and frustration, and underneath it all a kind of endless despair I could see, though I didn't want to.

"Mrs. Boyce," Hanger said gently, "I'm sorry this is so difficult. I'll try to ask the questions so it's easy for you to understand what you are permitted to tell. But if I throw you off, just remember that you can't say what Mrs. Sneed said, and you can't say what Mr. Boyce or anyone else said she said. The court has ruled that we can't introduce any evidence about what Mrs. Sneed said. While this may not make much sense to you—"

"Mr. Hanger," Swayne warned from the bench.

"Yes, your honor, I apologize," said Hanger. "As I was saying, Mrs. Boyce, because Mrs. Sneed isn't a witness in this trial, since she can't testify against her husband and the defense states that they decline to call her for reasons of insanity—"

"Your honor," protested McLean, "you see what he's doing. We want him—"

"Pipe down, Bill," said Swayne. "And Mr. Hanger, he's right. I see exactly what you're doing. Proceed with this witness or I'll do it myself."

"Yes, your honor," said Hanger gravely. "Mrs. Boyce, what did Colonel Boyce say after you told him of your conversation with Mrs. Sneed?"

"He said he would talk to Al."

"And did he do so?"

"Yes." Mrs. Boyce looked furious but she stuck to the rules.

"Did he tell you or anyone in your hearing what he said to Al?"

"Yes."

"What did he say he said to Al?"

"He said he told him how much he disapproved of his conduct with Mrs. Sneed."

It went on like that: When did Mrs. Boyce last see Al; what the Colonel said about keeping Al in Canada; when Colonel and Mrs. Boyce learned his whereabouts, etcetera. McLean was simmering with objections and sometimes came to a full boil. Hanger had to step carefully to extract the information he was after and sometimes couldn't get at it at all.

Mrs. Boyce tapped her fan faster and faster and her mouth got tighter and tighter.

"After the families became involved, did you talk to any family members about the problem?" Hanger asked.

"Yes, I spoke with Beal's father, J.T. Sneed, and also with Tom Snyder. I talked more to Tom Snyder because he visited the house twice to talk about it."

"Can you tell us about the first conversation?"

"Mr. Snyder came in while Mr. Boyce was shaving. When Mr. Boyce got done and sat down by the fire, Mr. Snyder said, 'Al, I'm sorry about this trouble. Why didn't you let me know before?' Mr. Boyce said that they had been trying to straighten it out and that he thought Mrs. Sneed and Al would grow tired of one another. I asked Mr. Snyder about the bruises I had seen earlier on Mrs. Sneed's neck and arms. He said that she had tried to keep Beal from phoning to notify him and Beal had had to force her away from the phone."

"What was the extent of the bruises?" asked Hanger.

"She was terribly bruised about the neck and arms," answered Mrs. Boyce, using the fan to point. "She had come to our house, but I didn't know she was there until she came into the room with Beal's sister, Mrs. Thompson. Can I not tell what she said?" she asked.

"No," said Hanger, Swayne, and McLean all in a chorus. I saw her knuckles go white.

Did she say I beat her? That I threatened to kill her? And why was my sister with her?

"What did you tell Captain Snyder about this incident?" asked Hanger.

"I told him that Mrs. Sneed had come to our house to phone Albert to leave Dalhart because she said both her father and Beal were threatening to kill Albert."

McLean didn't object, I suppose because he thought there was some use to the idea that I'd been fired up enough to want to kill Al and so had old man Snyder.

"Henry was supposed to take Albert away," Mrs. Boyce went on, her knuckles white but her voice unwavering. "But Albert wouldn't leave until Mrs. Sneed told him it was all right because he said she had no one there to protect her. The whole family had told Al he must go—I myself told him to move on—but he said, 'Go see what Lena says.'"

"What happened in the second meeting between Mr. Boyce and Captain Snyder?" asked Hanger. "Was anything said about insanity?"

"Yes," said Mrs. Boyce. "Mr. Snyder said they were going to take Mrs. Sneed off and that he was sure Mr. Boyce didn't want to know where. Mr. Boyce said he certainly did not. Mr. Snyder said they were going to say Mrs. Sneed was insane for the sake of her daughters. Mr. Boyce said, 'But, Tom, you know she's not crazy.' And Mr. Snyder said, 'No, but we have to take her off and report that. She's got to be taught to behave herself. She ought to be beaten. Beal Sneed ought to take her and beat her.'"

She paused and rapped the fan on her hand so sharply it must have stung. "I felt like taking her myself and putting her over my knee."

"Was Albert usually submissive and obedient?"

"There never was a better boy at home. He took less correction than any of the other children. He was considerate of others and slow to get angry and censure anyone, but when his mind was set he could not be changed. This woman had influenced him and he wouldn't obey me or Mr. Boyce."

"When did you last see Mr. Boyce?"

"He left Dalhart to attend a bank meeting on January ninth." She paused and briefly placed smelling salts wrapped in a black-bordered handkerchief under her nose. Then she went on, her voice steady. "I never saw him anymore until I saw him as a corpse here in the undertaking parlor." The fan lay still in her lap. The courtroom was entirely silent.

"No further questions."

As he began his cross-examination, McLean stood up respectfully, in contrast to the way he often approached witnesses. In the case we were making about the sanctity of the home, and mothers and wives, he knew better than to show anything but the deepest respect for the grieving widow—at least at the start.

"At the time of the first conversation with Captain Snyder, was any mention made of insanity?"

"No. Mr. Snyder seemed to think it could be smoothed over but that Beal Sneed would have to come back to Amarillo to complete his business transactions and that Albert should be kept out of the way."

"Didn't he say something to the effect that it would be like shaking a red flag for Beal to see Albert?" McLean asked in a mild tone.

"Yes, he said it would be. Mrs. Sneed had said—"

"Mrs. Boyce," Swayne interrupted, "please remember, you aren't permitted to say what Mrs. Sneed said."

"I'll tell the truth," she protested, looking at both Swayne and McLean, "but you don't let me tell all the truth." Behind me I could hear murmurs. By this time, I was pretty good at reading the crowd's mood, even if I couldn't hear the words, and this one was sympathetic. *Why* shouldn't *she say what she knows?*

"I'm sorry, Mrs. Boyce," said Swayne, sounding like he meant it. "I'm trying to make sure that this trial is a fair one for everyone's sake."

Mrs. Boyce nodded her head. For the first and only time in the proceedings, she looked ready to cry. The murmurs grew simultaneously louder and more sympathetic—as if some of the women wanted to give Mrs. Boyce a hug or an extra handkerchief. But the sound died right back down at a sharp look from Swayne.

McLean resumed cross, still using his mildest tone. "You learned from your husband that he and Mrs. Sneed had discussed how much alimony—"

"No, no," Mrs. Boyce broke in, looking irritated. "Mr. Boyce said Al would keep on until Beal killed him and Mrs. Sneed said, 'He won't kill him . . .'"

Because he's too big a coward. Is that what you thought?

"Objection," cried Cone.

"Mrs. Boyce," said Swayne, a tiny bit less cordially this time. "Please remember my instruction not to recount anything Mrs. Sneed said."

"I think I ought to be allowed to tell what Lena said," said Mrs. Boyce firmly. (This time the murmuring agreement that rose up must have come at least as much from curiosity as from sympathy. That crowd was dying to know what Lena had said.) "I talked to her in a motherly way, and in a stern way."

"I'm sorry, Mrs. Boyce," Swayne replied equally firmly, "but the court has ruled that you may not tell anything Mrs. Sneed said."

"If you will just answer the questions, Mrs. Boyce," chimed in McLean, "we won't keep you long."

"I am willing to stay all day," she answered, sitting up still straighter and looking McLean in the eye as if he were another of the obstinate children in the case. "It's the last thing I can do for Mr. Boyce."

"Tell me about the night of Al's whiskey rigor," said McLean, changing course and hardening his voice. "You went down to the Sneed home."

"Albert didn't drink much," said Mrs. Boyce, impatiently. "He wasn't a drunken son, as Snyder said. I went down in the evening to try to talk to them together, but they weren't there."

"Did you think Mrs. Sneed was insane?" asked McLean.

"No," snapped Mrs. Boyce. "She was nervous. Albert was nervous.

I was nervous. Everybody was nervous. There ought to have been more people nervous. Mrs. Sneed was a pretty strong woman," she said with a hint of sarcasm. "To have gone through what she has, she is pretty strong yet. If she was the least bit insane then, I think she would be a raving maniac by now."

"Had you known they were going to put her in a sanitarium where there were insane people, you would have objected, wouldn't you?" asked McLean.

"I thought it was the wrong step, and I still think so," said Mrs. Boyce. By this time, her dislike for McLean was palpable.

"You and Colonel Boyce felt such an interest in Mrs. Sneed—"

"And in Beal Sneed and his children."

"That you didn't want her put in a sanitarium."

"I didn't want her persecuted. I wouldn't have persecuted one of my own children that way."

"Is that why you didn't put Al in a sanitarium?"

"He was not a fit subject for a sanitarium. He was not insane."

"Don't you think a man who would run over and disgrace his mother and father and steal another man's wife, killing his little children—don't you think he is a fit subject for an asylum or a penitentiary?"

McLean had barely finished the question when Lynn Boyce sprang to his feet, knife in hand, and lunged at him. The lawyers at both tables rose in one movement. I was so startled I dropped my pipe. Several women screamed. Lynn's brother, Will, and a family friend from Amarillo, Frank Hovencamp, pinned Lynn's arms behind his back and wrestled him to his seat. The knife clattered to the floor in the little pile of paper strips Lynn made every day as he listened.

On his feet and shaking a fist at Lynn, Bill's father, Judge McLean shouted: "Will the court permit one of its members to be assassinated? We demand that this man be excluded from the courthouse."

Lynn hung his head, his face flushed bright red. Will and Frank stood on either side of him, each with a hand pressed hard on his shoulders. The spectators were on their feet, craning their necks and talking excitedly, and the reporters were all scribbling furiously while trying to keep an eye on things at the same time.

Throughout all the commotion, Mrs. Boyce remained still, only gesturing to the bailiff to hand Lynn her smelling salts. He couldn't look her in the face, but he took a half-hearted sniff from the bottle.

Judge Swayne peered down at him. "I'll fine you the maximum one hundred dollars and exclude you from the courthouse." he said sternly. "In addition, you will spend an hour in jail."

"The sentence is entirely inadequate, your honor," protested Judge McLean. His face was splotched red and he was breathing like he'd been running.

But the truth was, nothing better could have happened for us than having Lynn go crazy that day. It marred the good impression that Mrs. Boyce was making on everybody, including Kitty Barry: *Annie Boyce belongs to the pioneer type of American womanhood who could stand by the side of the fighters and load muskets when she saw her loved ones being shot down around her. No more magnificent evidence of the courage of the freeborn American woman has ever been given in this state.*

I read that in my hotel room that evening with a strange feeling.

It took me a minute to recognize it as envy.

50

To follow up on Mrs. Boyce's testimony, the prosecution read a letter the Colonel had written on January fifth to ask an old friend to help get Al released from the Immigration Hall in Winnipeg. The letter made the Colonel's attitude entirely clear: *I am very anxious that Albert remain in Canada. If Sneed and his wife can live together, and Albert becomes convinced that it is unsafe for him to cross the line on account of the state rape and abduction indictment, it will keep him and Mrs. Sneed forever apart. They claim that she is insane, but the woman is no more insane than I am—she is mean as the devil and smart as a whip. You can assure the Canadian authorities without fear that Albert will make them a good citizen. You know personally he is a good, law-abiding man.*

Once again, I remembered the real Colonel Boyce, who wasn't the one I shot. He wasn't the one in the story we were telling the jury. He wasn't the one I wanted to believe in. So I tried not to.

Later, as we were walking away in the rainy dusk at the end of another long day, McLean said, "Tomorrow we'll go to work on getting your temporary insanity evidence admitted."

I nodded. I knew it couldn't hurt. But part of me got to wondering again: *Am* I crazy? *Was* I crazy? I tried not to pay that any mind either.

"They'll say it ain't right," McLean continued, "that we're done with our case and we're not rebutting anything in theirs." He took a long, appreciative draw on his cigarette and blew a smoke ring into the dark. "It *ain't* right, but we'll see if we can get Swayne to go for it. It'll be good for that jury to think about walking in your moccasins again after Widda Boyce."

Johnson laughed ruefully. "I feel sorry for her, Bill," he said. "This ain't her fault. She's lost a husband and she's got one son she don't know when she'll see again and another who went crazy in court and you and me objecting every time she tries to tell her side of the story."

"Cone," said Bill, laying a hand on Johnson's shoulder, "you know how it is with me. If they ain't on my side, I don't like 'em, I don't trust 'em, and I *definitely* don't feel sorry for 'em. That jury feeling sorry for her is the biggest obstacle we've got. I, for one, will get down on my knees to thank the good Lord that boy of hers went after me. It distracted the jury and made it look like she's raised more than one hothead. They've got to be wondering what the father was like if one son ran off with another man's wife and another is in court jumping lawyers. When it's all over, and my client here is a free man—and he will be, you mark my words—then I might extend some sympathy to Mrs. Boyce. Until then, she and all her tribe are the enemy."

Cone looked pensive. "Yeah," he said, "I know. I'm just not seeing it that way right now. She's not much younger than my mother."

"Of course," said McLean. His whole manner softened. "I'd see it just like you do in your position. You give your mother my best when you talk to her tonight."

But as it happened, Cone's ailing mother died that night, while still more cold rain and snow swept down from the north. And that same night another man died after he got into an argument about the case on a crowded streetcar with our detective Ben Bell.

"That sonofabitch was liquored up good," Bell told us the next day at the McLean offices. "I don't care what his widda says about he's been off the stuff for a year. The whole car was talking about this thing and he was ranting about bitch this and whore that—excuse me, Beal—and I says, 'Don't talk like that about Mrs. Sneed,' and he shoves me into a corner and says, 'You wanna take it up with me, old man?' So I go to beatin' on him with my pistol and next thing you know he's pulled the trigger on hisself."

There was a silence while everybody considered his own opinion about the truth of this account. Bell had already shot a man to death who'd killed a county attorney, so we knew he wasn't averse. McLean just shook his head; the slain attorney had been his cousin and he was inclined to give Bell the benefit of the doubt.

"How does a man manage to get hisself killed on a streetcar over another man's wife?" Bell went on, shaking his head. "Hell, why is everybody on the streetcar talking about the thing?"

He shook his head some more so that his big moustache shook along with it like a toppled over parenthesis. "This whole damn town—this whole damn *state*—has gone crazy."

51

After Swayne denied most of the temporary insanity evidence, there was nothing left but the closing arguments. The courtroom had been full before, but now it was jammed, with hundreds more waiting in the cold outside. People had come from all over the state. Before the session even started, the clerestory windows were completely steamed up, the crowd pressed up against the railings and walls and hanging over the galleries. One woman caused a ruckus when she stabbed another in the back with a hat pin just to get a seat. The place smelled of wet clothes, stale smoke, Listerine, toilet water, and sweat. It made my head swim.

Right behind the bar on our side—they must have stood in line for hours in the cold—sat a couple as fresh off the farm as this morning's eggs. "We're praying for you and your family," he said quietly as she smiled shyly.

Cara and Marvin were seated beside them. Cara greeted me so warmly it was hard to believe the scene at my hotel had ever taken place. Marvin gave me a long hug.

District Attorney Jordan Cummings, as the official representative of the State of Texas, was scheduled to make the first summation. He was good-looking, tall, and well-proportioned, but even the regulars hadn't seen much of him previously; he'd spent most of the trial seated at the prosecution table with his back to the spectators. When he straightened his tie, cleared his throat, then rose from his chair with a sheaf of notes in his hand to approach the jury box, he made a forceful impression. I noticed some women paying particular attention—sort of like he was a surprise bonbon in the chocolate box.

Turning first toward Swayne and then toward the jurors, he looked down at his notes briefly, like a conductor checking his music. "Your honor, gentlemen of the jury," he began almost conversationally, "regard for human life is the ultimate test of a country's civilization." There was a faint rustling as people settled down to listen.

"In a barbaric nation, among savages," Cummings went on, "life is held cheaply. But in civilized countries, safeguards reduce justification for killing to the narrowest limits. This court has been engaged in hearing evidence to determine whether the defendant, John Beal Sneed, should be deprived of his life and liberty for the life which he took on January thirteenth. The state's evidence has shown that, as civilized men, this jury should convict the defendant of murder in the first degree, for the malicious and cold-blooded killing of Colonel Albert G. Boyce."

He wasn't loud, but there's nothing comfortable about listening to a man argue in favor of your execution. If he's good, and Cummings was, he can get you to where you just about want to hand him the rope yourself. I felt something like a squirrel stuck inside a wall; I wanted to scratch my way out and I couldn't. The jurymen were all intently focused. For the first time since I'd testified, Juror Strong had his feet off the railing.

Cummings never once referred to his notes, though he waved them around occasionally for emphasis or punctuation. He spent a little time on the basics—Al and Lena, the sanitarium, the elopement, etcetera—but quickly marched his audience to the scene of the crime. "Was Sneed cool and deliberate when he fired his pistol?" he asked rhetorically. "We know from his own testimony that he saw Colonel Boyce earlier that night. Manslaughter in such a case, as set in the statutes of the state, occurs if the killing happens at the *first* meeting after the killer has learned of insulting words toward a female relative." He paused to look at the jury significantly. "But in this case, *all* that Colonel Boyce had said or done had been conveyed to Sneed *before* he saw him in the lobby of the Metropolitan. And yet, Beal Sneed turned away and went to supper at Joseph's.

"Nor did this man kill Al Boyce Jr. when he found him in Winnipeg. And why not, gentlemen of the jury, if he was so incapable of calm reasoning, rational thought, and cool reactions at the thought of what this man had done to his wife? Because he'd heard Al Boyce Jr. had two bodyguards with him and he knew the laws in Canada would judge him harshly.

"This lawyer-defendant, this lawyer-witness, understands very well how to appeal to your sympathies and blind you to the facts in this case. His wife hasn't been on the stand. We haven't even been permitted to hear what she said, in conversations with Mrs. Boyce or others. This lawyer-defendant and his attorneys have told you that they have not called this woman because they believe she is insane.

"But members of the jury, you must ask yourselves, what's the real reason this woman isn't on the stand? Is it because she is morally insane? How can we not doubt that diagnosis, especially after listening to Dr. Turner?" Cummings waved his notes and rolled his eyes. There was some laughter in the crowd, though it died quickly.

"Or is it because she *won't* testify for her husband and they have to say she's insane to explain that? After the testimony we've heard—that he tried to kill her, that he beat her, that he had her locked up—who is to say what she might say if she were allowed to? I, for one, can have no doubt about why she wanted to leave him and go off with another man who might give her the love she failed to receive from her husband, regardless of whether I approve of her decision and behavior or not."

During most of the trial, I'd spent most of my time not thinking about Lena, except as a figure in the story we were telling, the poor unfortunate who'd been seduced and lost her mind. But now, listening to Cummings, I had to remember that she'd be happy to chime in about her manipulative, violent, short-tempered, intelligent, and opportunistic husband. I had to remember that she was nothing like what we were saying she was and neither was I.

"Colonel Boyce thought Beal Sneed's charges were unjust and without merit," Cummings continued, "the acts of a cowardly man who had been a lawyer and knew how to manipulate the truth and the law. Colonel Boyce would have understood and accepted Beal shooting Al in cold blood. But playing the lawyer game, charging an honest man with theft and with white slavery, these charges incensed the plainspoken, old-fashioned Colonel. He was an old man, and not in the best of health, as his widow has testified."

Cummings began to stoop and sag a little, so that he seemed to age before us. "He is seventy years old. He comes to Fort Worth and secures the dismissal of the false charges against his son, charges that would have caused his son to be extradited and brought back to Texas, rather than kept in Canada and away from Mrs. Sneed as his father prefers. He is an old man, used to the ways of the ranch, and away from ranch life too blunt of speech, perhaps. But he has succeeded in his mission. Where is the father on this jury or in the audience or in this world who would do less for his son?

"Now picture him." Cummings pulled a chair over from the state's table and placed it near the jury box. He sat down and settled himself into an old man's pose. "He has wired his old wife that he will be coming home that night. He is sitting in the lobby of the Metropolitan Hotel, feeling relieved and tired, chatting with his friend Throckmorton, who has, *most* conveniently for the defense, since died and so cannot tell us his memories of that terrible night."

Cummings paused, sagged a bit more, and smiled as if conversing with someone to his right. "Now, through the revolving doors comes the defendant, Beal Sneed. At first, Colonel Boyce doesn't even see him. Sneed crosses the room. He begins firing." Cummings clutched at his stomach and, groaning, staggered to his feet. "Sneed sees him rise, and keeps shooting. He comes closer and closer."

Cummings doubled over, staggered the few steps to the jury rail and collapsed, grabbing the rail as he went down. He lay on the floor and groaned for a few moments, then lay completely silent. You could have heard a pin drop. Several jurors actually peered over the railing like they wondered if he really was dead. I was trembling.

Cummings jumped up so suddenly that several women screamed and a few jurors startled visibly. "Now you're out of it," he sneered, pointing his notes like a pistol at the place on the floor where he'd been lying. That pose, too, he held a while, his lip curled in disdain, his right hand aimed at the floor. Somehow he'd made himself look shorter and stockier.

At last he straightened and grew into himself again.

"Turn this man loose," he said, looking somberly at the jury, "and you grant him immunity to kill Henry Boyce and Lynn Boyce and Mrs. Boyce and every person in Amarillo that ever spoke to his wife or of her."

He concluded passionately. "A man who kills in defense of his home or in self-defense stands his ground. He does not run away as Sneed did. We are not barbarians or anarchists. We are a civilized state in a civilized country. We are not swayed by high-priced lawyers, manipulations, and lies. I am confident that this jury, having weighed the evidence, will convict the defendant, John Beal Sneed, of murder in the first degree."

It felt like every single eye in the entire courtroom was fixed on me when I stood up as court recessed at noon. I grabbed Joe's arm like a life preserver. My father took my other hand and squeezed it. Hearing me vilified for several hours must have reminded him I was his flesh and blood, however disappointing and wrong-headed.

52

McLean spent most of the noon hour complaining about the theatrics—"taking unfair advantage of all that amateur theater he did"—and trashing Cummings' argument from the legal point of view. Joe and Marvin and the rest went at it from the human angle. My father was mostly silent and looked distressed. Cone sat in a folding chair in a corner scribbling notes and mouthing things silently.

"Don't worry, Beal," he said as we gathered our things to head back to court. "You'll feel a whole lot better by the end of the day." Eula met us outside the courtroom holding Lenora and Georgie by the hand. They rushed to hug me and that made me feel better immediately. Of course we'd kept them out of court in the morning, but it was important to have them there that afternoon.

When Cone rose from his seat, there was a rustling in the courtroom like a great flock of birds roosting and settling. But once he began to speak, you could hear the clock tick when he took a breath. The people were that still.

Cone was a nice-looking man but sort of loosely put together and a little rumpled, like he'd forgotten to hang his trousers straight the night before. But once he started orating, you just couldn't tear your eyes or ears away. His voice pulled at you like music. I don't recommend being tried for murder, but having a man like Cone Johnson defend you is like having the angel Gabriel speak for you in front of God.

"Gentlemen of the jury, ladies and gentlemen of the audience, your honor," he began, nodding in the direction of each. "Jordan Cummings has presented the State's view of this case, a view I am here to correct. This case may seem complicated, but truly there are very few propositions of law involved. The first is that the case must be viewed from the standpoint of the defendant—what he thought and heard, and the conclusions he reached. You must not consider the statements of Colonel Boyce against the affair, nor any other statement not communicated to the defendant. You must trace the river back to its source. You must consider every straw that made the load that broke the camel's back.

"The source of all this tragedy was the violation of God Almighty's written law—'Thou shalt not covet thy neighbor's wife.' That law is in the same category as the one that says, 'Thou shalt not kill.' And there is but one insult which Southern chivalry and Southern lawmakers say carries no limitation of time, that blow which strikes deepest in the heart—an insult to women relatives. Our lawmakers and our customs agree that no number of days or months or years is too long to carry the barb in one's heart."

Cone leaned on the rail, looked intently at the jurymen, and got to work on the walking-in-your-moccasins angle. "Have you stopped to remember the promise you made to your wife at the marriage altar? How you promised to stand by her in sickness and in health, and to cleave to her for better or worse, as long as you both shall live?"

He straightened and took a few steps toward me. "How few of us are willing to stand by our wives through evil report," he said, shaking his head woefully. "*This* man"—pointing—"remembered his vow." He passed a handkerchief over his face as if to suggest that all this was difficult and he was working very hard to contain himself. "There was a time," he continued, his voice starting soft and building, "under the old Israelite law, when it was a life for a life and a tooth for a tooth, and if a woman did wrong she was to be stoned to death. But the time came when One stood on the banks of Galilee, and when they brought a woman who had done wrong before Him, He wrote in the sand, 'Neither do I condemn thee—go and sin no more.' Since that time, woman's heart in every part of the world has been clamoring for equal treatment. If Sneed had done what his wife did, what would the world have counseled her? It would have counseled her to stand by him, as he stood by her."

Cone approached the jury again, his tone now almost conversational. "Beal Sneed didn't put his wife in a sanitarium just to keep her out of the way. Why, the man consulted the best doctors in the state, asking them what they thought of his wife's state of mind and what he could do to help her get well. How can the state contend that it was Al Boyce, rather than Beal Sneed, who wanted to protect her?" he asked incredulously, then paused and raised his voice to its best oratorical heights. "So far as my reading is concerned, Beal Sneed is the only man I have ever heard of since the days of Christ who has stood by his wife under all circumstances."

I glanced cautiously at my father, who looked startled, though you had to know him well to see it.

After all that, Cone made a show of getting down to actual evidence. He ridiculed the idea that the elder Boyces had no idea where Al and Lena were. He characterized them as millionaires trying to buy influence and control my wife. He spent lots of time on the Colonel's smutty talk. He said I'd struck a blow against anarchy by killing the Colonel.

And he wound up at full oratorical pitch, his voice stretching far beyond the jury. "I have said nothing of murder, ladies and gentlemen, because murder is based upon malice and malice was never born in a breaking heart. At each step of the way, straw by straw, barb by barb, the Boyces aimed to rob this man of all the happiness he and his little girls had known. Step by step, they drove him closer and closer to the brink of the precipice of desperation. He tottered over it the night he entered the Metropolitan hotel and heard the epithet, 'There goes the sonofabitch now.' Human life is not the highest consideration of our laws. Beal Sneed obeyed the highest law when he forsook his father and mother and stood by his wife. He ought not to be punished for being a living embodiment of all chivalry and honor toward women.

"They have *done it all*," said Cone, looking dramatically at the Boyce side of the courtroom. "It is Al Boyce's violation of God's almighty law that brought calamity on his family. I say to him in Canada today, 'You and your acts have brought death into your family.'" Then Cone turned and pointed directly at me. "If you believe that this man and his little girls have not suffered enough at the hands of the Boyces, then yield to their entreaties and send him to the penitentiary." Lenora squeezed my hand so tightly it hurt and Georgie laid her head on my arm.

Cone's eyes filled and his voice choked. "I am sorry that Sneed killed Colonel Boyce. I know Sneed himself would restore that old man to the bosom of his family if he could, despite the ill that they and that old man have done him. But I say to you"—the voice grew fierce—"this man has violated no law."

There was dead silence in the courtroom, except for the sound of muffled sniffling. Several of the jurymen were crying. Cone's words seemed to ring in the air as he sat back down and became ordinary again.

"That's all, your honor."

53

Back then, the court allowed multiple speakers for both the prosecution and the defense. The next few days were like a tennis match with two teams lobbing stories back and forth. Though I'd braced myself for County Attorney John Baskin's speech the next morning, it wasn't too rough. His job was to handle the technicalities: How often I seemed to draw guns, what Atwell was really up to, the way the defense kept changing its mind about what the defense really was. We didn't think the jury cared much about any of it.

After Baskin, my side had Judge Henderson from Cameron. He wasn't one of my lawyers, but he and my father went way back, and McLean *et al.* figured the personal note would help. My father cracked one of his rare smiles as Henderson walked to the jury box. "We're in good hands," he murmured.

Henderson's white hair and old-style beard were carefully combed and trimmed. He stood very straight and spoke in an old-fashioned style, pitching his voice like he was on stage or in the pulpit and using his hands as formally as his voice. "Ladies and gentlemen, gentlemen of the jury, I have known Beal Sneed since earliest boyhood. His grandfather was the Methodist parson Joseph Sneed, who came to Texas to fight the devil and preach the Word of God. On his mother's side, the defendant descends from John Beal, a well-known Indian fighter who helped make this land safe for all the great gifts of civilization we see around us. Can it be any wonder that, coming from such stock, this man would fight to uphold the highest standard of civilization—the family itself?"

I knew my father was delighted with a public recital of these proud facts about the family, after weeks of a sordid melodrama with his son in a starring role.

Henderson went on for some time about the happy home and the "dark shadow of another man," all of it pretty predictable. But he wound up going Cone one better. Striking his heart with his fist he proclaimed, "In this case, the blood of the deceased is not on the brave man you see before you. Oh, no. Rather, it is on Al Boyce. Al Boyce is the murderer of his own father."

It was a ridiculous statement, but I thought the jury would like it. They liked me and they wanted all the cover they could get for voting their feelings: *Look, he didn't really even kill the Colonel. Al did.*

"Let us imagine," Henderson went on solemnly, "that this jury has found Beal Sneed guilty and condemned him to hang. The people of this great state are aghast at what has been done in their name. His children weep for the fatherly embrace. We find his wife at his grave each day, crying over her loss and her weakness. One early morning she arrives at the cemetery, but this time a crowd is gathered round her husband's grave. She approaches fearfully as the sun's first rays strike a tall monument, one she has never seen before. Eyes dimmed by tears, she reads the words inscribed upon the stone, words which tell all the truth her heart or any other can know about this man and this case. A simple inscription, ladies and gentlemen, which says everything that must be said: "Beal Sneed—Hero.""

Lenora and Georgie, as well as any number of others, were sobbing. I fought to keep my face grave and modest.

By this time, everybody was wringing their hands over how much time and money the case was taking, and the jurymen were desperate to go home. Swayne decided to run a night session. Before the prosecution's next speaker—a Judge Hendricks from Amarillo—even got started, several jurors looked like they'd dozed off.

And then, after only a few minutes of trying manfully to get them to focus on telling details, Hendricks paused and clutched the rail of the jury box. His naturally ruddy face blanched. "Your honor," he gasped, "I am ill. Please excuse me." Then he bolted down the aisle.

"Did you put something in his dinner?" Cone joked to McLean when we'd got clear of the courthouse. But like Throckmorton's death, it was just another piece of good luck. It disrupted the flow and it was what the jury would most remember about the speech. Hendricks still looked peaked the next morning and then he made matters worse, out of loyalty to the Boyces, I reckon. "It is natural we should all condemn Al Boyce, but he was a rancher in Montana and the Pecos and he had limited experience with women. And you have heard testimony that this woman was brilliant."

Juror McIlrainey straightened his neck and started moving it around inside his collar like it had just seized up on him. The story was already a scary one for the jury, but not as scary as it was to think about their wives running away *and* running the show.

"Beal Sneed is the smartest man in the case," Hendricks continued. "He made a better speech from the witness stand than Johnson did on his behalf." It was another hopeless tack—that jury sure didn't want to feel that I'd outsmarted or manipulated them. As I held Lenora's hand, it came to me: *I've beaten every one of the three old men,* the only ones Joe and Henry thought could straighten things out. *I* was the one taking care of things, in my own way. Suddenly and surprisingly I found myself talking to Lena in my mind.

You're gonna end up mute. It won't be because your voice don't work. It'll be because no one can hear what you're saying.

54

And then came Bill McLean Jr. "There won't be a dry eye in the house when I'm done, I promise you that," he whispered to me. People were sitting on the spiral stairs that led to the gallery and standing clear up to Swayne's desk. Hats hung from the chandeliers: Stetsons, derbies, the women's feather- and ribbon-covered confections. Several boys dangled their feet from the ledge of the balcony.

"Ladies and gentlemen, your honor, gentlemen of the jury," McLean began. I felt a sudden rush of warmth for him. How far we'd come since that morning in the Fort Worth jail. "I don't know whether the Boyce millions or their influence is behind this prosecution, but it is the cruelest one I've ever seen." He looked meaningfully around the courtroom. "They say this case is about a killing. No! This case is about the breakup of a home."

He spoke his next words with slow force. "Every time a home is broken up, there ought to be a killing. When that's done, homes won't be broken up." There was another impressive pause.

"They say my client ought not to have killed the old man. And yet that old man helped murder those two little girls, using contemptible language about their mother. And what can we say about a man who was more hurt over a theft charge than anything else in this terrible case?

"I hope that my two little boys will never have to steal, but I would a thousand times rather they steal diamonds than some other man's wife. Diamonds I could replace, but all the toil and all the wealth in the world cannot replace the jewel of a woman's virtue." Another pause. "And yet, they say, Beal Sneed ought not to have killed an old man."

He went on for hours in that vein. Almost none of it had to do with evidence. Mostly he was touching up the story. And he was a real good lawyer. He understood his audience and he wound up strong.

"Do you know what will happen if you convict this defendant?" He looked at each of the jurors in turn. A few looked confused, like they were wondering if they were supposed to answer the question. They startled as a group when he struck his fist on the rail and thundered: "His deranged wife will get a divorce and go to Al Boyce. Beal Sneed's property and his children will find themselves in that despoiler's hands. Let us suppose you have sentenced Beal Sneed to the penitentiary. I wonder"—his voice became contemplative—"I wonder where little Georgia Beal is?" He looked somewhere in the middle distance, deliberately avoiding the girls and me. "Where is Lenora?" She burrowed her head into my chest.

I heard the rustling that meant people were pulling out their handkerchiefs. "I can see those little girls—no matter what kind relative takes them in—I hear them saying . . ." he paused as if he might need a handkerchief himself, "'Go get Papa.'"

There were audible sobs from one of the balconies. Lenora was crying as if her heart would break. Georgia really didn't understand what was going on, but on my other side she began to cry, too. I tried to whisper comfort into their ears but my own eyes had filled.

"I don't need to hurt this defendant or his children further by picturing what will become of his wife in the hands of the despoiler—you can do that for yourselves. Will your verdict sentence these innocent little girls sobbing in their father's arms, to cringe through their young lives before Al Boyce in the forests of Canada? I think I see them, in their little white gowns, saying their prayers.

'Now we lay us down to sleep,
We pray the Lord our souls to keep,
But let us die before we wake,
Rather than Al Boyce our young lives take.'

"Gentlemen," McLean finished in a quiet tone of voice, as if he felt what he was saying so deeply that any theatricality would be wrong, "let your verdict be, 'We the jury declare that the homes of this country must and shall be protected.'"

Before Eula took the girls back to Plano, McLean gave each of them a paper doll cutout book. "You helped your Papa more than you know, sweetheart," he said to Lenora. "I'm sorry you had to be here. I know it was hard. You two are very brave girls."

"It's all right, Mr. McLean," said Lenora shyly. "I'm glad to help my . . . my family."

"Me, too," said Georgie, in her sturdy way. "I'm glad to help my family, too."

"Good girls," said McLean, looking like he might cry at any moment himself and not the for-show tears of the courtroom. "I know your papa and your mama are both mighty proud of you."

"Our mama said she was when she came to see us," said Georgie. "She told us she loved us very much." Lenora flushed and hung her head.

"She does," said McLean, putting a hand on each girl's shoulder, "and your family will soon be right as rain. Just you wait and see."

"Yessir," both girls said in unison.

55

Hanger went last. He hadn't looked well for days, and when he reached the jury box, he supported himself on the rail. But his voice was strong and clear, sonorous as always.

"The defense," he began, "has argued that the trouble in this case has been the double standard, one for the Boyce family and another for everyone else. A greater trouble is the double standard for enforcement of the law. When a poverty-stricken man, feeling the skeleton hand of hunger upon his wife and children, meets a wealthy man and picks his pockets, there are no lawyers summoned from every compass to plead that he had not time for cool reflection. But if, as in this case, he has a comfortable fortune, backed by the First National Bank of Amarillo, things are different."

He went on for some time like that, pointing out—yet again—that the defense was "employing imagination and using it as fact. No man can conceive that the old man, sitting peacefully in that hotel lobby, happy that he could tell his patient old wife that the indictment had been dismissed, meditated any attack on Sneed."

Hanger looked paler by the moment, but that voice continued to flow. "Seven weeks ago today, the man who forty years ago pledged his life to her"—pointing to Mrs. Boyce—"was here in Fort Worth. Seven weeks ago today, this man"—pointing to me—"snatched her husband away. The attorneys for the defense have painted you the picture of one home. I ask you to look at another. No more the footsteps of that old father will be heard. No more will his voice be heard in admonition, in cheerful word, in sage advice—the defendant has stilled that voice forever. There is but one answer to the question of what penalty is proper in this case, and that is the penalty for murder."

Hanger sat down, wiping his brow. *Good,* I thought, *but not good enough*. I was amazed I was cool enough to judge it like a lawyer and not like the defendant.

"We got 'em," McLean said that night as we parted. "That jury'll do the right thing." He was wound up, talking even faster than usual. As he and Cone walked on, he kept chattering, as if shutting up terrified him.

I tossed and turned for a long while that night, remembering bits and pieces of the speeches and of the silence that was everybody paying attention. The crowd had refused to leave until it became clear the exhausted jurymen were going to bed. There in the dark, I went over Swayne's instructions and the choices he'd given them: Life sentence or hanging for first degree; not less than five years in the pen for second; not less than two and no more than five for manslaughter; or not guilty.

I'd left the courtroom smiling to the crowd and the reporters like I was counting on *not guilty*. People had smiled back at me and waved. Some even cheered. They made me feel certain I'd go free.

But alone in the dark, it was hard not to consider other possibilities.

56

"Goddammit," said McLean, striking the table in his office with his open right hand. "Dammit to *hell*. I thought we had 'em. My left knee was even doing that thing it does when I'm going to win."

Cone was sprawled in an office chair with his collar undone looking depressed, but he roused himself. *"What?"* he said. "Did you just say your left knee tells you when you're going to win?"

"Ask my daddy," said McLean, looking over at the old judge, who nodded but looked like he was busy thinking about something else and didn't want to be interrupted. "My knee is never wrong," Bill went on, "least not before now. It kind of quivers or trembles or something when the jury goes out if I'm gonna win."

"It *quivers*?" said Cone, sitting up straight in his chair. "Jesus, Bill, you make it sound like pussy. What in the hell are you talking about?"

"'Course I win a lot," said Bill, like he hadn't even heard, "so it does it a lot."

Cone just shook his head. "Well," he said, "I reckon you need to have the ol' knee worked on, cause it sure was quiverin' the wrong message." He sighed and pushed himself back in his chair. "Though in defense of your knee, I'd have to say I agreed with it. I thought we had 'em, too. And you *know* they ain't broke down on degree. When juries send letters to judges about 'We reiterate, with all the emphasis known to the English language, that we CAN NEVER agree'—it ain't over degree. Swayne's so mad he'd slap 'em all with contempt if he could."

"You're right about that," Judge McLean said. "I never knew a jury stuck like this except over acquit-convict. It's unusual," he went on in his academic, judgey way. "The whole case."

My own feelings were mixed. On the one hand, I was sort of relieved. I wasn't going to hang or go to the pen, at least not any time soon. That was a sure thing now and—no matter what we'd all said—it hadn't been before. But I was also upset. I was thinking about which of the jurymen hadn't bought our story. Who wasn't crying when I testified? I couldn't recall. It made me uneasy, as if my father or Colonel Boyce or even Cara had somehow joined the jury: *You don't fool me one bit.*

The room was full of smoke and gloom. And those lawyers weren't in despair over what a hung jury and a mistrial meant for my life or my family or the Boyces. They were in despair because they just flat out *hated* to lose.

Eventually, though, McLean started talking about next steps, and everybody perked up a little. "Now Beal," said McLean, in his most lecturing tone of voice, which visibly cheered him, "you got to act the whole time like you ain't disappointed. You know you're innocent, and the next jury will see that. You leave the expressing disappointment part up to me. Just remember that any man who reads the newspapers may be on your next jury. You comport yourself accordingly, y'hear?"

I nodded. Of course I knew all that, but it didn't hurt to let him huff and puff. He looked brighter by the moment.

He straightened in his chair and looked directly at me. "You know we'll win this thing in the end, Beal. Most everyone thought you were wrong at the start and now we got most of 'em thinking you were right. Look at the way they were crying. And all those phone calls about the verdict, not to mention the letters."

He pointed at boxes lined up against the wall where his secretary had stacked hundreds of letters, all supporting me. "Next time around, they won't be able to pick a jury in the state of Texas that'll convict you, no matter what that bastard Swayne wants."

It was Leap Day, February 29, 1911, before Swayne finally declared a mistrial. The jurymen's wives had been calling the court for days, furious at how long their husbands had been away from home.

Swayne wasn't happy either. But after all those years prosecuting Acre cases, he knew a dead end when he saw one. "I know that if it were a question of second- or first-degree murder which divided you, a compromise might be expected," he announced grimly, "but as it is, I realize that it is useless to keep you here." Foreman Strong raised his eyes and mouthed the words "Thank the Lord." Swayne shot him a warning look and Strong looked at the floor again right quick.

"I hope there is no man so low that he could have formed his verdict before he entered the jury box," Swayne said, looking searchingly at each man. Not one of them met his gaze. I'm sure he wondered. There were all sorts of rumors flying around that we'd bought ourselves a juror, or tried to. "This case has attracted the widest attention of any case ever tried in Texas. The world knows the testimony, and it has put Texas on trial. This doesn't look well for Tarrant County or the state of Texas.

"I hope you can go home to your wives and children, kneel at your bedsides, and say to your families and to God that you have tried this case according to the law and the evidence without other considerations, as you swore before God you would do." He paused for a minute, as if he hoped one of them would fess up. "Dismissed," he said at last, banging the gavel down hard. The jurors filed out, still without looking at him.

"What are your plans now, Mr. Sneed?" a reporter shouted as I made my way down the courthouse steps. I just smiled and shook my head.

"Anything you'd like to say to the people of Texas?" yelled another young man badly in need of a haircut.

"There is nothing he *can* say," McLean answered, taking hold of my elbow. "He made his announcements on the stand in the trial. Come on, fellas," he pleaded, "leave him alone. This has been an ordeal and we are disappointed with the result. We'll get an acquittal at the next trial—you mark my words."

After we'd shaken free, he said quietly, "That's as close as they're ever gonna to get to convicting you."

"How can you be so sure, Mr. McLean?" my father said with a

dubious look on his face. "Seems like we don't ever know how a jury is going to vote." It was obvious that he was thinking, *How would Bill know since Bill was wrong this time?*

"The tide's turned, sir," said McLean portentously, but with the respect he always showed my father. "I can feel it. They won't be able to find a single juryman next time who don't know about this case and, uhh . . . we won the storytelling contest. Our story is what people are going to remember." He stopped walking and faced my father directly.

"And your son, sir, is the best witness on murder one I ever had, just like I told you he'd be." He beamed at me like *he* was my papa. "Maybe I screwed up, or Cone did, or Atwell or Dr. Turner, but not your son. He's been perfect."

My father smiled, though with something kind of doubtful about it. "Yes," he said, "he did very well." He patted me on the back, and that felt doubtful, too.

The mood was sort of flat and mixed-up as we headed over to the McLean offices. The situation wasn't the sort of thing you break out champagne for, though there were some sandwiches and coffee the girls had brought in. McLean used the occasion to school everybody on what to expect and how to behave.

"Rumors are spreading like the Mexican fever about feuds and more killings," he said. "My girls tell me new ones every day. Y'all gotta act like it's *over*. No shenanigans of *any* kind." Everybody nodded. They were more than ready to act like life was normal again. They couldn't wait to get back to their own business and be done with mine.

"Beal, would you stay behind for a minute?" McLean asked as the group began to disperse. My father looked askance, but Joe took him by the arm and steered him through the door.

Once we were alone, I stuck out my hand. "Thank you, Bill," I said. "I know you did your best." We shook and he made the right noises, but he looked preoccupied.

"Beal," he said and cleared his throat. "We're at a real delicate point." He stared out the window. "Way more delicate than I was letting on. I'm not worried about what's already happened. If that retrial were held next week, we'd win. I'm sure of it. But there's a lot . . . well, that ain't certain." He pulled out a cigarette and chewed on it for a second or two.

"Sit down." He waved the cigarette at a chair, lit it, inhaled, and blew smoke out his nose before asking abruptly, "What are you going to do about your wife?"

"What do you mean?" I answered, though I had a pretty good idea.

"I mean she don't want to be with you," he said. "And she don't strike me as the type to just come on home quietly now that she's had her fun."

"No," I agreed.

"We got you painted in a pretty tight corner," McLean went on, intently. "We gotta make sure that when we get back to court your story still looks good. So . . . no more trying to kill her or beat her or nothin' like that. We managed to get all that explained, but it'll be a lot harder if you do it again. And forget about sanitariums for a while." He paused, pulled on the cigarette and coughed. So far he hadn't said anything that wasn't obvious.

"I like you, Beal," he continued, "and I feel for you in this thing. But I know you ain't the choirboy we been tellin' the jury about."

My first reaction was I felt attacked, but that was followed real quickly by a funny sort of relief. He was looking at me without a shred of distaste. "No," I said.

"That's normal," he went on, "as you know yourself. Defense tells a big yarn about the accused—at least eighty percent of it's bullshit." Waving his cigarette, he added hurriedly, "I ain't saying the percentage is that high in your case."

I nodded.

"I know you want your wife back."

I nodded again.

"That's fine. That's what we've said you want. But there are things you can do to try to get her back that will make it harder for us and things that will make it easier, or at least won't make it harder. I just want to make sure we're both clear about which is which."

I began to sense where he was heading. "No beatings, no threats in front of the wrong witnesses, no coercion, no confinement," I said dutifully. "No matter how pissed off I get, I can't kill her."

We both laughed.

"Right," said McLean. "You gotta look like a devoted, caring husband. She's the weak-minded wife you're trying to protect."

"I understand, Bill."

"Good," he said. "And I figure you also know you can't be killing Will, Henry, or Lynn Boyce, unless one of 'em happens to ambush you."

"Right," I said, "no stray Boyces." I thought about it a minute. "Do you think they'll come after me?"

"No," Bill said, looking interested, like it was a strategic question rather than one about my personal safety. "I don't. Despite all the talk, I think they understand that it would be a damn stupid thing to do right now. And I don't think those boys want to put their mother through any more trouble."

He fell silent, then stood up, stretched, and said, "That's as to stray Boyces."

He said it kind of lazily, but that was just theater. He was making his main point, the one he couldn't say out loud. *If you kill anyone else, make sure this time it's the right one.*

"Well," he said, still with that lazy tone, "I reckon we understand each other."

"I reckon we do," I answered. Both of us knew; *get the right one* and the whole case got easier. It showed I meant business. I hadn't just gone crazy and shot an old man because I was too afraid to go after his son. But both of us also knew it wouldn't be easy. A whole lot could go wrong, starting with Canadian laws and ending with the right one getting the wrong one—me.

McLean and I shook hands and went out onto the street where the rain was falling again in the twilight and a newsboy was hawking papers telling all about us. People were buying them up so fast he could barely keep pace. McLean and I pulled our hats low over our faces, shook hands again, and parted.

57

My father was already—of course—fretting about the cost of the second trial. He insisted we go to Waco the day after the jury went home to meet with an old banker friend of his. "I'll co-sign the note with you, son," he said, "but I want it structured so you're ultimately responsible for the debt. What this is costing the family is a burden you must face." His face showed the usual mix of disapproval and certainty. But at least he wasn't going on about I should give Lena up. He'd realized that there was now no advantage, financial or legal, to that course of action.

After we got things drawn up to his satisfaction in Waco, he went back to Georgetown and I went on to Plano to see the girls. "I told Lena she could see them when she comes to Fort Worth tomorrow," Eula announced to me nervously.

I considered whether it made good sense to forbid that entirely and decided it didn't. "You make sure she's never alone with them," I said. "I don't want her telling them lies." Eula looked—well, I'm not sure how I'd describe the look, but it was a complicated one. She opened her mouth, shut it again, and nodded.

I knew Henry was likely telling her every rumor he heard about Lena and the rest of the Snyder girls: That Eula was the only decent one of the bunch; the rest were she-devils of withered virtue; Joe and Lena had been lovers and Joe was the real father of one of my children; Pearl—Lena had been staying at her house in Lake Charles—was as bad as Lena, but it just hadn't come out yet; the Snyder females had a disease so no matter how much they got, it was never enough, and every one of them had a venereal disease, too, to go along with the other disease. Except Eula.

I reckon she knew she didn't have much choice but to tow the line and keep on doing whatever Henry and I wanted her to do. At times, I could see there was something she wanted to say about the girls and their mother and I made sure she never got the chance to say it. I could only deal with so much at one time.

From Plano, I went to Dallas to talk to Nellie and Billie Steele. I figured Lena might come see them again—they were kin by marriage—and try to work the angles. But when I mentioned it, Nellie reassured me. "I've made it clear to her that she's welcome in our home, but of course Billie and I will always support you in trying to reunite your family, and I shall tell her so." She stirred her coffee so furiously it almost splashed out of the cup.

Nellie was all for letting me know she wasn't one of *those* women. When we got to talking about the suffragettes in London who'd smashed up store windows and pulled policemen off their horses, she said pointedly, "And people think Texans are crazy. Those women don't sound like they have the good sense God gave them."

"Good sense and women don't always go together," Billie said jovially, and Nellie responded, "Oh, yes, and it's *such* a common combination in men," kind of sarcastic but affectionate at the same time, and then both of them pulled up short like they realized the topic might not be the best in present company.

"Speaking of women without good sense," said Billie, winking, "I see another one has got the Dr. Allisons indicted for doing to her what they did to Lena."

"They didn't do nothing to Lena," I said.

"I ain't saying they *did*," said Billie. "I'm saying this here Irene George says they did—kept her naked, wouldn't let her see her children, got her declared insane when she wasn't. So now she's suing."

And right then—I'll never forget it—we heard a pounding at the front door and a commotion of voices, and then Atwell rushed into the kitchen with a telegram clutched in his hand and his face paler than I'd ever seen, gasping. "Bad news, bad news."

"Lena!" I shouted. Atwell panted and shook his head and waved the yellow paper. His voice trembled: *"J.T. Sneed, Sr., shot to death at Georgetown Post Office."*

I couldn't breathe.

And then all hell broke loose. Nellie got on the phone and was hollering at the operator to put a call through to Georgetown and Billie was pumping Atwell for details he didn't have and the house girl was screaming, "Oh, Lordy, Oh, Lordy," and I was sitting on my chair, thinking over and over, *My father is dead.*

Of course, everybody assumed it was the Boyces. But it turned out they had nothing to do with it, despite all the rumors to the contrary. My father had complained for some time about one of his tenant farmers, an R.O. Hillard, who had some bad habits when it came to liquor and guns. My father had given Hillard a ride into town and fifteen minutes later, as my father was coming down the steps of the Georgetown Post Office, Hillard shot him twice in the back with a .45, then turned the gun on himself. He left a note for his wife saying that my father had caused him to lose his mind. Although I tried hard to pretend I didn't, I felt some secret sympathy—especially if that ride into town had involved a lecture.

But even if the Boyces were not involved, no one could deny the symmetry: The father in one family, then the father in the other. I imagined the grim satisfaction the Boyce boys must have felt, the comments about *the mills of the Lord* and *heavenly justice.* At the cemetery in Georgetown, water stood in the open grave and black umbrellas sprouted like mushrooms, much as they must have out at Llano when they buried the Colonel. Aunt Lillian snuffled away into a black-bordered handkerchief, a big black veil covering her face, just like Mrs. Boyce must have done.

Joe was crying openly, as his wife Zella clung to his arm. Marvin and Cara stood together with their heads bowed. Aunt Lillian's two grown children were holding hands. As usual, our sister Georgia was the rock. She stood entirely straight and the tears ran down her perfectly composed face like water sliding over a big, smooth boulder.

"A judgment on the family," I heard one townswoman whisper to another. She looked up and saw me and blushed to the roots of her hair. "We're all so sorry for your troubles, Beal," she said in her churchgoing voice. I just nodded.

Bill's father, Judge McLean, seemed genuinely affected. "A fine man, your father, a fine man," he said, dabbing at his eyes with a handkerchief. Bill was uncharacteristically subdued; of all the things that happened while he was my lawyer, I think my father's death was the only one that truly frightened him. Maybe he saw somebody coming after him the same way. Maybe he saw somebody coming after his own father. Or maybe my father's death and the manner of it was one of those things that didn't fit into any of Bill's predictions, and that unsettled him.

"It's a terrible thing," he said to me softly, his face open in a way I'd never seen before. I didn't know what to say because I didn't recognize him.

"Yes," I answered.

We were both silent for several minutes. Then he said, "We can have his testimony read into the record," and looked instantly ashamed. "I'm sorry, Beal. It's the lawyer in me. I can't help it. I'm sorry."

I looked at him and, for the first time in a few days, I smiled. "Don't worry, Bill," I said, "It's the shock." I patted his shoulder. "I understand." I did, too. I was thinking about the inheritance in exactly the same way, calculating what I'd get and when, and whether I'd still need that credit line in Waco.

For a long time afterwards, I'd believe I caught sight of my father every now and then, just the way I sometimes thought I saw one of the Boyce boys or Ed Farwell on a streetcar or coming round a corner. Only with my father I didn't worry he was trying to kill me. In fact, he seemed to be busy with something else completely, like he'd forgotten all about us and had a brand-new life. I'd start to call after him, "Father, Father," and then realize he wasn't really there.

I also had a recurring dream: My father was coming out the doors of the Georgetown Post Office and starting down the steps. Then Lynn or Al or sometimes even Mrs. Boyce shot him. It was the same dream every time; the only thing that changed was who did the shooting. I was always at the bottom of the steps, frozen in place, waiting my turn. I'd wake up with a sick feeling that the Boyces were somehow behind my father's death in a secret way no one would ever discover. During the day, I knew it wasn't so.

But the feeling of an invisible, malevolent power that couldn't be checked stuck with me.

58

A few days after the funeral, Bowman and I boarded a crowded streetcar in Fort Worth on our way to the McLean offices. We had to sit a few rows apart. As usual, we had our hats pulled low. On a seat between us, a man and a woman in their early twenties were talking.

"It's such a shame," said the woman in a girlish voice, a little husky around the edges. "Both those old men. He must feel terrible." I pulled my hat down even lower and slouched in my seat.

"He must be scared is what he must be," the young man said in a decisive tone like he was used to setting her straight. "We was laying odds the other night on who'll be next and they weren't real good for him."

"Oh, no, Hank, that's a terrible thing to do," cried the young woman. "It's a terrible thing to *say*. It ain't right to be betting on something like that."

"It may not be right," said Hank, sounding indulgent, "but everybody's doing it. Letty, it's the biggest thing going right now. And it ain't finished. *Everybody* knows that."

"What an awful thing," said Letty. She sounded like it really did trouble her, not like she was just saying it and meanwhile thoroughly enjoying all the drama.

When the car came to a stop, they bustled out into the rain and a tall, lean man came up the car steps with his hat pulled down over his face just like mine. I sprang up as I reached for my gun.

The man sat down and pulled out a newspaper and I collapsed into my seat with my heart pounding and my hands shaking and sweat rushing down the sides of my face.

Bowman and I got off at the next stop. Before he took off on his own errands, Bowman said in an even voice, "Beal, I think you ought to get a bodyguard." It was hard to read his expression. But I thought part of it said, *I don't want to be around if you do any more killing, especially if you start shooting strangers.*

I got right to it with McLean. "I had a bad experience coming over here, Bill. A man got on the car who sort of looked like Al and I was about to shoot him."

Bill stopped jogging his knee and drumming his fingers. "Dammit, Beal," he said, sounding both worried and exasperated. "I can't get you off if you do that."

"I know," I said. "I scared myself. But after what happened to my father . . . maybe I need a bodyguard."

"I think that's a fine idea," McLean said with obvious relief. He paused to light a cigarette and blow a smoke ring. "What about John Blanton? I met him the other night at the Royal drinking with Lena's brother Tom. He used to be a deputy in Amarillo. He knows all the parties and he's looking for work."

"As I recollect, he's a good shot."

McLean responded in his best *listen up, this here is your lawyer talking* voice. "We're not hiring him to shoot, Beal. And if he has to, we want it real clear he didn't have no choice—either you or him was in imminent, life-threatening danger."

"I understand."

"Beal," he repeated. When he used my name that often it meant he was truly worried. "How about you let Blanton do the gun-toting? I don't think Swayne would be real happy to learn you're armed."

"Come on, Bill," I said. "You've heard the talk. There was a couple on the car chatting about odds on who's gonna die next. Mine weren't good."

Bill sighed and puffed on his cigarette for a minute. "It's true," he said at last. "I've never seen anything like it. People come up to me and say all sorts of crazy things. The other day one old lady told me I was going straight to heaven for defending you, and five minutes later here comes another one to tell me I was headed the opposite direction."

He shook his head. "It worries me, Beal," he said. "It ain't normal." He paused again. "It's normal to find murder and adultery interesting, that's just human nature. But this . . . They were jawing about it at the Royal the other night. Every damn one of 'em, including the bartender. I passed this group going on about what was the trouble with Lena, or were you the problem, or was Al, like it was a matter of life and death. Two of 'em were so mad they were about to take it outside."

He stared out the window at something I couldn't see. "You got to ask yourself why grown men would be ready to fight over another man's wife they don't even know. It ain't normal," he repeated emphatically. "And it don't . . . well, it don't really have anything to do with you or Lena or the Boyces or anybody else who's really *in* it. It's like they're talking and arguing about something personal and get mixed up, and use all y'all's names to do it."

He turned to face me. "Sorry, Beal. I should shut up and keep my rambling to myself." But he was Bill McLean Jr. Shutting up wasn't his strong suit.

"It worries me," he went on repeating himself. "You get two ol' boys arguing in a bar over some strange twat that neither one of 'em has a thing to do with and you got stuff going on you can't control."

I couldn't help it. I started laughing.

"Oh, Jesus, Beal," McLean said. "Jesus, I am so sorry. That was completely inappropriate. I'm done with this subject. I apologize." He stood up and for the only time I ever saw, he was blushing. He stuck out his hand.

I was still laughing. I shook his hand and said, "Yeah, the problems *that* twat has, you'd think they'd want nothing to do with it, and instead they're arguing over it." Bill looked startled, like I'd suddenly gone crazy, too. Then he burst out laughing. In those few moments, I felt free. I could see half a dozen futures out there that had nothing to do with her.

But soon we got started on Atwell's federal white slave charges and how I should answer this question or that one, and those other futures evaporated like morning dew in August.

59

"I'm going to California," she said, just as cold as ice. We were alone in the Steele parlor, standing on opposite sides of a small table next to two chairs covered in rose-colored velvet. I almost didn't recognize her, she was so thin.

"You plan to meet him out there, don't you?" I wanted to sound as cold as she did, but instead I sounded angry and my voice broke a little. "Don't think I won't know. I know everything you do."

Her body stiffened and her hand strayed to her temple but that voice kept right on coming. "You're such a liar," she said. "Why that jury didn't see right through you I do not know."

"*You're* talking to *me* about lying? The woman who lay in my bed bleeding from losing another man's baby is talking to *me* about lying?" I grabbed her wrist so tight she couldn't pull away.

"You're hurting me," she said, loudly enough to be heard outside the room. "Let me go." I did. But I swear to God I wanted to beat her 'til she couldn't say another word.

"Listen, Beal," she said, but the ice was beginning to crack, she was trembling. "I can't open a paper without reading a story about a woman I don't recognize they call by my name. People say things no decent woman wants to hear about anyone, let alone herself. I need to get away from all of it, and I'm going to California and you can't stop me."

I looked her up and down with disdain, so she'd know just how bad she looked. "I can't stop you, but I can sure make it plenty unpleasant."

"You've already managed that," she said, sticking her chin out.

"I can make it worse."

"What else could you *possibly* do?" She sounded sarcastic, but she looked frightened.

"Well, let's see." I started to count on my fingers. "One, I can make sure you never get to see our daughters."

"You can't," she said dismissively. "Any court would permit me to see them."

"That's assuming we're in divorce or separation proceedings and the court gets involved. We ain't. Do you want to start now? That'll be a field day for the press."

She was silent.

"Two," I went on, counting off the next finger. "I'll teach your daughters to hate your very name, and I'll do it so they won't even know I'm doing it."

"They will *never* hate me," she said, her voice rising with indignation. "When I saw them a week ago, they begged me to take them with me. You're the one they'll hate in the end."

"We'll see, but I don't think so. I'm not the one who wants to break up their family."

"Family?" she almost shrieked. "You call this a family? You and I can't hardly be in the same room together, let alone talk."

"We're a family, and we'll stay a family. That I promise you."

"Hah," she snorted, "you have no idea what you're talking about."

"I think I do. Let me count it out again for you. One, you won't see your children. Two, I'll teach 'em to hate you. Three, if you're thinking staying in touch with lover boy will be easier in California, I wouldn't count on it."

"I told you," she said, "I'm going there to get away from all this awful talk."

"I'll arrange for Nellie Steele to accompany you on your trip, so you won't feel lonely."

"I don't *want* Nellie," Lena protested. "Cousin Cootsie's coming."

"No, she ain't," I said flatly. "And here's number four—your whole family knows the best thing for you is to stick with me. In fact, your mother is here to talk to you about it."

Lena shook her head in disgust. "She's in Clayton."

"No, she ain't. And just to make sure we're clear—five is I'll tear up

Clara Sneed

creation if you ever go near that bastard again."

She sat down abruptly in one of the little velvet-covered chairs. After a while, she raised her head and looked me straight in the eyes. "You don't know what's inside me. You think if you bully me enough or do enough bad things, it'll die or change or go away. It won't."

I didn't have time to answer. I heard her mother's tentative voice greeting the house girl. Lena looked startled.

"Daughter," Mrs. Snyder said as she walked into the parlor without looking at me.

Lena rose. "Mama," she said warily. But when Mrs. Snyder touched her face gently, Lena crumpled into her arms and began to cry. Mrs. Snyder held her and made comforting noises.

"Mama, it's so terrible. Make him stop," Lena sobbed, her voice muffled by her mother's shoulder. "Mama, please make them stop. I'm not a terrible woman, I'm not."

Mrs. Snyder looked stricken. "Let's sit down, shall we, honey," she said softly and led Lena to the sofa, where she quieted for a few moments, only to burst out crying again.

"Mama, what did I ever do to any of them that they say such awful things? They don't even know me." Her voice rose to a wail.

Mrs. Snyder looked up like she hoped I'd give her some help, but I just shook my head. She flushed and looked away. Her hand paused above her daughter's back for a second or two, and then she lowered it and began to stroke her like she was calming a small child. "Lena," she repeated gently over and over.

When Lena was quiet at last and her shoulders had stopped shuddering, Mrs. Snyder said softly, "Honey, I don't know why people do other people like this, but they do. I don't know why they'll do a woman like this, but they do.

"I don't think your father and I . . ." she started, then stopped, then started again. "I don't think your father and I did all we should have to help you understand . . . to make you understand how things are." I saw Lena's back stiffen. Her mother felt it too and stopped talking for a few seconds, then started again, her voice once more uncertain.

"We let you girls . . . we spoiled you girls," she said, with a note of relief when she hit the word *spoiled* like she'd found the right thing to gloss things over. "You ended up thinking you could . . ." She faltered again.

"Be happy?" Lena said bitterly, sitting up abruptly to look her mother in the face.

Mrs. Snyder pulled back slightly. "No, that isn't what I mean," she said. "But there are things . . . there are things . . ."

"What things? What are you talking about, Mama?" Her voice was cold again.

"There are things you just can't *do*," said her mother almost violently, or at least as close to violently as a woman like her could. "Some things just won't work, Lena."

"Oh, for pity's sake, Mama, you're blaming me for this?" Lena cried furiously.

"I'm not blaming you," said Mrs. Snyder. "I'm saying you're not judging the world or your position in it clearly."

"Mama," said Lena, "you don't understand and I guess you never will."

"I understand more than you think," responded Mrs. Snyder. "Watching you and Al together as youngsters, way back when, I thought you were right for each other."

That was news to me and apparently to Lena, too. She looked as startled as I felt.

"Why didn't you say anything, Mama?" Lena asked.

"Lena, look at yourself," said her mother, shaking her head, but speaking gently. "You don't listen if it ain't what you want to hear. You wanted to marry Beal and you did. Don't you remember? I asked you a few days before the wedding if you were really sure he'd make you happy."

Lena's pale face flushed. "You were right," she said eagerly. "I see that now, Mama. I was too young. I thought—"

"You thought he'd make you happy and he didn't. He doesn't." She made a point of not looking at me.

"No," Lena said, "and he hasn't for a long time. And Mama—"

"It's too late," she said. "It's all gone too far."

Lena just stared at her with her chin stuck out and started rubbing her temple again.

"Honey," Mrs. Snyder went on, "the world don't see men and women the same."

"It's not fair," cried Lena.

"No," said Mrs. Snyder. There was a moment of silence before she continued. "A decent woman can't live without her reputation, and you won't survive long as an indecent one."

"I could do anything if I can be with the man who makes me happy," cried Lena passionately. "Albert will protect me. We can live where no one knows us." She resisted when her mother tried to take her hand.

"It's too late," Mrs. Snyder repeated. "For your own sake and your daughters', and even for Al's, you've got to give up and make the best of it."

"No," Lena shouted. "You don't understand, Mama. It's my life, it's my heart and my soul. It's like asking me to cut off my arm or my leg. I can't." She started to cry again.

Mrs. Snyder's own eyes filled. She said again, "I understand more than you think."

"No, you don't," said Lena adamantly. "You don't or you wouldn't talk to me this way. You'd know—"

"I *do* know," said Mrs. Snyder, speaking with a kind of desperate determination. "You think I don't or you hope I don't or you pray I don't, but I do. You've got to give your lover up and settle down to your marriage. It's the only course that leads to a life that you, Lena Snyder, can actually live. You're not a woman who can leave her children behind without a second thought. You're not a woman who can build her entire life around a man you've given up everything for. You've been petted and pampered your whole life. You're not prepared to give that up, no matter what you tell me. Soon enough, you'd miss everything you left behind." This was a side of Mrs. Snyder I'd never seen. She was so clear she sounded like her husband.

"Mama, how *dare* you take Beal's side? How dare you? Haven't I proved to you what I can do?" Lena's hands were bunched into fists.

"Oh, honey," said Mrs. Snyder, heavily. "I'm not taking Beal's side. I'm taking yours. You're just too blind to see it. I wish you had married Al. But you didn't. And the man you did marry is as sly and stubborn as an old goat, and as murderous and devious a silver-tongued devil as any that resides in hell." She did look at me then. Her hatred was so pure it shot like a bolt of lightning across the room.

Lena seized her arm and shrieked, "Then how can you want me to stay with him?"

"Look at me," said Mrs. Snyder, her voice heavier still. "Look at me," she repeated.

Lena turned to her slowly, lower lip trembling.

"You've got no choice." She emphasized each word. "You do anything but go back to your husband and somebody else, maybe lots of others, will die."

There was complete silence except for the grandfather clock ticking away in the corner.

Then Mrs. Snyder said, "It isn't fair, it isn't right, it isn't just—whatever you want to say about all that, I won't disagree. But you got no choice."

Lena stood up in a fury. "Oh, yes, I *do*," she cried. "You always were a coward, Mama. You got no more spine than a jellyfish. And *you*," she said, turning to me and narrowing her eyes. "You think you can manipulate and twist and turn everybody and everything, but you can't. You're a liar and a coward and a cheat and a murderer, and one fine day the world will know it. I will not be stuck with you for the rest of my life. I will not."

Buoyed by her fury, she swept from the room. I looked at Mrs. Snyder, but she turned away.

"Beal," she said in a voice like an animal growling. "Let her go." Her voice rose. "For God's sake, let her go!"

Clara Sneed

60

I didn't, of course. Let her go, that is. By mid-August 1912, I had her and my girls on the Milam County farm where I'd been born. Marvin had inherited it after our father's murder. She'd come back from California. We'd been living together in Dallas. And Al was back in Texas.

Of course it was hot: The Gulf clouds piled up every morning and disappeared by noon, no rain in them at all. Dust coated the leaves of the grapevines that lined the dirt road to the farmhouse. John Blanton and I were out in that heat most every afternoon, winging bottles off fence posts for target practice. I worked hard on my draw. The cicadas were so loud we could hear them over the whining bullets and breaking glass.

On occasion, Blanton took the car into Calvert for supplies and I'd be on my own at target practice. One such evening, after I'd been shooting for a while, I headed down to the sharecropper quarters. Old Henry was sitting in a beat-up rocker on the little front porch of one of the gray wood cabins set among a bunch of post oaks. A cat was on his lap and a few skinny hounds lay in the dust beneath the trees. There were chickens scratching under the house and a swaybacked mule switching flies in the little corral out back.

When he saw I intended to come right up to the porch, Henry pushed the cat off his lap, took hold of the cane propped next to the rocker, and made a move to stand up. His dark fingers were so gnarled it looked like the cane had sprouted roots.

"Don't bother," I said and sat down in the straight chair on the other side of the entrance.

"That don't seem right," said Henry mildly, but he stayed put. I was silent. He'd stopped rocking. After a few minutes, he cleared his throat and said, "There's some cool water in the house."

"Don't trouble yourself," I said. "Do you want me to get you some?"

"No, Mr. Sneed," Henry said, "much obliged, but no." He said this easily, but of course he must have wondered. Like any colored back then, he knew how to keep a poker face when dealing with whites. But the colored folks always know at least as well as the white folks what's going on with white folks, and I reckon I made him nervous.

We sat in silence for a while. In a little bit, his chair started creaking rhythmically against the porch floor. One of the hounds under the tree commenced to scratch. Henry and I swatted flies.

"I suppose you've heard about my troubles, Henry," I said finally.

Henry answered in the same easy tone that hid whatever he may have really thought or felt, "Yassuh, Mr. Sneed." He paused. "I'se sorry yo' family been troubled some lately."

"I appreciate that, Henry," I said and sighed. "Sometimes I wonder if it's easier being black."

I reckon Henry had to think on how to deal with that ridiculous statement because he stayed quiet for some time. "Well, Mr. Sneed," he finally replied, "I don' suppose life is easy for many on this earth. That don' seem to be how it's laid out."

"You're right," I said. "It don't seem laid out like that."

More silence. I noticed some arrowheads lined up on a rickety table beneath one of the cabin windows. "How many years it take you to find all them arrowheads?" I asked.

"A good many," said Henry. "They plenty down there in the Bottom, but a body got to keep his eyes open."

"I wonder if it was easier being an Indian. They didn't have this black folks and white folks thing to deal with, for one thing," I said. "You must think some on that."

There was another pause. "Yassuh," Henry answered, betting on formula.

"Do you ever wish you was white, Henry?" I said, twisting around to face him directly. "Or do you ever wish you was Indian?" I was looking straight at him so he didn't have much choice about answering, but he came up with a way to avoid the direct question.

"I'se part Indian," he said. "My mother was part Seminole, and my daddy always said there was some Choctaw in his family. Other things, too." He meant white, but he wasn't about to say so.

He looked out of his old eyes at me directly at last and said, "Mr. Sneed, I see white folks with a lotta things I'd like to have, but lotsa times y'all don't seem so happy."

He paused again. "You please excuse me for sayin' so."

I stood up. "Nothing to excuse," I said. "It's just the truth." I looked around and added, "Anything y'all need, you let me know, y'hear?"

"Yassuh, Mr. Sneed, thank you." Henry said. Back to formula.

I stepped off the porch. The dogs followed me a little ways and then returned to their spot under the trees. I had to get out of there. I was afraid if I didn't I'd tell Henry everything.

Instead, I grew a beard and blackened it with shoe polish. Then I headed to Amarillo and rented a little cottage on Polk Street under the name of Stenson.

PART III

ON POLK STREET

Clara Sneed

61

September 14, 1912, Amarillo, Texas

That hard rain the other evening made a mess of Polk Street, even with the new pavement. And late last night, when he and Lynn were coming back from Groom, the automobile got stuck in the mud just south of town. They'd had to go pull it out first thing this morning. What with the late night and early morning, Al is tired. But as he shuts the door behind him, he feels the cool, invigorating September air. The leaves on the young trees in the front yard are now tinged with red. The year is turning.

These days, one thing often calls to another, it seems, and the present gets all mixed up with the past. The red-edged leaves bring to mind a wildfire licking at the edge of the horizon years ago out on the old XIT. He suddenly remembers it so clearly it's like he's still there, like there's a movie camera inside his mind recording everything, one that can capture color, sound, smell, and feelings, not just images in black and white. Sometimes he's just about certain that if he could only turn the corner into the sitting room quickly enough he'd find his father there reading the newspaper, spectacles on and feet propped up on the little stool Cousin Mary embroidered a cover for a few Christmases back. And if he walked over to the Tyler Street house, Lena would be there waiting for him.

He steps onto Polk Street now just the way he did back then. But the house on Tyler belongs to someone else; Lena is gone; his father is dead.

62

Back then, his heart pounded every time he removed his hat and smoothed his hair and knocked on her door. At the sight of one another they beamed like twin suns. And though their first conversations were casual, about the books they were using as an excuse for the visits, or people in town, or crops or cattle, or wet versus dry, the talk soon changed to dreams and secrets and flowed without stopping.

And then one day Beal phoned up from Paducah. Lena was flushed and angry, but trying to hide it when she returned to the parlor and sat down again on the sofa. Al said, "Are you happy?" It wasn't exactly a question.

She said nothing for a few minutes, just looked at him with those liquid dark eyes, so open that he caught his breath like he was in the presence of something vast and fleeting. Many things passed between them then for which words were useless.

Words are often useless is what he's found, or they're worse than useless, they actually get in the way. But on that sofa two springs ago, he and Lena had the luxury of speaking only with their eyes and they did. Finally, she said, "No, I'm not happy."

He placed his index finger gently against her mouth and felt her lips' smooth skin against his finger as a species of miracle. "You're meant to be happy," he said in a voice just barely above a whisper. "You of all people are meant to be happy."

"So are you," she said, just as quietly.

Al went back the next day and the day after that and the day after that, until Beal came home from Paducah.

"I don't have words for what I feel for you," said Lena.

"Shhh," said Al. "I know."

He never has needed words the way she does. But there is something about all the lies getting told that makes him want to find the right ones. How can people have words so ready for lies when he and Lena still can't seem to find a way to explain to people the one thing in this whole mess that isn't a lie? The bitterness that rises up in him at times is almost unbearable, but the worst of it is that he can't feel it as purely directed at Beal. It always falls back and spills over Al himself.

One afternoon, directly after his return to Amarillo, he'd gone out to Llano with his mother. A hard wind had set in to blowing and the cords running up the flagpole at the cemetery entrance snapped against the wood. Al helped his mother out of the car and they walked the short distance to his father's grave, set near Bessie's. Supporting her by the elbow, Al read the newly chiseled words: *Faithful to every duty.* To the west, lightning stretched its fingers down like a skeleton set on fire.

"Oh, Lord, I'm sorry," Al said in a strangled voice. The words hurt coming out, like he was spitting up glass. "Pa, I'm so sorry."

His mother trembled against his arm. "Ma," he said, without turning to look at her, "I'm sorry."

She just shook harder, so hard he feared she might fly apart, the bolts that held her in place shearing until they gave way and she scattered over the ground in a rain of broken pieces.

"Look," she said, her voice harsh with pain, pointing to a spot a few feet away. "There's your place."

"Ma, please," he said desperately, pleading with her—about everything, really— *"please."*

"There's your place," she repeated. She pulled herself away to face him. *"Jesus knows all about our struggles.* That's what it will say. I've already thought it through."

While Al stood shocked and silent, she walked to the car, where she stood with her forehead pressed against the passenger-side window. Her back shook so hard and so rhythmically it looked like she was crying at last, but when he returned to the car he saw her eyes were still dry.

"Get in, Ma, please," he said, opening the door. He helped her in, then stood for a moment listening to the thunder and looking out at the rain falling in sheets some miles away on the plains.

63

He and Lynn had agreed about the land they'd looked at yesterday: Too dry, too scrubby, overpriced. But after all those cold months in Canada with too little to do, the business of checking out land and cattle relieves him. If God ever created a time and place to inspire a man to get and stay drunk, he told Lynn, Canada in the winter is it.

Though he's promised Lena and his mother he won't drink again, privately he thinks Lena's talking is at least as dangerous. He's not a talky drunk, nor a belligerent one. If anything, he gets quieter. But Lena relieves the pressure by talking. She talks to try to explain, or convince people to help, or maybe just to feel better. And then the people she talks to decide it's safer to side with Beal. Al has noticed a definite pattern. He's got no confidence at all in that John Blanton—he's Beal's *bodyguard*, for God's sake—but Lena is convinced Blanton is secretly on their side. Still, Al has kept his word about the drinking—he's stone-cold sober and has been for a while. Neither of those women has any idea how hard it is.

During the trial, Beal's lawyers, especially Bill McLean Jr., had routinely referred to Al as "the whiskey and cigarette fiend."

"*Way* more than made the papers," according to Lynn. "It didn't matter how often Hanger objected."

They were sitting in Al's bedroom, gazing out at the spindly trees and the hot midday sun the way they used to before all this got started, though the trees had grown some.

"I wanted to *kill* that hypocritical sonofabitch McLean," Lynn said, talking about the day he'd caused the big ruckus. "He smokes twice as much as you do and I bet he sucks down whiskey like mother's milk. And I had to apologize to him. Henry and Will were so pissed off I thought they was gonna kill me."

That made Al laugh, which was something these days. He could imagine just exactly how pissed off Will and Henry had been and said so. "You have *no* idea," said Lynn. "Goddammit," he shouted, imitating Henry in one of his rare rages. "What the hell do you think you're *doing*? Jesus Christ! Attacking lawyers in court, running off with other people's wives. Jesus Christ on a quarter horse. There's days I don't blame Beal one bit, and believe me, if *I* feel that way, how do you think that jury feels?"

Lynn paced back and forth and pounded his fist on the wall a few times for emphasis. Al was laughing so hard he was choking. It sounded just like Henry when he got mad. He'd learned a lot from the old man about blowing his stack.

"Yeah," said Lynn, "and then Will piled on citing cases and precedents until I totally lost track of the argument except the part about I'd fucked up. Which I admitted right away but that didn't even slow 'em down. By the time they was through, I wanted to get ol' Swayne on the phone and tell him I'd stay in the calaboose the rest of my life if he'd just tell the sheriff I couldn't have no visitors, *especially* not family."

"I don't know how they stand it—do you?" said Al, wiping his eyes. They'd talked about this many times, and to do so again reassured him that some things stayed the same.

"No," said Lynn, "I'd go nuts if I had to sit around all day thinking about loans or lawsuits."

"It was terrible in Canada that way," said Al. "Cold all the time and dark most of it and I was stuck in hotel rooms with nothing to do. Lord, I wanted to come back home. And everybody was telling me not to; it would make things worse."

"Yeah," said Lynn, "it would have, although . . ." He trailed off. "*I* made things worse. I did, even though it hurts to admit it."

"You're not to blame," Al said. There was short silence between them.

"That sonofabitch," Lynn said.

"That sonofabitch."

Clara Sneed

Though he's heading downtown now, he mostly went uptown in the spring of 1911. Instead of turning left, he'd turn right at the Polk Street house gate, stroll down to Fifteenth, and head one block over to the Sneed house on Tyler. It got to be so familiar that sometimes even now he has to stop himself from walking that way. All the twists and turns things have taken since, life nothing like the straight-lined streets of Amarillo. Al's been thinking lately about one afternoon in particular, wondering about what hadn't happened then and what might have happened if it had.

He and Lena had been sitting close together in her parlor, clasping hands. She whispered, "I lie awake at night and I imagine you. I feel your mouth and your tongue. I smell you and taste you and it all feels right the way nothing ever has."

He kissed her. Everything in the room looked brighter and clearer afterward. "It sets the world right," he said, which was the best he ever did.

"But Albert," she went on in the earnest way she had when she was trying to put things into words that didn't go there easily. "I'm married. And . . . maybe it would be better for you to leave me alone. I think you can have a good life with another woman and . . ." She pulled herself away from him.

"Is that what you want?" he said, his insides clenching up.

"No," she answered, her face as open as a girl's. "I want to be with you forever. I want to have children and grow old with you and have grandchildren we spoil who laugh about the old folks behind our backs. But I don't want to see you suffer. And right now I love you enough to send you away." She turned as if from the pain she didn't want to witness. He tried to take her hand, but she pulled away. "Soon, I won't have the strength."

Then she faced him again and he saw agony in her eyes, as shocking as if she had just walked into the parlor naked. "I won't have the strength," she repeated. "I barely have it now . . ."

"You can't send me away," he said, taking her head in both his hands. "I don't want to go. We'll just have to get you divorced so you can marry me."

She started to cry. Partly it was from relief that they weren't going to say goodbye, and partly it was from shock at the idea of divorce—she'd never thought she'd be that kind of woman—but now he wonders if it was also because something inside her knew what was coming. Maybe all along there had been only one right action and that day they'd failed to take it. They'd left a hole in things and all the broken world had come in through it.

His mother certainly sees it like that. For her, the whole thing was nothing but sin right from the start. She doesn't understand that once there was nothing of sin in it at all.

By the time Lena came to see her on July 22, Al and Lena considered themselves married in the sight of God and Lena was speaking with a mystical sense of the truth of their union. Since his mother had always liked Lena, and her first question was bound to be what Lena thought, they'd decided she'd react better if Lena broke the news. Al went out driving to leave the coast clear.

It was Election Day 1911. They were voting on wet versus dry yet again and Al's father was out campaigning for Cone Johnson, an irony mentioned repeatedly during the trial. Al naturally didn't favor prohibition, but he wasn't thinking about that much, although while he was out he made sure to vote against it and for Cone.

Texas flags were waving and red, white, and blue bunting was everywhere. People passed by in automobiles and wagons with bullhorns and leaflets urging his vote for this candidate or that one. Some of the Carrie Nation types were standing at the edge of the Bowery proclaiming the benefits of going dry. The drunks, he noticed, had all vanished, except for one poor bastard who was passed out in the sun at the edge of the sidewalk. He'd wet himself and there was a pool of vomit a few inches from his head. Since he lay still and kept quiet, he was useful to the woman with a bullhorn who was pointing him out as an illustration of the wages of sin.

Taken by a sudden impulse, Al stopped the car at the corner and left it idling while he walked over to the man, picked him up under his shoulders and dragged him to the covered part of the sidewalk in front of a saloon. He wiped his face with a handkerchief and propped his hat on his lolling head so it more or less covered his eyes. Then he walked back to the car, tipping his own hat to the ladies.

The car backfired when Al shifted into gear, so he missed how his act was portrayed by the sisters. The Good Samaritan, possibly, but probably something angrier, along the lines of God Punishes the Wicked Sinner and Woe to Him Who Interferes. There was a lot of that going around, Al noticed. People seemed to love their punishing God way more than they loved the forgiving one.

Helping the drunk calmed Al's spirits and made him feel like somehow things would come out all right. But when he got back to the house, his mother called from the parlor, "Albert, is that you?" And he knew right away that they hadn't. Lena was nowhere to be seen.

"I sent her home," said his mother. She was sitting on the sofa in her perfectly erect way. The parlor was cool and dark, at least relative to the heat outside. Sister Bessie used to say their mother thought she had to *look* straight and narrow to keep her family on the straight and narrow. She was looking exceptionally straight and narrow now. It startled Al to realize how easily he'd believed something was possible that he should have known wasn't.

"Albert," she said firmly, "sit down."

"Yes, ma'am," replied Al, as he'd been taught to do since he could talk. He chose one of the old horsehair chairs they'd brought with them from Channing and tried to match her erect posture with his own.

"Albert, what can you be thinking?" she said. "Why didn't you talk to me yourself?"

"We thought it would be better this way, Ma." He wanted to explain more, but she shook her head.

"She's promised me she won't see you again," she said.

"*What?*" he said. "She did not."

"Yes, son," said his mother firmly, "she did. I told her how wrong it was and that you would both regret it. I told her that her children would suffer. I told her that you deserved to marry a woman who was free and hadn't been married before so you could start fresh."

He could imagine Lena hearing her own words in that last part.

"She's the one I want and love," he said stubbornly, bowing his head slightly and looking out from under his brows as he has since he was a boy when his mind is made up. "You had no right to make her promise that."

"*You* have no right to break up Beal Sneed's marriage," snapped his mother.

"It's no kind of marriage," said Al. "She's miserably unhappy. I'm sure she told you."

"Yes, she did," said his mother bitingly, "but neither one of you understands the first thing about unhappiness. She's been a charming, spoiled girl her whole life and now she's bored and you come along and she perks up and thinks life will be roses and violins with you and it won't."

"Ma," he pleaded, "it's not like that. I never expected to feel anything like this in my life. It's the same for her. Please, Ma. You have to believe me."

His mother's shoulders drooped then, the straight and narrow softening into what looked like hopeless and hurt him to see.

"It's hopeless, son," she said, like she'd heard his thoughts. There was something in her eyes he didn't remember seeing before that made her look old. "The love makes it hopeless."

"Then you *do* see we love one another," he said eagerly, seizing on that part because the rest made no sense.

She was quiet for a few moments. "I was hoping you didn't," she finally said.

"I don't think Beal is happy either," Al said, trying to make things clearer. "Lena says they've talked about separating. She says—"

"She told me," his mother said curtly. "She said she was your soul affinity, but I told her plainly that she was your mistress, and not to make it out to be more than it was."

"But Ma," he protested. "You just said—"

"So you *are* lovers," his mother cut him off again. "She wouldn't admit it."

"Neither am I," Al snapped, but it was too late. He was no good at this stuff. He knew how to say it like it was and how to shut up. He got all messed up with the in-between.

"*Please*, Albert," his mother said in exasperation. "I've lived a long time. I'll say to you what I wouldn't to her. I don't approve of adultery but it's one of those sins that . . . well, people commit quite a bit. It's not right but it's not the end of the world, and marriages often survive it. I've seen some that have thrived."

Al was shocked. He didn't think his mother knew about the things in town he knew about.

"You're shocked," she said bluntly, "but you shouldn't be. And I . . . I wouldn't be saying this if I didn't think this thing is more dangerous than adultery. Because—"

"Because we love each other?" Al said incredulously. "You would rather that I . . . she . . ."

"I would rather that this thing not destroy you," said his mother fiercely. "*That's* what I'd rather. You don't know, you're too young to remember, but I've seen others . . ." She started to cry and he didn't know what to do. He wasn't sure he even knew what they were talking about anymore.

"You don't know what you've gotten into," she said, looking up at him, still crying. "You're blind to it."

"Ma," he said, rushing to sit beside her on the sofa. He took her hand and kissed it. "I'm not blind. For the first time in my life, I feel like I can really see. It'll be all right, I promise you."

"You *can't*," she said. "You don't remember, you're too young. Old sheriff Gober's wife ended up on their bed with their tenant beside her. Both dead. I'm sure they didn't think they were blind either."

"Oh, Ma," Al said, relieved to be dealing with something specific. "Lena and I aren't going to end up dead on Beal's bed. He'll give her a divorce. He's as fed up as she is."

"We'll see," said his mother, sounding doubtful but looking like she'd stirred from whatever trance she'd been in. She resumed her straight-and-narrow position, which for Al was now a relief. "I want you to leave town for a while," she said in a voice that matched her posture. "Give her a chance to repair her marriage. It's what's best for her future, and yours."

"My future is hers," Al said. "And if it's better for her to be with Beal, I'll leave her alone. I want her to be happy. It's more important to me than anything else."

His mother stood up and smoothed her skirt. "I know," she said in a discouraged voice.

64

His boots strike the new sidewalk as he walks down Polk Street in the rain-cleaned, breezy daylight—that sidewalk is an improvement for sure. A boy in a cap and short pants pedals by on a bicycle, riding deliberately through a puddle. The muddy water splatters his bare legs, barely missing Al. The boy turns to check the damage with a look of guilt so delighted that it makes Al laugh. The boy shrugs his shoulder, grins, and pedals on, right past Lee Bivins, who is turning the corner at Eleventh. Al waves, but Lee doesn't see him. One thing leads to another; Lee had been a pallbearer at the funeral. And so, without wanting to, Al recalls the terrible night of January 13. Amarillo is now full of that kind of reminder.

He'd been at the Regina Hotel, pouring out his heart in a letter to Lena when he'd heard urgent pounding on the door and known instantly that something awful had happened. He was terrified it had happened to her. Then he found out it had happened to his father. He'd barely been able to finish the letter. *It will be my pleasure and duty to avenge him, I may return at once to Texas. I can't write more. I love you with all the strength I possess and will to my death. I love you, I love you. Good night.*

The fantasies of killing Beal had begun that night, though at first Al didn't consider them fantasies. They were more like prevision—Al had an obligation to kill his father's killer. But he soon realized things weren't that simple, and not just because Henry kept wiring him to stay put. The Canadian lawyer Murray, and finally Al himself, came to the same conclusion—let the public focus on Beal killing an innocent old man and not get distracted by Al storming down from the frozen north.

But staying put did damage to Al's sense of himself. The fantasies became part of trying to heal it. Often he imagined a confrontation on the streets of Amarillo; Beal drew first, but Al drew faster. Sometimes he pictured shooting Beal point blank, and damn the consequences. At other times he dreamed they were back in the '70s, when the plains were unfenced and no one would have expected him to do anything but shoot Beal. It would doubtless have started a feud—plenty had started over less—but it would have been *justice*.

All the feelings he'd had that night and in the days following got stuck in his heart and mind. They're like a patch of quicksand or a nest of cottonmouths—he tries to keep his distance but he knows they're there. There are times when it's hard to remember that he ever felt comfortable in his own skin.

"You're asking too much of love," Beal's brother Joe had told him when he and Al were at Mineral Wells early in the summer of 1911. They'd been sitting beside one of the indoor pools, their hair wet and their fingertips slightly shriveled from the water.

"I know my brother ain't the most thrilling husband a woman could have," Joe went on. "Hell, if I was a woman, I'd probably pick you, too. But Beal ain't . . . well, it just ain't gonna be simple with Beal."

Joe paused, but Al kept quiet.

"Nothing is simple with Beal, no matter how it may appear," Joe continued. "Give this thing some time. Go on back to Montana or you and Lynn get y'all a stake in New Mexico or just stay put in the Pecos. There's times if you let something alone, it'll come to you without you lifting a finger."

"You mean you think he might go on and give her a divorce if I ain't around," said Al.

"I think it's possible," said Joe, looking at his pale feet in the deck chair as if he were examining them from a telescope. "I know they ain't been getting along."

Al considered the proposition. He trusted Joe—he didn't think Joe would tell him a divorce was possible if he didn't believe it. But Al had an intuition, something warning him at funny times, in the dead of night when he woke up unexpectedly, or first thing in the morning. It told him that their best chance was to light out without telling anyone.

A few weeks after Mineral Wells, he and Lena were down at his family cabin in Palo Duro Canyon. The rising sun's light came through partly closed curtains. Wild turkeys gobbled just outside the window and mourning doves were calling. The room smelled of sweat and toilet water and come.

"What if we just ran off?" he said, feeling so happy that many things seemed easy which weren't. "Maybe to Cuba?" He danced his fingers down her uncovered thigh.

"What if we did?" she answered lightly, her mouth moving against his shoulder. She paused and then spoke more seriously. "It might be better to go farther. What about Brazil?" She rolled onto her back and looked up at the ceiling as if she could see Rio there.

Happiness seemed to rise before them the way the sun did, just that sure and magical.

"It might be safer that way," he said.

"I hate the idea of hiding," she said, still staring at the ceiling. "I want to shout all up and down Polk Street, *Lena Snyder loves Albert Boyce.*" She'd quit using her married name with him some weeks before. "I'm not ashamed of this," she went on. "It's my marriage that shames me, because it's a sham. *This*"—she touched his breastbone with her fingers and then touched her own—"is real."

"Yes," he said, kissing her softly. "It is. Still, there's that little piece of paper called a marriage license . . ." He smiled. It was hard to take it seriously at the moment. Every obstacle seemed as flimsy as that paper.

"I really don't want to run," she answered in a serious tone. "My girls would think their mother didn't love them. But," her voice dropped almost to a whisper, "I get so scared. Sometimes I think I made us up. When he's home and everything looks the way it always has, I wonder if I'm going crazy."

"Maybe if I bought you something like a locket?" Al suggested. "You could touch it when you get scared and tell yourself that all this is just that real and solid."

"You're so good to me," she said gratefully. "You understand me. I'd love a locket, but he might ask about it."

"I thought he wasn't noticing that way," Al said.

"He mostly isn't," she answered, "but every now and then he'll surprise me." She burrowed in closer to his chest. He could feel her slight weight in his arms.

"Well," he whispered, "what about my handkerchief? You can keep it in your pocket and when you feel doubtful, just give it a squeeze." He paused, then said in a normal tone of voice, "You might want to wash it first," which had the effect he'd hoped, of making her laugh.

"No," she said. "It'll smell like you, and you're what I want."

Clara Sneed

65

The Canadian papers had loved printing articles in which Al said preposterous things he would never have said, even if he'd agreed to talk with the reporters, which he hadn't. He frequently appeared with tears in his eyes, shaking his fist at the heavens and swearing revenge. The writers always managed to work in how taciturn he was—*a man of few words, with a steely gaze and cool manner that hint of danger*—but he sure did talk a lot according to the reports they filed.

In Texas, we hold life much less dear than we hold honor. My father was an honorable man, and Beal Sneed is not. I will avenge him. One of us must die. Things of that nature. Even if he thought some of it was true, he would never have said so to the reporters and he wouldn't have sounded so much like one of their serial stories saying it.

Before Beal found them, their hotel rooms had been like little gift boxes containing what they most needed: Time and space together. But those same rooms began to feel like prisons after she'd gone. Al had never liked being indoors much, but in Canada that winter there wasn't a whole lot of choice. The blizzards tore in just about every day. And even if the weather let up, he hated leaving the hotel because of the reporters. They'd be laughing and smoking and horsing around 'til they caught sight of him and then they were like a wolf pack, surrounding him in an instant, all hollering at once, "Mr. Boyce! Hey, Al! Hey there, Tex."

If he managed to get a taxi, they'd press their bodies and faces against it until the cursing driver hit the gas, and even then a few of them would trot alongside, clutching their pencils like magic wands they hoped would conjure him to talk. "Any comments on your father's death, Tex? Could you say a few words about your plans?"

All of it shocked him: The cold, the relentlessness of the reporters, the way he felt alone as he never had before. He asked Murray to arrange for Immigration to send him her clothes so he could smell under the arms of her dresses, her corsets and bloomers, the place where her hair had lain across the neck of her dressing gown. He thought it might restore him a bit. And it helped, but not enough. Sometimes Al thought it would be a relief to walk out into the blizzard and just keep going.

The worst was the day he read the reports of his mother's testimony and Lynn's attack on McLean. Part of him wanted to finish the job on McLean. Part of him wanted to holler, "Lock me up before I cause any more harm." And part of him felt like either of those alternatives was better than the torture of sitting in that hotel room, unable to do anything useful at all. He badly wanted a drink. But he remembered his promise.

The summer before, he'd been coming off a two-day drunk and had a bad case of the shakes when Lena had phoned to say that Beal had gone back to Paducah and the coast was clear. Though he showered and shaved and put on fresh clothes, he still stunk of whiskey and cigarettes and his hands trembled visibly. At the sight of him, her eyes filled. "I'm so sorry," she said.

"You've got no reason," he answered curtly. "I'm the one who's sorry—in more ways than one."

They were out on the gallery in the deep dusk; her girls were in bed. "Come on," Lena said, touching his face gently. "Let me get you a cup of coffee and then we'll walk around a while." In that moment, she reminded him of the angel in stained glass at Polk Street Methodist, touching her feet to earth and causing flowers to bloom.

They walked the streets for hours. When the worst of it had passed, he said, "Lena, I'm so sorry. It's just . . ."

"You don't know what to do," she said.

"No," he said. "And I'm used to knowing." He paused, then said decisively, "I won't get drunk on you like this again. It don't help." He tried for a light note. "I couldn't draw right with a fifteen-minute head start."

277

"Please don't joke about it," she said, clutching his arm.

"Shhh," he said, kissing the top of her head. "I won't do this again."

And he hadn't. Not like that. But after reading about his mother and Lynn and McLean at the trial, all he wanted was to drink 'til he'd warmed up inside and could pretend that everything was going to come out all right or that none of it mattered all that much, or some other comforting false thing. He fought the impulse for about an hour, but by then he could almost see the bartender's easy, practiced movements and smell the whiskey.

Wrapped up in an overcoat and mufflers, his hat pulled down, he tipped a room service waiter to let him out the kitchen door. Then he trudged through the snow to a little place on a side street he'd noticed a few days earlier. It was practically empty and the bartender—a stout, balding man about his own age with a thick moustache and a heavy lower lip that bulged like a peeled fruit—handed him his whiskey without any small talk. Al took the first sip with deep and silent gratitude.

He was fully clothed when he came to. The clock said 2:25 and Al worked out from the light coming through the side of the blinds that it must be afternoon. His overcoat was wadded up on the floor and his hat was lying upside down in the open doorway to the bathroom. When he first tried to stand, he had to sit right back down because he was so dizzy. Eventually, though, he managed to stagger to the bathroom and vomit. In the mirror, he saw a two-day beard and a bruise on his forehead he couldn't remember getting.

He tried to shave, but his hand shook so badly he went back to bed. It was dark when he woke up. On the bedside table was a telegram, wrinkled as if he'd crumpled it and then tried to smooth it out again. It was from Lena and he had no recollection of seeing, getting, or reading it. *Be careful. Best to leave Winnipeg. People near house.*

What is she talking about? He wondered. *Did I answer her?*

He was struggling to remember when there was a sharp rap on the door and a voice called, "Western Union."

Very worried. Wire you are safe, Al read once he'd managed to open the telegram. He felt her terror through the wire's terse conventions as if she were standing next to him.

Am sick, was what he ended up wiring back. It was the truth, but only part of it and he knew she would think he meant something else. *Leaving Winnipeg Weds.*

That very night, after he'd cleaned himself up and the shaking had subsided, he wrote her a letter. *Forgive me,* he began. *Please forgive me. I was drunk for a couple of days. I have no excuses.*

He'd read her answering letter with a sense of both relief and pain. *I want to write about you being sick, but oh, Albert, <u>I can't</u>. It almost killed me but I know the temptation was awful and that you have suffered as much as I have from it, and oh, precious heart, I know you won't <u>ever do it again.</u> I thank God you didn't drink very much and I know you wouldn't ever be untrue to me. That is the one thing I could never live with. Where a woman's love is her life, there is no need to ask forgiveness.*

It wasn't true that he didn't drink very much, but it was true he didn't do it for very long and maybe that was what she meant. He *was* sure there had been no other woman. His conscience was entirely clear, and he didn't think it would be if he'd cheated, even if he couldn't remember doing it.

One of the surprising things about his notoriety was how often he had the opportunity. Every few days, an unknown woman wrote him or introduced herself. They all said more or less the same thing: "You must be so lonely. Let me help you forget." He'd been taught to divide women into two groups—decent ones and soiled doves—but the women offering themselves appeared to be in some third category he didn't understand. They looked quite respectable and they never suggested charging him, but he'd never heard of a respectable woman offering herself to a complete stranger.

"I recognized you from your picture," said one young woman who stopped him as he was leaving a restaurant he'd managed to get to without any reporters spotting him. She couldn't have been more than twenty, tall and well-formed with clear, almost golden eyes. She laid a gloved hand on his arm and leaned in to say quietly, "I have such sympathy for you."

"Thank you," Al mumbled, trying to pull away as she inched closer.

"When I read your story," she went on intently, "I felt that we were destined to cross paths and you see"—she smiled at him—"that's what happened."

"Thank you," Al repeated with growing alarm.

"Oh, you are so welcome," she said. "I . . . I long to console you. I think we are destined to—"

"Excuse me," said Al, yanking his arm away and jumping into a cab so fast he startled the driver. As with the reporters, as time went on he'd gotten better at escape, but he remained confused and a little spooked by these women. What were they looking for and why did they think they would find it with him?

It was part of the crazy falseness passing for truth that had surrounded him and Lena for months now. He didn't know what part of the falseness the young women seized on, but they used it as a foundation and kept on building, constructing *castles in the air*, as his mother would say. The stock phrase had never seemed so apt. Sometimes he could just about see them, with their stairs that led nowhere and their off-kilter turrets, like the enormous headdresses Indian warriors wore on the cover of dime-store novels.

66

Now, months after that cold winter in Canada, this terrible year of 1912 is running toward its end. He's back in Amarillo, heading downtown with an unmailed letter in his pocket. Behind him, in the house on Polk Street, his mother waits, still dressed in deep mourning. On Sundays, she sits in their pew at First Baptist praying silently, all in black, black veil over her face, black gloves laid beside her. The only time he sees her smile in a way that looks genuine is when Lynn's wife Hilma brings the grandbabies to visit.

These two women—his mother and Lena—are the twin pillars his life seems to stand between. Except they're nothing like real pillars: They walk and talk and have minds of their own and can't stand one another. About the only thing they've ever agreed on is his drinking.

He sees his grim-faced mother at the house every day and Lena in his dreams every night. Sometimes she stands smiling at him from a snow-covered street in Winnipeg, dressed in the furs he bought her. Sometimes she's framed by the doorway of an adobe house in a place he doesn't recognize, with mountains behind her and a little boy by the hand. These dreamscapes still seem like pictures of the way things ought to be, but there is his mother, haggard and thin-lipped and dry-eyed, and there is his father, beneath the ground at Llano. And then there is Lena herself.

Sometimes I think I'm losing my nerve, he wrote a few weeks ago, *but when I realize what I must do for your sake and the sake of your children, I find my strength again.* The formula mostly still works, but more and more he wonders if it ought to.

"Beal won't give up," Henry had said not long after Al returned to the

Panhandle. "I keep telling you that." They were sitting in his office at the Dalhart bank.

"Neither will I," said Al, surprising himself with his tone, which was discouraged.

Henry raised his eyebrows. The heat was fierce, despite the drawn shades and the overhead fan. Al never complains about heat anymore, not after that cold in Canada, but Henry, who was plumper, fanned himself with a folded copy of the Dalhart newspaper. Beads of sweat stood out on his forehead.

"You could, you know," Henry said mildly. "You could let her go on and live with Beal. She'd be all right."

Al didn't say anything for a few minutes and neither did Henry, which was a relief. "Why do you think she'd be all right?" Al asked finally, but not like he was challenging him.

Henry pursed his mouth and tapped the folded newspaper gently on his thigh a few times. Al sat quietly. He didn't really think anything Henry said would make much of a difference, but it seemed to relieve him to imagine that it might.

"I know you and Lynn think what I do is just about the dullest thing going," Henry began. "But a banker learns to see what type survives misfortune and what type don't. It ain't always who you'd think. There's ol' boys who'll survive any bust, blizzard, drought, freeze you throw at 'em. And then you got folks who start out with everything and just as sure as shootin' they'll find a way to lose it.

"After a while, you can smell it on people," he went on, with pride so muted you had to know him as well as Al did to see it. He looked at the drawn shades and took out a handkerchief and mopped his brow. "Lena's one of them survivors," he said. "She'll be all right."

"But—"

"I know. She *looks* fragile and she's telling you Beal's mistreating her—which I'm sure he is—and that she loves you only—which I'm sure she does—and that you're the only one who can save her, and it's that last part that ain't true. She'll survive."

He said nothing more. *Henry had tact, was what it was,* thought Al. You didn't expect it because he spoke so directly and seemed so practical. But he knew when to shut up and he knew how to make difficult things sound as clear and manageable as a checking account.

There were a few moments of silence. "Well," Al said at last, "I reckon I should let you get back to work."

They shook hands across Henry's big desk, and Henry walked Al to the door and patted him on the back. Al turned around and hugged him. "Thank you," he said.

"Sure thing," Henry said easily. "Tell Ma I'll be down in a few days."

As his train chugged out of the Dalhart station, Al considered the idea: Lena could and would survive without him. He didn't know why, but he couldn't seem to look at it straight on. He'd get right up close and swerve away at the last minute, like he lived on a vast ranch that had once seemed endless but wasn't and he'd reached the fence line.

67

Lena had stayed with Pearl in St. Charles during most of Beal's trial—it was easier being in Louisiana and Pearl wasn't always yammering at her to give Al up. But once the trial ended, she wrote to say that nothing could stop her return to Canada: *Won't you please buy us a little home there?* she asked. *I never want to stay in another hotel.*

Al threw himself into finding a place. By then he was in Bassano, a tiny town in Alberta incorporated only a year earlier near the Bow River and within sight of the Rockies. It was still cold as hell, and the blizzards rolled in regularly, but the days were noticeably longer. When he arrived one afternoon to check out a rental cottage, he found the glittering icicles hanging from the eaves dripping into the snow with a muffled thud, one of the sounds of spring he recognized from his years in Montana.

The cottage was clean and simple, with well-waxed wooden floors and a big fireplace in the living area. The bedroom faced east and the newly planted spindly trees just outside the window reminded him of Amarillo. He imagined waking with Lena to the sun streaming in, imagined her once more beneath him with her pale and slender body arching up to his, the sound of his name in her throat.

"I'll take it," he told the agent. He searched for simple furniture, things he knew would suit them both, and when all was in readiness, he looked around and felt satisfied. It still needed a woman's touch, but she would soon be there to provide it. He wouldn't spend the night in the house until she arrived. That way it would be theirs and theirs alone.

He got her letter dated March 8 a couple of days later. *I saw Mr. Lattimore in Ft. Worth. He said that I must consider you and not do any-*

thing hasty, that not only Texas but the whole U.S. would tear up creation to find us and it would now be impossible for us to go anywhere in Canada or a foreign country. You are so far away, sweetheart, you don't realize the intense feeling over the affair—all Texas is divided over it. Lattimore advised me to establish a residency elsewhere. That way I can file for divorce somewhere else than Texas. And this is what I have decided to do. When you next hear from your girl, she'll be on her way to California.

"California?" Al said out loud.

He lay on the bed in the Bassano hotel—a two-story affair with sporadic housekeeping, bad cooking, and poor mattresses—and stared out the window. There was an eddy of torn brown paper and cigarette butts whirling against the fence across the street in the muddy chopped-up snow. The cold wrapped round his heart again.

He didn't answer her 'til the next morning and by that time his disappointment had turned to anger. *Is your husband paying your way to California?* he wrote bitterly. Though he couldn't work out exactly why, the anger made him feel better. He tucked into his steak and beans and biscuits at Bassano's one restaurant with real appetite and got to talking with a man at the next table who knew some of the same people Al had known years earlier in Medicine Hat. They had a long and restful conversation about running cattle on the southern versus the northern plains and about the Mexican fever.

Shorty seemed to know Al's story—he vaguely alluded to it a few times—but it didn't seem to matter or even interest him much. He passed right over it like it was Al's business and he'd judge him as he found him. When they ran into each other on the street the next morning, Al invited him for a cup of coffee and a late breakfast. Over the flapjacks Al said, "You know, a man in my position needs work."

"I reckon he does," said Shorty. He looked down at his plate. "It can't be easy."

"It ain't," answered Al, and that was the most the two of them ever said about the whole matter. It made Shorty the most relaxing human being Al had come across in months. After a few more minutes of working on his breakfast, Shorty said, "The cows'll be calving soon and I could use some help. The pay's no good and you know pulling calves can be dirty work, but I'd be glad for an extra hand."

"The pay ain't necessary," said Al, a formality they had to honor and dispense with. "I'd be proud to help." He couldn't imagine anything more soothing than hard ranch work; he would have paid for the privilege.

They went out to the place—a nice spread that ran down to the river—late that afternoon. Al looked it over from the ranch house porch with his practiced eye and nodded approvingly. Shorty was pleased but tried not to show it. They smoked while Shorty talked about his plans, pointing out this or that feature of the property. His dark hair was gray at the temples and his belly stuck out a little over the top of his trousers. His wife was a younger woman, with straight brown hair drawn up in a tight twist. She was noticeably pregnant, but neither she nor Shorty mentioned it.

Al gazed out over the land as it eased down to the river. The sun had just set behind the outline of the Rockies and the sky was lit up salmon and gold. *This is who I am,* he thought. *I work this kind of land and live in this kind of house and know this kind of people.* The newspapers and the lawyers had made him a false thing. Here was his soul again.

68

And now he's back in Amarillo, surrounded by the kind of land and people he knows. But except for the weather, things haven't improved much. Though the almanac predicts another hard winter, Al thinks it'll be a piece of cake compared to Canada. He'd learned pretty quickly not to say much about the Canadian winter; just about everybody in Amarillo has a story about *their* winter—the worst anyone could remember except a few real old-timers—and likes complaining about it. People didn't enjoy having that pleasure shrunk down by being told they hadn't been through as much as they thought.

There's old Mrs. Dillon, waving at him from across the street like she wants to chat. She's one of the many who've told him about the Dalhart woman who'd walked out into the blizzard to try to find her husband. "She was a solid block of ice," Mrs. Dillon said after church one day, with the hint of self-satisfaction he's noticed the elderly sometimes have while discussing untimely death. "Like all those cattle stuck up against barb-wire."

She's clearly poised to step off the sidewalk and make for him, but Al hurries on, miming regret at his haste. Once they corner him, these old ladies can be relentless in their efforts to get him to say something about *anything* to do with all his troubles. They use their age and sex, and his good manners, like weapons—they remind him of the *banderilleros* he saw in a bullfight just over the border in Old Mexico, jabbing and maddening the poor bull with their darts. Only the old ladies don't want to kill Al; they just want to get him to talk. He'd quickly learned that anything he did say would get turned into a story he didn't recognize, so—as with the reporters in Canada—he figures escape is his best option.

Lena had been right when she told him he couldn't imagine the strength of feeling in Texas. The Canadian reporters had been interested because they could twitter on about slow-spoken, bloodthirsty Texans sorting out their love troubles in northern climes. But in Texas, it's personal in a way Al can't fathom.

On a blazing hot morning right after he came back, he'd stopped for breakfast at a short-order restaurant in Fort Worth. He was staying at the Dixie, a second-rate hotel in the Acre—exactly the kind of place Beal's lawyers wanted people to believe he belonged, but exactly where they wouldn't think to look for him. Unlike his father, Al knows how to carry himself quietly.

As he inhaled the smells of bacon grease and waited for his coffee to cool a bit, two men sat down at a nearby table, making a bit of a ruckus with the chairs. "Well, she may be bad," one of them was saying, "and she may give you hell every other minute about every other thing, but at least she ain't that Sneed woman." Al's hands tingled. He stubbed out his cigarette savagely, grinding the butt into his saucer.

"It ain't her fault," responded the other. "She's weak-minded." He was a skinny guy, in his late twenties Al judged, with an already receding hairline and big hazel eyes with long lashes that were his best feature, something a woman could love.

His friend was a few years older, with a long, thick moustache that matched his dark hair. "That's not what I heard," he said to Skinny. "I heard that's what they're saying to save the family reputation. You don't think old man Sneed was going to let it look like his own son married a prostitute, do you? Families like that, money like that? They'll tell any lie just to look respectable. I feel right sorry for the Boyces. What I hear, that old man said the truth and only about half of it at that. As for his son, well, what would you do if you had the chance to run off with a woman"—he dropped his voice—"who just couldn't stop fucking?"

Only the thought of all that would surely go wrong kept Al from rising from his chair to pound the man.

Skinny laughed a low, dirty laugh. "Well, there's women that like it as much as men. Why would a man go to all the trouble to steal one out of a nut house and take her to Canada?"

"I ain't talking about women who like it as much as a man, son," Moustache said. "Not that you'd know," he added. "I'm talking about a *disease*."

"What do you mean, a *disease*?" said Skinny. "I ain't never heard of no fucking disease in women. Seems like that wouldn't be a disease, that would be an advantage. What in the hell are you talking about, Angus?"

"The disease is the *real* reason she went to the sanitarium," Angus answered, with an air of authority. "Beal Sneed is lucky Al Boyce stole her away because Sneed can say she went wrong under the influence of a bad man, but what I hear—I know some folks in Amarillo—what I hear is she was fucking every man she could, including"—he dropped his voice to a stage whisper—"niggers. I hear she likes niggers best of all, 'cause you know, son, generally, your nigger is bigger."

Al stared horrified at the butter melting into his grits. This must be the report Lena wrote she couldn't bring herself to put in a letter. He pulled a silver dollar out of his wallet, thumped it on the table and pushed his chair back so hard he almost knocked it over. Inside, he was shouting, "It's a lie. I'll kill you if you don't take it back."

He remembers feeling walloped by shame; he couldn't protect her, couldn't defend her. Today is September 14, 1912. Nine months and a day. He hasn't avenged that either. His right hand briefly grazes the gun tucked into his waistband beneath his jacket. It's a Lugar, unusual in Texas but plenty powerful, and it suits him. He's still one of the best shots in the Panhandle, but so far he's had no chance to prove it.

69

In the early spring in Bassano, he'd developed a routine: Work at Shorty's, call at the post office, return to his room grateful for the relief of tired muscles and a day spent outdoors doing something he was good at. If the postmaster handed him an envelope with Lena's big handwriting sprawled across it, he felt an easing, despite his frustration about California. The distance between them shrunk as if their hearts were beating oars on a big lake and carried them to one another.

But her letters were full of misery and didn't make for easy reading. She and Nellie Steele had gone first to Long Beach, but the ocean with its waves and noise and foggy skies terrified her, and there were people from Winnipeg at the hotel who recognized her name. So she and Nellie moved to Los Angeles. Though Al offered to pay for the apartment, Lena claimed it wasn't necessary. *Everything is so cheap. A five-story apartment, rooms complete, and all for $26 a month.*

The new location did little to improve her spirits. Sometimes Al longed for just a glimpse of that spunky woman who'd enjoyed firing guns at nice parties. But she had vanished, swallowed up by terror and despair: *I am getting to be such a coward. I am afraid of everybody and everything. Precious, please believe me: If I had returned to Canada, Beal would have followed and killed us both or hired someone. Now it's you I worry about. I have nothing except you.*

In Bassano, it was hard to take the idea of a hired killer very seriously. The town was so tiny that strangers stuck out and Al didn't think Beal could pay a man enough to shoot him in Canada where the man would surely hang for it. Henry agreed with Al's assessment, but reported that their mother did not. *Ma's afraid the same thing that happened to Pa is going to happen to you,* Henry wrote in his down-to-earth way. *Write often.*

Al did. But it was hard. Like Lena's, his mother's letters pained him.

I pray for the bitterness to leave my heart, but sometimes the injustice and folly of all that has happened rise up in me like poison and I can't swallow it down. I cannot help but feel, Albert, that in your deepest heart you would choose differently if you had it to do over again.

Al read that with a sick feeling inside him. *Would* he have walked away? The question gave him vertigo. Thinking about the future was the only way he could get it to stop. In the eyes of God, who did not grant such deep love without suffering, he and Lena were already married. Someday their love would make a place for itself, surely it would.

California is beautiful, Lena had written from Los Angeles, *but when we crossed the desert, I felt like I'd rather live in a little adobe house there with you than* anywhere *on earth.*

How much Al wanted to believe in such a future in such a place. But his father's death and all his family's immense pain stood in the way, like roadblocks he couldn't get around or remove. He told himself his father's death was on Beal's head. But he couldn't help hearing his mother's voice, saying all the things she wouldn't write. "I did not raise you to break up another man's home. Your father would rather have followed you to your grave than to see you do this. You weren't even here to follow him to his. That awful woman has destroyed two happy homes and families for her own selfish pleasures. Any man who could see clearly would give her up."

Al didn't have to imagine Lena's thoughts. She stated them directly: *I try to keep the bitter feelings down, but out of the whole world you're the only one who seems to think I've had anything to stand. If your mother could just see into my heart, and see the love I have for my boy, I don't think she would feel hard about me.*

You don't know my mother, Al thought. *She's made up her mind nice and tight just like she makes up a bed and she won't unmake it, no matter what.*

Though Al wrote his mother at least once a week, his hand dragged across the paper and he stared out the window a lot. There wasn't much to tell about his life in Canada. He couldn't say anything about

Lena. He knew there were only two things his mother wanted to hear—that he was safe and that he was giving Lena up—and he could only tell her one of them. Their correspondence devolved into a ritualized and painful struggle. Each knew what the other wanted to hear and said something else. What wasn't said just kept getting louder.

One night on the XIT when he was a boy, before they were all killed out, Al had heard a wildcat shriek. It sounded just like a woman, as people always said. His mother's letters reminded him of that, something out in the dark, beyond the lighted words on the page, screaming.

70

In the middle of April, after dinner one evening with Shorty and a couple of other ranchers, Al called at the post office and returned to his room with one letter from Lena and another from his mother. Lena had last written at the end of March promising to write three times a week and he hadn't had a word since. So he read her letter first. Then he read his mother's. Then he carefully laid both side by side on the bed and read them each again.

I have had such a dreadful rising in my head, Lena had written on April 6, *and have not been able to write you since Sunday. Last night is the first time I've slept a minute. The doctor said the rising was caused from headache and my not taking anything for them. My head and neck are still so sore I can't move them, but the dreadful pain is gone.*

Monday, I received your letters sent to Long Beach. You should have received mine by the time you wrote, but you had only received the one I mailed in El Paso and the first one from Long Beach. I thought sure I would hear from you today, so went into town this afternoon, but there was no letter.

The first time Al read that, he sort of rushed over it. The mails were slow under the best of circumstances and all the storms had made things worse. But the second time through, he felt as if the devil's own long fingers had brushed his spine. Could Beal possibly be messing with the mail again? A picture of the man, grinning maliciously, popped into his mind. Al looked out the window to try to clear it and watched a man he didn't recognize chatting with one of Shorty's friends. He waited 'til his heart slowed down. Then he turned again to his mother's letter.

Spring is beautiful this year, she'd begun, *on account of all the snow and rain last winter. I wish you and your father were here to share it with me. Sometimes I imagine that you both* are *here, along with Bessie, only gone from the house a little while.*

Al could see it, too—all of them striding through high grasses and flowers, heading out to a picnic to celebrate the return of warmth and sunlight, the way they used to, before anyone was dead. His mother was right—you could imagine things so clearly that it seemed they must be true or come true. But there was a barrier, something like a windowpane. On the other side lay all sorts of impossible-to-reach scenes you could nonetheless view with utter clarity.

Albert, his mother continued, *I have done as you wish and not spoken to you about her*—she couldn't even bring herself to write Lena's name—*although you know my opinion. But William was in Fort Worth at Senator Hanger's offices for a conference and brought us news I think you should know: Senator Lattimore reports that Beal is saying they are reconciled and she is returning to Texas to join him.*

The first time through, Al muttered, "He's lying," as if his mother were right there in the room. But by the time he'd read both letters again, he didn't know what to think. There was a week of Lena's silence to account for, and that was only the first of many things that needed explaining.

I may have made a mistake coming out here, Lena had written, *though I did what I thought was best. But I can't stay. Unless I hear from you that you have some definite plan, I may go back to Texas. I believe Beal thinks he will finally break me. Nell said today, if Beal would give me a divorce how much better it would be, but he* never *will.*

Son, his mother's letter continued, *I know you are loyal and honorable and you measure others by your own yardstick. But the woman has every reason to return to her husband. Even if the current report is untrue, I believe at the last she will do so. Others share my opinion. THINK on this, son, please. She has nothing left—not her children, her house, her things, her family, her reputation. If she returns to him, she regains most of it. With you, what will she have?* She ended the paragraph with that question.

Al took a long drink of water straight from the carafe, drew deeply on his cigarette, and tried to think clearly. Less than a month earlier, Lena had arrived in California full of brave talk about *establishing a residence.* Now she was talking about leaving. Although he hated to admit it, his mother's version of things made a whole lot of sense. *Put two and two together,* he thought. Lena hadn't drawn on his bank account for a long time. She must be getting money from *someone*, and that someone was probably Beal.

Precious, Lena had concluded, *you must think what is best for your poor miserable girl and I will do just as you say. They can torture me but they can never kill my soul. It is in your keeping and I know it is safe. But I can't live away from you much longer. Won't you please come and take care of me?*

Al read that last part again and again. About the tenth time through he found he knew what to do.

71

"My friend in Lethbridge will take you across," said Shorty. "It's pretty down there and no one patrols it. You can go over near the Milk, head to Shelby, and get the train." They shook hands and made the usual comments about "if you're ever out this way, out that way," but Al thought they both knew they would never lay eyes on one another again.

Al often remembers that trip and sometimes dreams about it, too. Shorty was right: It was real pretty country, with bluffs rising near the riverbed, full of birdsong and hawk cries and the sounds of running water. Shorty's friend Clyde was as quiet as Al, and they rode without much talk. Although it was chilly and the wind blew hard at times, Al fell into the rhythm of riding in open territory, of the gait of his horse and the creak of the saddle, of his own breath and the horse's, of the occasional snort, the snap of the reins or clink of the bit—a rhythm he'd known as long as he could remember. The smells of grassy manure and sweat and well-used leather soothed him.

They set up camp not far from the river in the protected curve of a bluff where the wind didn't blow too much. Apparently, the Indians had liked the spot too; the rocks were thick with pictures. Clyde and Al sat in front of the fire after supper and sipped coffee and talked a little about the pictures and about animals they'd known. There was a sliver of moon rising and the Milky Way stretched across the big sky like another river. The horses shied and started occasionally, so they decided to keep lookout just to be on the safe side. Clyde drew the first turn.

When Clyde woke him about two, Al stirred up the embers under the pot, poured himself some coffee, and then sat watching and listening to the white-churning river flow in the starlight while Clyde snored gently. Above him was the sky he'd viewed since childhood, stars and planets sailing slowly across it. Some part of him seemed to see and know everything, and even though the rest of him didn't, the two parts felt peaceful together.

They crossed into Montana mid-afternoon the next day. Al saw nothing to mark the border. "You're here," was all Clyde said. They camped that night by a stream in the hills and the next morning rode into Shelby, where Clyde turned back, trailing the horse Al had been riding behind him, and Al caught a train to Seattle.

72

Shelby to Seattle was stop-and-start, but after that, things picked up. It was strange to be back in his own country again, traveling on yet another train, under yet another alias, L.B. Moss. Lena's Boy Moss. *Let me gather it, let me live long enough in one place to gather it,* Al thought as he noted the bags under his eyes and the deep lines across his face in the bathroom mirror.

When he got to San Francisco, he hired a young man about twenty, with the body of a pugilist and something vaguely Italian-looking about his eyes and nose. His name, he said, was Alexander Smith, Al for short. Al didn't believe him for a minute, but it didn't matter. The boy was handy with his fists and a gun, both by his own account and that of several older men at the wharf where he'd been working as a longshoreman. Al saw the gun part for himself and was satisfied.

At the wharf, the gunmetal-colored bay and the fog and clouds all blurred together and Al remembered Lena's reaction to the overcast ocean in Long Beach. "Is it often like this?" he asked Smith, who grinned when he answered, "A lot, especially in the summertime." Al just shook his head.

"San Francisco native, born and raised," said Smith. "We love the weather."

"Come to Texas sometime," Al said. "I'll show you weather."

"No, thanks," said Smith. "You got tornados and lightning."

Al looked down the long street running from the wharf with its mix of brand-new buildings and lots still filled with earthquake debris. He raised an eyebrow and grinned.

"Oh, that," said Smith. "Well, no place is perfect."

"Were you here?" Al asked.

"Yessir, I was," Smith answered with obvious pride. "The shaking was bad—it threw me and my brother right out of bed—but the fires were much worse. Ma took us out to the park. Pa was gone as usual, and then home was gone, too."

Al nodded and considered things: Fathers who vanished; earthquakes versus tornados; the way a week or so earlier that sure thing, the Titanic, had sunk into the ocean. The earth itself could topple buildings. The sea could swallow you whole. The wind could blow your life to pieces.

He was silent and anxious for most of the train trip down to Los Angeles. Then just past Santa Barbara, the weather cleared and the ocean sparkled with light like another world altogether. And when he stepped into the warm air outside the station in Los Angeles and his body relaxed instead of tightening against cold as it had for months, the intense blue of the California sky hit him like a jolt of hope.

He figured his Texas accent was likely to be memorable, so he had Smith ask a few questions to get oriented. Then they hustled onto a streetcar outside the station and got off at a park a few blocks from Lena's apartment. Al dictated a note asking Lena to set a time and place to meet that sounded like it came from Smith himself, and which Smith wrote out in his halting hand.

"Get a boy to deliver it and wait for an answer," Al instructed. "And make sure the other woman clears out, or wait until Mrs . . . uh, Boyce comes out of the apartment—however you do it, just make sure the other woman don't see."

Smith looked perplexed. "How do I tell 'em apart?" he asked.

Al fished a photo of Lena out of his wallet, taken shortly before all the trouble. It was folded in quarters and just about falling apart at the creases. Al spread it carefully on his knee and smoothed it so that Smith could see. "She's thinner now," Al said, "but you can't mistake those eyes. I'll wait here."

Despite his worries, he was so worn out that he fell to dozing in the sun on the park bench. When Smith tapped him on the shoulder, Al startled and went for his gun. "Goddammit, boss," Smith cursed as he jumped back. "I didn't sign on so you could shoot me."

"I'm sorry," Al said perfunctorily. "Did you see her?"

"Yeah," said Smith. He pulled a note out of his pocket with obvious pride. "I saw her looking out the window and then the other one came out, looking real exasperated and slammed the front door. That was my moment. I said to the boy I'd found outside, 'Take this note up to that lady in the window and wait for her to write an answer and bring it right back and there's two bits for you. No monkey business.'" Smith shook his finger, imitating the way he'd spoken to the boy.

Al heard all this like a buzz in the background while he read Lena's words again and again, written just a few minutes—not five or six days—ago:

I am watched every minute and it would not be safe for you to meet with me. I will be at the Orpheum this afternoon at 2:15 in the balcony, second row on the right-hand side. If you receive this in time, be there where I can see you, but don't *try and speak to me. I will have on a navy blue dress, a blue hat with a red band on it. Wear a red flower in your buttonhole and if you have a letter for me and can give it to me without anyone seeing you, please do so, but don't run any risk.*

Al's eyes filled. He didn't know whether it was from gratitude that he was in time—she was still in Los Angeles—or whether it was because at last he would see her again, or because even here, when for the first time in months they were near one another, they couldn't speak, and she was leaving him again.

He turned to Smith, Lena's note still open in his hand. "How did she look?" he asked.

Smith got a funny look, like he felt sorry for Al all of a sudden and it threw him. "Well, boss," he said, more slowly than usual, "she looks tired." He paused. "And thin, like you said. But you know, I didn't see her close up or nothing."

Al heard what Smith meant: She looks awful. "You know she's a beautiful woman," Al said because he felt his usual urge to protect her and for once there was a tiny opportunity to do something about it. "She has suffered so much."

"Sure," lied Smith respectfully, "I could see she was beautiful."

They were both quiet for a few minutes. Al took out his watch. It was a little after noon. "We should get to the Orpheum," he said.

73

They seated themselves in the balcony by the flickering light of black and white images. Al was so nervous he'd barely noticed the name of the movie, let alone what was going on in it, but Smith sat with his eyes glued to the screen, munching a sandwich Al had bought him. The lights came up at about two. Al looked around, his heart going hard and his mouth dry. There was a good crowd on the main floor, but the balcony was relatively empty. And then there she was.

He saw her blue hat with the red band first, but he would have known her without the hat, he could tell her by the way her head moved and the set of her shoulders as she climbed the balcony stairs. After all these months, he was no longer imagining her, he was actually seeing her. It was Lena herself who glanced up, saw him, and stopped dead in her tracks with a look he had never seen on the face of another human being in his life. Tears began to run down her face and she tottered, stretching out a hand to the back of a seat for balance. The feathers on her hat quivered as if the birds they had belonged to were still alive. She scurried into a seat across the aisle.

Once the lights went down and the music started again, she turned to give him a tiny, wavering smile. He smiled back, pursing his mouth up to form a kiss, but that terrified her and she turned abruptly back to the screen.

A few minutes later Al and Smith got up. Smith pretended to stumble, excused himself in a hoarse whisper, and dropped a note into Lena's lap. There was a muffled curse three rows up. Al wanted to reach over to touch her shoulder—she was just two seats in from the aisle—but he felt her no as if she'd said it aloud.

Smith waited outside the apartment for hours that Saturday night. But Nell never left and Lena never came down. Then about nine on Sunday morning, Nell came out church-dressed and headed for a streetcar. Smith corralled another boy and sent him up to Lena, who pressed a few coins into his hand and whispered, "Tell him to meet me at the Southern Pacific at two this afternoon on the Sunset Express platform."

So Sunday afternoon, while Nell was off doing some last-minute souvenir shopping, Al at last met Lena again. The bustle of porters and passengers and conductors, the sound of trains pulling in and pulling out, the shouts of greeting and farewell all bounced off the high ceilings and walls to produce the usual big-station din. Al and Lena faced the tracks a few feet apart and tried not to look at one another. Smith was at an awkward distance, close enough to protect them but also to hear snatches of their conversation.

"Why are you leaving now?" asked Al. He'd meant to ask it gently but it came out sounding harsh. "Now that I'm here, stay. We'll work something out."

She turned to him briefly. There were tears brimming in her eyes. "Don't you think I want to? Don't you think—"

"I don't know. I don't know what to think anymore."

"You don't understand," she answered in an urgent whisper. "You don't see how much danger we're in. You *still* don't know what he's really like. I—"

"How can you say that?" Al interrupted heatedly though he kept his voice low. "He killed my father. What I don't know is why you're going back to him."

"Who said I was going back to him?" Lena turned toward him with a shocked look. "That's not true."

Al stared at the track, his face stony. "Someone who should know," he answered. "Beal is telling people that you two are reconciled."

"That is *not* true," Lena said emphatically. "*Who* told you that?"

"Someone who should know," repeated Al.

"It's your mother, ain't it?" said Lena with a tiny flicker of her old spirit. "She would do anything in her power to separate us."

"It ain't my mother," said Al. It was the first deliberate lie he'd ever told her.

"I don't believe you," she said quietly.

It hurt him. But he had no intention of telling her the truth because—he suddenly realized—he'd come to believe she was lying to him.

"Well," he said after a few seconds, *"I don't believe you."*

"Albert," she said, her voice breaking, "Albert . . . you don't understand. Everything I'm doing is to protect you. I don't care about anyone or anything but you."

Despite himself, he answered, "Then stay in California. To be away from you has been . . . you don't know what it's been like."

"I do," she broke in.

"Lena," he said in what would have been a cry if it had been safe to cry out. "We can't keep on like this."

"No," she said, "we're not meant to be apart." They fell silent in the echoing din then turned simultaneously to face one another. He saw again all the damage in her face and knew she saw the same in his.

Then she said, "What are you going to do?"

"I don't know. Maybe go back to Canada."

"Don't," she said.

"Don't go back to Texas," he answered.

"I'll come back to California," she said, "I promise."

"Don't make promises you can't keep."

"Are you going to give me up?"

"You're giving me up."

"*No.* No, *no*, no."

Al was suddenly exhausted by all the emotion. "I don't know what I'm going to do. But I have to think this over. For both our sakes."

"Get on the train with me," she said abruptly, her eyes fixed on the track.

"*What?*"

"Buy a ticket and get on the train," she said. "We can meet that way. I can come to your cabin."

"That's a crazy idea," he retorted.

"They don't know who you are. They're watching me, but they don't expect you."

"They'll have photographs. If you want to see me, you can stay in California."

"Albert," she said in a harder voice, "I know you're thinking about leaving me." When he glanced at her, surprised by her words, she was still staring straight ahead, her jaw clenched. "I know your family is pressuring you and maybe you don't want to go through all this anymore." Her eyes filled and her voice softened. "But I have to hold you at least once more. I can't face it otherwise. If you ever loved me, buy a ticket and get on the train. I can't . . . I just can't . . ."

And so, he did.

It wasn't a long train—a dining car, a few sleepers—and he took a berth in the car next to hers. From behind a pillar near the edge of the platform, Al watched as Nell and Lena boarded. Nell was smiling and laughing, obviously relieved to be leaving. When the conductor issued his last "All aboard," Al and Smith rushed up the steps into their car.

74

"My dearest, my darling, my angel," they whispered. Even as they kissed feverishly, everything relaxed and slowed. She stopped trembling. When he opened his eyes again, he recognized the world around him as he hadn't for months.

"How long can you stay?" he breathed into her ear, drawing her down to the berth.

She pulled back, looked him in the face and answered, "I want to stay forever." She said it simply, the way she used to say things, so that he believed her. They kissed again, sliding down onto the berth until he was half on top of her. But when he began to fumble with her skirts, she tensed and pushed his hand away.

"It's too dangerous," she said, "I have to go soon or Nell will get suspicious."

He turned over and stared at the underside of the berth. He felt angry again without wanting to. All sorts of things popped into his mind, but all of them were hurtful so he said nothing. For a few moments, they lay together silently. Then he said, "Please come back tonight."

"I'll try," she said, but her jaw and shoulders tightened and he knew she was afraid again. She placed her hand on his cheek and stroked it gently. "You look so worn out," she said sadly.

Al sighed. "We're both worn out," he answered, and they were quiet again.

Then she said, "I have to go. Nell will be looking for me any second if she isn't already."

Al didn't know if it was what she said or the way she said it, but he suddenly saw what it had really been like for her all these months. He felt dizzy from the view. He sat up, tucking his head to avoid hitting it on the upper berth, then stood, extending his hand and pulling her to her feet. She pressed her face into his chest as if she wanted to burrow inside and never come out again. He tapped lightly on the door, the signal to Smith—smoking in the aisle near the window—to open the door if the coast was clear. Lena slipped out, smiling wanly at him. Within the hour, Smith brought him a note: *I can't come back tonight.*

After Smith fell asleep in the upper berth, snoring loudly, Al stood at the window and smoked, watching the moonlight fall uninterrupted out of the sky and onto the arid earth. He wondered if Lena was asleep in the next car and doubted it. The absurd drama of their position struck him as shameful, something a real man would have managed to avoid. He felt all his usual emotions—the ones he'd been feeling for months—but he felt something else, too. *I've got to make a decision,* was how he spoke of it to himself. *We can't go on like this.*

One way or another, he thought, he'd been saying yes to her since this thing got started. Yes, I'll go to New Orleans. Yes, you go on and tell Beal you want a divorce, we won't just run off. Yes, I'll get you out of the sanitarium. Yes, I'll stay in Canada. Yes, all right, you're going to California. Yes, I'll come to see you. Yes, okay, you're going back to Texas. Yes, I'll get on the train.

Lena couldn't seem to keep herself fixed on one course of action. Deep down, Al didn't exactly believe the reconciliation rumor, but Lena was a wreck, just like she'd said. She wavered and changed her mind constantly because her primary aim had changed. She believed that what she most wanted was to be with Al. It wasn't. Not anymore. What she most wanted was to stop hurting.

How badly both of them had underestimated Beal. He was more than capable of sticking to a course of action without wavering. *He must actually enjoy it,* Al thought, *or at least find it relieved his pain.* That busy, prairie dog mind of his. What about his heart? What could you say about his heart? It was a monster. There wasn't one thing the man had done in this whole business that sprang from love for Lena, not in any way Al understood the word.

He remembered wanting her happiness above all else. What a mess he'd made of that. And inside the pain of his own conclusions, the words came to him: *It's not just Beal. It's all three of us. We're turning one another into monsters.*

With the sound of the train in his ears, swaying a little and smoking cigarette after cigarette, Al gazed at the moon-soaked landscape. He felt like a man bleeding from the inside out.

First thing the next morning he wrote her. *I'm deciding where to get off the train. It may be best for me to return to Canada.* Smith stuffed the note in the cubbyhole near the ladies' room they'd agreed on as a hiding place the afternoon before and within the hour handed him Lena's answer, scribbled on the back of a tourist photo of her and Nell standing in front of the S.P. station. Lena looked miserable beneath her broad-brimmed, beribboned hat.

Go where you are safe, but I don't want you to go to Canada.

Al forced himself to say, "Where you want me to go doesn't matter." He didn't really mean it yet, but he was closer.

According to Smith, Nell was in the dining car having breakfast. "She'll take her time," he said to Al. "I think she's as tired of her as she is of her." Despite everything, Al laughed. Smith could never bring himself to use either woman's name, and at times the results were comical.

Smith paused, then said quite formally, "Excuse me if I've offended you by saying so."

"Not at all," said Al. "This ain't Nell's fight . . . she just got drug into it."

Smith nodded a bit too emphatically. "I'll step outside to wait," he said. A few minutes later, the door opened and Lena threw herself into Al's arms. He'd tried to air the place out after all the cigarettes, but everything still smelled like smoke. They embraced for a long minute. Then he led her to the berth and sat down beside her. "I love you," he said quietly, "I will always love you."

She started to say something but he shook his head.

"Let me finish."

She nodded.

"But this thing is destroying us both."

Her head trembled but she looked straight into his eyes and stayed quiet.

"I don't know what I expected when I came here, but I didn't expect to see you so . . ." he struggled for the right word "So . . ."

"Ugly?" she said, with great sorrow. "I know I'm ugly now, I'm so thin and..."

"No," he said, "you're not ugly. You can't be ugly to me."

Tears filled her eyes and remained there without falling.

"But you are . . . you're at the end of your strength, Lena. This isn't what I wanted for you or for me."

"But for us," she said, "in the end it will all be worth it for us."

"I don't know that anymore, Lena," he said, exhaustion from the previous night's sleeplessness clear in his voice. "I need to consider things on my own just like you've been doing. Because I don't . . ." He paused.

"You don't trust me," she said, with an effort to keep her voice even, but the next second the tears came rushing out. "After everything I've given up for you," she said, sobbing, "after all the things I've stood being said about me, my whole family turned against me except for Pearl because I love you, and you don't trust me after all that." She was wringing her hands.

He sat silent for a few moments while she wept. "I need to make some decisions," he said doggedly, "and I need to make them alone."

"We need to make our decisions together," she said. "We're married in the eyes of God."

"Well, we ain't married in the eyes of the State of Texas," said Al, with an edge back in his voice. "That appears to count for more than I thought."

"You truly believe I'm going back to that devil," Lena said furiously. "I will die before I live with him again."

Al sighed. "Lena," he said heavily, "you keep saying how you can't stand this and you won't do that or you'll die before you do the other, but you seem to keep on standing and doing and not dying."

She looked as if he'd punched her. "Oh, God," she said, and tried to stand up, but couldn't.

"I don't want to hurt you," he said. "But look what this is doing to us both."

She straightened up and looked directly at him for a long minute. Her face changed as if she saw him all over again, not as her lover, but as a man separate and distinct, caught in his own torment. "I'm sorry," she said, in a different voice. "You deserved so much better than this."

"We both did. We both do." He fell silent.

"I don't know where I'll go," he said at last. "I'm going to get off the train somewhere and then decide."

She tried to be brave. She told him she would abide by his decisions. But by the time she wrote her next note, she was as panicked and desperate as ever. *Oh, precious,* Al read, *I can't live and stand it. Are you going to give me up?*

With the note in his hands, he stared out at the desert. After a few minutes, he realized he was crying.

75

They met one last time in his berth. They held one another and he inhaled the smell of her hair and her skin. "I'm going to get off tonight," he said gently.

She stiffened in his arms. "Albert, please, can't we—"

"No, it's too dangerous. We've been lucky so far, but our luck won't hold. We don't seem to have much luck, you and I." In his voice, the bitterness was faint but unmistakable. "I'm getting off the train. The trail will go real cold for your husband and—"

"He's *not* my husband. *You* are."

"Lena," Al said forcefully. "Stop it. We haven't got much time." She stood stiff but silent in his embrace. "I don't think he knows I've crossed the border," Al continued. "And I want to make sure he don't find out." He knew she'd hate the next part. "The only way is not to write you anymore."

"I can't live if you don't write me," she said.

"Yes, Lena," he said, exhaustion filling his voice, "you can."

"But I . . . Albert, you don't know what you're asking." She pulled away, sat down abruptly on the berth, and put her head in her hands.

"I do know, sweetheart," he said, "Do you think I want it to be like this?"

She took her hands from her face and looked at him. "I don't know," she said. "Are you leaving me." The words hovered somewhere between a question and a statement.

He didn't say anything. He didn't think he could leave her, but deep down, he was hoping that if he didn't write her, if she didn't write him, if he could go to work and feel like some kind of man again, maybe he'd find the power to leave her somewhere inside him. Just to have that power. Just to have it.

"You're thinking of it, aren't you?" she said.

"No," he lied. "But things have to change. It's too dangerous, and we're . . ." He paused. "You could stay in California. You could get Lattimore started on a divorce. You could do anything but what you're doing." The anger spilled out in his voice.

"I've tried to explain to you," she said, sounding frightened. "You don't understand."

"Maybe not," he said, "but I understand that it don't make no sense for you to go back to Texas unless you're going back to him."

She pulled away and snapped, "I told you it's not true." Once again, Al saw a little of her old fire. It made things easier.

"We've got to stop," he said firmly. "Maybe Beal will simmer down and decide he wants a divorce. Maybe he'll get convicted at the next trial. But regardless, we're done for a while."

She stood up and glared at him, hands on her hips. "He will never be convicted. You don't understand. No Texas jury—"

"Maybe not. But since you're going, you can figure out your marriage problems. You'll have free rein, because I won't be around."

She bunched her hands into fists. "How *dare* you! I've lost everything because I put you first."

"How dare *you*!" he responded coldly. "Your husband shot my *father*. I keep defending you to my mother and my brothers when I got his death setting on my heart like a boulder and I can't do *nothing* about it. I've been stuck in a godforsaken, frozen part of the world, just living for your letters, and meanwhile reading every terrible thing they've said about me in the papers. I begged you to come to Canada and you didn't. I've begged you not to go back to Texas, but you're doing it. You can beg now all you want, but I'm getting off this train and I'm not going to write you. And I want you to destroy all my letters—"

"No," she cried. "I can't do that. Please, Albert, I have to have something." Her anger had disappeared completely and with it her strength.

He turned away from her and stared out at the bare Arizona landscape glowing in the late sunlight and felt the train rock.

"I'm so sorry," she said, "You're right. I have been so—"

"Don't," he warned.

"Albert," she said, crossing the short distance between them. She took his hands and looked up into his eyes. "I don't know what to say," she finished, sounding sad and surprised.

"L.B. Ogilvie," he said quietly, calculating quickly what he could give her without giving everything away. It was a name on his mother's side of the family. "I'll send you a note about where to write before I get off."

"Thank you." She sagged into his arms with relief. "I'm more afraid of something happening to you than I am of anything else in this world."

Smith's warning tap on the door came a moment later.

Within thirty minutes, Al had scribbled a note: *C/O General Delivery, Pasadena*. Within thirty more, she'd replied. Still smelling her faintly on his clothes, he wanted to believe every word she wrote: *If you stay in Pasadena, I will come back to Los Angeles. I will be back in Cal not later than June 1st and maybe the 15th of May.*

"Tucson," the conductor sang out. It's as good a place as any, Al thought.

76

The train picked up speed and grew smaller as it headed east. Only a few other people had gotten off and they slowly vanished in the darkness. In Al's vest pocket, the watch that had once belonged to his father and that his mother had sent him in Bassano ticked away, marking the minutes of their latest separation. *If she's looking out the window, I'm now invisible.*

After he and Smith conferred and agreed they hadn't been followed, he booked two separate rooms at the hotel across the street. He needed a night to himself. Then he drew a hot bath and soaked in it until the smell of cigarettes and the train and Lena herself had all disappeared. He was glad to be somewhere that wasn't moving.

They headed back to Los Angeles the next day. There, Al bought Smith a ticket to San Francisco, gave him a bonus, and reiterated the importance of keeping his mouth shut. Al said nothing of his own plans. He made sure Smith got on the train and then wired Ira Aten in El Centro: *Arrive this evening on Los Angeles train to see about cattle. Joe Bush.* Aten was an old XIT division foreman and a relative on his mother's side who'd taken to California and had a spread near the Mexican border. Al thought Aten would recall the Joe Bush name—one the Boyce boys had come up with as kids—and figure things out. Sure enough, when he got off the train in Heber, there was Aten. "Welcome to California, Mr. Bush," he said and winked.

For the first time in a long while, Al felt free. There would be no letters with bad news from Henry or unspoken complaints from his mother. Lena would write, but he'd have to head up to Pasadena for her letters. And Aten knew when to keep his mouth shut, which was more of a relief than Al could ever before have imagined.

In the evenings, they reminisced about days on the XIT—now

rosy-colored with time and distance—and laid out plans for Al to ranch with Aten, or go out on his own. They both believed that if he stayed in California, Beal would leave him alone.

"He's got enough trouble—not to mention blood—on his hands," said Aten. "And if he was dumb enough to come out here, you could shoot him and say it was self-defense. Any jury would buy that, because you'd be here minding your own business far away from him and his wife." He considered things for a moment. "Well, at least any California jury would buy that," he amended.

Al believed he could get used to it all. He could buy some of that cheap land and a few head of cattle, and learn some Spanish to talk to the hands. Early May in El Centro was the most moderate weather he'd experienced in months, and his body relaxed and unfurled in it like a budding leaf.

When he looked at himself in the bathroom mirror, he saw improvement. The sun had begun to bring color back to his face. He was eating again and sleeping better. Every day, he and Aten worked hard around the ranch, mending fences, moving cattle, tending to the calves. Al didn't think about anything except work which, ironically, made him feel like he was on vacation.

Sometimes, at night, he woke and saw the sky full of stars outside the window and swam into a great, deep calm as if it were a vast lake. The world was so much bigger than any passion a man or a woman might feel, and even something bigger than passion, whatever that thing was he couldn't find words for...well, the world was bigger than that, too.

That calm was so deep and true that he didn't realize how fragile it was. Or maybe it wasn't fragile—maybe it was just difficult to get to, more difficult than it seemed while you were there. In any case, he ended up believing he could take the train up to Pasadena, call for his letters, read what she'd written, and not mind too much.

But when he asked the clerk for mail for L.B. Ogilvie and his mouth went dry he knew he'd been wrong. *What if she didn't write?*

She had, though. It was a funny mix of feelings that made him wait to open the first of her two letters until he was on the train heading back to El Centro. But still his heart soared at the sight of her big, familiar handwriting sprawled across stationery from the Crockett Hotel. *Facing Alamo Plaza,* the legend read. *Absolutely Fire Proof.*

I am here in San Antonio and hardly know which way to turn but Pearl thought it best for me to go to a San, for a little while anyway because I am so sick. Everything and everybody is trying to push me to Beal. They all say I am only making my life miserable by loving you so, that you care nothing for me. They go over and over all the things your people have said about me. But that isn't you. I know my boy loves me. I close my eyes and think how you kissed me. But, oh, precious, how am I to live through the days and no word from you?

By the time she'd written the second letter, she was at Dr. Johnson's sanitarium in Fort Worth. Dr. Johnson was kin to Cone, if Al recollected right, which might not be such a good thing. On the other hand, Lena reported that the head nurse was Miss Bridges, *a good friend to your family.* Al remembered her. She'd been a Christmastime guest a few years back—a taller-than-average woman about Al's age with dark hair and eyes and one of those nurse-type manners, kindly but firm in a way that could veer into bossy as she deemed necessary, which might be more often than Al would agree with. She and his father had gotten along like a house afire; Lena probably couldn't have ended up in better hands.

But the next part of the letter was true to form. It seemed no matter what Lena said or promised, she always found a reason to change her mind. *Miss Bridges told Mr. Hanger where I am and he said for God's sake to keep me until this trial comes up if she had to tie me here; that as long as I was here I wouldn't be watched and neither would you. I feel also that you are safe in the U.S. as long as I am here. If I leave I will be followed and couldn't get to you.*

She closed by begging. *Please just send a blank sheet of paper or a flower*—anything *to let me know where you are—in an envelope to Miss Bridges. Oh, darling, send me some word by May 19th. When I think of how happy we were last summer, I almost die.*

In the end, once again, though it took him some time to get there, he did what she asked.

77

A week or so later, he made a run in Aten's automobile to the post office in Heber, where his Pasadena mail was now being forwarded. He thought he'd have a letter from Lena, but he didn't. Instead he had a letter from Henry: *Atwell will be forced to dismiss the federal slaving indictment. Ma has been worried about you so we are glad to have an address.* Henry didn't say how they'd got it, but it could only have been through Lena. Al had a moment of irritation—why could the woman *never* keep her mouth shut?—but his relief outweighed it.

"What will you do?" Aten asked mildly when Al told him the good news.

They stood outside the ranch house in the late afternoon sun and gazed toward Mexico. "I don't know," Al said. "I feel an obligation to . . . to try to ease things for my mother some."

"You know you're welcome here as long as you like," Aten said. "It might be a relief to her to know you're somewhere . . ."

"Away from Lena and Beal," Al finished the sentence.

"Yeah," said Aten laconically, still squinting at Mexico. "That about sums it up."

"I need to think things over," Al said.

Aten just nodded.

Al returned to the post office a few days later. When the gruff little postmaster handed him a letter and he recognized Lena's handwriting, Al felt relief like a body blow. It had been two weeks since her last and he'd begun to understand how she'd felt when he didn't write.

I knew you loved me and would not let tomorrow go by with no word. I am your wife through eternity, he read and felt a clear sense of their truth once more. But it vanished like spring snow as he read on. Eula had phoned the sanitarium in tears to tell Lena that Beal planned to kill her. The only cheering item was that when Beal had come to visit, Miss Bridges told him in no uncertain terms that Lena wasn't to be bothered. Beal hadn't even tried to argue.

Al had a hard time believing that Beal planned to kill Lena. It made *no* sense from a strategic point of view, which seemed to be the main one for Beal, and yet it sounded like Eula was convinced. Once again, Al's fantasies of killing the man sprang up, graphic and complete, like sexual fantasies, with different scenes and set-ups, though they always ended the same way: Beal bloody and lifeless, frequently on a street, but sometimes in a chair like Al's father. Those fantasies made it easy for Al to decide.

I am coming to Fort Worth, he wrote Lena.

The day before he left, her letter arrived begging him not to. *Go to Dalhart. If you go to Dalhart, no one can say you hunted trouble.*

"No," Al said aloud.

Aten saw him off at the station. The sun was hot and a few vultures wheeled around in the blue California sky as the train chugged into view. "I hope to see you out here again," said Aten. "You know you're always welcome." He stuck out his hand.

"Thank you," said Al, shaking it. "For everything." He meant it. "I'd like to come back out under better circumstances." He meant that, too.

"Sure thing," said Aten.

Once again, Al changed trains in Los Angeles. And in Tucson, once again, the moonlight silvered the desert and the mountains rising out of it. Al could almost see ghostly prior versions of himself and Smith as they stepped off the train, and of Lena weeping and desolate in her berth, and of a fed-up Nell, counting the minutes 'til she got off in Marfa. Then the train pulled out and headed east again, passing from Arizona to New Mexico. Some hours later, it pulled into El Paso. Al got out to stretch his legs and mark the moment—after more than six months, he was back in Texas. The station smelled of trains and the tacos a Mexican woman was cooking on a little stove at one end of the platform and of the cigars two men nearby were smoking. Al wondered if he would ever return to a time when coming to a place like El Paso would cause him to think first of the troubles of the place itself—revolution and Juárez across the river—rather than of his own particular and peculiar problems.

Before We Turn to Dust

78

Calling himself Mr. Ogilvie, he took a room at the Dixie Hotel in Fort Worth and sent word to Miss Bridges, naming a restaurant near the sanitarium and asking her to meet him at three the next afternoon.

He made a number of stops and turns on the way, keeping an eye out for anyone who might be following him. Officially, summer wasn't scheduled for a few more days, but the Fort Worth streets had reached the egg-frying stage by late morning, and the near-empty restaurant's ceiling fans were turned on high, the shutters closed against the light. Al chose a table in the corner where he could keep an eye on the door.

Miss Bridges entered at precisely three o'clock, blinked a little as her eyes adjusted from the brightness outside, and closed her parasol. She smiled when she spotted him. He stood and politely pulled her chair out as she approached. She extended her hand.

"First of all," she said, clasping his hand without addressing him by name, caution he noted and appreciated, "let me express to you my deep sympathy for the loss of your father. I've not had an earlier occasion to do that. He was a great man." Her eyes were deep brown and sincere. She was so tall they looked straight into his.

"Thank you," he said, formally. "His death was a terrible blow." As he spoke, he realized how few of these moments he'd had—almost no opportunity to ease his grief and shock with any of the usual well-marked rituals of communal mourning. His eyes filled.

"Of course," she said quietly, "and so senseless."

They sat down to order from the lone waiter in the place—a strawberry blond, pale-eyed young man with a sunburn and a few whiskers that had escaped the razor—and then Miss Bridges said quietly, "I did as you asked. She doesn't know you're in town or even back in Texas."

"Thank you," said Al. "I . . ." He hesitated. "The situation is so dangerous."

"I am very glad you see that," Miss Bridges responded almost eagerly, or as eagerly as a woman who radiated dignified self-control could. "She is so worried about you. It's all I can do to keep her even moderately calm."

"I know," said Al. He was tempted to commiserate about dealing with Lena's nerves, but decided that in this, as in most situations, it was best to keep his mouth shut. He stirred his iced tea.

"I am very concerned about her," Miss Bridges went on after a few seconds. "Her position is so precarious."

Al registered the word "position," which likely covered more than Lena's health. Miss Bridges took a sip of her tea and patted her mouth with her napkin. "She loves you . . ." She looked away. "I've never seen a woman love a man the way she loves you." She sounded almost wistful. Al's heart relaxed a little. *She doesn't deceive me.*

"Her husband," Miss Bridges went on, "is not like you."

Al kept his face neutral and merely nodded his head.

"He doesn't want what's best for her. I'm not even sure he wants what's best for *him*," she added with asperity, "because I don't see that having a wife who can't stand you is any kind of advantage."

Al raised his eyebrows slightly. "Yes," he said, a shade less guarded, "we all wonder about that."

"He's a devil," Miss Bridges said with what seemed real conviction. "When he came to visit, I told him she was a guest in my house and that he had to quit tormenting her. He never opened his mouth." Her pride in shutting that gabby liar up was clear. Al's heart eased open a bit more.

"She wrote me about that," he said. "We're both grateful to you."

Miss Bridges' brown eyes, suddenly sad, gazed into his. "The problem," she said and stopped.

"The problem is he ain't gonna quit," said Al directly.

"Yes," Miss Bridges responded, looking relieved, "that's *exactly* the problem. She's my patient and, truthfully, I don't know how much more she can stand. To be confined the way she is, never to see you, hardly even to hear from you, to be separated from her children and her family, to be afraid for your life or hers, to know that she's talked about so . . . so . . ." Miss Bridges' brown eyes filled. "So unjustly," she finished. "It's—all of it—killing her by degrees. I . . . well, I try to think clearly about what is best for her." A businesslike note crept back into her voice. "I believe that to be part of my job, because she is not capable of thinking clearly for herself right now."

"No," said Al, relieved once more to find his own observations confirmed, "I've noticed the same. Coming back to Texas, for instance—"

"Oh, she had to do that," interrupted Miss Bridges, with a conviction that struck Al the wrong way.

"I don't necessarily agree," he said stiffly.

"No, she told me you didn't and I can understand your thinking, but she made the right decision," Miss Bridges said emphatically. "She was falling apart out there. She doesn't want to feel responsible for your father's death, but she does, you know. She blames herself for all of it, even when she pretends she doesn't. Don't you realize that just about *everyone and everything* make her feel wrong for loving you?" She stopped, her eyes flashing.

Al was shocked by her ferocity. There was something personal in it, but he couldn't quite pin down what it was.

"We both want her health and happiness." Miss Bridges gestured to include herself and Al. "Her husband doesn't. Therefore, you and I must decide a course of action that makes sense for her." She paused very briefly. "Under the circumstances."

A strange image—given the heat—sprang up in Al's mind. He was crossing a frozen pond, testing each step, afraid the ice was too thin to sustain his weight. He nodded at Miss Bridges, as if he agreed with her, which by now he wasn't at all sure about. "What do you suggest?" he asked, noncommittally.

"Your mother shouldn't have to suffer any more than she already has," Miss Bridges responded. It sounded like a change of subject but Al knew it wasn't. "I'm the one who suggested Dalhart."

"I figured as much," said Al, which wasn't exactly true, but it did seem obvious now that he was talking to her.

"I still think it the best plan."

Al didn't answer.

Miss Bridges looked down at her glass and fidgeted with the teaspoon. "You know I would like the two of you to be happy together. I want the best for her."

"Yes," said Al, impatiently, "as you've said."

"And the best," said Miss Bridges, "is for her to be happy with you. She wants that more than anything."

Al relaxed a tiny bit. "Yes, that's what we both want."

"Sometimes," said Miss Bridges, "the best has to be the best possible." She seemed more uncertain than she had the entire time, still fidgeting with the spoon and looking down. But her basic point was obvious to Al.

"You want me to give her up," he said. "You think that's the best possible. You want me to tell her we're finished. You want us all to . . . just pick up the pieces from the mess we've made and pretend like none of this ever happened." He started out angry, but by the end he just felt sad.

"Maybe he'll get tired of it if you mind your own business," said Miss Bridges. "She says they were talking about divorce last summer."

Al shook his head. He'd been hearing that theory for far too long. "He ain't gonna give her up."

"It would be better if it were different," said Miss Bridges, not quite responsively.

"Something might happen," Al said.

Miss Bridges looked at him directly. "What do you mean?"

"Things can happen," Al said. "He could have a heart attack or crash his automobile or something."

"Well, yes," said Miss Bridges, "but we can't plan around *those*." She took a deep breath, looked him straight in the eye some more and then said, "You're right. I think you should give her up. She can't stand much more." She gave him a look of frank appraisal. "I don't know that you can. I think you know that Eula believes he intends to kill her."

"If he did that . . ." Al said, shaking his head.

"It frightened me, too, but I'm satisfied he won't if you leave her alone," Miss Bridges said in her all-knowing nurse tone.

"I have left her alone," answered Al. "You know that yourself. She begged and begged me to write."

"I know," said Miss Bridges. "She slept with that letter on her pillow for a week." She sounded sad again. "You truly love her. He doesn't. That's why I'm appealing to you. I'm afraid for her life or yours if you two keep this up. I don't think there can be anything worse in this world for her than your death."

She looked down as if that might lessen the directness of her words. "Excuse me for being so blunt," she said when she looked up again.

Al shook his head to indicate she wasn't to worry.

"And it would kill your mother, too. Go back to Dalhart. Write her a letter care of me and tell her that for her own sake you're giving her up."

"She'll never believe that," Al said.

"She may not," said Miss Bridges, "but I'm satisfied she'll finally get used to the idea and go on back to her husband and her children. Everything and everybody," she repeated, "except for you loving her and her loving you, are pushing her that way."

"That bastard," Al said, without bothering to excuse himself. "He don't deserve her."

"No," said Miss Bridges, "but she doesn't have many choices."

"I could give her more," said Al passionately, "I could—"

"Don't," she warned.

79

"You did *what?*" Al said into the telephone in a small hallway off the lobby of the hotel. The stench of smoke and spilled beer wafted out of the bar. He felt lightheaded.

"I convinced her to return to Dallas with Billie Steele. Beal will meet her there," Miss Bridges' voice repeated. "I thought it for the best." There was a long pause. Then she said emphatically, "The most important thing is to prevent more trouble. I don't want to see any more bloodshed over this." There was a note in her voice that Al hadn't heard before and recognized as fear. "I am . . ."

"You're afraid you'd be implicated," he said, with something new in his own voice, a combination of sarcasm and despair that made an ugly sound. He was surprised at his sudden acuity—it was so Beal-like to see people as pieces on a chess board and know which moves they might make and which ones they couldn't or wouldn't. "It's your own skin you're saving."

"No," protested Miss Bridges, "I honestly believe—"

"Either that or he got to you," Al said, as if she hadn't spoken.

"He did *not*," said Miss Bridges, sounding offended.

"Sure," Al said and hung up. He stood in the foul-smelling hallway, with his hand resting heavily on top of the black telephone. Inside him, something was falling apart like a building just dynamited. He waited while it collapsed into rubble. Then he returned to his room in the Dixie and scratched a pen into paper on the banged-up bedside table. It was early evening, the long days of summer upon them again.

You swore you'd die before you lived with him again. I have cherished and respected you as my wife. And this *is how you repay me? My mother is right about you: You care about* nothing *but satisfying your own self-centered desires.* Why did I ever love you?

He was underlining things like Lena herself, scratching the pen so hard that finally the point broke. He pounded it on the paper, leaving a trail of ink that smudged half of what he'd written. When he stopped, he saw that his hands were covered with ink and the letter was blurred to illegibility.

He told himself he'd leave her alone now that she'd returned to Beal. But not a week later he was writing to a Lake Charles lawyer, enclosing a generous check and asking him to deliver a letter to her sister Pearl. Four days after that, an envelope from the lawyer arrived at General Delivery at the post office in Fort Worth for the imaginary man Al had become this time. Inside were several nested envelopes and a cover letter and inside the innermost envelope was a letter from Pearl.

Yes, Al read, *She is living with him again. He has worn her down to a bone. They all torment her so, but Eula and Mama are sorry now for taking Beal's part and I think Mama will come to join her soon. She heard you'd returned to Texas. She cries for you every day. Come visit, we can talk better.*

Who'd told Lena he'd returned? It must have been Miss Bridges. What a mistake trusting her had been. But then Al had a more chilling thought: What if he'd been spotted? And regardless, if Lena knew, why had she gone back to Beal?

He headed to Lake Charles the next day. East Texas and Louisiana were ghostly with prior versions of things, just like Tucson had been. The previous summer on the trip to New Orleans, Al had stood beside his father at the end of the same train. "Son," his father had said with his usual bluntness, "no good ever comes of sticking your peter where it don't belong."

"It's not like you think," Al answered, staring out at the tracks. A faint smell of brackish water and things left stranded in mud mixed with the smells of the train. The heat made everything at a distance shimmer and undulate.

"It's *just* like I think," his father had responded in the no-nonsense voice he used to dress down a cowhand or a division foreman who'd failed or disappointed him. "You're sticking your peter where it don't belong."

Al felt just as strong and stubborn, maybe more so. "Pa," he said firmly, turning to face him, "you don't understand." His father looked ready to say something, but instead turned back to the scenery. There was a silence so long it might have seemed the subject had changed when he said, "Time has a way of straightening things out." He'd said it in an odd voice that Al didn't recognize or know quite how to interpret.

Remembering all that, Al got up and walked to the back of the train to stand in the place he and his father had stood. He had an eerie sensation that his father was standing beside him, just at the periphery of his vision. Al didn't dare turn his head for fear of driving him away. "Pa," he whispered, but his voice had the same effect; his father vanished.

"Time has a way of straightening things out," Al whispered, taking the dictum up in his mind, examining it like a box with secret chambers, shaking it to see if he could dislodge whatever was rattling around inside—some kernel of wisdom, a skeleton key to unlock the hard doors of the place in which he found himself. "Pa," he whispered again. His eyes filled.

From the preachers on Sunday morning to the drunks on Saturday night, everyone said the same thing: "He's in a better place." Al wondered with a new sense of urgency if it was true. *It's a lie,* he found himself thinking. *All that's left of my father is rotting in the ground out at Llano.* A sudden view of the civilized world as a mountain of falsehoods rose before him like a volcano spewing up out of the sea. He shivered, despite the day's heat.

80

"You know," Pearl said in her self-assured way, which reminded Al so much of how Lena used to be, "there's only one solution." They were seated in the parlor. Pearl's husband A.J. was nowhere in sight. "She must come here, and . . ." Pearl paused and again looked at Al intently with something in her eyes that also reminded him of Lena. "She's so unhappy and worn out."

"It's terrible," agreed Al. "I was shocked when I saw her in California. I tried to convince her—"

But Pearl cut him off just like Miss Bridges. "Yes, she told me, but she could never have seen you there and she was so weak and ill."

"How is she now?" Al asked, assuming she was no better, despite coming back to Texas.

But Pearl answered, "She's a little better. She's in a place she knows and she's with her children and our mother will come to stay with her, and she had the advantage of the time in the sanitarium and Miss Bridges."

Al could find nothing to say.

"I know what you're thinking," Pearl continued in a no-nonsense way that also reminded him of Miss Bridges. "You're questioning why she's living with him if she loves you the way she says she does."

"It doesn't seem—"

"You don't understand the way he torments her, the way people stare and talk." She spoke passionately. "You don't know what that does to a decent woman. You don't, you can't understand. You're not a woman."

Al's jaw tightened and he turned to look out the window, where a sweat-soaked mule hitched to a laundry wagon was plodding along.

"I've offended you," Pearl said in a slightly softer voice.

"Look," said Al, turning back to her, his exasperation clear. "I've said I'd move aside many, many times, and she has answered every time that she loves me more than life itself and hates the sight of him. Whether she's a woman or a man or a one-eyed mule she can't have it both ways. She can't live with him and have me and she can't have me and live with him."

"No," said Pearl decisively, "I do agree with you about that."

"Well, then," said Al, only slightly mollified.

"She wants *you*," said Pearl, "that's what she's wanted since the day y'all fell in love. Living with him is temporary."

"How is it temporary?" asked Al with an edge to his voice. "Unless you mean that everything turns out to be temporary with her."

"Not her love for you," cried Pearl, tears springing into her eyes. "I have never seen a woman love a man the way she loves you."

"She has a funny way of showing it," said Al bitingly.

Pearl looked toward the closed parlor door. For a few minutes, neither she nor Al said anything. Al's anger drained away. He felt flat and gray inside.

Finally, Pearl took a deep breath and turned back to him. "You know he'll kill you if you don't kill him first," she said.

The shock Al felt went through him like lightning. Following the shock, so immediately as to be almost indistinguishable from it, came a flooding sense of relief. The words were in the air now, spoken aloud.

"Yes, but there may be some other possibilities," said Al, because a picture of his mother's face rose in his mind.

"Not if . . ." Pearl began and stopped. Al waited. "I'll try to convince her to come here," she finally continued. "It would be best and I think she could manage it—he can't prevent her."

Al felt dubious. "I need to go see my mother," he said.

"Please tell her—"

"Y'all can write me in Amarillo care of Lucien Hughes. L-U-C-I-E-N. Hughes like Hughes. General Delivery. Separate envelope. Somebody else's handwriting on the outside," he rattled off automatically. Lucien—nicknamed Nuts—was a dog-loyal friend from high school Al knew he could trust, both with secrets and a gun.

Pearl took his hand. "You know I believe in happiness," she said earnestly. Then she hung her head and began to cry. Al did his best to comfort her, though he wasn't sure what had suddenly made her so sad.

A.J. came through the door a few minutes later to find his wife wiping her eyes and clasping Al's hand. Al registered the irony: Here he was holding hands with yet another Snyder girl when her husband walked into the room. A.J.'s eyebrows rose and his mouth turned down. "What's all this about?" he asked brusquely.

"What do you think?" snapped Pearl. "My poor sister and her brute of a husband."

81

Now, on the other side of Polk Street, Frank Wolflin strides along, passing a slow-moving old woman. He tips his hat and Al tips back. The old woman's shoulders are hunched and she looks mostly at her feet, as if to be sure she doesn't trip. Watching her, Al remembers with a jolt of pain how shocked he'd been at the sight of his mother when he returned to Amarillo.

Henry had tried to warn him, but it was far worse than Al had imagined. "Oh, son," his mother said, rising slowly from her chair in the sitting room. She seemed unsteady, unable to stand without holding onto something. All the blinds and curtains except on the north window were drawn. When she stepped into the light, he saw deep lines that hadn't been there before. Her hair, once dark like his, had gone completely gray.

"Oh, Ma," he answered and took her in his arms.

"Thank goodness you're home," she said under her breath, as if she were talking not to Al but to God himself. Her back was hard and knotted. She smelled different, too, though he at first he couldn't say exactly how. Then he realized he missed the faint smell of her toilet water—an old-fashioned, lavender-scented thing he had associated with her his whole life.

"Ma," he began, but didn't know what else to say. He felt tears rolling down his face, yet again, and his body shook, just enough for her to feel it, he supposed, because she said, speaking into his shoulder, "I haven't cried. I still can't cry."

She sounded . . . she wasn't like Lena. She didn't go to pieces like Lena did. She held herself taut and didn't break. But he heard terror in her voice, as if her own control frightened her.

"Ma," he said, "I'm home. You can cry."

"I can't," she repeated, as if she hadn't made herself clear the first time.

He didn't know what else to say. So he just stood with his arms around her, and felt things he had no words for.

That night, William and Lynn and their wives and children all came for supper, but afterward, there was only Al and his mother. He felt her presence as if she sat on the window sill in his bedroom, though she had retired to her own.

Two days later, Nuts showed up at the door of the Polk Street house with a letter that Al knew—without even looking—was from Lena. *You are all I have,* she'd written. His heart still warmed at the phrase. But part of him said loud and clear: *No, I'm not. You have your children and your husband.*

82

And that was how the summer began. Al went to Dalhart to see Henry and found more letters from Lena when he returned. They argued by mail but got nowhere. Beal had dragged her to one hotel after another. Dallas, San Antonio, Fort Worth. Finally he'd rented part of a house on Reiger Street in Dallas to make things easier for the girls, according to Lena. Al bought the Lugar. A couple of times, he went to Dallas and Fort Worth and haunted the streets and imagined what would happen if he ran into Beal. He knew it was crazy, all of it. But that didn't stop him from agreeing to meet Lena at the rented house when Beal left Dallas for a few days.

Had it worn thin? Even with all his suspicions and jealousy, it seemed not. To touch her again—fingers meeting there in the dark on the porch, his hand clasping hers quickly because she was afraid, as always, that they were watched—brought him back to earth or back to himself or back to the truth, however he might express it, and he no longer knew how he might express it; words had become less and less adequate.

"*Why* are you here?" he whispered urgently, having to fight the desire to yell.

"I did it for you," she said.

He snorted and stepped away from her. "How big a fool do you think I am?" he said, no longer whispering, but still talking low.

"You don't understand," she said.

"Try me." He crossed his arms and was silent. They'd been through this in letters but it wasn't the same.

"Miss Bridges . . ." she began haltingly and stopped. "Miss Bridges told me you were in Fort Worth. She was sure someone would see you and tell Beal. She believes the only way to keep you safe is for me to live with him again."

Al said nothing. Lena tentatively touched his hand. "You don't believe me," she whispered.

"No," he said coldly, "I don't." But a part of him did, even though he wasn't ready to admit it.

"I don't know what to do," said Lena. For once, it sounded like she was talking to herself alone.

"Never," Al began. He paused and took a breath to steady himself. "Never tell me again that you're leaving me or living with him to protect me. Do you understand?"

"Oh, God, I'm so sorry," Lena said.

"Never," Al repeated.

It was at that point that Mrs. Rogers and Mrs. Castleton, the sisters who lived upstairs, came down the path from the street.

"Good evening," called out Lena in a bright social voice that startled Al with its apparent ease. "I'd like to present my brother Tom," she continued as the two women reached the porch and stood gaping at Al.

"Charmed," said one.

"A pleasure," said the other.

Neither looked all that fooled to Al, and they hustled into the house immediately. A few moments later, the porch light went on. Al cursed under his breath and moved into the shadows while Lena rushed inside, the screen door banging behind her. The light went off a few seconds later. Al sat down quietly in the porch swing.

"What will we do?" Lena whispered to him in the newly restored darkness as she sat down beside him. He knew what she was waiting for.

"There ain't but one thing," he started.

"It's all that can be done," she whispered.

"I don't see *how*," he said. "That's the problem."

"It can't look like you started it. It has to look like self-defense."

"Or an accident," said Al. The swing creaked a little in the dark. The moon had waned to next to nothing and the stars were bright.

"How could it look like an accident?" asked Lena.

"I don't know," answered Al. "I haven't gotten that far."

"The first thing they'll do is try to blame you," said Lena.

"We'll need to leave the country. Your girls . . ."

"Maybe we could have him kidnapped by some of your friends," Lena interrupted. "You could make sure you were seen in Amarillo, so people could swear you weren't part of it, and we could get away and then . . ." She stopped. "Oh, God," she burst out in a few seconds, "if I never, ever had to see his face again."

"A lot could go wrong," Al said.

"They could dump him in a river, make it look like he drowned by accident," she said. "Or make it look like he shot himself."

"He ain't the suicide type. People would see right through that."

"How about if they forced him to write a fake suicide note before they killed him?"

"Why would he agree to do that? If he knew they was gonna kill him anyway?"

"They could threaten to torture him if he didn't write it." Her voice was an emphatic whisper. "I think that would work."

Al was silent. The conversation shocked him, even while he was engaged in it. What had it cost to get to the point where talk of murder and torture sprang up so naturally . . . what hadn't it cost?

"Lena," Al said after a minute. "You surely don't want—"

"He's tortured *me*," interrupted Lena, speaking low. "Not physically, that's the only way he hasn't, but he would if he could get away with it. He's done every other thing he can think of. If you boil it all down to the very bottom of the pan, the only wrong *I've* done *him* is I don't want to be married to him anymore."

She wound down to silence and sat pushing the swing angrily with her foot. He could hear her breathing. He recognized—without being able to frame the thought completely, more as animal instinct—that her hatred formed some kind of bridge between her and Beal.

After a few minutes, she stopped pushing the swing and turned to face him. "You have to go," she said. "The longer we sit out here, the more dangerous it gets. We can talk or write later. Go."

So he did, but with feelings mixed up and shaken that had no business sharing the same container: His bones, flesh, breath and heartbeat, and the lightning flickering through his brain.

Clara Sneed

83

On those occasions when he left Amarillo and went to Dallas or Fort Worth, Al never told his mother where he was going. He only said, "I'll be gone a few days." To pretend she didn't know or didn't guess was a fiction, but neither of them disturbed it. Her self-control prevents her from questioning him; he's a grown man and hasn't had to account to her for his movements for more than a decade. But also—he sees with pity that tears at him—she fears that if she questions him he'll leave the house and never come back. When he walks in the front door, no matter whether he's been gone a few days or a few hours, he sees the relief in her face, stark and shockingly naked.

Until mid-August, Nuts had showed up almost every day with a letter from Lena. Al's mother never hid the letters, never destroyed them, never read them. If he was gone, she laid them neatly in the center of the little desk in his room. She never asked about them either, a continuation of the policy she'd adopted in her own letters, with much the same effect: Her silence quickly became far louder than words.

Lena's letters were the usual litany of love and need, the usual recounting of new alliances, people on her side, on *their* side, as she put it: Mrs. Rogers, Mrs. Castleton, John Blanton, and her own mother. *Mama is so pitiful. I can almost believe this is worse for her than for me and she is more afraid of B. than I am. I truly believe when B. goes away again you can come here and she won't open her mouth against it. And oh, Albert, if you come, could we have our little baby? A little baby would be such a comfort and the start of our family.*

Al had read that letter with a brief and acute sense of its utter preposterousness. These people she believes are on her side, on *their* side, will all betray her—he knows it—and there couldn't be a worse time to get her pregnant. It's like the kidnapping/fake-suicide scenario: Ridiculous, the stuff of bad melodrama, and completely doomed to failure.

More and more, however, his sense of the absurdity of their plans was supplanted almost instantly by a *whatthehell* voice inside him. Why not try to kidnap Beal? Why not get Lena pregnant? What did it matter? It was all so messed up anyway.

And so when Lena finagled Mrs. Rogers into wiring a coded message to indicate the coast was clear, Al took the train to Dallas and walked in the late evening's deep dusk to the Reiger Street house for the second time. The porch was dark. Lena's mother answered the door looking terrified. Neither Mrs. Rogers, Mrs. Castleton, John Blanton, nor the two girls and certainly not Beal, was anywhere in evidence.

"She's in there," Mrs. Snyder whispered, gesturing toward a doorway down the hall to the left, and then scuttling up the darkened stairs into the gloom above.

Al went to the door she'd indicated and knocked quietly. Lena opened the door, pulled him into the unlit room and fell into his arms.

84

As he steps off the sidewalk at Ninth, Al spots Pastor Jenkins coming out a side door at First Baptist across the street. It's the church Al's mother attends and the faith she raised her children to. On Al's side of the street—up there at Polk and Eighth—is First Methodist, where Al's father and the Sneeds had worshipped together, and by whose rites, the ones Al had missed, his father had been buried.

Sometimes those two churches—both soaring glory-to-God brick structures, one tawny, the other red—feel to Al like towering versions of his mother and father, the block between them a gauntlet of shame and sorrow. All the pain this love has caused.

His right hand grazes the Lugar once more. Superimposed on the sight of Jenkins, who is whistling and looks happy to be out in the September air, there's the image of the shootout again. Al and Beal meet on the street; Beal draws first, but Al draws faster. He still dreams of it. But the world has moved past the time of men meeting on dusty streets in bright Western sunlight to fire Colt .45s at one another. And anyway, Al is old enough to know that—no matter how those cowboy novels tell it—in real life it mostly never happened that way. Mostly it was lurking and planning and waiting. Just like now.

And in the end, even if he killed Beal . . . even if by some miracle he and Lena escaped and managed to marry one another . . . even then . . . Beal would stick around. He'd lurk in the bedroom, sit down to supper in the kitchen, wriggle into private moments, a persistent ghost. Things have gone too far. They're all stuck with one another now, no matter what, dead or alive.

85

"You're a father," Lena had told him that night in Dallas. "You can't know that," he'd said.

"I do, though," she'd answered. In early August she'd written that it was official—morning sickness and no monthly, although she didn't state either fact directly. "Our secret," she called the baby. By that time, her mother had headed back to Clayton, too frightened by her daughter's behavior to stick around.

And then the letters stopped. The last one was dated August 10. A few days later, Mrs. Castleton wired to report that Beal had suddenly hauled Lena and the children away.

Al hasn't had a word from her since. Most nights he reads that last letter at least once, breathing in the dimming fragrance of its pages—now smelling more of Al's cigarettes than of the toilet water on Lena's wrist as she scratched pencil across paper in the upstairs rooms at Reiger Street. She'd written right at the top, above his name and the date, *Please destroy this letter.* But he couldn't. He didn't destroy her last letter 'til he got her next one and there had been no next one.

After Mrs. Castleton's wire, he'd gone straight to Dallas. He took Nuts and a case of guns, hired a big parlor at the Southland Hotel, and headed straight for the house on Reiger Street. The inquisitive faces of Mrs. Castleton and Mrs. Rogers peered at him through the screen door.

"Oh, do come in off the street," the one Lena had introduced as Mrs. Castleton said urgently, grabbing him by the arm and pulling him into the entryway. "Isn't it *terrible?*" Her dark blonde hair was piled in a tight knot and she smelled faintly of violets and cooking oil. "We are both so distressed," she continued, "my sister and me—"

"Do y'all know where he took her?"

"No," both women cried in unison, gazing at him with their sympathetic, eager eyes, the pale honey-colored ones of Mrs. Castleton and the blue ones of Mrs. Rogers. Mrs. Rogers said, "She was crying when she came running upstairs. He comes storming up behind her not two minutes later and yanks her by the arm so hard she hollers. Then he drags her away. We were watching out the upstairs window. She was still crying."

"She was crying harder," added Mrs. Castleton, helpfully. Al's body tightened at the picture.

"We," began Mrs. Rogers, "my sister and me"—she clarified unnecessarily—"are so very sorry for your troubles."

"Y'all were made for each other," breathed Mrs. Castleton. "I have never seen a woman love a man the way she loves you."

"And the other way around," Mrs. Rogers chimed in, smiling at Al, her eyelashes fluttering over her big blue eyes. She put a plump hand on his other arm, the one her sister wasn't holding. The two flanked him like a military escort. "Mr. Rogers will be home soon," she added. "You dare not be here when he arrives. He has warned us and warned us to stay out of this business, but we—my sister and me—feel such an interest in your troubles and we are so distressed, and we don't—"

Mrs. Castleton interrupted, "We try to think where he might have taken her, and we—"

"Georgetown?" cried Mrs. Rogers. "Or maybe New York? Paducah?"

Al put his hand to his temple where he felt a headache coming on. "Could we . . . ?" he began.

The two women stopped chattering as if they'd been shot. Mrs. Castleton recovered first. "Sit down?" she trilled. "Oh, of course. Where are our manners, sister?"

"Of *course*," echoed Mrs. Rogers vigorously. "Mr. Rogers is *not* sympathetic, I'm afraid, but we still have a few minutes 'til the baby wakes up and he comes home." With her sister following close behind, she took his hand, drew him upstairs, and waved him onto the divan. Baby toys, picture postcards and snapshots of family were scattered everywhere. The only relief Al found from the clutter was in two mounted photos on the wall across from him, one of the Alamo, the other of a monument to the Confederate dead.

Al said politely, "I don't want to impose too much on your hospitality."

"Not at all," said Mrs. Rogers. Mrs. Castleton appeared with a cup of tea which she set before him. "Don't give it another thought," she said. "We're here to listen and help if we can."

"You're very kind. Thank you," said Al and took a sip of the tea. There was a brief silence in which he felt awkward and considered keeping his mouth shut as usual, but there was something alluring about unburdening himself before these two ordinary and not especially intelligent women with their avid greed for sensation. The impersonal nature of their interest spurred him on. It had a whore's appeal: Shallow, temporary, responsive, and expressive.

"It don't seem possible," he began.

"No," the women chorused. "He's a brute. How could he do such a thing *again?*"

"I don't mean it that way, exactly," said Al. "I mean it don't seem possible that it's only a little more than a year ago when things . . . when things . . ."

"Began?" suggested Mrs. Castleton.

"Well, yes," said Al, "but what I meant was, it don't seem possible that we were all there back then and now we're *here* and it ain't been all that long."

Mrs. Castleton and Mrs. Rogers pondered that in silence for a second or two. Then Mrs. Rogers opened her mouth, but before she could get started Al went on, "They looked like a happy family. No one would have guessed. *I* didn't guess. When I saw her at that party . . . I could never have dreamed her husband would shoot my father. Who could ever have thought of a thing like that? We were all such friends. Did she tell you?" He turned to the two women with an urgency he didn't understand.

"She surely did," said Mrs. Rogers.

"So tragic," added Mrs. Castleton. "But love has a way . . ."

"*Does* it?" said Al. "Sometimes I think we've all been cursed."

"But," cried Mrs. Rogers and Mrs. Castleton, practically in unison.

"You *love* each other," said Mrs. Castleton.

"Her husband *won't* understand," said Mrs. Rogers, "He *can't* because you two are blessed with such a rare love."

"Oh, love," said Al. "My mother tried to warn me but I didn't listen. I can't stop. She can't stop. We *can't*," he said, the desperation so clear in his voice that the two women said nothing, just looked uncomfortable.

"But," said Mrs. Castleton with fear in her pale eyes, "love is . . . it's the greatest thing in the world, it's what—"

"Makes the world go round?" Al said with a harsh laugh. "Oh, yeah, it makes the world go round all right. It makes the world go round' til you don't hardly recognize it. That's what love does. Or maybe it's what the world does to love. I don't know. But I don't recognize—"

He stopped. He'd been about to say he didn't recognize the world anymore but he realized that what he meant was, *I don't recognize myself*, and that seemed too intimate, even with all the truth he was spewing out. Mrs. Rogers and Mrs. Castleton looked startled and uncomfortable. Mrs. Rogers got up to look out the window.

"I see Mr. Rogers coming up the street," she exclaimed with obvious relief. "We'll let you out the back. There'll be trouble for sure if he sees you."

There's nothing but *trouble when people see me,* Al thought.

86

After a few days of poking around, Al had come back from Dallas without any better idea of where Lena was than he had when he'd left Amarillo. He tries to act like he did when he believed things were sturdy, but nothing seems so anymore. Sometimes Amarillo itself looks like a scrim on which a whole city is painted. Yet here he is, walking its streets. He can't seem to work himself free.

Because it pleases her, he goes to First Baptist with his mother on Sundays and listens to the preacher talk about Jesus—whose opinions apparently more or less line up with those of the deacons. It's not exactly how Al sees it. He doesn't know what Jesus might say about his situation, but he doesn't think Jesus condemns him and Lena simply for loving one another. Al believes what Lena does. God had given them a clear set of instructions: *Love and cleave to one another.*

Or Al had believed that. He just doesn't know anymore. He tells Lena he believes it, and often he tells himself he does, but right this minute, as his boot heels thud against the brick pavement and his heart beats a rhythm that seems steadier than anything else around him, he acknowledges to himself the truth: He's outlived all his firmest beliefs, including the deepest conviction of his life, the one about him and Lena.

There are moments that still ring and ring inside him, like bells summoning or mourning or maybe just reminding. Who or what? He doesn't know. Those moments on the Milk River watching the stars wheel by. Those moments when at last he'd entered Lena again.

Her fragrance filled him, the way she and she alone smelled. This was all there was, is all there is, all that has ever been, all that is meant to be. She is moaning into his ear and he cries out, too, quietly, because they aren't alone in the house, although he barely remembers that, and can't really believe it matters. She is saying his name over and over and he is saying hers. He becomes her and she becomes him, indistinguishable for as long as it lasts, which is to say as he says to her, *forever,* until the end of time, as she answers him, *forever,* until the end.

And those moments go on ringing. But he can't connect them anymore to the things he once believed they meant. Sometimes he finds himself dreaming of ordinary life again, of another ranch and another woman he can have babies with and love—not the way he loves Lena, but enough—and Lena and Beal living elsewhere, picking up the pieces as best they can. But those dreams waver and vanish before his eyes—he can't seem to hold onto them.

I am no longer the man I wanted to be. I came to the truth of my life and somehow I failed it. And now . . . He suddenly sees that wildfire sweep across the plains again. *It's burning my life up.*

The worst of it is that fire feels like the only real thing left.

The letters in his pocket, even the Lugar in his waistband—they're gestures toward his place in a story he no longer really believes. One of the letters is to Lena, though he has no way to send it directly. It turns out she's on the Milam County farm, the one Beal's younger brother Marvin inherited when old man Sneed was killed. Al had heard from Pearl this morning: *John Blanton is out there guarding her, but she managed to get word to me while he was attending to a call of nature. Beal hasn't been there for a few days and she don't know where he is. She's worried to death about you.*

As he'd left the house, his mother put her hand to his face. He'd flinched the way a horse does at an unexpected touch, however gentle, the hide rippling as if it were a pond into which a pebble is thrown.

"Will you be back for supper?" she asked.

"Yes, Ma," he answered. "I ain't going out for long. Only downtown and back."

"Maybe Lynn and Hilma and the babies can join us," she said.

"That would be fine." He wanted to tell her something that would make her happy. "Lynn and I plan to buy some of that old XIT land."

She smiled dimly. "Son," she began and Al braced himself but she said nothing more, just looked at him for a few seconds from the hollowed-out pits of her eyes. Then she said, "I'll see you shortly."

"Yes, Ma," said Al, "You will."

"Goodbye," she said, in the formal way she so often has with him now. "I'll phone Hilma up about supper." She turned away and he headed out the door.

Now he's closing in on First Methodist at Eighth and Polk. There's Mr. Robinson, who did the service for Al's father, heading for the steps into the rectory with a couple bags of groceries. Al always feels awkward around him. Robinson has never been anything but tactful—that's his business—but Al feels the weight of a whole lot of unspoken opinion backing the man up like a posse.

"Howdy-do," says Al, seeing that it's too late to cross the street and avoid the man.

"Howdy-do," says Mr. Robinson. "It's cooler today, ain't it?"

"Yes," says Al. "It's getting to be the fall of the year."

Robinson sets his groceries down and fumbles for his key. The same kid who'd peddled by on the bicycle earlier is now headed back the other way holding a package on his handlebars. As he whizzes by, Al catches sight of a man crossing the street. He looks like a tramp, with a dirty black beard and old clothes. Maybe he's on his way over to see about a handout, which will give Al the chance to escape talking any more with the preacher. But something about the tramp's walk draws Al's attention. He's carrying a long, odd-looking wooden box and he's crossing the streetcar tracks, which glitter and shine in the afternoon sun. As Al turns to say a polite see-you-later to Robinson, something thuds against the brick pavement.

There's a flash of light—not sun on the tracks—and Al knows who it is.

He can't change how slowly his body reacts. The Lugar feels a thousand miles away. There's a crack like thunder and a rain of buckshot spatters into his right arm then pelts into his chest. He crumples to the sidewalk. In the big stained glass window above him, the angel descends. She flutters before his eyes for a few seconds and flowers bloom beneath her feet. He knows she's real. And very shortly after that, he doesn't know much of anything at all.

87

Beal knows he got him. This time there's no need to stop and check. The target practice sessions at the farm, the disguise, the fake name, the cottage he rented opposite the church to wait and watch—it's all paid off. He doesn't cross much farther than the tracks, and barely registers Mr. Robinson shouting from the top of the rectory stairs. Turning away, he scoops up the wooden case, drops the shotgun back in, and heads on downtown, leaving the cottage, Al's shot-ridden body, and the corner of Eighth and Polk behind him.

Inside him is jubilance: *I've won.*

It will only be later this evening—when he is once again sitting in a jail cell waiting to get bailed out after killing a man, this time in Amarillo rather than Fort Worth—that some part of him will begin to recognize that he doesn't feel quite so free this time. That feeling is like a snake lurking somewhere far away in a wide field of sunny grasses. He can't see that it has much to do with anything and he ignores it.

It will be many years more—so many that it can sometimes seem like none of this ever happened—when he hears a curious thing: That for a drunk, the first drink comes as a revelation of freedom, and that every drink after is a search for that freedom, which never returns. His mind flashes back to the Fort Worth jail. He's not the type to dwell on why he'd suddenly remember a night spent in jail decades earlier in the course of an idle conversation about drunks, since he isn't one. Still, he notices. But all that is yet to come. For now, he continues down Polk Street with that triumph in him.

Hundreds of miles away, his wife sits down at a roll top desk to write a letter. Their daughters are playing outside. It's hot, but at least it's a little cooler than it was in August. She has just a few hours left of this particular dream, but she doesn't know that.

Lena takes a deep breath, fans herself, picks up a pencil, and begins.

September 14, 1912. Milam County, Texas

Before We Turn to Dust

AFTER

Clara Sneed

Habeas Corpus Transcript

Witness C. J. Collier
Pages 193 – 195

  I was on the first floor of the Neal house, 800 Tyler St., and did not see any of the shooting but heard it. I went to the porch and saw the excitement and went running to the corner of Polk and 8th in front of the Methodist Church and saw a man lying near the east steps against the pier of the church.
  A laundryman was there who drives for the Amarillo Steam Laundry and he told me he did not know who the man lying there was. I spoke to the man and asked if I could help him but he did not answer anything and by that time about 15 people were there and nobody seemed to know the man lying there and I asked some of them if they knew him and no one knew him.
  His face was toward the steps and he had a letter in his right coat pocket, and in trying to find out who the man was I took out this letter, and looked at the address and it was addressed either Mrs. or Miss Snyder. I am not positive where it was addressed to but think it was LaGrange, Texas, but it might have been New York.
  I also saw another letter in his inside coat pocket and it was open at the stamped end. I took it out and it was addressed to A. G. Boyce, written with blue type.
  Presently, Deputy Speed came up and Mrs. Boyce also came about then, and Mrs. Boyce, as soon as she came, shook her fist and said,

Before We Turn to Dust

"Show me the man who killed this man," or words to that effect and someone asked her if he could do anything for her and she said all she wanted was to see the man who did the killing and reached over and brushed his hair back and said something about if only her boy could speak to her, and reached over and got the letter addressed to Mrs. or Miss Snyder, that I had seen and I did not see her get any other letters, and she held it folded in her hand. Deputy Speed told her not to interfere with the body, that it was necessary to be examined before removing it, but I heard no reply from her.

Witness Jim T. Green
Pages 58 - 59

  I did not recognize the man. On this day he was dressed, I could best describe it like a Russian Jew: overalls and some rough clothing, a thick black beard all over his face — his general aspect was — he did not seem to be a man of Beal Sneed's stamp at all.
  He spoke to me and Jackson when he passed, calling him by initials — I forget his initials — he said, "Hello Green." I did not say "Hello Sneed;" I did not know who it was; I said "Jackson, who in the hell is that?" Jackson said, "That is Beal Sneed, Jim," or "Green." I forget what he called me. I disputed it and said it could not be, and he said, "That is him all right."

351

Clara Sneed

FORT WORTH STAR-TELEGRAM

*EXCERPT FROM MONDAY, SEPTEMBER 16, 1912
AMARILLO, TEXAS*

After the shooting, Sneed hurried to the jail where he gave up the automatic shotgun and two automatic pistols he had carried in a box with brass hinges. He had paused about a block away to refill the gun, possibly expecting an encounter with some of the Boyce brothers.

This he narrowly escaped. Will Boyce, who assisted in the recent prosecution at Fort Worth, was in the office of District Clerk Mart Hardin at the time the shooting occurred and had just left without hearing about it. Had he been one minute later he would have encountered Sneed as he hurried to the jail adjoining the courthouse. Lynn Boyce was also on the scene almost instantly, running down Polk Street with a Winchester and dashing into the crowd that gathered about his brother's body, but Sneed was already gone.

Mrs. A. G. Boyce, Sr., widow of Sneed's first victim, was the first of the family to reach Al. Dropping in the mud at his side she wiped the blood away from his forehead, exclaiming, "How much more of this can I stand?" She then was overcome and is in a serious condition at her home to which the son's body was taken Sunday morning.

Her condition, pitiful as it is, has the value at least of insuring against a further outbreak. Setting aside thoughts of vengeance, the three remaining sons have set themselves to the task of caring for their mother. "It wouldn't bring them back and mother, I am afraid, could not stand another shock," said Henry Boyce Sunday when the possibility of further trouble between the families was mentioned with the urgency that he help restrain Lynn, whose outbreak at the trial in Fort Worth was one of its exciting features.

One of the crucial moments already has passed. Joe Sneed, brother of Beal, reached Amarillo Saturday night. Sunday he saw the Boyce brothers, though of course, they held no conversation. The passing, however, did not provoke hostilities.

Curious crowds thronged all day Sunday about the Methodist Episcopal Church, commenting upon the affair while services were going on within and looking for the bullet marks that scarred the building in many places.

EXCERPT FROM SATURDAY, SEPTEMBER 21, 1912 CALVERT, TEXAS

Mrs. Lena B. Sneed, whose escapades with Al Boyce, Jr., have caused the killing of two men and wrecked the lives of members of three families, today for the first time discussed with close friends the tragedies in which she has played the principal part.

Mrs. Sneed is despondent over the killing of Boyce by her husband at Amarillo last Saturday and made no effort to conceal the fact to her friends. To them, it is said, that she appeared heartbroken and declared that Al Boyce was the only man she ever loved and that the reason she consented to reconciliation with her husband two months ago was because of her children and her need of financial aid.

EXCERPT FROM TUESDAY, DECEMBER 3, 1912
FORT WORTH, TEXAS

On Tuesday, John Beal Sneed was found not guilty of the murder of Capt. A. G. Boyce in the Metropolitan Hotel lobby Jan. 13. The jury was unanimous in its verdict on the first ballot Monday night and withheld its report only because it was too late to go home. After Judge Swayne's stiff charge to the jury, the verdict came as a surprise to even the defendant's counsel.

The jury had retired to its room Monday afternoon at 5:30 o'clock with one of the most unusual charges ever read to a Texas jury. It excluded man-slaughter and self-defense and instructed the jury that it must find Beal Sneed guilty of murder in the first or the second degree or acquit him.

"I don't see how they could have done it," commented Judge Swayne afterwards.

Walter Scott and William P. McLean, Jr. of defense's counsel were fined $50 each because they shouted and threw their hats over the chandelier when the verdict was announced. Sneed shouted as loud as any of them, but he went unpunished.

Jubilant almost to the point of hysteria,

Sneed was too moved to talk. He silently accepted the congratulations of the friends that swarmed about him and when little Lenora, his daughter, came running up to him to throw her arms about his neck, he held her close for a full minute and kissed her hair.

Mrs. Sneed and Georgia Beal were out shopping when the verdict came in. Mrs. Sneed heard the tidings on the street and she hurried to the Court Hotel, where she has been in practical seclusion since Friday.

"She hasn't heard the news yet, but I know she will be elated and happier than she was before," a woman relative ventured soon after the verdict was returned. "Of course, she doesn't want to talk for publication. She is happy over the verdict and she loves her husband and children."

With the windup of the trial came a revelation of how those twelve men who decided to let Beal Sneed go spent their evenings. They danced—the old-fashioned, country square dance. "I could hear them calling the turns," Barney Fitch, deputy sheriff who guarded the jury, said Tuesday. "They had not music but they clapped their hands and patted their feet. All of them danced and they seemed to enjoy it."

EXCERPT FROM FRIDAY, FEBRUARY 21, 1913 VERNON, TEXAS

The sorrow of a woman bereft of husband and son was bared in the testimony of Mrs. A. G. Boyce, Sr., Friday afternoon in the trial of

Beal Sneed for the murder of Albert G. Boyce, Jr. Lawyers for the defense protested in chorus when she commented bitterly on the tragedy; even the admonition of Judge Nabers could not stop her.

"Mrs. Boyce, in justice to the defendant," Judge Nabers said, "you must just answer the questions and not tell all that you believe because everything is not admissible under the rules of testimony."

"Then this is just a trial for the living," Mrs. Boyce responded, "and there is no trial for the dead. Why can't I tell the whole story? I can't cry but my heart is dripping blood."

EXCERPT FROM TUESDAY, FEBRUARY 25, 1913 VERNON, TEXAS

John Beal Sneed was found not guilty on the first ballot this morning of the charge of murdering Al Boyce, Jr. at Amarillo, Sept. 14. "Call it a three-minute verdict," a juror said. "It took just about that long to write out the ballots."

Despite Judge Nabers' severe warning against demonstration before the verdict was read, the clerk had proceeded no further than the word "not" when Sneed leaped from his chair and clapped his hands.

"Who did that?" Judge Nabers asked, craning his neck to see into the group about the defendant.

"I did it, judge," Sneed answered, stepping forward, his face crimson with joy.

"I fine you $30, Mr. Sneed," Judge Nabers said smiling. Then in the same breath: "No, I won't either. No, no, I won't."

Applause broke over the entire audience and Sneed was carried toward the door of the district clerk's office by the press of the crowd eager to shake hands with him. He remained in Vernon today to attend to some business affecting his Cottle County farm. He will take the midnight train to Fort Worth and proceed to Waco, where his wife and two little girls are.

POSTSCRIPT

Annie Elizabeth Boyce outlived her husband and all her children. She died on July 19, 1929, a few months after Henry Boyce, the last to predecease her. She is buried in Llano Cemetery in Amarillo with her husband and all her children except Henry, who is buried in Dalhart.

John Beal Sneed and Lena Snyder Sneed remained married as long as they both lived. Although Lena was reported to be pregnant at the time of Al's death, there is no evidence that a child was ever born. And though they lived many decades more, and Beal had a few more scrapes with the law, the events recounted here must have been the defining ones for their marriage—likely a ghost-ridden affair ever after. Beal died on April 22, 1960. Lena died on March 7, 1966. They are buried in Hillcrest Memorial Park in Dallas.

SOURCES

The most important of the primary sources used in this novel are:
1. Letters of Lena Snyder Sneed to Albert G. Boyce Jr.;
2. The transcript of John Beal Sneed's habeas corpus hearing in Amarillo;
3. Reports published in the Fort Worth Star-Telegram.

Lena's letters are quoted almost verbatim, as are the portions of Al's letter written from Canada after learning of his father's death. With few exceptions, courtroom testimony, summations, and judicial rulings or comments are taken directly from newspaper accounts and the surviving transcript, though I edited for clarity and concision. The biggest exception is in direct testimony about Colonel Boyce's salacious comments. In accordance with journalistic standards of the time, these were not published.

The transcript of the habeas hearing—which includes some testimony from the first Fort Worth trial and a few of Al's letters to Lena—is the only surviving transcript from the relevant legal proceedings. Because Judge Browning in Amarillo denied Beal bail after he killed Al, a transcript was required for an appeal to the Texas Supreme Court in Austin, which reversed Browning's decision.

It is impossible to overstate the debt I owe Albert G. "Pete" Boyce, the great-nephew of Albert Boyce Jr., for allowing me to read and transcribe letters in his family's possession that Lena wrote to Al. Without them, the novel would have been entirely different.

Finally, despite the frustration expressed by characters in the novel about the press, I want to express my gratitude to the mostly nameless reporters who struggled to make such detailed accounts of Beal's trials, particularly the first one in Fort Worth. To Kitty Barry—the one reporter with a byline—and the rest of the "tribe," wherever you may now be: Thank you.

ACKNOWLEDGEMENTS

Any writer who researches and writes about a complex historical episode knows that few endeavors rely so much on "the kindness of strangers," nor demand so much from editors, family and friends.

In the case of a decades-long project like this one, that is especially true. There is a melancholy aspect to thanking many of the people most helpful to me in the research stage, begun so long ago that they have passed on.

Chief among these: My father, Joseph T. Sneed, who gave me his own research materials and never tired of talking with me about this and other family stories; my Amarillo cousin Joe Pool (voluminous archives, ideas, and time); Mary Kate Tripp, long-time book editor and columnist for the *Amarillo Globe-News* (deep knowledge of the story and a wicked dry wit); Katy Antony, research librarian in the Amarillo Public Library (A good research librarian is like having a personal angel.); E. P. and his wife "Mike" Taylor (One More Time bookstore and a whole lot more good times); Bill and Patricia Kirkeminde (XIT ranch headquarters at Channing and the path to Albert "Pete" Boyce); Frederick W. Rathjen (editor of the *Panhandle-Plains Historical Review* who steered *Because This is Texas* to publication); and Charles Emmett Warford of Warford Walker Mortuary (generous guide to better understanding Black life in Amarillo and the Panhandle).

I also owe an enormous debt of gratitude to the people who helped wrestle this manuscript into shape, which was no small task: Jane Anne Staw (a writing, editing, counseling, loving treasure); Victoria Prior (agent, editor, wise one); Diane Grimes and Robert Earl Williams (dialect consultants); Diane, Jo Brookter and Michael Miller (consultants on use of racially charged language); Wendy Lane, Jared and Trish Goldin, Pascale Roger, Susan Wickens, Candy Lochridge and Chris Klem (readers who slung feedback and caught typos); and of course the great crew at Blue Handle, Ricky Treon (editor—we writers love him; he's one of us); Madison David (publishing, marketing, publicity—all that and editing, too); and Charles D'Amico (putting muscle, money, and imagination into a new publishing model).

My mother Madelon—a beautiful visual artist now also passed on—never stopped believing in and encouraging me as a writer. My sister, Carly, is a generous and inspiring voice of reason and elegant badass. Chris, tragically dead far too young, was an enthusiastic early reader. My son has been living with this project since he was small; thank you for your patience, Sam.

I've also been lucky to have in my corner mi familia mexicana (Gracias por el amor y el apoyo.); Rollins (BFAM); Stanley and Stephen, who never stopped asking how the book was going, despite signs that maybe it wasn't going at all; and Trish, who makes me laugh when I've been crying.

Thank you all.

And finally to Kirk, writer, editor, advisor, friend, collaborator, and husband. Thank you from the bottom of my heart.

Clara Sneed

Clara Sneed was born in Texas and never got over her it, despite a peripatetic childhood that landed her in California.

She earned a Bachelor of Arts and an Master of Arts in English literature at UC Berkeley, raised a son, managed IT systems for a San Francisco law firm, and had a successful second career as a tutor for writing and Spanish—all the while working on her own writing.

Though she began as a poet, she loves complex historical stories that require a lot of research, and the events depicted in this novel more than qualify. Her nonfiction account, Because *This is Texas*, was published in the 1999 *Panhandle-Plains Historical Review.*

Sneed and her husband split their time between Berkeley and Milam County, Texas.

Clara Sneed

Milton Keynes UK
Ingram Content Group UK Ltd.
UKHW041306291124
3267UKWH00012B/22/J